NO QUARTER

LINDSAY MCKENNA

Blue Turtle Publishing

No Quarter
First edition 2023
Original Copyright © 2015, R. Eileen Nauman
ISBN: 978-1-951236-43-4, Print Edition

Excerpt from *Unforgettable*
Original Copyright © 2015, R. Eileen Nauman

This edition is published by arrangement with Blue Turtle Publishing Company.

Dear Readers,

Welcome to my latest romantic military suspense series, SHADOW TEAM!

You've met the Shadow Team in *Last Stand*, Book 1, and Book 2, its sequel *Collateral Damage*. Readers have fallen love with the strong secondary character, Ukrainian combat medic, Alex Kazak. They have clamored for his book and here it is: NO QUARTER, Book 3 of the series. The tall, muscular medic who looks like a threatening giant to sniper instructor Lauren Parker, is a shadow over her life through no fault of his own. From the time they met at Shield Security, Alexandria, Virginia, she has avoided him at all costs.

They are thrown together in a mission to Peru, to Alex's old stomping grounds when he ran with a Russian team fighting Latin drug lords for turf and territory. Nearly killed by his team, Alex barely survives. To Shield employees, he is a hero. To the Russian mafia in New York City, he is a turn coat and wants him dead. The mission is one of finding the five Russian leaders of the teams in the jungle part of Peru, and Lauren is to take them out while Alex is her spotter.

Lauren's tragic childhood comes back to haunt her as never before. Alex has artlessly fallen in love with the dynamic and courageous Lauren and cannot understand why she looks afraid of him when he's never done anything but treat her with respect and admiration. The past is alive and a monster to Lauren: when she knows the whole story about Alex, she no longer sees him as a traitor to the American military, but a hero.

Little by little, Alex pieces together Lauren's reactions toward him and it staggers him. His beloved sister, Kira, reacts the same way and she was gang raped by Russian terrorists when she was in the Russian Army. Both she and Lauren have the same type of reactions. Knowing that? He begins to earn Lauren's trust, the very thing that had never grown between them. Until now.

Is it too late? His enduring, silent love for her is going to be tested. On the field of combat, Alex has saved many lives, but when Lauren is kidnapped by his old Russian team, there is only one of two out comes: Lauren's life hangs in the balance. Can he and a Special Forces team find her in time? His heart is shredded because he loves her and will do anything, including giving his life, to save hers.

Warmly,
Lindsay McKenna aka Eileen Nauman

Dedication

To all the readers who love romantic military suspense!

CHAPTER 1

LAUREN PARKER WAS going to cry. She shut the door to her guest room and stood tensely, fighting the tears burning in her gray eyes. The past had taught her that tears did nothing but make her foster father angry. And they sure as hell didn't win her a reprieve from him or his ugly, sick, incestual intentions toward her. With a muttered curse under her breath, she took a swipe at her eyes. Her anger was focused on Alex Kazak, an ex-Spetsnaz operator from Ukraine who had joined the Russian army as a combat medic. Damn him! Why couldn't he just leave her the hell alone? She wanted NOTHING to do with the six-foot-four soldier. He was a common criminal, who had worked in the past for the Russian mafia down in Peru. Why Jack Driscoll, head of Shield Security, the outfit she worked for, had ever even hired the man was beyond her.

Moving around the beautifully appointed bedroom, Lauren thought back on how she had come up here to visit Cal Sinclair and his fiancée', Sky Lambert. They'd invited her, and unfortunately, Alex Kazak, to share their happy news with. Sky was four months pregnant and they'd just found out it would be a girl. Lauren walked over to the large picture window that overlooked the rocky hill atop which their huge cedar home sat in the Virginia countryside. Shield Security was a ten-mile trip, each way, and Lauren loved the quiet of their home.

Below the bedroom, in the dusk light, she spotted a doe with a new fawn at her side. The fawn had lost its white spots and stepped confidently along at the side of her White Tail deer mother. Lauren placed her hands on her hips, watching the twosome down below. They were probably heading for the oval-shaped meadow that was on the other side of the hill. There was a creek running through the middle of it and, most likely, they were going there for a drink before starting their nightly foraging. This did little to soothe Lauren's anger toward Kazak. How could it? Who did Alex think he was?

She pushed her red hair off her shoulder, digging into the pocket of the olive-green cargo pants she always wore, and found a rubber band. Quickly gathering her long, slightly wavy red hair up into a pony tail, Lauren let it settle between her shoulder blades. Moving away from the window, she looked around the suite. Cal Sinclair, an ex-Navy SEAL, and someone she worked with at Shield Security, had hand built this incredible two-story cedar home over a seven-year period. It was his way, she supposed, of ramping down from constant deployments into combat in Afghanistan or their eighteen-month cycle of grueling, continuous SEAL training.

The bed was queen sized, a bright quilt across it. Lauren thought it was probably her best friend, Sky, who had brought this splash of vibrant color into the otherwise subdued reddish-gold cedar bedroom. A soft knock came at the door.

Lauren turned, scowling. Who? It was nearly nine p.m. and everyone was retiring for the night. Her lips tightened. It had better not be Kazak. She'd had enough of him for one day. Too bad he worked at Shield Security in Gage Hunter's Sniper Department. She could never quite escape his presence because she was a sniper instructor at the company.

Opening the door, relief flooded through her. It was Sky. She stood there in her white linen slacks, a soft purple top and white leather sandals. "I wanted to see how you were," Sky said, giving her a concerned look. "Is it too late? Are you going to bed?"

"No... come on in," Lauren said, stepping aside. Sky was five foot seven inches tall with sun-streaked blond hair, and the most unearthly blue eyes she'd ever seen. Their bond with one another was tight. At one time, Sky had been an Army Black Hawk Medevac pilot, black ops, and had served in Afghanistan until she was shot at Camp Nichols, a forward operating base near the Pakistan border. Sky had almost died, as Lauren understood it, but had survived. It had been Cal Sinclair, a SEAL, who had saved her life. And now, nearly three years later, they were about to be married.

Closing the door, Sky sat down on the cedar chair near the small desk in the corner. Lauren thought she looked so fragile at four months pregnant. Sky had been through hell. Three weeks ago, Lauren had been part of the Shield Security team that had freed Sky from the captivity of a Russian mafia drug lord who had kept her at his villa in Costa Rica. "Aren't you tired?" Lauren teased a little, sitting down on the edge of the bed, palms on the firm mattress as she stared across at Sky.

Shrugging, Sky smiled a little. "Too excited to go to bed just yet. Cal's finishing cleaning up in the kitchen. I just wanted to drop by and see how you were doing."

"I'm fine," Lauren deadpanned. She trusted few people, but Sky and Cal were two whom she did. The caring expression on Sky's delicate features touched her. Lauren allowed few people in behind the walls she put up to protect herself, from men in particular.

"You didn't look fine late this afternoon," Sky observed quietly, clasping her hands in her lap. "When Alex called you 'Little One', you looked like... well," and Sky looked up, searching for the right word, "I guess, like you were going to cry. I could tell that what he told you touched you deeply, Lauren. And since then, you've been upset. I just wanted to come and see if I could be of help? Maybe an ear to listen?"

Lauren nodded. "He caught me off guard, Sky. What he did, what he said, came out of nowhere. I guess," and she rubbed the back of her neck, a sign she was upset, "he shocked me." She saw Sky's calm face turn sympathetic. Lauren didn't know how Sky could bounce back so quickly from a month held captive by Yerik Alexandrov. She had been tortured. And she'd survived, Lauren thought, because of the love Cal had for her. Lauren had never seen a love like theirs. Sky was pregnant when captured, had gone through a grueling month of hell, had been broken through torture and, yet, she sat here looking serene. Lauren, Cal and the Shield Security mission team, plus that damnable Ukrainian employee, Alex Kazak, had rescued Sky. It wasn't as if life had dealt Sky a good hand when Lauren knew it hadn't. And that is what bound Sky and her so tightly to one another: abusive childhoods.

"Mmm," Sky said. "I don't think Alex said it to upset you, Lauren. You've known him for what? Three months now since Jack hired him into Shield Security? Cal and I think he really likes you."

Needled, Lauren growled, "Well, it's friggin' one-way, Sky." The anger leaking out through her husky voice. "He has NO RIGHT to say anything like that to me. Who the hell does he think he is? God's gift to women? Well, he picked on the wrong woman this time."

Sky made an unhappy sound and stood up, then came and sat next to Lauren on the bed. "Listen, Alex is a combat medic. He's getting recertified through Army Delta 18 schooling."

"Yeah, he's taking Delta courses right now. But then he has to go through the advance course, for eighteen months. I think because he is ex-Spetsnaz, they're letting him leapfrog a lot of classes and jump straight to the nitty-gritty of the advanced eighteen-month course."

"Well," Sky said wryly, "Alex saved my life down in Peru. I got an up-close and personal look at him as a medic."

"You had malaria," Lauren muttered. "If he's a medic, putting aside him working with the Russian mafia down in Peru, he was charged with caring for you."

"And he did," Sky said, holding her gray gaze. "He stopped Vlad Alexandrov from charging into that hut where I was hallucinating with a hundred-and-five-degree fever, and raping me. Alex stood between me and Vlad. I didn't know it at the time, of course, because I was unconscious. But later, because Vlad had captured me to rape me, Alex turned against his own team and helped me escape."

"I guess that makes him a good guy," Lauren muttered. "He's still a criminal. He worked for the Russians." She saw Sky give her a sad smile and reach out and touch her slumped shoulder.

"He really is a nice person, Lauren. I know he's made some bad decisions, and he had reason to. But who hasn't?"

Snorting, Lauren bit out, "He's stalking me, Sky. I'm a sniper, dammit, and I can FEEL it. Ever since that meeting where Jack Driscoll, our boss, introduced him to the employees three months ago, he's had it in for me." She opened her hands, frustration in her low voice. "I took one look at him and he scared the living bejesus out of me, Sky. When he joined our meeting, Alex lorded over me, and I couldn't take it. I just spun around on my boot and left the damned room. I didn't want to shake his hand or be around him." Her nostrils flared as she bent her head, shaking it. "I didn't want him hunting me."

Gently, Sky rubbed her tense shoulder. "He likes you."

"I want NOTHING to do with him!" They'd been forced to drive up together to visit Sky and Cal. It was the most torturous half hour Lauren had ever spent, with the medic that close, that big, that overwhelming, and pushing every terror-filled button deep within her. And she'd done it because Sky had asked them to come up together for an important announcement. Lauren had bitten the bullet and caved in, and had agreed to ride with him. Because Sky was her closest friend, someone who had a military background like herself, who had worked in black ops, suffered a rotten childhood and somehow survived it, she had driven with Kazak. More than anything, Lauren respected Sky because she was a survivor like herself.

"I guess," Sky whispered apologetically. "I shouldn't have begged you to drive up here with Alex, then. It would have gone better for you two to have driven up separately for our news and dinner." Sky reached out, squeezing Lauren's hand. "I'm really sorry. I know someone his height and size scares the hell out of you because of your past. I should have thought it through better."

"Hell," Lauren muttered, standing up, "don't blame yourself, Sky. You're three weeks out of captivity and torture. I don't blame you for anything. Okay?" and she turned, giving Sky a pleading look. "None of this is your fault…"

Sky watched Lauren pace, her friend's face tense, her gray eyes stormy with a lot of emotions she had never released and rarely spoke about. "I guess my relationship with Alex is different from yours, Lauren. I just didn't completely think this meeting through." She smiled a little. "We were so excited to find out I was carrying a little girl…"

"Don't beat yourself up," Lauren told her, taking the upset out of her tone. She pulled out the chair, turned it around, and hitched her arms over the back of it, staring at Sky. "I WANT to share happy moments with you and Cal. God knows, you deserve some happiness after all the shit you've gone through and survived."

Sky rallied a little. "Cal and I were talking earlier, after you two went to your guest rooms. We're going to try and get married again."

Lauren felt her heart squeeze in sympathy for her friend. Sky had been captured by Alexandrov's men one day before the wedding had been set to take place in Coronado, California. Cal's SEAL Team 3 friends, whom he'd fought beside for years, were going to be there as well. It would have been such a happy occasion. And Lauren had been slated as Sky's maid-of-honor. It had been such an upper for Lauren. She didn't believe in happily-ever-after. She didn't believe in love because she'd been taught otherwise growing up. But Cal and Sky had something special, something so beautiful and strong between them, that Lauren had been devastated when her friend had been kidnapped. "That's good," she told Sky, seeing the happiness banked-up in her eyes. "When? And where?"

"Well," Sky said, hesitating, "Cal wanted the wedding here, at our home, before the baby comes. Nothing fancy like we had planned before. Just you, Alex, and Jack Driscoll, and us. Cal's SEAL buddies are on deployment again. None of them can make it. I was just… well… worried if you'd consent to come or not because we'd invited Alex, too. And then, next June 16th, we'll go back to Coronado, when all his SEAL team buddies will be back off duty, and hold an 'official' wedding."

Lauren saw how important it was to Sky that she be in attendance. "I'll be there for both of them," she promised Sky. "I'll just ignore Kazak." Instantly, Lauren saw relief in her friend's face. Sky never could hide an emotion, unlike herself. Lauren had learned to put on a game face starting at seven years old. She cracked a grin. "Am I still your maid-of-honor?"

Sky made a happy sound, rose, and walked over, giving Lauren a swift hug. "Of course you are!"

"Do you want me to help you find the right flowers for your bouquet again?" Because Lauren enjoyed the details. As a sniper, details ruled her life. And she'd had so much fun with Sky choosing from hundreds of flowers from the San Diego florist, for the blooms she'd wanted for her wedding.

"Would you? There's a great florist in Alexandria, Virginia. I thought, maybe, if you had time, you could drive up next week and we could go look at them?"

"Sure. Are you still going to wear that beautiful wedding dress we picked out?" Lauren had gone along to the bridal store and had driven the seamstress crazy with small details to make sure it fit exactly right on Sky's willowy, slender frame.

"Well," Sky laughed, placing her hands over her belly, "I don't know if it's possible. Look at me: I'm four-months along and I can't button my jeans anymore."

A smile tugged at Lauren's full mouth. "Get an appointment with the bridal seamstress at that shop? We'll go over and see if she can create some magic for you? That dress is drop-dead gorgeous on you, Sky. And you've already bought it. It would be a shame not to wear it. In fact, if the fitting can be done? You'll be able to wear it twice. Once here, and then again next June for the 'real' wedding at Coronado. You won't be pregnant then, and I know the dress will fit you beautifully."

"I know," Sky sighed, smiling softly. "I just wanted a magical and wonderful wedding so badly…" She shrugged. "I guess that during my time spent in the closet of my parents' home I dreamed a lot. I'd be in there for hours and, after I'd get done sobbing my heart out, I'd dream. It would take me away from all of it."

"And you dreamed of a big wedding?" Lauren remembered her harrowing midnight visits once a week down in the basement with her foster father. She wished she had the ability Sky did to remove herself from the pain and suffering, but she didn't. Reality was a bitch. And it hurt. Always.

Sighing, Sky nodded. She stood by the large window, looking up, seeing the first stars twinkling in the coming night sky. "I had my doll. I would hold her, sing to her for hours in the closet. I felt safe there, Lauren. I loved reading. I read all the King Arthur fables about white knights rescuing damsels…"

Lauren held back her own black response to that info. Sky was hauntingly fragile and yet, somehow… and God only knew how… she had survived her terrifying childhood far better than she, herself, had. And Sky was still an idealist. "Cal was your white knight on his horse riding to your rescue."

Sky laughed a little and turned, her blue eyes radiant with happiness. "Well, he really was. He's saved my life twice." And then she became serious. "And the second time, it was your Shield Security team who rescued me. I'll be forever grateful to all of you, Lauren. You all put your lives on the line to rescue me out of that hellhole."

Nodding, Lauren said, her voice thick with feeling, "It's the only time I feel really good about myself, Sky. When I'm rescuing someone. Taking out an evil guy with one shot, knowing he will never hurt or kill another innocent human being, makes my day. I'm not an idealist like you." And then she gave Sky a warm look. "I wish I could be. It would go easier for me. Wouldn't it?"

Sky opened her hands, aching for Lauren, for the loads she carried invisibly on her shoulders from her dark past. "Being able to daydream helped me survive," she admitted quietly. "I didn't realize it then of course, as a six-year-old." Her voice lowered with feeling and understanding for Lauren. "I wish... I wish there was some way to help you, Lauren. I don't know how you handle carrying all that stuff... all those memories. You never cry... you rarely talk about it..." She sighed. "If I couldn't talk about it, if I couldn't cry, I think I'd implode. I just don't have the internal strength you do to handle it and keep a lid on all of it and do what you do as a black ops sniper. You are amazing and so strong to me."

"Stick to your idealism," Lauren said, "because my way isn't good, either." She grinned a little, wanting to stop Sky from looking so glum. This was a happy time in her life and Lauren hated being a downer to her best friend. "Tell you what; You daydream for me, okay? Keep those good thoughts coming my way."

Laughing a little, Sky came over and patted her shoulder. "Do you mind if I daydream a knight in shining armor riding to your rescue on his white stallion someday, rescuing you? Would that work?"

"Not likely," Lauren muttered, but she grinned up at Sky. "But who am I to say it doesn't work? Look who you dreamed into your life: Cal. And you two are so much in love with one another, I can't believe it. I never knew that kind of love ever existed."

"I didn't either," Sky admitted, "until Cal found me two years after I was shot. I ran, like I always did, Lauren. Jack's investigation and research found me in Peru, and then Cal came and got me. At first, I was so scared of him and, in truth, I was afraid of myself. I was so drawn to him two years earlier in Afghanistan, but I was just too fearful to take that step toward him."

"Good thing Cal was a SEAL," Lauren murmured. "Once one of those guys sets his sights on a goal, they don't veer off course from getting it. Hell could rain down on that guy, but he'll get that goal." She looked up at Sky. "In this case, he fell in love the day he met you. He followed his heart and he wasn't going to let you walk away from him, either. So, yeah, you bet he'd come after you once Jack located your whereabouts. I'm glad he did." Lauren reached out, gently pressing her hand against Sky's belly. "And look at you now. You're happy. You have a baby on the way. Cal loves you so much..."

"Well," Sky said, smiling down at her, "then I will dream that you meet a man who loves you so much that he can't ever turn away from you."

"Now," Lauren growled, "don't go there. You KNOW I don't believe in love for myself."

And Sky knew why. "I know. But you're so beautiful, intelligent, and accomplished."

"Yeah, don't remind me, okay? I don't WANT their attention, Sky."

"I understand," she said. "But you can't go through life alone, either, Lauren. I can't tell you how lonely and alone I felt. I was like you: prepared to live a life like a hermit when Cal walked in. My few experiences with men scared me off. They scared ME."

"It wasn't like you didn't know they couldn't hurt you, because they did. Why on earth would we run toward what gave us pain, Sky?"

"I know... but I guess I felt so damned alone, that I let Cal inside my walls I had put up. And he knew. He knew I liked him. He was a SEAL. Their sensing is so powerful, their intuition, and he knew I liked him. A lot."

Grinning, Lauren said, "And he didn't let you walk out of his life. He came and found you. It was a nice fairytale ending for you two, and no one's happier than me for both of you. If anyone deserves happiness, it's you and Cal."

Patting her shoulder, Sky walked toward the door, realizing almost an hour had flown by. "YOU deserve happiness, Lauren. And don't you dare give me that narrowed-eyed look and pabulum about how happiness is a crock of bull."

"Okay," Lauren said lightly, her grin widening, "I won't. But look, I'm here for you and Cal. I'll be at your wedding, whenever you set it, unless I'm called out for an op. I like to see happy people because there's so few of them in this sucky world."

"You're a brutal pessimist," Sky teased.

"But it keeps me alive," Lauren sardonically said, giving her a wicked look.

"Yes, and for that," Sky said, opening the door, "I'm more than grateful."

"See you tomorrow morning for breakfast," Lauren said, standing up and putting the chair under the desk.

"I hope you have a good night's sleep."

Grimacing, Lauren said, "You know how that goes."

"Well," Sky said in a whisper, leaning back in through the narrow gap of the door, "if you need to get up, then go out to the kitchen and make yourself some chamomile tea, sit in the living room and look at the Milky Way up in the sky, do just that."

"You're SUCH a dreamer. Good night, Sky. Love you."

"Love you too, Lauren."

Lauren didn't feel she deserved someone as nice, warm and open as Sky. She understood why Cal loved the woman so much. Sky had been an incredible friend to her, as well. Walking to the bed, she sat down and began to undress. There was a huge bathroom at the end of the hall and she loved those two shower heads that behaved as if warm rains were coming down from the sky onto her skin. When Cal had built this cedar home, he'd thoughtfully cobbled it together. Even the glass surrounding the huge shower was frosted, and he'd hand-etched beautiful nature scenes into it. Yes, Sky, the dreamer and Cal, the artist, certainly deserved one another.

She placed her combat boots at the head of her bed, folded up her cargo pants and dark-green t-shirt, laying them over the chair by the desk. Lauren hated bras, never wore them, and chose a silk camisole instead. Shimmying out of her utilitarian cotton panties, she laid them on the bed. Grabbing her small suitcase, she opened it, took out her dark-blue cotton robe that hung to her knees, and pulled it on. She drew out a Ziploc plastic bag that contained her toothbrush and toothpaste and headed out the door.

And ran into Alex Kazak, nearly colliding with him.

Lauren's nostrils flared and she gasped, not having expected to meet the medic. Her heart leapt and adrenaline poured through her veins. He was so tall, his shoulders so broad that he filled the low-lit hall with his bulk. And, instantly, the past flashed in front of Lauren. She didn't see Alex. She saw her hulking foster father enter her bedroom, in the dark, tiptoeing softly toward her bed. Walking toward her. And she could feel him wanting her sexually. She knew he was going to lift her out of bed, and that no matter how much she cried or struggled, he'd soothe her, kiss her and hold her gently in his arms, telling her he had candy in the basement for her.

Lauren slammed into the wall, the terror screaming through her. Her breath came in gasps. She gripped her robe closed at her throat, a reaction to protect herself from Kazak's startled gaze. And then, just as swiftly, Lauren saw him. Saw Alex Kazak, not her sexual predator foster father.

"You scared the HELL out of me!" she nearly yelled. Her voice echoed down the hall.

Alex Kazak tensed. He instantly backed off, seeing the terror in Lauren's shadowed, narrow gray gaze. "I-I am sorry. I did not know you were coming out at the same time I was…"

Cursing to herself, Lauren launched herself away from the wall, barefoot, the cedar floor cool beneath her soles. "Get the hell away from me!" and she spun around, heading for the bathroom. She saw the instant apology in the medic's square face, his hazel eyes wide with surprise and then, Lauren thought she saw sadness. Dammit! He'd scared the living hell out of her! She'd thought it was her foster father. A PTSD flashback that had overlayed reality. All she'd seen was her foster father, not Kazak. A fine quiver moved through her as she quickly opened the door to the bathroom, wanting desperately to escape and be away from him. Snipers were super-sensitized to everything. They knew, better than anyone else, that, once they'd acquired their target, they couldn't follow their movement through the scope or their target would sense them nearby. Lauren could literally feel his gaze on her back.

She shut the door and then leaned against it, breathing unevenly, her heart pounding with the rush of unexpected adrenaline. Pressing her hand against her throat, feeling her chest tighten with the fear vomiting up from her past, holding her prisoner in the present, Lauren fought to get herself under control once more. Kazak was like a bad penny: he showed up at the wrong time with her, every time. She swore to God the man had telepathy and knew exactly when she'd be at every certain place and show up there as well.

Dammit!

CHAPTER 2

ALEX KAZAK TRIED to remain a shadow at the kitchen island where Cal Sinclair was fixing them breakfast. It was impossible. There were four red leather stools at the black granite island. The sun was shining brightly through the open-concept kitchen-living room area as Sky worked with Cal to create a breakfast for the four of them. Alex sat at one end, coffee in hand, watching the two very-in-love people work flawlessly together at the counter. Where was Lauren?

Ever since nearly smashing right into her in the hall last night he'd felt frustrated by her reaction toward him. The terror that had been in her eyes as she'd looked at him tore him up. And it was real. Very real. He'd never done anything to her to make Lauren look at him that way. It hurt. He was interested in her personally. Yet, Alex saw nothing but huge, unscalable walls standing between them. She was a good person who was running hard from something in her past. Frowning, he moved the bright red ceramic mug slowly around between his large hands. Farm hands, as his sister, Kira, often said, pride in her voice. Yes, he had grown up in Ukraine, in a farming family that, for generations, had been growing wheat, plowing and harvesting. He'd been like his father, who was six foot five inches tall, a giant in the family, but he'd been one inch less in height than him. And Alex, because of his size and strength, had done the hard jobs around the farm that few others could.

He glanced toward the hall off the left side of the kitchen that led to the guest suites. The smell of bacon frying, the scent of coffee, always made him feel good. It was almost like being back home on his family farm before it was destroyed by Russian terrorists when he was nineteen years old. Wondering if Lauren was purposely avoiding him by not coming to breakfast, he moved uneasily. The horror in her eyes had deeply disturbed him. She was five foot eleven inches tall, he was five inches taller, and she had nearly screamed when she'd barged out of her bedroom, not realizing he was walking down the hall. His chiseled mouth pursed.

Cal had told him not so long ago that Lauren had survived a very bad childhood. That her foster father was a big man, like him. Cal thought that perhaps Lauren's avoiding him, always being clipped and cold toward him, had something to do with that. Glancing at the hall entrance again, it remained empty. Feeling bad that Lauren was probably avoiding him due to the embarrassment he'd caused her last night, Alex felt sadness. Was Cal right? Was Lauren hating him because he reminded her of her foster father? Could she not separate those two things? See him for who he was? There was so much he wanted to speak to her about, to calm the waters between them because, sooner or later, they would be assigned a mission together. And they'd have to work, out in the field with one another, whether Lauren wanted to or not.

Alex didn't mind working with Lauren. He'd never forget the day he was sitting in the Mission Planning room, the other contractors, men and women who were all ex-military, filing into the room for a meeting. When Lauren arrived, he'd felt as if someone had struck him in the chest with a sixteen-pound sledge hammer. She was tall, curvy, confidence dripping off her, and beautiful. Her red hair was in a ponytail between her proud shoulders. She wore a form-fitting, black, men's t-shirt that showed off those proud, full breasts hidden beneath it. The olive-green cargo pants hid nothing from Alex, even though they were bulky and loose-fitting. But then, as a Spetsnaz sniper as well as a medic, he was trained to notice the smallest of details. Lauren had nice, wide hips, the kind a man could hold onto, and wrap his hands around. Her legs went on forever, and Alex had to imagine how firmly curved and long her thighs were, how tight the muscling was in her calves. She walked with feminine grace, but with a solid confidence he rarely saw in other women.

When he'd sat with Gage Hunter, manager of the Sniper Division, a vaunted ex-Marine Force Recon sniper, Alex had been stunned to realize that half of the employees were women operators. These women came from three of the four US military services and had been trained in the field for a year by the Marine Corps and then assigned to different black ops teams. Some were with Special Forces, others were with SEAL units, or Delta Force teams. Even the Army Rangers. All these women had seen combat for three years in a row; six-month deployments in forward positions around the world and six months stateside, continuing to hone their skills.

Alex had asked Gage about Lauren. She had been the first women to break the all-boy ranks of Marine Force Recons, and was the best that Gage had in-house at Shield. Alex had become excited about that because, as he had told Gage, within Spetsnaz women were being trained to be snipers as they were better shots than males. Which was true. He'd worked with one for two years and had great respect for her. Gage had shown him a computer screen that brought up the twenty-five employees who worked for him at Shield. He'd instantly honed in on the red-haired woman with her stubborn chin lifted up slightly, her cool gray eyes staring out at him, unsmiling. When Alex had pointed to her photo on the screen, asking her name, Gage had told him that she was Lauren Parker, their best sniper and instructor. Alex had smiled. He wanted to meet this woman.

The meeting, Alex decided forlornly, had been a disaster. Lauren had spotted him down at the end of the fifteen-foot square walnut table and frozen. Her calm expression had hardened. Her sharpened gaze had reminded Alex of that soft gray color just before dawn on the eastern horizon, then had become colorless ice shards as she stared malevolently at him. Her lips had parted. And then, she'd snapped them shut, glaring back at him, as if silently daring him to say a word to her. She'd taken a seat at the opposite end of the table, refusing to meet his gaze. At first, Alex figured she just didn't like him. When Gage had introduced him to the Shield crew, Lauren did not welcome him. Alex knew he was a big man. Most of the operators at Shield were less than six feet tall, lean and honed. He supposed he stood out because he probably looked like a bumbling ox in comparison to a herd of gazelles. Maybe he looked ugly and repelled her? Alex honestly didn't know. When the meeting broke up, after he'd been introduced to the group, he'd gotten up to try and meet Lauren. He'd gotten close enough to extend his hand toward her, but she froze him out with a glare that said: back off. So, he did, flummoxed.

Now, three months later, Alex thought he had some of the answers about Lauren. She tolerated him at Shield. She was the lead sniper and trained others in Krav Maga, an Israeli defense force method, besides teaching sniper techniques to her charges. There, she was cool, professional and, if he got too close to her, she'd move away from him, as if he'd infect her like a virus or something. Everyone else at Shield was glad to have him onboard. The sniper-trained women were all pleasant, trading jokes with him, black humor and swapped stories with no problem at all. Lauren refused to engage with him except when forced too. Driving up to Cal and Sky's place yesterday afternoon in her red Jeep Wrangler had stressed them both. She was tense and snappish. He couldn't talk to her because she always took everything he said the wrong way. Granted, English was a second language for him and he was trying desperately to learn it and learn it well. But American slang got him in a whole lot of trouble. Especially with Lauren. So, they had hardly talked.

"How many pancakes, Alex?" Cal called over his shoulder as he worked at the Wolf stove.

"How many can I have?" he asked, grinning. He heard Sky laugh as she cut up onions, green peppers and ham for the coming Denver omelets.

"Sky's the limit, Bro," Cal replied.

"Six? Is that all right? I do not want to take them away from others."

Cal shrugged. "Hey, it's easy to make more pancake batter."

"You probably want nine?" Sky turned, bringing the coffee over and pouring more into his cup. "A dozen?" she teased.

"Nine sounds good." And then he added, "Hey, I am a boy growing."

Sky smiled sweetly at him. "Slang would be a 'growing boy,' Alex."

"Oh," he muttered, "I turned it around again, eh?"

"Just a little. But it's okay. I knew what you meant."

Cal was chuckling darkly, sliding Alex an evil-humored look over his shoulder.

Alex took his faux pas in stride. English was a very hard language to learn in comparison to Russian. Even Quechua, the Incan language down in Peru, had been easy enough to learn. But not English.

He heard a door open and close. Lifting his head, Alex saw Lauren walking slowly down the hall toward them. Eastern sunlight shot in huge shafts through the massive living room, through the kitchen, and highlighted the hallway where she walked. Wondering why Lauren always wore the same outfit, the same color, he thought it was a shame. She was twenty-eight years old, in her prime, and she was a gorgeous woman with a body so hot it made him ache to want to touch her. Alex knew she'd probably deck him if he confided in her that he wanted to make long, slow, delicious love with her. The thought of strumming her body like the fine instrument it was, to hear her sighs and moans, to feel her confidence as a woman challenging him on every level as they made love to one another, teased him. All heated dreams, he knew. But even though he felt she wore men's clothes, bulky and ill fitting, to hide her beautiful, curvy body, it didn't work. At least, not with him.

"Hey, Lauren," Cal called, "hungry?"

Lauren ambled into the kitchen, moving to where the coffee pot was. "Not so much," she said, pouring herself a cup.

"Cal and Alex are having hubcap-sized pancakes," Sky told her. "I'm making a Denver Omelet for myself. Does that sound good to you?"

Lauren sipped her coffee, refusing to look toward the island. She could feel Alex like a bad cold coming on. She wished mightily he'd stop staring at her because she could feel his gaze on her as if he'd reached out and touched her. It made her tense. Jumpy. "Yes, that sounds fine. Do you need help? Want me to break eggs and add some cream?"

"Great," Sky murmured, scooping up the onion, peppers and shredded cheese and putting them into a nearby bowl. "Thanks, come join me. We'll be a team."

Alex watched from the island. He didn't expect Lauren to engage him. She'd only do so if forced to. More sadness moved through him. She had been hurt so badly in the past by a big man. And now, it seemed all he did was remind Lauren of her horrific past. Shaking his head, he sipped his coffee, feeling trapped and unable to know how to undo such damage that stood between them. Damage he had not caused. But Lauren didn't seem to be able to separate him from the man she hated.

"Okay, Bro," Cal said, bringing over a plate of six hubcap-sized pancakes, "start on these."

"Thanks," Alex murmured, taking the huge red ceramic plate. He smelled the scent of vanilla in them. Cal was a chef, not a cook, he'd happily discovered when he was invited up here to stay a weekend with the couple. He was grateful that they treated him like family. Maybe because he'd saved Sky from getting raped by Vlad Alexandrov, and cared for her when she'd had days of malaria, were the reasons they were so grateful to him. Later, when Cal had found them, Alex had created a diversion with the other Russian mafia soldiers staying in the village, and that had enabled them to escape. Sky and Cal's affection for him was genuine and, being in a foreign country, he was indebted to them for their care and their love. And it was love, he knew. They reminded him of the Ukrainian people who took care of others. If there was a disaster, nearby farming families would come and help out, to support those who had lost so much. That was a form of love, also.

Alex ate alone and enjoyed watching Sky and Lauren work together like a well-oiled team to create their two omelets. When Sky came over carrying the two plates, and Lauren with the silverware and napkins, Alex wondered where Lauren would sit. Sky solved that problem by sitting next to Alex. She smiled over at him.

"Wow, you're eating in a hurry, big guy. Hungry?"

He grinned, his gaze on Lauren, who refused to look at him as she sat down across from Sky. "Yes. Starved. I have never heard of pancakes being hubcaps, but they are that big."

"They must be putting you on the obstacle course every day," Cal said drolly, bringing over another six pancakes and shoveling them onto his own empty plate.

"I am putting myself through it," Alex said. Although the interior of Shield Security was hidden within a three-story Virginia farmhouse from the 1850's, Jack Driscoll had used the woodlands in one area to create a SEAL obstacle course for those who had to stay in shape. It was hidden within the woods, an area carved out to place the daunting, challenging course on. In one section, Jack had duplicated the dreaded and infamous obstacle course found at Coronado, where men were trained to become SEALs. The first time Alex ran it, he was winded. But within three months, he had his body finely honed like a sharpened knife blade, back into the shape that an operator needed to be in in order to work at peak efficiency.

"You're a glutton for punishment to run the O course daily when you're here," Cal muttered, shaking his head and returning to the stove.

"Ah, a new slang," Alex said. He pulled out his iPhone and pressed on the note app. Opening it up, he wrote the slang term down. The only way to learn all the thousands of American slang sayings was to keep them in alphabetized details. "What does this mean?" he asked Cal.

"Means you're crazy for wanting to do it daily, something that is punishing or hard to do."

"Oh, I see," and he jotted down the explanation. "So, I am a pig?"

Sky choked. She coughed, holding her hand against her throat.

Cal chuckled. "No. A glutton, someone who eats LIKE a pig. Overeats. Greedy. You're NOT a pig, okay? Nobody's calling you names."

Alex poured more syrup on his pancakes, scowling, trying to marry together all the adjectives Cal threw at him, and come up with a picture that he understood. "But when I run the O course? I am not eating. And I do not run like a pig, either."

Sky patted him gently on the shoulder, after taking a drink of water to clear her throat. "Alex, we use the word 'glutton' in more ways than just describing the eating of food. It could mean, like what you're doing by taking that very tough O course daily. It's not something most people could do."

"Except SEALs," Cal noted proudly.

"Yes," Sky said, "SEALs do run that O course all the time. It keeps them in good shape. Which," she smiled up at Alex's confused-looking face, "is why you do it. It is a very punishing course. It is not something many would put themselves through."

"Okay…," Alex said, thinking he had a handle on the slang. "So? If I clean all my weapons in my armory locker every day? Does that make me a 'glutton for punishment'?"

Cal grinned. "Well, being operators, we know the importance of keeping our weapons clean and in great working order. Think of this in different terms. Anything you would do that is extreme. Running the O course every day is extreme."

"Oh," Alex said suddenly, "such as plowing a field with a team of horses? If I have plowed the field once and it is fine and I go back out and do it again? Is that being a glutton for punishment?"

"Bingo," Cal murmured, giving him a proud look. "You got it." He brought over three more pancakes and sat down next to Lauren.

"Did you really plow fields with horses?" Sky asked.

"Yes," Alex said. "Our farm family was poor when I was young. We could not afford a tractor. The other farm collectives had them, but we were very far out into the country. Not easy to reach. My family owned a thousand acres. We had a huge multi-generational family. Boys like me, who were big and strong for their age, always got to handle the plows in the fields with our heavy draft horses. They were very tall and large," he said, "and they were a beautiful strawberry roan color. They would weigh around fourteen-hundred pounds, and were fifteen hands high."

"Wow," Sky said, amazed. "You have such an interesting background!"

Alex didn't want to go there. He gave Sky a fond smile and said, "Please, eat your omelet while it is hot?" And then he happened to glance up and Lauren was studying him intently, an odd expression on her face. It wasn't anger, which was her usual expression for him. Maybe interest? Unable to interpret it, Alex looked away, unsure of why she was staring at him. Lauren usually refused to make eye contact with him at all. Women... they were confusing to him at the best of times. Lauren was like an intricate Chinese puzzle; so many levels, twists and turns within her. Just when Alex thought he understood her, she'd destroy the confidence he'd just gained.

"I just got a call from Gage earlier," Cal said between bites, getting Lauren and Alex's attention. "He said we just got awarded a huge Defense contract."

"What does that mean?" Alex asked. Since joining, he'd spent the last three months training, getting in shape and learning American weapons systems, and spending a lot of time out at their firing range.

"It means missions are going to be handed out to us," Lauren said. "We're gaining a reputation among the US civilian agencies for being good at what we do. I worked with Gage on that contract and we won it. Shield has enough people onboard to take outside contracts from time to time, and this is one of them."

"Good," Alex said, pleased that she'd responded in a husky tone that did not have anger in it. "Maybe Gage will reward me? I will be given an assignment? I am tired of sitting around. I need the action."

Cal chuckled. "Spoken like a true operator. Don't worry, Hunter will put you on a mission when he thinks you're ready for it, Alex. He's a very good planner, and knows how to choose the right crew for an op."

"Maybe my lucky day, eh?" and Alex grinned, anxious to get back into the fight.

THE NEXT MORNING, when Lauren walked into Shield's front office, Mandy, the receptionist, handed her a note. That meant a mission. Lauren felt relief, wanting to get out of the office and back into the field. Away from Kazak.

Finally. She thanked Mandy and breezed through the side door, walking down the white-tiled hallway to Gage's office.

"Hey," she called, entering with a knock, "you got a mission for me? I'm dying to get into the field." Gage Hunter was thirty years old, a Marine Corps sniper with nine years of combat experience under his belt. He lifted his head from his papers in front of him.

"Yeah, have a seat, Lauren," he invited. "Got something hot from the Defense Department contract we just won. Your partner will be arriving shortly."

Lauren sat down at a small briefing table near Gage's desk. She pulled out her laptop from her ruck and opened it up, ready to type in information. "Great. Where are we going?"

"Peru."

She raised her eyebrows. "I've not done anything in South America. Sure you got the right sniper?"

"Positive," he said, typing some keystrokes on his computer.

Lauren was busy opening a document when she felt someone enter the office. She raised her head. Her eyes narrowed. Alex Kazak stood uncertainly in the doorway.

"Mr. Hunter? Am I at the correct place?"

"Sure are, Alex. Call me by my first name?" Gage lifted his hand, waving him in. "Sit over there with Lauren. Shut the door, please?"

Panic hit Lauren as she saw Alex enter. Each contractor was given a company laptop in which mission planning, and anything related to it, was available on file. What the hell was Kazak doing here? She scowled.

"Why is he here?" she demanded of Hunter.

Gage didn't even look up, hands flying over his keyboard, inputting intel. "He's your partner. Have a seat, Alex."

NO! Lauren's eyes grew huge as she stared disbelievingly at Gage. He KNEW she didn't like the Ukrainian! What the hell did he think he was doing? The words nearly ripped out of her mouth. She saw Alex advance toward the small table. His bulk and size filled the room. And he was giving her an apologetic look, making her feel like shit. She didn't dislike him. It was just his damned size. Alex was a daily reminder of her painful past. He was salt, tearing open the wounds of those horrifying memories she had effectively suppressed until he showed up at Shield. Then, all those memories had come erupting upward, making her life miserable. She looked away from him, her mind running full-tilt. Somehow, she had to convince Gage to give her another partner. In order to do that, she'd have to hear the mission briefing from him first.

Alex took the chair at the end of the table, as far away from Lauren as he could get. She looked shocked. As an operator, his senses were finely honed. He felt more than shock. Running it through himself, he felt the terror within Lauren, even though there was nothing suggesting it on her calm-looking game face. He opened his laptop and turned it on. This was his first assignment at Shield. And he wanted to give a good account of himself, show Hunter and the Driscoll employees who ran the firm, that he'd been a good choice to hire.

"Okay, boys and girls," Gage said, pulling his laptop in front of him. "Go to File A."

Lauren opened it up. Brad Galloway was the Director of Mission Planning. She knew from his input that Gage, Cal Sinclair and others, did the mission planning and briefing for Shield. Brad's name was on this one. Mouth thinning, she said nothing, waiting for Gage to begin.

"The Defense Department has suddenly discovered that the Russian mafia is in utter disarray since Yerik Alexandrov was killed down in Costa Rica. Rolan Pavlovich has taken the reins of the Russian mafia in New York City and is the leader of it." He glanced up at them. "This isn't news to you two, because you pulled the mission to rescue Sky. A Special Forces sergeant killed Alexandrov."

Alex nodded. "That throws all the mafia teams in Peru into instability as well? They get their orders directly from Alexandrov, who was Mafia boss in New York City. Now he is no longer there, the new boss has been installed. Does anyone know if the Peru drug gang will be resurrected by Pavolvich?"

"Right question to ask," Gage murmured, pleased with the Ukrainian's grasp of the situation. "And this leaves the Defense Department wanting to drive a Mack truck right through the current instability this branch of the mafia is currently experiencing in Peru. Your job, Alex, because you were down in Peru for two years with one of those groups, is to go locate the other five Russian groups that were put together by Yerik Alexandrov. The Defense Department wants the leader of each one killed, to create more chaos among them and, hopefully, stop Pavlovich from reforming all of them and doing what Alexandrov could not. By doing that," and he looked over at Lauren, "you're cutting off the head of the snake. The Army is preparing to put in five Special Forces teams, three men each, to locate, capture and retrieve, or arrest, or kill, the members of these other four groups. The Peruvian government requested our assistance in this matter. This is your mission."

"And the Peruvian government is behind this?" Lauren demanded. It was a federal offense to be found with a military-style weapon in Peru. It meant a long jail sentence in a prison at ten thousand feet where it was cold and miserable, for up to twenty years, with no hope of getting out early for good behavior.

"Yes, they're backing this fully and we have their blessing. You won't have to worry about being caught with military weapons on you."

"Why is Peru okay with this?" she asked.

"Because the insertion of the Russian Mafia is creating an ongoing drug war with the two South American drug lords who already own that turf. A lot of innocent villagers are being killed, raped, or wounded in the crossfire. Peru lacks the funds and high-tech ability to hunt these Russian groups down and eradicate them. They've asked our federal government for direct intervention and help."

"Better the enemy you know," Lauren drawled.

Gage nodded. "Alex can tell you first-hand: The Russian Mafia intruding into established drug lord turf has turned the highlands of Peru into an ongoing blood bath. The Peruvian government is more than happy to have you two coming in. Lauren, you are the sniper and Alex will be your spotter, to hunt these pack leaders down."

Alex nodded, but said nothing. If Hunter wanted him to comment, he'd ask. He noticed Lauren had shifted into briefing mode. She was asking a lot of good, important questions.

"Okay, here's the meat of your mission," Gage said. "You're going down there undercover. You're going to pose as tourists on an extended vacation from the U.S. You are married. Lauren, you're a botanist. Alex, you're her husband who lets her do whatever she wants, including looking for rare orchids in the jungle, which just happens to be in the same area these five groups are operating within. You will pose as a paramedic with the New York City Fire Department. We'll make sure your credentials hold up, should someone get curious."

Lauren's head snapped up.

Gage held up his hand and said, "Hear me out, Lauren, and then I'll answer any questions you have."

Chastened, Lauren realized she had allowed her emotions to get the better of her. She prided herself on always being in control; never allowing her feelings to get in the way of an op. Gage wanted her to pretend to be a couple, to be married and undercover, with Alex? Her mind spun and Lauren scrambled inwardly. In her wildest, worst-nightmare scenarios she had never dreamed Gage would team her up with Alex.

"Your base of operation is Aguas Calientes, the small Peruvian town at the foot of Machu Picchu. You'll rent an apartment there. Townspeople will see you out and about as a tourist couple. You'll eat at a number of restaurants in order to be seen and, Lauren, you'll be letting people know you're a botanist interested in finding rare or new orchid species. Spread the word and hand out money to the poor, who will be more than willing to show you where there are orchids, as part of your ongoing cover. Alex, in reality, is going to be your spotter. Undercover? He's going along as your doting husband who only wants to make you happy. He is going to offer his paramedic services to the small medical clinic, Helping Hands Charity, that is located there. It's a good way to pick up useful info on Quechua Indians coming down from the highlands for medical treatment. Furthermore, it will indebt the locals to you and you may pick up some more intel. There's a CIA agent contact for you there, as well, and he will give you the details on your mission briefing after you connect with him. Plus, you'll have daily updates from Shield, via scrambled and encrypted satellite phone conference calls, as well as via encrypted emails. Alex is going to be tasked with finding each group. He speaks fairly decent Quechua, as well as Spanish. And then, once you are able to establish where a group is located, you'll be flown in by a black ops Nightstalker helicopter. After being dropped close to the nearest village where they're located, Alex will speak to the chief, and hear what he knows about the situation."

Gage looked up at them. "Lauren, once Alex is able to confirm where a group is at, you'll go into stalk mode. Learn where it's best to set up a shot after Alex is able to identify the leader of that group. Then, take him out, fade into the jungle, get back to Aguas Calientes and resume your undercover life for a few days or a week until things settle down. Then, go after the next group. Same way. Same outcome. Okay. Questions?"

CHAPTER 3

LAUREN'S GUT WAS a mass of writhing snakes by the time Gage had finished his briefing with them. She could barely think through it all, typing in pertinent intel almost by muscle memory. Alex had asked a lot of good, in-depth questions, things she should have been asking, but she had not been focused. *At all.* It was an hour before Gage ended the details of the briefing. Alex gave her a worried look once, but said nothing, and left the office, heading for the lockers located in the basement. He had to get his weapons ready for transit.

Lauren watched Gage's oval face. The ex-Marine Recon sniper had dark green eyes with large black pupils. He always spoke quietly, and had laser-like eye contact who whomever it was he was speaking to. And, typical of any sniper, he had a game face on. Lauren knew she had to get her own shit together enough in order to convince him that she wasn't the right sniper for this op.

"Gage?"

"Yes?" He looked up after putting photos into a file on his desk.

"I'm requesting to be taken off this op."

His brows fell. "Why?"

Lauren compressed her lips, took a deep breath and said, "I just don't feel I'm the best qualified sniper to go on it. I have NO experience down in South America. I don't know Spanish, much less Quechua." She tried to appear relaxed, but her heart was pounding in her chest and she wondered if Hunter could hear it. Opening her hands, she added helpfully, "Surely one of the other women snipers has field experience down there? Speaks Spanish? Wouldn't that be a better fit with Kazak?" Her throat was dry. She was desperate for a drink of water. And Hunter's face was utterly unreadable. Lauren would never want to come up against this operator in a fight.

Gage folded his hands, evaluating her reasons. "You've been working here a long time, Lauren, and never ONCE have you asked to be taken off an op."

Grimacing, Lauren said, "I know. But this one is different."

"Different how?" Hunter demanded. "You've gone on ops in areas you've never been in before. Nor did you speak their language. You never cried foul."

Edgy, Lauren felt the focus of his eyes on hers. As if he could feel what she was really thinking: Wanting to bail on the op, wanting nothing to do with Alex. "Who among the other snipers speaks Spanish?" she challenged quietly, holding his unblinking stare.

"Two. So what?"

"Well," she stumbled, "why not one of them and not me?"

"Because Alex speaks Spanish and Quechua. Besides, those two snipers are both out on other missions, otherwise I'd have chosen one of them for this assignment. He's the total package. He'll translate for you," Gage replied smoothly, unruffled.

Desperation raced through her. Lauren cast about for a reason; one Gage would accept. "Look," she growled, "I don't feel comfortable around Kazak. Okay?"

"So," Gage said, "that's the truth?"

Anger flared in Lauren. "Yes," she snapped.

Gage folded his hands on his desk, head down in thought for a moment. When he finally raised his head and studied her, he said, "Is this a personality clash? A mismatch?"

"It is." She saw Hunter give a bare shake of his head. His black hair was military short. He pushed his fingers through it, sitting back in his chair, rocking it ever so gently.

"From your end? You're the one asking to bail."

"Yes, it's from my end," she growled back. Gage didn't scare her at all. No man did. Except Alex. "I won't be able to concentrate or focus like I have to."

"Only one person can handle that rifle at a time," he drawled. "You dial it in like you always do. Kazak isn't going to be sitting there, chatting idly away with you when you're in the zone. He's a trained sniper himself. He'll be your spotter on this mission, helping you by feeding you the information that you need to dial in."

Frustrated, Lauren said, "I know that."

"Then what the hell is this really all about?" he demanded, sitting up in his chair, his voice tight.

Chin jutting out, Lauren glared at him. "I don't trust him!" Well, that WAS the truth.

"In what way?"

Nostrils flaring, her hands clenching on each side of her laptop, Lauren snarled, "In EVERY way. He was a damned mafia goon for two years in Peru. How the hell do you think I feel about working with someone like that?"

"Because he was a mafia convert?"

"Hell yes! He ran with common criminals."

Hunter snorted and glared back at her. "Never mind that he saved Cal and Sky's life? Never mind that he turned on his own group of ex-Spetsnaz soldier? Do you even know he took a bullet for Cal and Sky? To get them safely out of that Indian village?"

Her eyes widened. "What are you talking about? All I heard is that he rescued them."

Gage smiled a little, his voice turning deadly quiet. "It was Kazak's idea for Cal to shoot him with a through-and-through in his lower leg, the calf area. That way, he'd told Cal, once his friends in the group found him, he could convince them he'd been unable to stop Sky from escaping. And," Gage went on, nothing casual about him now, "Alex misled the group and sent them in the opposite direction of where Cal and Sky had gone to escape. As it turned out, the leader, Vlad Alexandrov, couldn't find them, and he turned his rage on Kazak. He nearly beat him to death, Lauren. When the Special Forces team found Alex, he had a broken nose, cracked ribs, not to mention the fact that his mafia friends had left him to slowly bleed out from that leg wound. They left him to die and never gave him any medical help whatsoever. They could have, but didn't."

Lauren looked down, processing the information. "I didn't know that," she muttered lamely.

"Alex turned against them to save two lives," Gage went on, rolling his shoulders to rid them of accumulated tension. "He was a bad guy who did the right thing. So now, he's a good guy. I have no doubt where his loyalties lie, Lauren. The only family he has left is his sister, Kira. The State Department granted them political asylum in our country, and both are on their way to earning their green cards to become citizens probably about six-to-eight years down the road. I vetted Kazak personally because I wanted to make damn SURE he wouldn't turn on us. And I'm confident he's one of us."

She gave him a narrow-eyed look. "Just how sure?"

"He can have my back any time he wants. Is that good enough for you?"

Stinging beneath his warning growl, Lauren knew when an operator said the person could have their back, it implied trust. Total trust. That the operator was good and wouldn't screw up in the midst of a hot firefight. "Yeah, it's good enough."

"I've got a dirty suspicion you're not really coming clean with me regarding this op," Hunter said, holding her stare. "And I think what it comes down to, is your attitude. You've been in the Corps and have gotten saddled before with people you didn't like, but you damn well worked with them anyway. And you successfully carried off those ops without a hitch."

Anger riffled through her. She stiffened. "I have told you the truth!"

Gage shook his head. "No... no, I sense something more is behind this, Lauren. And frankly, I could give a shit less what that is." He jabbed his finger toward her. "You've got your orders. YOU make this mission work, whatever your issues. I need my very best sniper on this op, and that's you. So, if you want to get pissed, get pissed at yourself because you're so fucking good at what you do. Dismissed."

AN HOUR LATER, after Alex had finished cleaning all the weapons he'd pack for the op, he decided to go back and talk to Hunter. Alex saw the door was open, knocked lightly and stuck his head in. "Do you have a moment, sir?" he asked his boss.

Hunter scowled. "Not you, too?"

Alex gave him a confused look.

Hunter made a sharp gesture for him to get his ass in the office. "Get in here and close the door."

Alex stood close to attention in front of Hunter's desk. "Sir," he said, "I respectfully ask to be removed from this op." Alex knew he could be fired over this. He could lose the job he loved, and desperately needed. He had no other source of income.

"Shit."

Alex looked down at Hunter, who was shaking his head. "You know what? I don't know what the hell is going on between the two of you, but you're damn well going to address the issues and fix them. Do you understand, Kazak? If you've got a personality conflict with Lauren, then FIX IT. Got it?"

Gulping, Alex came fully to attention. "Yes, sir. I will, sir."

"Now get the hell out of here. You're wasting my time."

"Yes, sir." Alex did a smart about-face and reached for the door knob.

"You'll find her out at the firing range."

Alex hesitated, and then twisted the knob and opened the door. "Yes, sir," he said again, quietly.

"Leave the door open, Kazak."

"Yes, sir."

Alex girded himself. He pulled the black baseball cap out of his pocket and settled it on his head, walking out through the rear of the facility, toward the firing range. That meeting hadn't gone well at all. Obviously, Lauren had talked to Hunter earlier. And that probably hadn't gone the way Lauren had wanted, either. Grimacing, Alex followed the concrete walk toward the bunker area. The firing range was above and below ground. State of the art. The above ground section was for rifles and sniper shooting. The pistol range was located on the first of two underground floors. His senses told him Lauren was on the upper firing range. Probably putting center-mass shots into the paper target, and visualizing it was his face on that cardboard cutout.

The morning sunlight was bright and he wore wraparound sunglasses. As he stepped into the bunker area, huge walls of dirt in all four directions, looking like massive earthen dikes, he spotted Lauren below. She was firing a .300 Win mag sniper rifle. The boom of the rifle, when fired, echoed like rolling thunder within the enclosed area. He was sure she had earplugs in because the sound would destroy a person's hearing over time. She lay prone, legs spread, her baseball cap on backwards, the brim brushing between her shoulder blades. She was shooting at a thousand yards, and Alex watched as Lauren caressed the trigger, and then the ripple effect throughout her entire body as the bullet left the chamber. It was a big, powerful rifle. She was tall, and heavier than most women, and Alex could see her entire body absorb the powerful recoil from the shot.

He walked around from behind her so she could easily spot him. She did.

Alex saw Lauren's head suddenly snap up. She had dark glasses on, so he couldn't see the anger that he was sure was in her eyes. As he approached, she sat up into a kneel, resting back on the heels of her combat boots. He slowed, making sure there was plenty of room left between them. Taking off his sunglasses, Alex crouched down in front of her. The way her mouth was set tight, the tension in her body, told him to be prepared.

"We need to talk," he began quietly, opening his hands. "We cannot go on this op like this. I think you know that, Lauren." He watched her grow more tense, if that was even possible. The feeling radiated off her, like a tidal wave, toward him. He felt her fear, her frustration and hatred. So many dark emotions. All aimed at him. "I know you hate me," he began awkwardly, casting around in his head for the right words in English. This was a struggle for Alex because, if he had been speaking in his mother tongue of Ukrainian, he'd have been far more eloquent and persuasive and, most likely, would have been able to win a reprieve from Lauren. Right now, he felt foolish, unsure of his words, feeling her rage aimed at him. "I do not hate you. I respect you, Lauren. You are a woman of many skills and I admire you—"

"Dammit, I don't hate you! So, let's just get that off the table, shall we?" Lauren jerked off her dark glasses and tucked them into the upper pocket of her cammies. Pulling the cap around, she jerked the bill down, shading her eyes from the sunlight.

"Oh…" Alex swallowed hard. "You do not hate me?"

Lauren scrambled to her feet, dusting off her knees and lower legs. "What did I just say, Kazak? Are you hard of hearing, too?"

Befuddled by this sudden, unexpected admittance, Alex remained crouched. Something told him to seem smaller than he normally did. He suspected Lauren was scared of his height and bulk. She stood there, breathing harshly, her hands on her hips, glaring down at him. "No, I hear okay," he said, keeping his voice low and even. Lauren was like a wild steppe pony from the rugged, mighty Mongolia in Central Asia. Or perhaps like the steeds the Russian Cossacks rode: those hardy, wild-eyed, hot-blooded horses who were akin to the mustangs here in America. "I just asked Mr. Hunter to remove me from this op," he admitted. He saw Lauren's mouth drop open. She quickly shut it. "But," he offered sadly, "he said no. He said we must talk to one another and do... well...," and he searched in his mind for the word.

"Sort it out," Lauren provided, the anger draining from her voice. She stared at Alex, seeing how open and vulnerable he was toward her. She had been ripping into him with a passion. What was wrong with her? The guy had just tried to remove himself from the op because he knew she was uncomfortable around him. *Shit!* Turning, Lauren walked away about ten feet, her mind and emotions in utter turmoil. She hated herself for taking her issues out on Alex. The guy didn't have a clue as to why she couldn't stand being around him.

She swiped her jaw, sweat standing out on her face from the rising July heat hitting the region. What to do? There were no options. Hunter would have her ass in a sling if she screwed this op up. And he'd have every right to do so. And then, Lauren realized the enormity of what Kazak had just done by going to Hunter, requesting to be removed. He was their newest member here at Shield. He still had to prove himself. To go in and ask to be relieved on his very first mission sent a very bad message to Hunter. Even though they were no longer in the military, Shield was run as if they were.

She groaned inwardly, shutting her eyes for a moment. Alex had literally put his job on the line for her. Lauren felt pulled in two different directions inwardly. He did NOT deserve to be fired for what he'd just done. And, as far as she could tell, it looked as if Hunter had ordered them to kiss and make up. Some relief trickled through her. Lauren turned, walking back toward the Ukrainian. He remained in his crouch, balanced on the toes of his boots, long arms resting relaxed across his thick, long thighs. Licking her lower lip, she asked, "Did Hunter threaten to fire you?"

Surprised, Alex said, "Uhh... no. Why?" Lauren's expression was suddenly readable to him. She wasn't hiding behind that game face of hers anymore. He sensed her worry, concern and anger. At least that sense of hatred wasn't there right now and he drew in a deep, grateful breath.

"You do realize by going in there and asking Hunter to remove you from this op, he could have kicked your ass right out of Shield? Fired you?"

Giving a slow nod, Alex watched Lauren's face closely. She was concerned for him. That touched him deeply. It surprised him because she'd never shown any care toward him. Not even as a fellow employee. Her mouth, that sinner's mouth of hers, was pursed. He could feel her thinking, balancing something, but he didn't know what. So, he remained patient and quiet.

"You knew I asked to have you removed."

"I found out when I went to Mr. Hunter's office. He said, 'you too?'"

"But you made your request anyway?"

"Of course."

"What do you mean, 'of course'?!" Lauren demanded, striding closer to him. "You had no reason to do that! You could have lost your job!"

Her breathing was ragged, her nostrils flared and her face red with anger as she glared down at him. Alex maintained his calm. Lauren was certainly a wild, temperamental steppe pony, no question. "I do not like to see you suffer. When I am around you, I feel pain in you, Lauren. I do not know where it comes from; only that I cause it." Alex frowned and shook his head. "I do not know what I have done to you to make you react like this toward me. I did not want to see you in pain during this op. I do not wish to continue to hurt you."

Growling in frustration, Lauren's heart tore open over his simply-spoken words, the honest unvarnished truth in his eyes, his large hands open toward her in supplication. Maybe as an apology for breathing. *Shit!* She stormed away, walking a good hundred feet before she stopped, breathing erratically. How bad did she want a job here at Shield? The military was all she had ever known since age eighteen. It had saved her life. Given her goals. Aspired dreams within her of being like her Marine Corps sniper father, who had been a real hero. Lauren knew she had to make this work. If she fucked up on the op, Hunter would go after her. Rightfully so. She was the one wanting out. Alex had put himself in the line of fire to protect her in his own way. *Damn.* Running her fingers through the hair by her temple, Lauren tried desperately to sort all this out in her mind.

Alex was a man of integrity. He had morals. Values. She hadn't known he'd nearly died, nearly given his life, in order for Sky and Cal to escape Vlad Alexandrov and his thugs. He'd shown a loyalty that Lauren respected. Her two best friends wouldn't be here if that Ukrainian crouched on the ground behind her, begging her to try and work things out with him, hadn't stepped in and nearly sacrificed himself for them. She felt horrible about how she'd been treating Alex. Wearily, Lauren rubbed her face. She turned, slowly walking back to him.

"Get up," she growled, gesturing sharply for him to rise. Lauren halted, watching him slowly unwind upwards, all male grace. Alex's face was open. He trusted her. She didn't trust him. Licking her lower lip, Lauren tried to sound reasonable, not angry as she usually sounded toward him. "I don't hate you. I never did. It's just… that… well…" and she choked, her throat tightening up. Dammit! Her emotions were running rampant through her, out of her control. Being around this big Ukrainian always made her feel like he was dismantling the walls that had shielded her up until now, from everything and everyone. She shut her eyes, wrestling to get the words out.

"Someone hurt you very badly, Lauren."

His low voice filtered in through all her turmoil. A voice filled with sympathy, understanding. She snapped her head up, her eyes narrowing on his. All she saw in Alex's hazel eyes was compassion. For her. "How…," she croaked. "How could you know?" and that scared her even more. Was this guy a telepath? Reading her mind? Lauren never wanted anyone to know what she'd lived through. What she'd survived. And yet, the kind expression on Alex's face, the look in his eyes, made her tremble inwardly. Even worse, tears burned at the back of her eyes. Lauren blinked a couple of times, willing them away.

"I have watched you with other men. I know you work with them, but you are never tense or angry around them. Only when I walk in, do you go on guard." Alex wasn't about to tell her what Cal had told him. That would break a loyalty between them, and he wasn't going to let that happen. "I feel… sense… a man, perhaps my size, hurt you very badly, Lauren. It is the only logical reason for your consistent reaction toward me. I have never given you cause to be afraid of me. Or angry. I have always treated you with the respect you deserve."

Lauren whirled around away from him, her eyes tightly shut. She felt a fist of emotion shoving up through her, shutting off her breathing. Her heart felt like a tortured animal in her chest, so much pain radiating outward around it. Pressing the heels of her hands against her eyes, she forced herself back under control. Finally, and she didn't know how long it had taken, she slowly turned back toward Alex. He was standing exactly where she'd left him. His hands were loose and relaxed at his sides. His expression was kind, but now concerned. He was concerned about her.

She cleared her throat and walked closer. "Okay," she rasped, her voice coming out strained, "You're right, and that's all I'll ever say about it. And don't ever bring it up to me again. Not EVER."

"Okay," Alex agreed gently. He saw the terror, the anguish, in her stormy gray eyes. Heard it in her husky voice. He knew Lauren was struggling to be honest and fair toward him. She knew she had to make this op work, too. For both their sakes, but for different reasons. "What can I do to help you then? I do not mean to scare you. Is it my gestures are too fast? Or coming up behind you and you do not hear me approach? Tell me, Lauren, and I will change it." And he would. Alex would give her his life if that's what she wanted, but he could never know that. So much stood in the way between them. Her past, whatever it contained, was a mountain range between them, not just a wall. Alex had no hope it could ever be crested. And that gutted him. Because he felt like a man without water, and Lauren was water to drink, to allow him to live, not just exist. He'd never met anyone like her, and the moment he'd seen her, he'd secretly given her his heart.

Giving a jerky nod, Lauren whispered, "Yes, to all of those. You can't come up behind me. It scares the living hell out of me."

"Okay, I will not," he promised her solemnly. "What else?"

"No sharp gestures if you can help it." She closed her eyes, remembering. Not wanting to remember. Sharp movements of her foster father's hands, pinning her arms above her head, stopping her from striking out to try and get away from him...

"You know we are married under cover. How...," he groped with words again, "how will you feel if I touch you out in public?"

Yeah, Lauren thought, they are supposed to be a happily-married couple. That was a complete joke. "It's okay if you put your arm around me every once in a while."

"Kiss you?" Alex wanted so badly to do that. But he saw the disgust come to her eyes. "Well, perhaps a kiss on the hair," and he gestured toward his head, "to give the appearance?"

"That would be okay. Not often." Because Lauren knew if Alex kissed her mouth, her whole carefully-constructed inner world would explode and fall apart around her. She was drawn to the Ukrainian. Didn't know why. Never had been drawn to a man before him. And she didn't know how to handle it, or how to deal with Alex. She was more afraid of herself, if he kissed her, than of him.

"We must be in the same room together."

Nodding, Lauren shrugged wearily. "I won't sleep with you." Then why did she feel such intense, unexpected longing to be in his arms, to be held by him? It staggered her, and Lauren had no defense against the yearning hunger that was now coming to life within her.

"No... of course not. I will take the floor. You take the bed. Yes?" and Alex saw just how exhausted she really was because Lauren completely dropped those shields of hers. Alex saw a woman who had been pushed into a corner and was now trapped. And there was no way out for her. It would be like going to the dentist and getting a tooth drilled without Novocain, he thought.

"May I hold your hand from time to time? People who are in love often do that. My parents did up until they died. My grandparents held hands, too."

Lauren heard a sudden lurch of pain in Alex's low voice. Saw sudden anguish in his eyes but it was gone as swiftly as it had arrived. He was good at hiding too, she thought. "Yes, that's fine. Just... not all the time...," because she might get used to it, and the reality was that it was undercover work. *Pretend. Not real. Fake.*

"Yes, I will be mindful of it," he said. The change in Lauren was staggering. She'd gone from being a Harpy Eagle, the large eagle that killed monkeys in South America, one of the most aggressive of all predators, to a terribly exposed, stripped, vulnerable woman. This was who hid behind those powerful walls she'd erected. Alex found himself enamored with the real Lauren. She was hesitant. Unsettled. Not boldly confident like before. He saw her casting adrift, upset, her emotions clearly etched into her lovely gray eyes. Wincing inwardly, Alex stared at her soft, wide mouth. Right now, her lips were compressed, as if holding back words, maybe emotions. Alex wasn't sure.

"Is there any way I can help you?" he asked, searching her eyes, wanting so much to stop hurting her. "To take away your pain?"

Lauren managed a derisive half laugh. "I wish you could, but you can't." And then, more darkly, "No one can help me. What's done is done. We just need to move on, focus on the op." The tender look Alex gave her damn-near unstrung the massive control she was holding over herself. Why did he have to be so damned open? So readable? Such a good human being? A man who would give his life so others might live? Her view of him was changing minute-by-minute.

"Very well," he said, his voice husky with emotion. "But you tell me if you need something, Lauren? I do not wish to continue making you feel pain by my presence."

Wearily, she walked over and picked up her rifle, checking its chamber and then safing it, before she pulled the strap across her shoulder. "Come on, we've got a lot of stuff to get done before we leave. Gage will have the receptionist give us our new identities, credit cards, driver licenses, and all that stuff. We need to commit it all to memory."

Alex forced himself to move toward her. He could see Lauren working through her fear, standing her ground, allowing him to come closer to her than he ever had before. "I am sorry," he whispered, meaning it, holding her gray gaze. "I wish... I wish things were different between us."

Lauren shook her head. "So do I. Come on, we got a ton of things to do before we're wheels-up."

CHAPTER 4

ALEX THOUGHT HE'D probably looked like a deer caught in the headlights, staring as he had at the most beautiful woman he'd ever seen. He stood in the lobby of Shield five hours later, waiting on Lauren's imminent arrival. She had gone home to her apartment to dress and pack. And he didn't know what to expect. When she walked in through the sliding glass doors in a pearl-gray linen pant suit with a white silk tee beneath it, her eyes were still the first thing he looked at. They were a dove-gray, black pupils huge, a thin crescent of black around her irises, emphasizing their luminosity. Her hair was swept up and twisted around at the back of her head, a long, curved silver comb studded with white pearls holding it all in place. Soft crimson tendrils touched her temples. The silver-stud earrings with white pearls set in them made her look elegant. *A model.* Alex had seen some magazines on racks in the grocery store and he thought Lauren could be on the front cover of any of them. She was simply breathtaking.

Lauren saw the look in Alex's eyes as she arrived with her white leather purse over her left shoulder. She felt nervous, stomach fluttery, beneath the heated inspection he gave her. There was no missing how she affected him. And, for whatever reason, over the past few hours, she had made a little bit of internal peace with Kazak. He was a hero. He wasn't a turncoat, as she'd previously thought. And he was no longer dressed in cammo pants and a black t-shirt, either. Instead, a pair of bone-colored chino pants, some comfortable sneakers and a green polo shirt that drew out the emerald tint in his hazel eyes made him ruggedly good-looking. He was clean-shaven, no more of that stubble that had made him look dangerous to her. As Lauren drew near, she caught the scent of what she thought was Ivory soap combining with his male fragrance. It did funny things to her lower body. Sensations she'd never felt before. And, as he dipped his head, his well-shaped mouth drew into a slight smile of admiration as he greeted her.

"You could be on the cover of any fashion magazine," Alex told her, unable to tear his gaze from hers. Lauren had such long, long legs. Alex wondered what they looked like bare, imagining, and feeling himself begin to react inappropriately. He did not need an erection right now. Not with her. She was a sniper. She'd notice everything. *Everything.*

"Thanks," Lauren muttered, lowering her lashes, unable to stand the frank appraisal he gave her. "Stop staring at me like a slobbering dog, okay?" and her lips twitched with irritation. "If we're supposed to be married, you gotta stop looking at me like I'm meat on the hoof."

Alex felt heat rush to his face and he had the good grace to give her an apologetic look. "I am sorry. But," and he gestured toward her where she stood six feet away from him, "you are... you look like the queen of England, wearing her pearls. Truly."

It was her turn to feel heat in her face because Alex's cheeks had also turned a ruddy color. "Well," Lauren managed, "you don't clean up so bad yourself." And he didn't. That polo shirt stretched across his broad shoulders and chest, silently told her just how strong he was. He wore a linen sports coat of the same color as his chinos over the polo shirt. She could tell his biceps were thick, but he was not obtrusively muscled. There was a sprinkling of dark hair peeking out from the neck of his polo shirt.

His masculinity was screaming at her and she felt destabilized by it. This time, however, she wasn't reacting to him because of his height or size. It was the quiet masculine power that surrounded Alex; as if he could handle any situation, no problem. And gazing up into his square face, his boyish smile curving the corners of his mouth, his crooked nose, his straight black eyebrows across those large, intelligent eyes, all served to make Lauren feel shaky inside. In her lower body she felt a gnawing sensation. Lauren wished she could call Sky. Ask her what was going on with her. Now she regretted never having had a long-term relationship with a man before. Those two boys in high school had cured her of that. Now Lauren felt ignorant of her own body's behavior, and of how to deal with Alex's raw admiration that was burning in his eyes for her.

"This is probably a stupid question," she said, "but have you ever flown first class on an airline before?"

"No." Alex added with a shrug, "I'm used to helicopters and transports. Not commercial airliners. Is there something I should know?"

"Yeah," Lauren said wryly, "but I'll teach you as we go along. Just stick close, and I'll tell you in a low voice. That way, you'll look like the savvy traveler you're pretending to be."

There was an amused gleam in her gray eyes. Oh, he wanted to stick close, all right. If Lauren could have read his mind, she'd have snapped right back into that aggressive defensive posture of hers. The change in her was startling. Shocking, in the best of ways, for Alex because he'd never seen Lauren all dressed up like this before. He liked her this way. She wasn't smiling, which was what he wanted more than anything else, but if he couldn't have that, at least she wasn't looking at him like he was the bogeyman anymore. And she was softer toward him. Best of all, she had lowered some of those walls she always hid behind. Lauren was now so much more approachable. She was behaving somewhat as she acted with the other Shield employees. Would she ever joke with him? Laugh with him? Alex could hope.

Gage Hunter sauntered out, giving them the once over. "Where's the ring, Kazak?"

"Oh…," and Alex grinned bashfully over at Lauren while he dug into the pocket of his sports coat. He drew out a small red jewelry box. "I picked these myself from supply. I hope you like them?" and he opened the lid.

To Lauren's everlasting shock and surprise, there was a plain silver wedding band within, and a beautiful white pearl engagement ring. The latter would go well with her outfit. He beamed as she came forward.

"How did you know?"

"Know what?" He saw amazement in her eyes as she looked up at him.

"That I was going to be wearing pearls?" and Lauren touched the single strand of them around her neck.

Gage chuckled and ruefully shook his head. "You two are a pair, I gotta tell you. You oughta be doin' stand-up comedy together," and he laughed heartily.

Lauren gave Hunter a dirty look. And then, before she could say anything, Alex picked up her left hand, holding it very gently between his long, calloused fingers, and slipped on the first and second ring. Her flesh grew hot, prickles of absolute pleasure tingling throughout her hand anywhere his roughened skin briefly touched hers.

"There," Alex said, smiling and releasing her long, spare hand, "now you look perfect."

Hunter came over and stood next to Alex. "Yeah, you clean up well, Parker. Wish you'd do it more often," and he gave her a teasing grin.

"Get lost, Hunter. We're undercover. I have to play the part of a botanist. Remember? Don't you think a botanist would prefer pearls over gemstones? Something that is living? Organic?" Lauren glared at him before he could answer. "I sure as hell do."

Gage held up his hands in surrender. "Hey, you look very nice, Lauren. Really, no bull."

She snorted derisively.

"Wait here," Alex pleaded, as he hurried up to the receptionist's desk.

Lauren frowned at Hunter.

Hunter shrugged.

"What's he up to?" she growled.

"Got me," and he gave her an evil grin. "Probably up to no good, by the look on his face."

Alex came back and held out a white orchid with a fuchsia and gold lip on it. "Here, I thought about your cover. That you love flowers and plants. Would this orchid not look right for you to wear? We are on vacation. Right? And you cannot bear to be without your flowers?"

Lauren's heart somersaulted as Alex tentatively held out the orchid in his large hand toward her. There was a small plastic vial at the end of its stem, wrapped all around in white satin ribbon to hide it. The orchid would look appropriate for the trip. "T-this is beautiful...," and Lauren briefly brushed a finger across one of the waxy petals.

"Pin it on her," Gage ordered Alex. "Left lapel. Nice touch, by the way."

Alex nodded, but he looked gravely down at Lauren. "Do you mind if I do this?" Because he knew she didn't want him very close to her or touching her any more than necessary.

"Don't you feel like you're going to the prom?" Gage unmercifully teased them. "Boyfriend is gonna pin his girlfriend? Don't stick her with that needle, Kazak."

"Shut up, Hunter. Don't you have anything else better to do?" and Lauren gave him a withering look. Alex looked as if he didn't know how to pin it on her and she wasn't going to let Gage ride Kazak. He did often enough, anyway. But not today.

Gage grinned. "Okay, I'm leaving. Corky, your driver, is coming around with the car to take you two lovebirds to the Regan International Airport to pick up your flight. When you reach Lima, check in."

"Roger," Lauren muttered. She saw the helpless look Alex gave her, extending the corsage toward her.

She scooped it up and muttered, "It's okay. Most guys don't know how to pin a corsage on a woman's lapel, anyway," and she quickly affixed the orchid to the gray linen lapel.

"That looks very good on you," Alex said, nodding in approval, smiling.

"Thanks... that was a thoughtful idea." And it was. Alex appeared to be an easygoing, somewhat bumbling farm boy from Ukraine, but she was beginning to understand there was a hell of a lot more intelligence to him than what had first met her eyes. Would any other of her mission specialists going on this op with her have thought of an orchid to complete her cover? She sure didn't think so. It told her about the level of detail Alex was accustomed to utilizing. He was black ops, undercover, and was showing her that he understood the depth and details of being just that with her on this mission.

"My pleasure," he murmured, seeing the pink blush spread across her high cheeks. Lauren's eyes were exotic-looking to him. He'd been on missions in just about every part of the once-upon-a-time Russian Empire, and beyond. Women in some countries had slightly tilted eyes, and he always thought that made them mysterious-looking. It certainly did with Lauren. Like the orchid, which was also exotic, the flower and her eyes belonged together, but Alex didn't think she'd want to hear him wax poetic about his thoughts to her.

"There's Corky, our driver," Lauren muttered, pointing to the black sedan pulling in to park at the front doors.

Alex picked up his calf-leather briefcase. "After you," he said, gesturing toward the door. Their luggage had already been put in the trunk earlier.

Lauren was about to open the car door, but Alex got there first, opening it for her. His eyes sparkled with humor as he said, "We are married. I will always open a door for my wife."

Giving him a weak grimace, Lauren scooted in and said nothing. Kazak was quite the charmer when he wanted to be. Lauren sternly told herself, as he climbed in beside her, that it was all a charade on his part. *That was all.* Yet, her heart skipped for a moment. First, the rings with the pearl in one. Then, the orchid corsage. Now, he was opening doors for her. It was almost too much to take in. She was glad it was a half-hour ride to the airport. It gave her time to collect herself.

THE AMERICAN AIRLINES jet took off right on time from Washington, D.C. enroute for Lima, Peru via a Miami, Florida stopover. There, they'd land and have a two-hour wait for another flight to take them on to Lima. Lauren noticed Alex insisted, as they took their seats in First Class, that he sit on the aisle of their large, wide row. She got the window. And, even though he appeared relaxed, she knew he was sensing, listening to other conversations around him, watching everything discreetly, not being obvious about it in any way. When the flight attendant came around offering wine, he declined it. So did she. They were working. Alcohol was a bad partner on an undercover op like this.

Once they were at altitude, and had been served a snack, he leaned toward her and said, "I like that they let us keep our real first names for this op."

Lauren nodded, feeling the nearby heat of his body. That quiet power rocked her from a feminine standpoint. She saw his hazel gaze sweep appreciatively across her. They had held hands as they had boarded. It wasn't as bad as Lauren had thought it would be. In fact, she had liked it. Maybe a little too much. "If they can, they will. It makes it easier for us."

"You smell good," he murmured, meeting her gaze. "Like vanilla and cinnamon."

Amazed, Lauren quirked an eyebrow. "I just washed my hair with cinnamon shampoo and took a shower with vanilla soap. You're pretty good, Kazak."

"Alex," he murmured quietly. "You should call me Alex. We are married. You would not call me by my last name, especially not my real one." and he gave her a lopsided, teasing grin.

"Okay," Lauren sighed. "You're right."

"Are you happy with the rings I chose?"

Now, he was serious. Lauren saw concern in Alex's eyes, as if he honestly cared about the rings. "I like them very much," and she moved her left hand, noticing the luminescence of the pearl. "Is it a real one?"

"Yes. I told the woman who runs supply that I wanted a real ocean pearl, not a fresh water type. You deserve fine things, not cheap counterfeits."

Lauren could almost hear the pride in his voice and the corner of her mouth lifted slightly. "I guess I never expected that from you." It was tough not to call him Kazak. In the military, a person's last name became the only name that everyone knew them by. That, or a nickname. She watched Alex puff out his chest a little, happiness shining in his eyes. He was so readable. *Open.* Lauren envied him that.

"I think it's amazing you chose a pearl for me," she admitted, still reeling from that intuitive choice he'd made. Operators were often highly attuned to their partner, but she'd never expected that from Alex. Not with the all battles between them since they'd known one another.

"It felt right," he told her seriously, looking at her rich, thick red hair piled carelessly upon her head. Lauren was elegant, yet he saw the girl in her, too. Perhaps the little girl trapped inside her was really a wild steppe pony? He hoped one day to find out because Lauren was always so serious. He'd never seen her play; be goofy or funny as other Shield employees were with one another from time to time. Always serious. Never smiling. What he'd give to see that luscious mouth of hers lift into a genuine smile. He'd probably, as went the American slang he'd picked up from Cal earlier, "die and go to heaven". Alex grinned and spread out his long legs, appreciating First Class flying. A man of his height needed a big seat with a lot of leg-room.

Lauren closed her eyes, suddenly very tired. The day had been grueling from an emotional point of view for her. She leaned her cheek against the plush seat, facing Alex. There was a sense of safety that embraced her. Nothing jolting, just an invisible warmth, as if he were holding her, as if she were fragile, in his large, strong arms. And that was the last thought she had, spiraling into much-needed sleep. Because sleep rarely came to her. The night was not her friend.

Alex felt his heart opening as Lauren slept and her head slowly found a resting place against his wide, broad shoulder. She was so close and he turned, inhaling her wonderful fragrance. Some strands of her hair tickled his jaw. How badly he wanted to lift his arm and embrace her, draw her close to him. Keep her safe. Lauren was incredibly stunning as she slept. Gone was all the tension she normally held on her face. Her red lashes were long and thick against her cheeks... those full lips of hers, slightly parted.

She moved, tucking her knees beneath her, cuddling more securely into the side of his seat and large body, her hands resting in her lap, more like a child. In some ways, Alex sensed Lauren had never been a child. Somewhere, somehow, she hadn't been given the gift of being allowed to be one. He found himself aching to give her that experience of becoming a child once again, even though she was now an adult. Alex knew how to be a child inside as well, and he would be good for her. He knew he could draw that wild steppe pony child of hers, out to play.

But she was barely civil to him, and Alex constantly reminded himself that she was an actress playing a part with him right now. Gone was the snarly Lauren. Alex reeled internally because the change in her was that dramatic. But it was all for show. When he'd slipped his hand into hers, he'd felt her tense for a second and then, she relaxed. But her hand had remained damp and cool as he'd held it, telling him she didn't want to be touched by him at all. If only... and Alex turned once more, studying her, absorbing the velvet of her skin, the soft pink across her cheeks, all natural.

Everything about Lauren was real. What you saw was what you got. She had resisted make-up. He liked the way her thick red hair twisted upward to show off her slender neck. He found himself wanting to kiss the sensitive nape. Alex knew she was ice on the outside and red-hot lava inside. He'd met military women like her before, who'd all had very cool exteriors. There had been a number of them over the years and he'd found out just how hot they ran under the hood. All of them had been like a blooded thoroughbred. Lauren would be no different, his experience told him.

Alex saw the orchid was being crushed by the way Lauren had leaned into him as she slept. Gently, he coaxed the two trapped petals from beneath the fabric with his fingers, releasing them. A sudden thought hit him and he wondered if Lauren had been crushed in her childhood as well. Now, he wished Cal or Sky had known more about her past. Because Alex sensed strongly that it was the key to Lauren.

"*MALEN 'KAYA*," ALEX whispered near Lauren's delicate ear. It was a Ukrainian endearment that meant "little one". It was reserved for a man who loved his woman, his child or his baby. "Lauren?" he rasped, his voice a little more insistent.

"Mmmmph…," and Lauren moved, her lashes barely lifting. In her drowsy state, she was completely vulnerable. She felt Alex so very close to her, his lips inches from her ear. She felt his moist breath flow across her brow. She realized she had tucked her legs beneath her, leaning into Alex's body, his shoulder a pillow for her head. Lauren suddenly snapped wide awake. She jerked away; Alex too close. Too tempting. Blinking, she uncurled her legs, her heart skittering. But it wasn't from fear. Alex had felt good to her. She had felt safe. That was a laugh, Lauren thought drowsily, her fingers moving to her hair, making sure it was still in place.

"You were about to fall out of your chair and onto me," he told her, watching how fetching she looked while waking up. Her black pupils were huge, the crescents of gray pushed to the outer rims of her irises, her lower lip soft, kissable, and so available. All he had to do was lean forward and he could easily curve his mouth in upon hers. Several tendrils of her hair stuck to her cheek and, without thinking, Alex gently grazed her flesh, brushing them aside. For a moment, Lauren froze. And then, she relaxed as she straightened her wrinkled pant suit and tried to wake up.

"Oh," she muttered, pulling her seatbelt tighter, "I dropped off the face of the Earth." What must Kazak think of her now? The way she'd fallen asleep and leaned on him like the big teddy-bear pillow he was? Why couldn't she have leaned the other way, using a pillow against the bulkhead instead?

"You slept long and deep. I am sorry I had to wake you. I did not want you falling off your seat," Alex told her, watching her fuss with her clothes. Her fingers had a lot of white and pink scars all around them and they were so long, her nails cut short. No sniper had long, polished fingernails, that was for sure. Still, her long hands were graceful and Alex found himself wondering what her fingertips trailing across his flesh would feel like. Frowning, he had to get his mind out of the ditch. Disconcerted, Lauren was more of a distraction that he'd first realized. Much more than what was allowed. Alex swallowed and forced himself to stop responding to Lauren on such a level. It could get them killed in the wrong circumstance.

By the time she awakened, Lauren felt calmer. More centered. She wasn't sure if it was Alex's nearness or not. Something had changed remarkably between them. Had it been her? It had to be, because Alex was his same-old self.

"You are very tired," he noted. They sat in a two-seat row and he was glad they had no one else nearby.

"Yeah," she grumped, "I don't know what happened. I was down for the count."

His eyebrows drew down as he studied her. "You do not sleep well at night?" She almost always had slight smudges beneath her eyes when Alex would see her in the morning at Shield HQ.

Shrugging, Lauren muttered, "I don't like the dark. The night."

He smiled a little. "How do you operate as a sniper, then?"

"Oh, that." She made a face. "That's not a problem. I'm focused. I have a target. Everything in me is honed like a laser on my tango."

"Then? Between ops? When you are at home in your apartment? You do not sleep well?"

Needled by his continued interest, Lauren scowled. She refused to look at Alex because, when she did, she went all sort of mushy inwardly, feeling longing for him. And it wasn't lost on her at all that women were extremely interested in Alex. He was a tall, damned ruggedly good-looking man. And yes, he was eye candy. Worse, she was affected by him, too. "I just... sometimes... don't sleep. I toss and turn. I'm restless."

"Nightmares? PTSD?"

Wincing a little, Lauren heard the sudden gentleness in his low voice, felt his gaze upon her. Damned if she didn't feel like he really cared about her. It was part of the act, she told herself. Mouth quirking, she said, "Yes, I get nightmares." But not what he thought they were about. And she wasn't going there with Alex. Not ever. She flexed her fingers, feeling nervous for no reason. The flight was not full. There were no other people right near them and that was good.

"Comes with the territory," Alex agreed.

Lauren nodded. "I guess I should warn you now."

"About what?" Alex asked, meeting her grave-looking gaze.

"Sometimes," and Lauren sighed and shook her head, "I scream out at night. I'll probably scare the living hell out of you when it happens." She saw his eyes narrow upon her, felt a sudden powerful sense of protection emanating from him to her. And she'd not been safe in her life. Not ever. But the feeling was so delicious, so comforting and tender, that Lauren felt her heart respond, warmth flooding her chest.

"Flashbacks?" Alex wondered aloud, wanting to reach out and touch Lauren, to make her feel protected and cared-for. Because he saw the momentary terror come to her eyes. And then, she pushed it away, hiding it again. Hiding so much.

"Yes, flashbacks."

"Do not worry, Lauren. I get them myself. It is not pleasant." Alex shared a tender look with her. "But if you have one, I will hold you until you feel safe."

"No," she hissed, "don't you ever touch me when I'm having one!"

Blinking, his smile dissolved. Lauren's voice had gone hoarse with terror. And, just as quickly, she had choked everything back down. He watched her fight it. Whatever 'it' was. The sense he got was that it was so terrifying that she was helpless, and had no control. Frowning, he rasped, "I will not touch you."

"You can't," she whispered, anguished. "This isn't' going to work."

"What is not going to work?" Alex heard the desperation in her voice, saw the wildness in her eyes for a split second. And then, she was back under that icy exterior, game face on.

"Us. Staying in the same room together. It's not going to work."

Alex felt the powerful emotion she was experiencing. And it was a mix of desperation and anguish so raw that he damn near reached out and dragged her into his arms. But he remembered. *Don't touch her. She'd fight.* Alex knew it. What little trust he'd established with her wasn't enough to risk blowing it. "Let us take this a step at a time," he advised, his voice low and soothing. "We have to focus on why we're going to Peru. You will feel better once we get on the ground." He saw her lift her chin and give him a look of disbelief.

"Okay," Lauren uttered, her shoulders collapsing, exhaustion tunneling through her. "I'll try not to fall out of my seat this time." and she turned her back on him, pulling her legs beneath her, hugging her pillow against the bulkhead.

Alex sat there, feeling like someone had just gutted him. He thought of his sister, Kira, who was three years younger than he was. That LOOK that had flitted across Lauren's face was exactly the same look that Kira's had been after she'd been gang-raped by terrorists at the forward Russian field medical facility where she'd been a nurse. Cursing to himself, he rubbed his brow, an ache coming on.

No... Alex wanted to reject the idea that Lauren had been hurt in that way. Kira was a shadow of her former self, as if the rapists had stolen her soul. No longer did her beautiful light-green eyes light up with joy. When Kira had smiled, Alex had always felt like the sun had suddenly come out from behind a cloud, warming him all the way to his heart.

Kira... Now she was safe in the U.S.A., trying to rebuild her life in San Diego, California. The ocean was helping her heal and she loved walking the beaches. She had been a registered nurse in the Russian Army. After her unit was attacked and overrun by the enemy, all the wounded men in the medical facility, were killed at point-blank range. The doctors were killed in the same way. All the nurses were herded into one tent and the twenty men, armed with AK-47's, had their way with them over a twenty-four-hour period. Alex dragged in a painful breath. Misery flooded him as he recalled everything regarding his little sister's situation.

Alex had felt guilty about having been out of the country when Kira had been gang-raped. He'd been notified, and had gone through hell to get back to St. Petersburg Hospital where she, and the other women survivors who had been severely traumatized, were recuperating. Some of them had gone catatonic. Kira was somewhere in between those two states as he'd knelt at her bedside, crying, wanting to hold her. She'd screamed and fought his arms from going around her. Because he was a man. And men had torn her soul from her by their heartless sub-animal actions. His heart ached without reprieve as he recalled that first year after Kira's rape. She'd quit the Army, quit being a nurse, and quit living, a hull of her original self.

And when he would visit Kira, he always saw that terror banked up in her wide, guileless eyes. Her beautiful red hair, once so long and feminine, had all been chopped off. She looked more like a young boy to Alex than the beautiful, twenty-year-old woman who was his warm, loving sister. Kira's personality had been violently stolen from her. She was so internalized, wary of all men, hurting inwardly, unable to speak of her trauma to him. Alex stopped trying to count how much and how often he'd cried for his sister. Lifting his head, he stared at Lauren's back. She was asleep once more. Perhaps it gave her some of the peace she so richly deserved.

More than anything, Alex sat there feeling like the earth had moved beneath his feet and that he was tumbling out of control, in shock. Cal had said Lauren had had a bad childhood. Whether he liked it or not, Alex couldn't help but compare Lauren's experiences with Kira's. Unwillingly, he looked at the possibility that someone had raped Lauren. Hurt her badly. Stained her life just as Kira's was now stained forever. That was why Lauren had reacted so strongly, with such fierceness, when he'd said he'd hold her if she had a nightmare. If she was dreaming of being raped, of course she wouldn't want ANY man to touch her. Much less hold her. Now it all made sense.

Not only were they hunting an enemy who was deadly in their external world, Alex now suspected that Lauren saw him as the enemy from her past, overlaid on the present, and on him. He would have to be in the same room with her. There was no place for her to relax. To honestly rest. IF she had been raped. And he had a wretched feeling that she had been. But how to find out? How to confirm it? Alex knew it was vital to understand what was fueling

Lauren's reactions to him. If he couldn't find out, that left them both open to getting killed on this op. Because, in this business, a team trusted one another without question. And they didn't have that kind of trust between them. At all.

CHAPTER 5

LAUREN WAS EXHAUSTED from the nonstop traveling over the last twenty-four hours. They'd landed at the Chavez International Airport in Lima at 0400. At 0600, they took a local flight deep into the Andes and arrived at Cusco about two hours later. The city sat in a raw, dustbowl-shaped area nearly twelve-thousand feet above sea level, the rugged Andes rising around the once renowned Incan fortress, where the emperor Pachacuti had resided. She was grateful that Alex knew Cusco and Peru so well. He got them a taxi and they went to the railway station where he bought two first class tickets, and then they were on their way down to Aguas Calientes, that lay at six-thousand feet of elevation. From the train window, she saw the brown, barren land where Cusco sat. Literally, it was naked desert, with nothing growing in the dustbowl except for the Incan-built city at the center of it. As the train rocked gently back and forth, clicking and clacking, heading down to the world heritage site of Machu Picchu, she saw bare rock and soil slowly transition to dark, verdant jungle vegetation. By the time they reached Aguas Calientes, the town sitting at the base of Machu Picchu, it was mid-morning and she was exhausted. Maybe it was because of the severe altitude changes, or her new fear of Alex being in the same apartment with her, hearing her scream at night if she had a nightmare. She felt trapped.

Alex guided her out of the train and onto the busy terminal station, a long concrete platform with a dark-green tin roof overhead. Even though she was tired, Lauren felt the vibrancy of the jungle area surrounding them. She saw teenage Peruvian boys quickly hauling the luggage off the train for the tourists. They formed a continuous line from the train to a roaring river that divided the station from the town below it. Alex led her over to the edge of the platform, and pointed at a churning feeder river that spilled into the nearby powerful Urubamba River that snaked in and around the area. The boys balanced themselves, and the luggage they bore, carefully, leaping from one massive, smooth, wet rock, to another. They nimbly crossed the dangerous river.

"Sometimes," Alex told her grimly, "a boy slips. Those kids are young and their families are hungry. They take this dangerous job because it means money to feed all of them."

Alex stood near her and, for whatever reason, Lauren appreciated his quiet strength, feeling the heat from his body, so close to hers. Now, they really had to be undercover. "That water is so swift. The current's fast."

"Yes," he said, his mouth flexing. "These boys sometimes fall in. They are dead. No one can rescue them because the river runs so swift. If they do not die from striking those big boulders throughout the river, they will die in twenty minutes from hypothermia because this is glacier water from the Andes."

It wasn't a pleasant thought.

"Are you ready?" Alex asked, leaning over enough to catch her weary gaze. "We need to walk from the train station, down that hill to a bridge that leads into the plaza of Aguas Calientes. From there, we will walk up a sloping concrete road. Our apartment is located at the top of it."

"Yes, I'm ready."

"You are very tired, Lauren. When we get to the apartment, you must rest," and Alex gently slid his hand beneath her elbow. This time, she didn't tense. Was it because she was playing her role as his wife? Alex didn't know, but wished that he did. He felt Lauren lean into him and that's when he realized she needed a little care. She had slept through most of the flight. It had been a restless sleep for her, though. He wanted to do something to help her, but he didn't know what. She stumbled a few times going down the dirt hill littered with endless sharp rocks. And, each time, Alex gripped her elbow a little more firmly to steady her.

Lauren forced herself to stay alert. This wasn't the first time she'd been severely sleep deprived. As a sniper, she would catnap, five minutes at a time, and then continue her watch for her target. The plaza was a huge square of flat, carved stone tiles. At one end of it was a Catholic church built out of gray stone, reminding her of the 1800's style of Spanish churches. The small restaurants, pizza parlors, hairdresser and grocery store ringed the busy plaza. She liked that there were planters full of colorful flowers, and bushes at its center, with many park benches where a person could sit and take in the sights, sounds and smells. Alex cut his stride for her benefit as they began the long walk up the slope of the concrete street. There were donkeys with carts, hundreds of tourists, the sidewalks lined with one- and two-story businesses, all designed to lure in the curious tourists and take their Peruvian soles or US dollars.

"You know this place well," she said.

He nodded, casually looking around as a tourist might. What Alex feared the most was unexpectedly running into one of the five Russian teams he used to be a part of, who were constantly roving across the area. With Vlad as their leader, they usually dropped into Aguas Calientes about once a month. Most of the men took prostitutes, drank beer, got good Peruvian food in their bellies, a hot shower, and badly needed rest. He and his best friend, Nik Morozov, the other combat medic, had only ever showered, ate and slept. They never took a prostitute. "Too well," he murmured, keeping her close, liking the way her body sometimes brushed against his. Monitoring Lauren, Alex didn't feel any tension in her from his close proximity. Closer than he'd ever been before. It was bittersweet, because he wanted to show her that a man could be gentle toward her. It was all a dream, much like the thin, twisting, white, filmy mists that moved in slow motion through the jungle surrounding the town.

"Are you worried you'll meet someone you'll know?" Because Lauren knew from the briefing material that all five Russian mafia teams came here to recharge and rest up.

"Yes."

She could feel a fine tension thrumming through Alex. To casual passers-by, he looked like a tourist, nothing more. But he was on guard. Working. Alert. "What's the plan once we reach the apartment?"

Alex gave her a quick glance. "You are going to get a shower and then, rest up. I am going to that small airport nearby to pick up our weapons bags. I will bring them back to the apartment and we will get set up."

"I can help."

"No. You need to rest."

Her mouth thinned but Lauren didn't argue. The scent of spices and food cooking, the blaring of horns, the pounding of deep-throated drums and raspy Andean flutes from bars created a cacophony of sensory overload. The quiet of the jungle was being violated by commerce and awful noise pollution, she thought.

"Here," Alex said, gesturing to a three-story yellow stucco building. "We are on the third floor. He guided her to the concrete steps that would take them up to their apartment.

Lauren found the climb a little tough, her breath coming quicker. She knew her body had to acclimate to the altitude. Where they were going, the jungle was at six to seven thousand feet at times, but Alex had told her they would be up at ten thousand feet sometimes, to reach some of the Quechua villages in order to talk to the chiefs to find out where the Russian teams were currently operating.

Alex said, "Stay here. I will come back with the key."

Nodding, Lauren was content to lean against the black wrought iron rail and observe the busy, noise-ridden and colorful traffic below. She was glad they were high up; the disjointed music clashing far below them and muted to a degree. She saw mighty Machu Picchu towering above the town, rising like a French loaf of bread stood on one end. The raw, sharp, black lava flanks of the mountain were covered with thousands upon thousands of jungle growths, bromeliads, orchids and spindly trees. There were two other similar-looking mountains, the fog's wreath-like white, sinuous necklaces, weaving in and out among them and always moving magically as if guided by an unseen hand. She felt the peace of this area and silently absorbed it. She heard Alex rapidly climbing the stairs. He must be as tired as she was, but he looked fresh and alert. Now, Lauren was getting a taste of what a Spetsnaz operator was made of.

He smiled a little at her. "Beautiful, eh?" and he gestured toward the loaf-like mountains. "There is Machu Picchu, 'old mountain', right in front of us," he said, gesturing upward, "and, to your right, Mama Putukusi, and between them, Huynu Picchu or 'young mountain'."

"Almost magical." She moved out of the way so he could open the bright-yellow door. Lauren noted it had no window in it so see who might be standing outside. No peephole, either.

Alex said, "Let me clear it first."

Lauren remained outside as she watched him move like a silent shadow through one room after another. Within minutes, Alex returned, gave her a nod, and gestured for her to come in. She locked the door behind her and turned, appreciating the spare living quarters. The floors were a reddish, polished wood, the stucco walls white, allowing the large, square room to be bright and filled with indirect sunlight. The furniture consisted of a rattan couch, two chairs and a coffee table. A bright, woven Peruvian rug lay beneath the furniture.

Wandering into the kitchen, Lauren watched with curiosity as Alex examined the small refrigerator, the stove, and the double sink and white laminate counter. He checked out everything, every cabinet, opening and closing them. He was thorough. Even the lamp fixtures, where a tiny camera or microphone could hide, he went over. He found no bugs.

"Go get your shower," he told her. "No bathtubs in Peru," and he grinned a little. "There are towels, but no washcloth. They don't use them here. I packed some in my suitcase. If you want one, open it up and get it."

"No tub," Lauren muttered, shaking her head. "And I absolutely need a washcloth." How was one to get truly clean without one? She saw him smile and it made her feel good, her heart automatically opening to Alex. He was sunlight, Lauren decided. When he smiled, his whole face lit up and those hazel eyes of his gleamed with humor. She wished she had his ability to smile.

There was a sharp knock on the front door. Lauren instantly tensed, wishing she had a pistol on her. Right now, without those weapons bags that had been flown up by the Army Black Hawk pilots from Lima, they were unarmed. Alex held up his hand.

"Let me get this."

Lauren watched as he went to the window facing the stairs, and peeked out of it to see who was standing there.

"It is the boy with our luggage," he called over his shoulder, opening the door.

Lauren saw a thin, fifteen-year-old boy with long, straight black hair cut in a bowl shape around his head. He wore a white jacket, and clean black slacks, with his badly scuffed and worn sandals. She heard Alex speak to him in Spanish, pulling out several twenty-dollar US bills from his wallet. The boy almost literally glowed as he saw how much he was receiving as a tip. Alex took the luggage and closed the door.

"You made his day," Lauren murmured, coming over to pick up her luggage and carry it back to the bedroom.

"I gave him two twenty USD." Alex slid his wallet into the back pocket of his chinos. "A US dollar is equivalent to three Peruvian soles. That money will keep his family well fed for the next six months."

She gave him a thoughtful look. "You're an operator with a heart."

He shrugged and took her suitcase from her hand. "Maybe. I will do the heavy lifting around here…"

She was too tired to argue. Her heart felt warm after seeing how Alex had treated the Peruvian boy with respect and kindness. And he was a generous person, no doubt. It made her feel good about him. She'd badly misjudged Alex. She'd thought he was a traitor who couldn't be trusted. But she had heard only part of the story. Now… well, now, she saw Alex in a completely different light. A better one.

Unsure if she wanted to follow him into the only bedroom of the small apartment, Lauren lingered at the door. The bed was queen-sized, the room fairly large, with a green jungle plant in a ceramic pot on the mahogany dresser at the foot of it. She watched him pick up the suitcases with ease, place them on the white chenille bedspread, and open them up. He dug around in his own for a moment and then offered her a dark-blue washcloth. She pushed off of the door frame where she had lingered, and took it. Their fingers met.

Alex straightened up. "You get the bedroom," he told her, making it clear he wasn't going to argue with her about it. "I will sleep in the living room, on the couch."

She stood aside as he eased out past her through the door. He had to duck because he was too tall for its frame. "But," she began lamely, "that rattan couch isn't long enough for you."

Alex halted and partially turned in the hall. He gave her a crooked grin. "That floor looks comfortable. I was used to sleeping out in the jungle, which is much worse. I will be fine. Do not look so concerned. All right?" Because he saw she was worried about HIM. Despite Lauren's wounds from the past, she was unselfish, thinking about her partner. That was a good sign to Alex.

Shrugging, she murmured, "Okay. I see what I have to look forward to out there in the jungle," and she took the washcloth and disappeared down the hall to the bathroom to take that hot shower.

ALEX RETURNED TWO hours later with the two huge, dark-green canvas bags, one over each shoulder. He unlocked the door and quietly stepped in. Earlier, he'd took a run down to the local grocery store in the plaza and bought enough food and supplies. He'd made Lauren some fragrant hot coffee, scrambled up some eggs with some tasty purple and yellow Peruvian potatoes, and onions, and they'd eaten ravenously, like wolves. She'd then gone to bed.

He quietly closed the door, setting the weapons bags on the couch. He'd changed into jeans, put on a black polo shirt and his hiking boots. Alex knew how to prowl the backstreets and alleyways to reach the makeshift airport. It wasn't much more than a grass strip, usually muddy and wet because it rained here in the jungle every day. There was an old Russian helicopter, a couple of modern civilian planes, and the man whose job it was to keep track of boxes and other gear coming into the town. He had led Alex to the locker where the bags had been stowed beneath a hefty padlock.

Going to the sink, he quickly washed his hands. Drying them on a towel, he didn't hear even a peep from Lauren. She had to be asleep. At least, he hoped so. Moving silently down the hall, he saw that the bedroom door was ajar. Through the gap, he saw Lauren curled into a nearly fetal position, the bright-red wool blanket around her shoulders, sleeping deeply. She had released her hair and it flowed like a crimson river around her face and shoulders. His heart lurched and he ached to walk into that room, lay down beside her and love her. Worse still, he was getting an erection. With a grimace, Alex turned away, quietly closed the door and walked to the living room. The weapons would need to be checked out, each of them well oiled, cleaned, and their jungle hunting gear gone through carefully and prepared for eventual use.

LAUREN FELT DRUGGED when she woke up. The sun had been in the east, toward Machu Picchu, when she'd dropped off to sleep. Now, the bedroom was grayer, the light low. What time was it? She sat up with a groan, her hair falling around her face as she looked blearily at her watch. It was 1700! Five p.m.! Scrambling, she got off the bed, barefoot, and hurried out of the bedroom.

Lauren halted at the entrance to the living room. Alex had a cleaning cloth laid out on the floor, field-stripping her sniper rifle. There were all kinds of weapons, two dragon vests, rucksacks, two harness vests, ammo and other jungle gear spread neatly around him.

He looked up. "Feel better? You slept a good six hours." She looked delicious. Damn, all he had to do was be around Lauren and he went into an instant ache, his mind spiraling into heat, arousal and wanting her. He continued to rub the barrel down with the light oil to protect it from the high humidity and constant rain.

"Yeah," she muttered, wiping her eyes. "I can do that…"

"I want you to rest," he told her. "I like cleaning rifles." Because it would keep his hands off her. Keep him focused on their mission. *Not her.* Alex saw how drowsy Lauren looked, her eyes heavy-lidded, their irises that soft dove-gray which he was finding meant she was calm and at peace. Her eyes turned nearly colorless when she got focused, angry or defensive. He wondered how her eyes would look if he kissed her. *Whoa.* Alex gave himself a severe, internal shake. That wasn't ever going to become a reality because Lauren would never permit it, role-playing or not.

"I need to wake up," Lauren muttered, stumbling toward the kitchen.

"I just made a fresh pot of coffee," he called over his shoulder. Alex heard a muffled sound. Clearly, Lauren was endearing when waking up. She was mussed, drowsy and vulnerable. Gone were her walls. He felt such a burning sensation move through his heart. He knew he could make Lauren happy. He knew it in his soul. Frowning, Alex continued to lightly oil all the metal parts to protect them from the constant rain they'd endure every day in the jungle. He heard a cupboard door open and shut. The clink of glass against ceramic. Smiling to himself, he could just picture Lauren sleepily fumbling around to find a mug and bring the coffee pot to its rim.

"Do you want some?" Lauren called from the door of the kitchen.

"Yes. Thank you." Alex warmed to her. She was thoughtful. Lauren cared. That wasn't role-playing. That was her. Despite her harsh life, she was a person who cared for others. He'd seen her worry about the boys crossing that river with their assigned luggage. Real concern, not play acting. In a way, this op was going to test him in ways he didn't want. In another, more positive way, he was getting to see the real Lauren, the woman who he had known all along was much softer than those hard walls she hid behind. Now, he was privileged to see her open up. *Bloom. Like that orchid.* She'd thoughtfully placed the orchid he'd given her earlier in the small bowl of water he'd found sitting on the counter upon arriving back with the weapons bags. He felt hope. Realistically, Alex told himself his dream of someday loving Lauren was exactly that. Yet... he was seeing cracks in her defenses. Maybe even a little trust extended toward him. Or maybe it was because she was so sleep deprived and was struggling to wake up?

Alex set the cloth aside and took the mug of coffee Lauren handed him. She looked like a little girl, with her feet bare as they were, and he smiled.

"I wonder, did you run through the grass barefoot when you were a little girl?"

"Never," she said, her voice a husky whisper. Lauren took a seat on one of the rattan chairs, curling her legs beneath her. She pushed her thick, long hair off her shoulder, cupping the mug and gratefully sipping the steaming, dark, rich coffee. Watching Alex sit on the floor, his masculinity right in her face, that polo shirt showing off his upper body, Lauren felt her own lower body flex, as if hungry. That same gnawing sensation returned as she skimmed his shoulders, chest, and those long, muscular, arms with her gaze. He had stubble now, and it accented the angular lines of his square face and that rock-hard chin of his. Her gaze drifted back to his nose. It had been broken by Vlad. Because Alex had sacrificed himself, turned decoy, and that had allowed Sky and Cal to get away. To stay alive. Her heart turned and Lauren felt warmth spilling through her chest once again. Alex was focused on his work, his profile rugged and sharp. There wasn't anything else a woman could want from a man. Alex was the complete package.

"Do you have a relationship with someone?" she wondered, sipping her coffee, watching him over the rim of her cup.

"No. I have been busy since returning to your country. My sister, Kira, is my focus. She was a registered nurse in Ukraine, and now she is living in the state of California. She is working to fill the requirements that will allow her to work at a hospital once more, and that is a good sign. She loves the ocean, and walking the beach, too." He frowned. "She is three years younger than me."

"I can hear the love in your voice for her."

Startled by her insight, Alex reminded himself that Lauren was a sniper. They, spotters and trackers; enemies called them predators because, when it came to noticing details, their intuition honed to an almost mystical level, any slight change, even hearing or sensing emotions in a person's voice, was picked up and noticed. He cocked his head in her direction. Lauren was relaxed. And she looked like dessert to him, her bare feet tucked up beneath her body, her hair loose and free, as it should always be. It was the tender look in her gray eyes that told him she was sincere. There was that care of hers again. He'd been wrong to judge too soon on her ability to be a team player and a partner on this op. He finished oiling the rifle and started piecing it back together. "When I was nineteen, our farm was overrun by Russian separatists," he told her gravely, not looking at her, focused on the rifle because it was easier to talk about all this that way. "My parents, my grandparents, and two of my aunts and uncles were murdered that night."

"Oh, no...," Lauren choked, sitting up, stunned. She saw the sadness in Alex's face as he turned toward her. His eyes were filled with anguish. "H-how did you and Kira escape being killed, too?"

"I was in Spetsnaz training, and had come home on leave, and Kira was needed at a neighbor's farm, ten miles away. The wife was birthing and Kira went over to help. I had driven her over there." Alex frowned. "No one knew anything about the attack until we drove back the next morning." His mouth tightened. "It was carnage." And he would never forget seeing the photos that had been taken of his parents' farmhouse and of them murdered in their kitchen. A police officer had turned swiftly, kept Kira out the station's briefing room, told her to not come in. At least that man had spared her those haunting dark images that were always with Alex. She never saw the photos of their slain family.

"Alex, I'm so sorry." And Lauren was. Life had not treated him well, either, she realized. "So, Kira is all the family you have left?"

"Yes. And you can understand that my heart, my focus, is on her right now. I have no room, no extra place in my heart for a relationship with a woman." *Except for you. And I can't have you. You will never trust me enough because I am a man....*

Closing her eyes for a moment, feeling his tragedy deeply, she choked out, "I'm so sorry. I wish... I wish I'd known this earlier..." Because she'd judged him harshly, been so cruel toward him, so... uncaring... and insensitive... Lauren felt guilt eating at her as never before. Through it all, Alex had treated her kindly, with respect, remaining open toward her despite how much she'd angrily taken verbal swipes at him, and been rude to him, treated him like he was unimportant as a human being. She had so much to make up for to him. And more than anything, Lauren knew she owed him a humble apology.

"What happened to your farm?"

"The state came in and bought it." He shrugged. "My family had built that stone farmhouse two hundred years ago with their own hands. So many generations had lived there..."

"I-I can't imagine the pain you and Kira went through having to walk away from that kind of wonderful life."

Shrugging, Alex said, "It pushed me to graduate and become a combat medic and a Spetsnaz sniper operator. Kira went to university and became a nurse. She then joined the Russian army, following in my footsteps. She loved helping others, healing them."

Lauren saw his brows fall as he packed her rifle into the nylon sheath that would protect it from the harsh jungle elements. "Your voice," she said warily, "Did something happened to Kira?"

Alex's brows drew down even further. He stood and put the rifle in the corner, coming to sit down on the couch opposite Lauren. "You have ears like a wolf," he accused her darkly. "But you are a sniper." Leaning his elbows on his thighs, hands clasped between them, Alex studied her. Lauren, amazingly, was still being open to him. There was a new softness in her gray eyes and he felt it as well. It gave him the courage to tell her what had happened to Kira. Opening his hands, he warned her, "This is going to be very disturbing for you to hear, Lauren."

"I want to hear it." Because she cared about Alex and had never seen him look so distressed as right now. He was hiding nothing from her. "Please?" She saw his mouth tighten and he looked away for a moment, as if considering things she knew nothing about. Finally, he turned back and held her gaze.

"Kira was at a forward Army field hospital when it was attacked by twenty Russian separatists who are terrorists," he told her in a flat, unemotional tone. "They killed all the wounded soldiers where they lay in their cots. They killed all the doctors." His voice died and he swallowed hard, not realizing just how tough it would be to tell another person all of this. Looking down at his tightly clasped hands, Alex rasped, "They herded the twelve nurses into a tent. They raped them repeatedly..."

"Oh, no...." Lauren felt her stomach grow tight. Nausea burned in her throat as she stared disbelievingly at Alex. His face was one of grief. Anger. Guilt. "H-how old was Kira when it happened?

"Only twenty-three," he managed, swallowing hard. He saw Lauren's entire expression become stunned. Her eyes widened and he saw tears in them. For Kira. "I was away on a mission, in another country, when it happened," he added, frustration in his low tone. "I fought my commander to be released from the op in order to get to Kira's side. To... help her... I do not know... do something..."

Lauren sat there understanding exactly what Kira had gone through. Only, it hadn't been a bunch of animal-like soldiers who had repeatedly raped Lauren herself. "How was she doing when you saw her?"

"Two days later, I arrived at the hospital in St. Petersburg where she was being kept along with the other injured nurses. Kira was in a ward with her friends who had also been raped. Three died during it. Half of those who survived were catatonic. They were… not there… in shock… their souls torn from them…" Alex heaved out a sigh and said, "Kira was not like that, but she was traumatized and in deep shock. It was… well… it was painful for her and for me. I was a man," and he looked up, helplessness in his expression. "It had been men that had hurt her so badly."

"She was afraid of you even though you were her brother?"

His shoulders slumped. "Yes." His throat tightened. "And we had always been so close. I watched out for Kira because she is my little sister. I was supposed to protect her but," and Alex wiped his mouth, shook his head and muttered, "I failed her. I was not there when she needed me the most…" and he looked away because tears burned in his eyes.

Alex didn't realize the profound guilt and sorrow he carried until he'd spoken the words out loud. And then, he abruptly realized what Lauren had just asked him. How could she know that Kira feared him because he was a man and because men had harmed her? Studying her anguished features, Alex felt thunderstruck as another realization about Lauren exploded into his awareness.

CHAPTER 6

LAUREN TRIED TO plug her escaping emotions, her grief for what Kira had experienced. Alex continued to suffer, just as Kira did, but in a different way. "Listen, Alex, you can't gig yourself for not being there. That's not logical. I'm sure, knowing you like I do; you've done everything humanly possible to help Kira."

His sense of helplessness, rage, and frustration churned through Alex. Only Lauren's suddenly husky, soft voice took some of his pain away. He studied her, and the silence grew between them. But it wasn't a tense silence. Maybe, some sort of unspoken understanding passed between them. His heart tumbled into deeper anguish. Lauren didn't deserve to have been injured like that, either. Two women in his life who meant the world to him, had both had their souls murdered by men who were monsters.

Alex rubbed his face, unable to hold the understanding look in Lauren's eyes. "I carry that," he told her gruffly. "I will always carry it. It was my duty to be there for my little sister. Kira was innocent... unable to fight back, to defend herself. She had no one to come to her rescue..."

Lauren felt a chill within her. His words were low and emotional, as if torn from him, not wanting to be given voice. She thought about her own experiences. Knew what it felt like to be abandoned. Help had never come to her, either. The pain she carried never stopped. That, no matter how much she'd screamed for help, no one had ever heard her.

Something within nudged her to get up, and Lauren moved beyond her own pain. Walking over to Alex, she leaned down and slid her arm around his broad shoulders. She hugged him with all her woman's strength, her cheek resting against his head. "Alex, don't do this to yourself. Kira understands why you couldn't have been there for her when it happened." Tears caught in Lauren's throat, her voice strained as she whispered unsteadily, "It's more important that you are there for her now. The BEST thing you can do for her, Alex, is to love her. If she'll allow you to hold her when she cries, that will mean so much to her. Just let her talk. Be her witness, and you will help her healing process along."

Lauren reluctantly withdrew her arm from around his sagging shoulders. She straightened up, quickly wiping away the tears that threatened to fall. She did not want Alex to see her cry. It just wouldn't work. And she was far too vulnerable because of what he'd just shared with her. Moving around the coffee table, Lauren sat down across it from him.

Alex was struggling, his head bowed, his hands clasped so tight between his legs that his knuckles were turning white. She could feel the massive load of grief and guilt he carried for his forever wounded sister. And Alex had no one to turn to, either. Not his parents. Nor his grandparents. *No one.* Neither of them had anyone who could support them emotionally. They were more alike than Lauren had ever imagined: wounded, shattered human beings just trying to survive the day they were in. They shared a similar trauma, a darkness that bled through their collective souls. Rape not only harmed the woman, but injured her family as well. They ALL suffered. Lauren understood Alex's helplessness. And maybe, in some small way, she could become his witness to it, because it was clear that he deeply loved his sister and was loyal to her in ways she rarely saw between two people.

Alex slowly raised his head, pushed his damp palms down his thighs and studied Lauren in the silence. "Thank you for your kindness." He'd never expected it. That Lauren had the remarkable courage to step outside her own wounds and extend her care to him, stunned Alex and made him reel internally. Emotionally, he felt like he was unraveling, never having expected Lauren to aid him in such a moment of private and personal grief. But she had. He'd felt her arm, so warm and strong and steadying, wrap around his shoulders, her brow pressed against his temple, her warm breath soft against his cheek and neck. And her words had been so low, and fraught with ragged feelings. It was the most emotional he'd ever seen Lauren, except for those times when she'd been angry at him.

Dragging in a torn breath, Alex managed a twisted grimace as he held her glistening gray gaze. It looked as if she were going to cry. For Kira. For himself. He didn't know many people who had that kind of rock-solid resilience. Humbled by her selflessness, Alex felt the tenderness Lauren had hidden from him until just now. There was such a profound softness to her heart. That heart that she hid from the world, but had just gifted him with.

"One day," Alex said, his voice rough, "I want Kira to meet you. I think you two would like each other very much." *Because you are mirror reflections of one another in so many important ways.* "You would like Kira's healing ability. Whomever she touches, they respond. They always get better, sooner," and Alex smiled faintly, remembering how open, how effervescent, Kira had been before being gang-raped. It were as if someone had stolen the life-giving sunlight from her, and had hurled her into total, ongoing darkness for the rest of her life.

"I'd like that," Lauren murmured. "She sounds like a wonderful person. Doing good in the world, and helping others who are suffering is commendable. She is trying to ease their pain." Even though hers would never be eased. Rape didn't go away. It was a toxic stain on the woman's soul forever; like an acid eating into her every day 24-7-365. It never stopped.

Nodding, Alex slowly rose, feeling bruised internally by their discussion. He gave her a thoughtful look. "And you know that I am here for you, Lauren? I know I am a man, but I can be here for you anyway? If you need me?" Because, God help him, Alex wanted to walk those few feet between them, sweep Lauren into his arms, and just hold her. Hold her, and let her feel safety for once in her life. She'd turned tragedy into victory. Instead of being a victim, Lauren had done something positive with her life. Her decision had been to become a sniper, to become the hunter. Instead of having control ripped away from her, she now controlled the life and death of her target. Alex was finally beginning to understand the inner foundation of Lauren. Piecing her together, a little at a time. Seeing the larger picture of who she was, and who she had become. Why she acted the way she did. How she saw the world through the distortion of her wounds. That gave him hope that, perhaps someday, Kira could emerge from that visceral shadow that still controlled her. He knew that his sister had strength like Lauren. Alex felt relief so deeply within his heart, that it actually gave him a tiny glimpse of hope that Lauren could, someday, learn to trust him. As a man.

ALEX, THAT EVENING, took Lauren to a restaurant, Feliz Navidad by name, to eat. They needed to make their faces known to the locals, so that the populace would come to recognize them and, from then on, think nothing of their comings and goings. It was dusk, the heavy white clouds descending rapidly like fog from hundreds of feet above the bustling town. Machu Picchu was clothed in a white raiment, only the lower levels still visible. The wide concrete ramp between the tightly-packed buildings was crowded with the nonstop foot traffic of tourists. Protective of Lauren, Alex placed his hand lightly on the small of her back, intent on keeping her close to him. Some tourists watched where they were going. Most did not, enamored with the sights, sounds, and small businesses offering so many distractions. Alex quickly glanced over to see if Lauren minded his contact. He got his answer when she moved a little closer to him, no stress in her expression. Role-acting? Or real? How he wanted it to be a genuine reaction from Lauren toward him. Because Alex had promised to himself, on his life, that he would never let her be harmed. His life for hers. It was an easy choice to make.

Always, Alex watched out for any Russians among the crowd. He didn't know all the mafia groups who used this town as R&R, rest and relaxation, but that didn't matter. As a Ukrainian, he could sense and recognize anyone who was Russian whether he knew them or not. Plus, operators had a certain stride, a confidence, even an arrogance, that the civilian populace would never own. He was watching, firstly for that kind of body language among the hundreds of people wandering the street, secondly for any facial identification, if possible.

"You're tense."

His hand became firmer against her back for a moment and then Alex relaxed it. "I am watching for my own kind," he told her wryly.

"What are the chances?"

"Very good."

"How can I help you spot one?"

"You know how operators swagger. Keep your eyes on the man who walks like that. Let me know and I will double check you on it."

"How many guys did you know in the two years you were down here?" Lauren saw the light from the streetlamps shadow Alex's face. Now, he was operational, and she could feel him sensing, sifting through hundreds of possibilities to either keep or reject. They all did that when they were 'on.'

"Many," Alex admitted.

"Are there any more like you?" and she looked up at his rugged face, the shadows deepening the angularity of his features. It made him look fierce. Indomitable.

"Just one, Nik Morozov, my combat medic friend who is also Ukrainian. We were considered misfits in Vlad's group. We would not partake in the rape of a woman. We would not harm anyone. Lucky for us, we were their combat medics, so they did not force us to do the things they did. We would have refused, if they had. Nik and I grew up together, our wheat farms near one another."

"I think you're lucky you weren't killed by Alexandrov because you refused to participate."

"We would walk away from the village. There was nothing we could do, Lauren. If we tried to stop the raping, Vlad would have pulled out his pistol and shot us both in the head. We hated it, and we felt helpless, guilty, and it became harder and harder to bear over time."

Lauren saw sudden pain comes to his eyes. And then, it was gone. He instantly shifted into hunting mode once again. "How did you two stand it?"

Alex shook his head. "The only way we could have really stopped the Russians was to put a bullet through their heads."

"Why did you join the Russian mafia?" She saw him frown, his mouth thinning. Lauren was beginning to understand his facial signals. The question was painful for him.

"At that time," Alex admitted hoarsely, slowing his walk, pulling her to the side, near the edge of the walkway, his hand resting against her back, "Kira needed therapy. We were poor. I decided to join the mafia to make a lot of money quickly so my little sister could get the psychiatric help she needed." He shrugged, casually looking at the slow-moving, milling crowd. The noise-level was high. There was a lot of laughter. These people were on vacation, with no worries in the world. He looked back down to see Lauren's reaction to his explanation. His heart wrenched. Her eyes were swimming with tears that she was valiantly trying to stop from falling.

Without thinking, he lifted his hands, framing her upturned face, gently removing the tears with his thumbs. "Why tears?" he demanded, his voice thick. Never had Lauren looked as vulnerable as she did right now. And he couldn't stop himself from continuing to frame her beautiful, shadowed face with his hands.

"B-because you love Kira enough to do anything you can to help her," Lauren whispered, blinking, trying to stop the tears. "You put yourself in harm's way to do the right thing for her. And you suffered a great deal by doing so. I can't even begin to imagine what you went through, Alex. Your sister had been raped. And then, to join a mafia team where the leader condoned it..." She gave him an anguished look. "I just can't imagine how that tore you up." Lauren was transfixed by the hooded, burning look in Alex's eyes. He didn't scare her any longer and that was simply amazing to her. She hungrily absorbed his unexpected touch, his calloused hands against her face, gentle, not controlling. The people ebbed and flowed around them, but she heard nothing except for his deep voice, drowning in the understanding in his eyes as he held her upturned gaze.

"I do not regret my decision. Kira received her therapy and she improved remarkably. And I was able to help Cal and Sky escape." His eyes grew dark and he added, in a husky tone, "And I have met you, *malen 'kaya...*"

Little one. The endearment he had called her by that one time when they were at Cal and Sky's home. He'd told her then that it was a Ukrainian man's way of telling the woman that he loved her. For a moment, Lauren thought he was going to lean down and kiss her. She could see it in his eyes, feel it all around him. And what stunned her the most was that she WANTED Alex to kiss her. Lauren lacked the bravery it took to make the first step, to simply lean upward and brush her mouth against his. The molten energy spun between them, and her lower body clenched. Hungry. Needy. Wanting Alex. No one else.

"Come, you must be hungry?" and he released her and took a step back. How badly Alex wanted to kiss that full, soft mouth of hers, and taste her. Lauren had actually wanted him to kiss her! That staggered Alex. Never, would he have thought he'd ever see that look of longing, that yearning, in her face. Her lips had parted and he'd groaned inwardly, desperately wanting to close the distance and kiss her. It would have been good cover, but Alex knew better. If Lauren really did want to kiss him, she had to make the first move. Otherwise, it could become a certified disaster, and any trust he had cobbled together with her would be instantly shattered.

Looking away, Lauren was too shaken to say anything. The comforting feeling of Alex's large, splayed fingers settled against the small of her back once more, made her feel good. Made her feel her body awakening in a new and different way. His touch was sending tiny tingles from her spine, straight down to her lower body. It felt good, as if some magical, unexplained transformation were slowly taking place within her. Lauren felt Alex standing there, patient, waiting for her to reply. Did he sense her? How she was feeling? Did he know she had wanted to kiss him? Lauren felt unsure of herself and the speed of the changes that were happening between them.

Clearing her throat, she met his warm gaze and whispered, "Yes, I'm ready to eat."

BY THE TIME they had finished eating their meal of Peruvian stew, night had fallen. Now, outside the small restaurant, Lauren felt the damp coolness of the night. She hadn't worn anything all that warm.

"May I?" and Alex lifted his arm as if to see if she would allow him to place his arm around her shoulders, draw her near, and keep her warm against him.

Nodding, Lauren moved closer. Heat radiated off Alex like a sun. As his arm settled around her shoulders, light, not heavy or trying to control her, she wrapped her arms around herself and relaxed. Lauren could feel his latent strength as he drew her gently against his body. It felt reassuring to her as they slowly walked down the wooden path toward the main street.

"Okay?" he asked, dipping his head enough to catch her shadowed eyes. She had drawn her arms in around herself in what Alex suspected was a defensive gesture. Did Lauren feel threatened by him? Forcing herself to play her role for the good of the mission? He knew Kira would not have been able to do so. He had no desire to make Lauren suffer like that. There was no need, and he would not do that to her. He started to lift his arm from around her shoulders.

Lauren whispered, "It's okay, Alex." And then she added, "You're like a big, warm teddy bear to me. Did you know that?" She saw the worry leave his eyes, saw yearning replace it. For her. There was something seductive and sensual going on between them. Was this how a woman felt toward a man they liked? Lauren had experienced none of these feelings before, and was now lamenting on why she hadn't forced herself to get at least a few relationships under her belt in the past. But her fear... well... it had just been too daunting to try. The past too raw. Never put to sleep. Always there. Until now. *Until Alex.*

"So, your arms around yourself?" he probed gently, as they melted into the flow of the tourists, "is to keep you warm? It is a defensive body-language gesture, too."

Lauren nodded. There was nothing weak about Alex Kazak. He was all hard solid muscle, no fat, over a frame of large, sturdy bone. Alex took the cold away from her. "Yes, to keep warm."

"Who is a teddy bear? Is that American slang?"

She saw how serious he was. "No, it's not slang. It's a favorite, soft fuzzy toy of American children. Often, parents give their child a teddy bear. It's like a loving friend. Someone you can hug, hold onto, and be loved in return because it has fleece for a body. Children hold onto it when they feel frightened. Or alone. It makes them feel safe. Secure."

"Oh?" Alex said, suddenly giving her a wicked, teasing look. "I am YOUR teddy bear?" He saw a flush sweep her cheeks and she suddenly became rattled as never before.

"Well... uh, no... it's a toy, Alex."

"But you called me YOUR teddy bear." He saw Lauren blush furiously and lick her lower lip, sending a pang of yearning through him. The woman made him ache.

"It's a manner of speaking," Lauren provided hastily. "Not real. Just... well... words."

"Oh," he murmured, disappointed. Alex would have liked nothing better than to hold Lauren. Make her feel safe. He liked the idea of being her teddy bear. To say she was embarrassed and scrambling would have been an understatement. His grin widened because he'd never seen Lauren as rattled as she was right now. "Is it okay if I consider myself to be your teddy bear when you need one?"

Lauren managed a shy smile, melting beneath his gentle teasing. The amusement dancing in his darkened hazel eyes made her yearn even more to kiss that mobile mouth of his. "Yes, I guess it's okay."

Alex halted her in front of a shop where Peruvian shawls, ponchos and scarves were hung in rainbow colors. "Here, allow me to buy you a poncho," and he pointed at a colorful bunch of them hanging nearby. He smiled over at the older Peruvian woman who wore a black dress, her black hair in a severe knot at the base of her neck, a brown bowler hat on her head. Speaking Spanish, he asked the woman how much it was for a poncho. Her eyes lit up with hope and she hurried forward, sensing a sale.

Lauren ran her fingers through the soft alpaca wool. Alex's arm was still around her and it felt good. Warm. Wonderful. She listened to him speak in flawless Spanish. And then, he switched to another language she didn't know, most likely Quechua. He and the woman proprietor spoke fluently in it with one another. Lauren was impressed with his linguistics skill.

"So?" Alex said, turning his attention to her. "Which one calls to you? What color do you like best?"

Lauren picked up a dark-green poncho. It had a hood to it, too. "I like this one."

Alex removed his arm. "Try it on? See how it feels to you?"

Lauren handed him the strap of her purse. As she pulled the poncho over her head, the warmth was immediate. "Oh, this IS warm," she murmured to Alex, surprised. Moving her fingers across the delightful weaving, she added, "I like this one."

"Good choice," he agreed. "Keep it on. I will pay the señora."

Lauren took back her purse, pulling the white strap across her shoulder. The poncho was divinely warm. She didn't want to admit to Alex that he was just as warm. And she found herself preferring him over the poncho. He paid the woman, who was delighted and thanked him over and over again. Turning, Alex slipped his arm around her, drawing her near as they continued to walk up the slope. "Thank you," Lauren said. "This is a beautiful, practical gift."

I would buy you the world if you wanted it. Alex kept that to himself. He squeezed her shoulder gently, "I like to see you happy, Lauren."

Lifting her chin, she drowned in his hooded gaze, his husky voice awakening a storm of longing built within her. He meant it. Sensing Alex wasn't role playing, she only nodded, her words choked up in her tightening throat.

They continued to walk up the slope, the tourist crowds thickening at dinner hour. She suddenly felt Alex tense. It wasn't obvious outwardly. Instantly, Lauren lifted her eyes toward the crowd. Alex turned to her, his eyes narrowed and hard. And, without a word, he leaned down and curved his mouth against hers, his arms drawing her hard against him, his back to the crowd.

Startled, Lauren started to resist, but felt danger. Urgency. *What was wrong?* Her mind spun as his mouth warmly took her lips, kissing her as if his life depended upon it. She felt the power of Alex's arms holding her protectively, her breasts pressed against his chest, her heart taking off at an erratic beat. His mouth moved caressingly against hers, coaxing open her lips. Lauren lifted her arms without thought, sliding them around his thick neck. The heat of his mouth plunged her into a cauldron of sudden, unexpected fire. Her mind weakened. Spun. She felt the urgency in his mouth against hers, taking her, claiming her and... she responded. Alex positioned her a quarter circle to the right, as if keeping his back toward something. Or someone? Her mind flitted between being alert to what was going on around them, and dissolving into the vat of scalding heat his mouth was evoking from hers.

Alex eased his mouth from hers, watching intently across Lauren's shoulder, gaze trained on a man threading his way through the crowd below where they stood. He felt Lauren quiver in his arms, but was unable to attend to her needs right now. The bald-headed man, who had just passed within feet of them, was a ruthless Georgian killer. He was a soldier from Vlad Alexandrov's old team. Alex felt Lauren sag against him, her head pressed against his chest, hands gripping his upper arms as if she were going to fall. Tearing his focus from the Russian, he looked down at her, abject apology written in his expression. Lauren's eyes were dazed-looking as she stared up at him.

"What's wrong?" she asked, her voice wispy. She saw Alex glance down the street, his eyes narrowed, focused on someone. "Was it a Russian?" Her knees felt weak. The man's kiss had blown through her like a blast furnace of unexpected heat. Pleasure skittered wildly through Lauren's lower body which now glowed with a throbbing life of its own. The sensations left her stunned and confused in the wake of his life-changing kiss. Alex's arm slid around her waist. He held her protectively against him, as if he were her shield.

"Yes," Alex gritted out, fury in his low tone, "Gavril Burak." He turned Lauren toward the upward slope. "Come, we must leave right now." He gave her a quick glance. "I am sorry I had to kiss you like that, Lauren. The man came out of nowhere, heading right for us. He would have identified me. There was not time to explain or do anything else."

Lauren nodded, her whole body continuing to melt in the wake of his mouth taking hers. She wanted to dissolve into the darkness, against Alex. "It's okay. It was good thinking," she managed, her voice still sounding far away... somewhere else...

Alex was on full alert. If there was one Russian, there had to be several more. Perhaps many more. Some of the mafia groups were small; others much larger, up to twenty men. He quickened his stride a bit, pulling Lauren along. He made a beeline for their apartment building at the top of the hill. Right now, he needed to disappear. Otherwise, he might be identified. And then, things could turn ugly in a heartbeat. And they had no weapons on them. Alex couldn't protect Lauren like he needed to.

By the time they reached the stairs, Lauren was huffing. She'd nearly been running at times to keep up with Alex. He guided her in front of him, wanting to protect her. She realized the urgency, and quickly dashed up the steps.

Alex shut the door once they were safely inside the apartment. He locked it and made sure there were no lights on. Going to the window that overlooked the busy street below, he cracked the venetian blind, studying the crowd with practiced intensity. He was peripherally aware of Lauren moving around. He heard her slip off the alpaca poncho. And then, her shoes came off. She was still breathing hard, the altitude getting to her.

"What do we need to do?" she demanded, out of breath.

"Remain here for now," he murmured, seeing two more Russians coming across the street. "It is a group coming in. I count two, three, four... more..."

Her mind had changed direction a hundred and eighty degrees. Alex was watching intently, standing far enough away from the blind so as not to be detected by any onlookers below. The apartment was dark, except for the light slicing through the blinds from the town below them. They had weapons here. She spotted her Glock 19 on the coffee table. Alex had put a magazine in it earlier, and it was ready for use. Lauren began to shed her clothes as she hurried down the hall to climb into her cargo pants, hiking boots and t-shirt.

Her mouth tingled wildly in the wake of Alex's life-affirming kiss. Her heart was pounding, not from fear, but from that delicious and unexpected kiss. Lauren understood he'd used it as a ploy to hide his identity from the advancing Russian man. These kinds of things came with undercover work. Use what was available. Don't run. Stay, and blend in. And he had. He'd kissed her, efficiently hiding his face so that he could not be recognized. But, did Alex realize just how much the kiss had affected her?

CHAPTER 7

"I AM GOING to recon," Alex told Lauren. He turned from the venetian blind and faced her. She stood tensely in the living room and was all business now.

"Check out who has arrived? How many?"

Alex nodded. Going to his gear bag, he pulled out some clothes. "Exactly."

"I'll go with you."

He shook his head, sitting down and removing his boots. "No. It will be bad enough for me. I cannot just stroll down the street to the hotel where they always stay and recon. I am too tall." He gave her a wry look. "The Indian population here is about five foot three inches tall. I am six feet four inches tall. Too obvious. I will slip behind this apartment building and move into the wall of the jungle and make my way down to where I know they are staying."

"But I could blend in. I could—"

"No." Alex gave her a frown. "They will possibly see you soon enough when we go into the jungle for orchid hunting. They will know you are American. It will be dangerous enough. I cannot risk you in a situation like this. I will do the recon and come back and let you know what I have discovered."

Lauren felt him being overly protective toward her. She worried that Alex would be recognized by his old colleagues who, she knew, probably wouldn't take him suddenly showing back up here all that kindly. Or would they? She didn't know. He had to keep a low profile in Aguas Calientes. "Do ALL Russian mafia groups know you on sight?"

"No. The five different teams all operated in specific areas. We did not meet with one another. I know this team because they operated parallel to our area." He dropped his boots aside and stood up, pulling off his polo shirt.

Lauren saw the power implicit in his naked chest, and the light sprinkling of dark hair across it. She didn't want to be affected by the masculine beauty of his upper body, but she was. There were several old, and some newer, scars fanned across it and she felt her heart contract with pain for him. He reached into his gear and drew out a black, long-sleeved skin-fitting shirt, swiftly pulling it on. His hands went to his belt and he looked over at her.

"I don't mind undressing in front of you, but you might," he said, giving her a crooked grin.

Lauren quickly turned her back, feeling heat fly into her cheeks. It was a good thing the room was gray and shadowed, because she doubted he could see her blush. She heard him sit down and heard the chinos he wore fall to the floor. He had chosen a pair of black cargo pants from his suitcase that would blend well into the night.

"You can look now."

She slowly turned; mouth thinned. Alex was sitting down once again, pulling on his combat boots, his fingers flying over the thick, black leather laces, tightening them up. He was all hard, massive muscle and she was mesmerized by his male grace. "What else do you need?"

"Get me my knife sheath? My pistol?"

Crouching down, Lauren dug through his gear, locating both weapons. She stood and handed him the sheath. He quickly strapped it onto his left, lower calf. The way he pulled the blackened blade from its nylon sheath, and tested the blade's edge with his thumb, impressed her but she said nothing. He was an operator. Alex knew how to kill in a hundred different ways. He seemed satisfied with the blade's sharpness and sheathed it. She handed him the MP-445 pistol. It was a sleek .40 caliber weapon that had a helluva stopping power to it. Alex stood up, and she handed him the drop holster that went with it. He quickly belted up, tugging the strapped Velcro into place around his lower thigh. She'd never seen him prepare for stealth before, but knew he would be lethal. There were no wasted movements with him. His game face was now firmly in place. Lamenting that all-too-recent time together when he had still been vulnerable to her, Lauren stepped around the canvas gear bag on the floor.

"What else do you need?"

"My camouflage paint."

She found it. He sat down and quickly smeared black, dark green and gray over his face and neck. White skin would stand out on a dark night like a sore thumb, and Alex needed to completely blend into the environment.

"What's next?"

"My camera."

She found a small, square digital camera and handed it to him.

"What else?"

He tucked the camera into a leg pocket.

"Nothing else." He smiled grimly. "Just my eyes and ears."

"Do the groups go to a specific hotel when they come here?"

"Yes." Alex took a black baseball cap from the bag and settled it on his head, along with a pair of NVGs, night vision goggles, which he hung around his neck.

Lauren was used to being around operators. Gone was his easy-going manner. He placed the MP-445 in its holster after putting a round in the chamber and unsafing it. If he ran into trouble, seconds would count. Seconds between surviving or dying. "What do you want me to do?"

"Stay here." Alex pulled the Velcro cover over his watch. The cover hid the radium dial from potential enemies. "It is 2100, nine p.m. The hotel where they stay is cheap and it is poorly-built compared to the other hotels in this town. I am very familiar with its location. There is a jungle wall and trees that grow within feet of the rear of that building. I will climb one of the trees, watch, and recon."

"No set time you'll return?"

"I will return by 0400." He reached down and pulled out two radios from his gear bag. "These radios work roughly for a mile. Are you familiar with how they work?"

Relieved, Lauren took hers and nodded. "Yes."

"Once I am in position, I will give it one click, and that means I am hidden in a tree. I will not speak into it."

"Right," she murmured, turning the radio on. It was a small, hand-sized model. One of several radios they had brought along.

"If you need something," and his voice lowered, "if your life is in danger, give me two clicks. I will come back here as soon as I can."

Lauren nodded. "I think I'll be very safe, warm, and dry here."

"Usually," Alex said, nodding back at her, "when a group comes into town, they are focused on getting cleaned up, eating hot food, drinking vodka, and then finding a prostitute."

"You probably know where the brothel is," she deadpanned. His eyes sparkled for a moment.

"Yes. It is right next door from that broken-down old hotel they stay in."

"I think I remember that hotel. It's on the left just where we started to climb the hill?"

"Yes, a gray two-story stucco building sitting right up against the jungle wall."

"We'd call that a flea-bitten hotel," she told him. "Dirty. Cockroaches. Cheap rates. Filthy, dirty mattresses," and she wrinkled her nose.

"More slang," he murmured, grinning. "Flea-bitten. Yes, the mattresses there are very old, musty and I have slept on them. I'd rather sleep on the ground, it is cleaner. Every morning I used to wake up with so many bites. Fleas among them."

"Sounds awful."

Alex looked around the semi-darkened apartment. "You call Hunter by sat phone. Fill him in. When I come back, I will give him my report, and I'll have digital photos we can encrypt and then send to him from the laptop."

She watched him tuck the radio in another pocket. "Just be careful?" Because Lauren knew if the Russians ever found Alex, they would torture and kill him. He was a traitor in their eyes, and she was sure his name was well-known among the groups loyal to Vlad Alexandrov that prowled this region.

"I will be."

"If you get into trouble? How will I know?"

"I will return here by 0400. No later. If I do not show up, then you need to find me or find out where I am being held." His mouth turned down. He reached out, placing his hand on her shoulder. "Lauren, if that happens, and I do not think it will, you must call Shield for back-up. Get the Special Forces team headed up by Sergeant Mace Killmer, who is on stand-by in Cusco, just in case. You cannot go it alone if I have been captured."

She saw the worry in his eyes, felt his fingers move restively across her shoulder. Her flesh tingled wherever they grazed her. "I don't work stupid," she told him. "We have that Special Forces teams available. And that CIA agent that we haven't met yet? After this stage is over, we need to reach out to our contacts."

Alex had planned on meeting the agent tomorrow morning at a predetermined time and location. "I agree. Okay," he said, somewhat relieved. "I am not going to get caught, so stop looking at me like that."

"Looking like what?" Lauren demanded, already missing the touch of his hand as he removed it from her shoulder. She saw his mouth flex, amusement in his gaze.

"I think you are a big worry-wart about your partner. Yes?"

"Always," she muttered defiantly. "Nothing wrong with that."

"You are a hen's mother, Lauren," he teased, trying out American slang.

"Alex, it's 'mother hen'. Okay?"

He chuckled. "I always get them mixed up. Your crazy Americans and your crazy sayings," and he reached out, briefly touching her cheek. "I will return, *Malen 'kaya*."

And then he was gone. For a man of his size and weight, even Lauren was impressed with his stealth. The door shut silently behind him.

She locked it.

Her heart started to pound with fear for Alex. Lauren grumbled to herself as she zipped up his gear bag and dragged it into the bedroom, where it was unseen and out of the way. She felt her heart respond to the endearment he'd whispered to her: *Malen 'kaya. Little One.* She swallowed nervously, feeling as if being with Alex was like living in another time and place. He was all business, and then that game face dropped away and she saw the real man beneath it. Whenever that happened, she felt as if she were the most important person in his life as he devoted his full attention to her.

Shaking her head, Lauren hauled her own gear bag to the bedroom as well. She had to put her feelings aside and get down to business. First, a call to Gage Hunter to give him a 'sitrep' situation report, an update… This mission now had legs, and Lauren sensed that things were going to start moving fast from here on out.

ALEX QUIETLY ENTERED the apartment, slipping inside, closing the door behind him. It was 0400. There were no lights on, but he could see well enough from the glow of the streetlights below shining upwards against the drawn blinds. He saw a soft light peeking through the gap of Lauren's partly-opened bedroom door and continued silently down the hall. As Alex slowly pushed the door open, he saw that Lauren had a night-light on. She lay across the bed, on her belly, facing away from him. There was her Glock 19 on the bedstand within easy reach if she needed it. He saw the sat phone and the radio on the mattress, near her hand. His heart went out to her. She was curvy and all-woman despite the masculine clothes she wore. He saw she was prepared to spring into action, her combat boots still on as well. That red hair of hers was tamed into a long ponytail, laying across one shoulder as she slept.

Alex gently closed the door, not having the heart to awaken her. He knew she was sleep deprived. He needed to grab a shower and wash off all the paint and sweat.

Later, as the light of dawn was crawling across the massive edifice of Machu Picchu, Alex was in the kitchen, making breakfast. He heard Lauren's bedroom door open. He saw her shuffle around the corner, rubbing her drowsy eyes, her hair tousled.

"You made it back okay?" she asked, her voice thick with sleep. Alex was dressed in a pair of Levi's, a dark-blue t-shirt and his hiking boots. She could smell the fresh shower he'd taken. His face paint was gone, and he was clean-shaven.

"Yes. Are you hungry?" and he smiled over at her as she leaned against the door, watching him. He felt himself stirring. Lauren looked soft and approachable. She was struggling to wake up. "Maybe some coffee first?" he suggested, giving her a wry grin. He saw her wrinkle her nose and push off from the doorway with her shoulder.

"Yeah, for sure. What did you find out?" she muttered as she walked barefoot into the kitchen.

"A lot," he murmured. "How many eggs?"

"Two, please." Lauren yawned and shook her head. She never woke up very fast; it was just her nature.

"Go sit at the table and drink your coffee."

"Good idea," Lauren mumbled, shuffling over to the small round table at one end of the kitchen. "I didn't mean to fall asleep on you. I never heard you come in."

"It is a sign you have confidence in me and my abilities," he told her, cracking six eggs into the black iron skillet.

Raising an eyebrow, Lauren said nothing. She was glad Alex was all right. "Normally, I don't sleep like the dead," she offered, sipping the hot coffee. It tasted good and would help her wake up. "That was a terrible black joke," she muttered, brows bunching. "Especially on an op," and she gave him an apologetic look. All he did was shrug, unfazed.

"Do you not think you slept well because you trust me just a little?"

"I do trust you," Lauren murmured, seeing him give her a quick glance. His mouth entranced her, and she hotly remembered it covering hers last night. She couldn't get that moment out of her mind. It kept replaying the kiss. How Alex had monitored his strength against her mouth, how he'd coaxed her lips open, and the response he'd drawn from her. Clearly, he knew how to kiss. She didn't. But now that she'd tasted Alex, and had liked the pleasure he'd brought her, Lauren found herself curious, and eager to explore him even more. Yet, fear and memories kept her curiosity in tight check. Still… the man was sexy as hell, animal sensuality oozing out of his pores. She'd have to be dead not to respond to it, she reluctantly admitted to herself. Another black joke of ill-fortune. She needed another cup of coffee.

"Really? You do trust me, Lauren?" Alex slid two eggs onto her plate and four others onto his own. He set the skillet back on the stove, and added the potatoes he'd fried earlier, along with a large, ten-ounce beef steak.

"Why wouldn't I trust you?" Lauren demanded, watching him as he brought their plates over. His shoulders were so broad. He made the kitchen appear smaller. She thanked him and realized he'd already set the table earlier, as if expecting her to have breakfast with him.

"This is our first op together," Alex said, adding toast and some strawberry jam that he'd brought down with them on this op in his suitcase. He sat down opposite Lauren, absorbing her sleepy features. Did she realize how innocent she looked to him? Alex thought this is how she might have looked as a young girl growing up; carefree, not worried what her hair looked like. He imagined her as a barefoot youth, soft and trusting. He was relieved to see her walls weren't coming up this morning. Something had obviously shifted between them. As he cut into his thick, medium rare steak, he wondered if the kiss between them had unlocked her trust toward him. He thought it had, but couldn't be sure.

"Yeah, it takes time to get in sync with a new operator partner," Lauren admitted. The eggs were perfectly cooked for her as she liked them: medium well. How did he know that? Her stomach grumbled. "What did you find out on your recon?"

"This is Vlad Alexandrov's original, old team. The men who were with him are now the core of group two. Group one was destroyed by the Special Forces teams in the area, and only two got away: Lev and my friend Nik. I took photos and we need to download them into your computer. You can send them by satellite link to Gage Hunter."

"Did you know these men?"

Alex nodded and gave her a grim look. "Yes."

"Who's leading the group now?"

He snorted as he slathered strawberry jam across two pieces of toast. "An ex-Spetsnaz officer: a Captain Anton Petrov. He was Vlad Alexandrov's second-in-command and he is an enforcer."

Lauren saw and felt Alex's response. His voice was low, almost a growl. She saw worry in his eyes. She said, "A bad dude?"

"He is a monster, just like Vlad was," Alex said with distaste. "If Vlad wanted information from a chief of a Quechua village, Petrov was the one who would find one of his daughters. And he was the one who would tear her clothes off, throw her on the ground, and rape her in front of everyone." He didn't want to tell Lauren all that, but she had to know the type of men they were dealing with. The look on her face was a mixture of disgust and terror. Most likely, for herself. He'd learned quickly from Kira's experience that just mentioning the word 'rape' would send her into a terrible emotional state. Now, Lauren was reacting similarly. He was sorry he'd had to tell her about Petrov.

"I read Cal's report on Vlad," she said, her voice tight. "I couldn't believe it…"

"Do," Alex warned her. "These men are hardened veterans from their at-tempts at destroying the Chechen rebels. They hate those who are not like them. They always took revenge when the Chechen's would attack on Russian soil."

"So, Petrov is the leader of Vlad's old group," Lauren murmured, thinking as she ate. "How many men did you see at that hotel?"

"There are five. It is a small group." He shrugged. "Small means they are far more mobile, logistically. They don't have to worry about finding enough food or water for a lot of men, things that slow larger groups down."

"When you were with Vlad, there were twenty of you. Right?"

"Yes."

Lauren looked at him. "I don't know how you were able to handle it, Alex. I really don't." She saw his face go expressionless, but his hazel eyes betrayed raw, unspoken emotions.

"I have done things in the Russian mafia I am not proud of, Lauren. I am not a good man any longer. My hands are stained with the blood of people who did not deserve to be murdered," and he scowled, breaking eye contact with her.

"At heart," Lauren said quietly, "you are a healer, like your sister Kira. She's a nurse. You're a combat medic." She watched as Alex seemed to flinch, his gaze on his plate, hands stilled over it, his mouth tight.

"I wish," he rasped, forcing himself to hold Lauren's sympathetic gaze again, "that I was the hero you make me out to be. But I am not." He didn't deserve someone like her, even if she wanted him. And he knew she didn't, for obvious reasons. So why did she look so heartbroken when he'd said that? Alex couldn't figure out her reaction.

"You told me yesterday you tried to help those women who the Russians raped. You and Nik tried to stop them."

Alex gave a one-shouldered shrug, cleaning up what was left on his plate. "I tried. So did Nik. After Kira was raped, I understood what it did to a woman. I found myself sickened, I should have done more."

"What?" Lauren demanded, "and get killed by trying to stop Vlad and his men? You were there to make money to help Kira with. It wasn't your fault those men did what they did."

Alex stared hard at her. "I did not stop them. Therefore, I am complicit."

"Short of putting a bullet into each of their heads, what could you have done?" Lauren replied, frowning. "And that was impossible because they'd have turned around and killed you and Nik. You weren't the leader. It would be different if you had been, and hadn't ordered them to stop. But Vlad was in charge, Alex. You did the best you could."

"I have thought about this hundreds of times," Alex admitted. Getting up, he took his now empty plate and flatware and set them in the sink. Pouring himself more coffee he came back and sat down. "My parents raised me to know right from wrong, Lauren."

"War has no morality, and you know that," Lauren argued quietly. "NOTHING is fair in war, Alex. Especially in a combat situation. You and I both know that from personal experience."

"It does not relieve me of the guilt I carry. It is mine to carry. I had choice. A woman suffers the rest of her life because of the choice I made. These are the facts."

Alex was too hard on himself. Lauren kept that thought to herself. She picked up a piece of toast and took a bite on it. Alex had already demolished five other slices. He'd worked hard last night, burning up a lot of calories, the adrenaline making him even hungrier. "That's not the man I see right now. The man I know," she said, giving him a challenging stare.

"I worry about you," he admitted. Gesturing, Alex said, "Those men, Petrov and his second-in-command, Tamryn Volkov, are rapists. If they ever captured you…" and he shook his head.

"I'm not going to get captured."

"I'd kill them if they EVER tried to lay a hand on you."

Startled by the powerful emotions in his voice, Lauren felt shaken. "We're on a sniper op, Alex. It's called being unseen and undetected. It's what I do best. I've never been compromised in all my years of doing this kind of work."

"Yes, but you do not know Peruvian jungle. It is impossible to move through some portions of it. The position you must choose to shoot from will be challenging to find. It leaves you vulnerable and open to being seen. Perhaps, caught." And Alex would give his life, in a heartbeat, if that happened because these soldiers he knew too well. They were depraved and sub-human. They had no morals, integrity or values, stripping them of their humanity. Women were routinely taken and raped without any afterthought. Petrov and Volkov cared nothing for how a woman felt or, worse, how it would stain her for the rest of her life.

"I'm not going to be caught," Lauren gritted out. "So, let's just get off the topic, okay?"

Nodding, Alex said, "Tamryn Volkov is second in command to Petrov. He is a blond-haired man. Women consider him to be good looking. I fought with both these men. I saw them lose their hearts, their souls. Now, they are monsters. And we need to eliminate BOTH of them, not just Petrov."

"You need to talk to Hunter about that. He'll make that decision."

Alex knew that orders came down from Hunter, and the Department of Defense. He was sure he could persuade his new boss to allow Lauren to take out both men. With Lauren, he was carefully watching his words to describe Petrov and Volkov. Hunter, a man, would want the raw, unvarnished version and Alex intended to lay it out in no uncertain terms to him as to why these two Russians needed to be removed. The world would be far better off without them.

"I will call him now," Alex told her, picking up his coffee mug as he stood.

"The sat phone is on my dresser," she told him. Alex was upset. He had his game face on once again but, for whatever reason, Lauren still sensed his feelings. There was a hatred in him when he spoke about his former comrades. A small shiver went through her. Soon, those men would be back on the hunt once they left for the jungle again. Lauren watched Alex head down the hall. The kitchen felt empty without his vital presence.

Mulling over his reactions, the guilt he carried, Lauren wished she could just hold him and make this mission go away. Alex was a good person, caught in a terrible vise. War destroyed a person's humanity. She rubbed her face wearily, hating men like these Russians. For her, it would be a righteous kill: eradicating evil off the face of this earth. Protecting innocent women and children from their kind. She hoped that Gage sent down permission to take both of them out.

CHAPTER 8

"WE NEED SOME groceries," Lauren told Alex at lunch, five days later. He'd wanted to remain indoors, not out in public where the Russians who were in town on R&R could identify him. This was the only group who could. As for the other four teams: he could pass right by any of them with impunity around Aguas Calientes and never be identified. "I'm going to walk down to the grocery store and get some stuff."

Alex scowled. He hated being cooped up like a chicken in a henhouse for five days straight. Fresh air, sunshine and the elements made him feel alive. Vital. The only good thing about all this wait was that he had Lauren as his company. And, in those five waiting days, they'd settled into a companionable resonance with one another. They should leave tomorrow morning. He damn well didn't want one of those ex-Spetsnaz men to catch a look at Lauren. It could mean trouble.

"Do you want dinner tonight?" she drawled. "We have NO food. And I'm not going to eat MRE's if I don't have too. It's a short walk. Tons of tourists around. I'll be okay."

"I worry."

She came and sat down opposite Alex at the table. He had his cleaning cloth spread out and was oiling his pistol with quick, familiar movements. "Now who's the worry wart?" she teased. There was stubbornness in his face. She could feel him resisting her leaving the apartment.

Flicking a glance at her, Alex swallowed hard. Lauren was naturally beautiful. Her thick, red lashes were the frames around her large, intelligent, gray eyes that calmly studied him. She reminded him of a sharp-eyed eagle. "Yes, I am."

"You're a hen mother," she teased, grinning, reaching out and touching his muscled forearm.

His heart opened. Lauren was smiling. Alex's hands halted over the pistol as he stared at her. The corners of her mouth lifted, and that dimpled smile went all the way up into her eyes, which danced with amusement.

"What?" she demanded, removing her hand from his arm because, if she hadn't, she'd have wanted to slide her fingertips up even higher, to feel his muscles leap beneath them.

"Your smille," he said thickly. "I have never seen you smile like this before."

Lauren felt her chest tighten. The look on Alex's face was one of utter honesty, his eyes burning with desire—for her. Her smile dissolved and she whispered, "I guess I don't smile very often, do I?"

Alex shook himself. He wanted to lay the pistol aside, wipe off his hands, and frame her face and take that lush mouth of hers. He dreamed of kissing her every night. He'd wake up on the rug, the blanket pulled over him, lost in some dream that involved her.

Forcing himself to continue cleaning the pistol, he rasped, "I wish you would realize how it makes me feel. It is as if the sun has come out from behind dark clouds. It makes me feel warm. Good." Lauren's smile told him how much she was relaxing and feeling at ease around him. It was a miracle in itself and for that, Alex was more than grateful.

"I guess I've always been too serious. At least, that's what everyone tells me."

"I feel here, in my heart, when you feel safe, you will feel more free. And when a person feels that way, a smile is easy to share with others. Yes?"

His simple words sank deep into her, bringing up both good and bad memories. Lauren stood up and said, "You're probably right. I'm going to grab my civilian knapsack, play botanist, and go to the grocery store."

Alex frowned. "Take a pistol."

Lauren hesitated. "Alex, I don't dare. The local police… if they see it or find it on me… all hell will break loose."

He lifted his chin. "If Petrov or Volkov see you, approach you, you may not have a choice."

"What?" Lauren scoffed lightly, trying to tease him, "they're going to shoot me out in the plaza because I'm an American? There's tons of Americans here in Aguas Calientes." She patted his broad shoulder. "I'll be fine."

"At least take the radio."

He was upset. His full lower lip was compressed, his voice a growl like that of a male wolf that had been disturbed and was close to biting anyone who got too close to him.

"Okay, a radio I can do." she said.

Lauren looked forward to getting out of the apartment. She hefted the dark-green knapsack over her shoulders. And, wearing the same color cargo pants, a pair of hiking boots, and a black tee underneath her long-sleeved white blouse, she knew she'd blend into the tourist traffic. The radio was in her left cargo pants' pocket, out of sight, but handy if she needed it. When she ambled by the kitchen, she saw Alex get up. His eyes were narrowed. And yes, he was clearly concerned for her sake.

He went to the door and opened it. Fresh, humid air tumbled languidly through it into the air-conditioned apartment. "You stay safe. All right?" Her hair was in a ponytail. She wore the kind of floppy hat that she'd thought a botanist out in the jungle might wear. No matter how well Lauren blended in, her beauty could not be hidden or dimmed. The men Alex had worked with for two years always went after the young, beautiful girls in the Quechua villages. Lauren far outshined them. She was a target of another sort.

"I promise," Lauren said, slipping out the door. "This won't take long…"

Descending the concrete steps, Lauren focused on the crowd below. Alex had taken photos of all five Russians. She'd memorized their faces. She knew their names. What they looked like, how tall they were, and their personalities. Being midday, tourists were pouring into the town after having just arrived off the Cusco train. Many different throngs of them were slowly snaking in and out of the plethora of shops. She chose the side of the street with the most people, and kept her pace slow. If she hurried, she'd stand out and possibly be spotted by someone, someone like a Spetsnaz operator. The sun was hidden behind the humid, fog-like clouds that drifted slowly across above the town. The humidity was always high. Lauren could hear the buses firing up, their diesel engines bellowing, preparing to take tourist groups up the winding dirt road to the top of Machu Picchu where the Incan temples were located.

Often, she was bumped, because tourists were looking everywhere except where they were going. With her dark glasses on, Lauren could swing her gaze around and no one would realize what she was doing. Sunglasses were a major asset in the field. Leaving the hill behind, she saw a group of Indians at the front doors of the Catholic church, waiting for the priest to open them. Mass was held at noon five days a week, she had discovered. On the opposite side of the street she was walking along was the hotel where the Russians were staying. Lauren looked long and hard, seeing none of them around the opened doors to the entrance. Maybe they were all sleeping? Or, as Alex had politely put it, daylight was for prostitutes, nights were for drinking beer, playing poker, and smoking their cigarettes.

The grocery store was opposite the church and she pushed her way inside, seeing that it was fairly crowded with tourists. Taking a small basket from the counter, she threaded in and out of people from many different nations. There was a group of Chinese. Rounding the corner, she ran into a cluster of Germans. In another aisle, Lauren could hear the musical lilt of French being rapidly spoken. Machu Picchu drew the world, and she could see why.

Going to the meat department, located at the rear of the store, she saw the butcher. He was a Quechua Indian, if she guessed correctly, and she hoped he knew a little English. Her Spanish wasn't great. Unlike U.S. grocery stores, meat was cut from a side of beef hanging off a huge hook. She smiled, and greeted the butcher in English. He gave her a blank look and shrugged his shoulders. *Damn.* Gesturing across the counter, she pointed at what she wanted: meat cut fresh from the dangling side of beef.

He shrugged and gave her a pleading look, speaking in his language. Probably Quechua. She wished Alex was here. *Okay, plan C.* She set the basket at her feet, and pulled open her right cargo pants' pocket, hauling out her English-Spanish dictionary.

"Perhaps, Señorita," a voice rasped from behind her, near her ear, "I can translate for you?"

Lauren gasped, whirling around. Her eyes went wide as she recognized the blond-haired, blue-eyed Tamryn Volkov. He grinned and bowed his head. He smelled of beer, cigarette smoke and sour sweat. He was unshaven. His pale-blue eyes narrowed on her. "You scared the hell out of me!" she snapped, backing away from him.

Volkov's smile remained. His eyes flickered as he moved his gaze slowly from her head down to her feet, and then came back up to rest on her breasts, hidden beneath her white cotton blouse. "Today is my lucky day," he murmured in thick English, rubbing his chin, holding her furious stare. "I am always drawn to women with red hair."

Panic coursed through Lauren. *Oh hell!* The Russian was six foot two inches tall and muscular. He wore a blue chambray shirt with the sleeves missing. The muscles in his upper-arms were thick, and told her he was in top condition and probably worked out with heavy weights at a gym. The black tattoos around his biceps were snakes. She hated snakes. He wore a pair of very old Levi's that were dirty and threadbare. Lauren saw that he had an erection under the denim, and it disgusted her. Shoving her own personal reactions down deep inside her, she knew she'd better get the upper hand here, or this drunk bastard would try something stupid.

"Thank you," she gritted out, moving closer to him, leaning down and picking up her basket. "I'll figure this out on my own. I don't need a translator."

As she straightened back up, Volkov's hand shot out. His fingers wrapped around her upper arm, efficiently stopping her from pulling away. "I'm VERY good at translating. You look new to this place. Are you American?" His eyes became hooded as he looked back down at her breasts.

Lauren felt stripped. Panic rose in her again. His fingers were hurting her. She saw the coldness in Volkov's eyes, that fixed smile of a snake. She hated that he was looking at her like she was a piece of meat. "Let go of me," she growled, glaring up at him.

"Surely, you have a name? And yes, you are American. I hear it in your accent."

The smell of beer and sweat assailed her flaring nostrils. Nausea churned through her tightened gut.

"Señor...," a man called, hurrying down the aisle toward them.

"Get lost, Enrique," the Russian snarled, his gaze not leaving hers.

"B-but... she is a customer, Señor Volkov. She is merely buying food. Please, can you leave her alone?"

Lauren saw Enrique, the fat proprietor in black slacks and a white short-sleeved shirt that stuck to his sweaty body. He was balding, wore glasses, and was wringing his hands, his expression pleading.

"Leave us," Volkov whispered to him. "Before it's too late..."

It WAS too late for this smug, arrogant Russian bastard. Lauren grabbed the Russian's thumb from the hand he had on her arm, rotating her hand above its knuckle. In a swift move, she locked his thumb down with her own. And then she turned and pushed his hand upward. The move was so swift that the Russian couldn't react fast enough. Lauren saw the sudden surprise in his eyes, and heard his grunt of pain. Before Volkov could do anything else, she swept out her booted foot, smashing it into his right knee.

Volkov went down like a roaring bull, rolling across the red-tiled floor, grabbing at his knee, grimacing and cursing in Russian.

Lauren spun around, running down the aisle, dropping the basket at the door, pushing out into fresh air, and losing herself quickly in the thick crowds. Breathing hard, she slowed down, taking on the pace of the tourists around her. Heart pounding in her chest, she ducked in between two stores and flattened herself against one wall, taking a quick glance back toward the grocery store. Volkov limped out of the store, cursing and screaming in Russian, his face twisted in rage, looking around for her. Lauren waited to see which way he was going to go. He limped badly across the plaza and disappeared inside the flea-bitten hotel.

Trying to slow her breathing, she closed her eyes and forced herself to relax. That had been close. Alex was going to be pissed. And they still had no food on top of all that. Lauren opened her eyes, deciding to remain on this side of the street. Sweat was trickling down her temples and between her breasts. She shakily wiped her brow and pulled her hat a little lower. Slipping back into the crowd, she quickly became a part of the great tourist mass.

ALEX HEARD THE apartment door being opened. He left the kitchen table, and swiftly met Lauren as she came in with several brown bags of food in her arms. "You took a long time," he said worriedly, closing the door and locking it behind her. Something was wrong. He saw it in her eyes. Her hair looked mussed. More than it should be. He reached out for the sacks of food, taking them from her arms.

"What happened?" he ground out.

Lauren threw off the hat, took off her sunglasses, and shrugged out of her knapsack, dropping it on the rattan couch. "Don't get pissed, but Volkov trapped me at the meat counter of the grocery store."

Freezing, Alex stared at her. "What?"

She shrugged, feeling dirty and in need of a shower to remove the sour, stinking smell of her assailant from her skin. "He surprised me from behind. I was trying to get the butcher to cut a certain piece of beef off the side. He didn't speak English and I didn't speak Quechua. I got my English-Spanish book out and the bastard came up behind me, whispered in my ear he'd like to be my translator." Lauren grimaced. "It all went downhill after that." She quickly told him what she did to escape and then added, "I hope I broke the bastard's thumb. Or his kneecap."

Alex felt terror rip through him. He walked to the kitchen and placed the sacks on the counter. "Where is he now?"

"He limped back to that fleabag hotel," Lauren muttered, pulling off her blouse. It reeked of the Russian's sweat, and the beer he'd been drinking. She would wash the blouse out in the shower she was about to take.

"No one followed you?" He saw Lauren was pale. Her eyes were dark, and he sensed the terror within her, no matter how good she was at hiding it from him.

"I made sure of that. I loitered between two buildings opposite their hotel for ten minutes to make sure. Then, I faded into the crowd, stopped at a restaurant up near the top of the hill and got us some take-out dinners." Lauren saw the anger in his expression. "I'm all right." She held up her hands. "I damn well know how to defend myself, Alex. So don't even go there. I'm upset enough. I don't need your anger aimed at me, too."

Cursing to himself, Alex advanced upon her. Lauren lifted her chin, jutted it out, up into Alex's face, and refused to step back away from him. The fire in her eyes, the glittering quality of her gray, ice-like gaze was something he'd never encountered before. Now, she was behaving like an operator. And he felt the steel in her spine as he slowed and halted in front of her.

Gently, he placed his hands on her upper arms, keeping his voice low, without any anger in it. "Lauren, I know you can take care of yourself. But I am your partner. I have your back. I am angry at myself for letting you go out there without me. My gut told me it was dangerous for you, and I dismissed it because I allowed you to convince me otherwise." He saw her blink, the fire in her eyes doused, the expression in them turning a little regretful now. Taking advantage of this, he added, with a slight smile. "I will NEVER be angry with you, *Malen 'kaya*. We will talk. And we may argue, but I will never raise my voice toward you. All right?" and Alex forced himself to release her arms. If he didn't, he was going to do something tragically stupid: kiss her senseless because he was terrified that he could have lost her to Volkov. The bastard could have just as easily snapped her neck. His close quarters combat skills were equal to Alex's own. And few were swifter or quicker at killing than them. But Lauren didn't know that. He then reminded himself that she was a Krav Maga instructor, and that is why she had gotten the upper hand on that bastard.

The adrenaline burning through her was starting to crash. Lauren felt suddenly shaky, and she didn't want Alex to see her that way. He'd see it soon enough. Right now, he was upset for the right reasons. His voice had been low, fraught with emotion… care…

She grimaced. "Okay, you're making sense. Next time you get a gut-check like that, you need to be more upfront about it with me. I'll listen."

He nodded. "I will make myself VERY clear next time. Volkov is dangerous, Lauren. He's one of the best at close quarters combat techniques. If he…" and he shook his head, terrible scenarios running through his mind. "If he had decided to engage you, he would have killed you," and he met and held her stare.

"You don't know me," Lauren growled. "He didn't stand a chance! I took him down in a heartbeat. You forget, I know Krav Maga. It's a street-fighting technique and, believe me, he collapsed to the floor like a bull that had just been castrated."

His mouth quirked. "I wish I had seen it. That is a first. Volkov is a master of CQC."

"Well," Lauren muttered defiantly, "so the hell am I! I'm going to take a shower. I want the smell of Volkov off me!"

Alex watched her storm off, her mouth set, her eyes blazing with justified anger. He probably could have handled that conversation with her better. Lauren had looked hurt because he hadn't thought she would have bested Volkov in a real fight. Running his fingers through his hair, he realized, too late, that he'd allowed his emotions to leak into the mix. Because he cared for Lauren. Because he didn't want her hurt. He was clearly being over protective. Smothering her. Or, maybe him not putting enough trust in her abilities as an operator was the real reason?

·

Lauren came out of the bathroom half an hour later, wrapped in a towel, her damp hair bunched up on her head, anchored in place with a tortoise-shell comb, the steam from the door behind her escaping and surrounding her in a misty cloud. She spotted Alex at the large window that overlooked the street below. He had the blind barely cracked and was watching for Russian activity below. Angry that he didn't think she could take care of herself, Lauren walked down the hall, leaving wet footprints in her wake.

Alex was putting the food in plastic containers on the table when she emerged later from her bedroom. Her hair was dry, twisted all up on top of her head, only this time with that beautiful silver and pearl comb she'd worn on the flight down to Peru holding it in place. She wore a black tee, olive-green cargo pants, and her feet were bare. It was such a study of contrasts, Alex thought. She looked like an elegant model from her slender neck upward, a soldier in the middle, and a child in bare feet at the bottom. His lips twitched, but he said nothing. Lauren was complex. But complex women always intrigued him, made him curious, and he enjoyed discovering the multi-faceted layers of such a woman. Lauren was his ultimate challenge and he met her cool gray stare as she stood in the doorway, her arms folded across her breasts.

"Do you feel better?" he inquired, going to the drawer and taking out flatware.

"Not really. I'm really pissed, Alex. At you."

Alex stood and faced her, his hands at his sides. "I must apologize to you," he admitted. "I questioned your ability as an operator. I was wrong to do that." He managed a cutting smile, aimed at himself, not her. "The fact you are here, unhurt, tells me who the best operator was in that confrontation. Volkov is the one with either a broken thumb or busted knee cap. Not you."

All of Lauren's anger dissolved. Damn but the man knew how to stop an argument cold in its tracks. She saw the abject apology in his eyes, and heard it in his voice.

"I don't meet many operators who can find it in themselves to say they're sorry about anything," she admitted, her voice brittle. Lauren waved her hand wearily, feeling exhausted from the adrenaline crash. "Thanks for the apology. I had it coming and I appreciate you having the balls to tell me."

Alex gave her a wry grin. "You are a badass, Parker."

"Damn well better know it, Kazak. Come on, let's eat. I'm starving to death." They ate in silence. Lauren watched Alex eat as much as two people. But he was a big man. She also ate her fair share and, between them, nothing was left but a huge pile of chicken bones on each plastic plate.

"So," Alex said, breaking the silence, "Volkov went down like a castrated bull?"

"Yes, he did."

A grin edged his mouth. "I would have given anything to have seen that. I am sure he is back at the flea hotel nursing his knee with ice bags. I wonder if he told his team how it happened?"

"Probably not. He didn't look like the kind of operator that had any humble pie in him. Most likely lied and said he fell and twisted his knee or something stupid like that," she said, grinning sourly and leaning her chair back on two legs.

He studied her. "You are a highly complex woman. Do you realize that?"

Lauren felt heat move in her. Alex was giving her that look that made her feel shaky and needy. Wanting something... not knowing what... Whatever it was, he seem to trigger her feminine side and it was all at once as exciting as it was terrifying to her. "I've led a complex life." Lauren gave him a challenging look. "And you aren't exactly simple, either."

"Then we deserve one another. Yes? We can understand one another because we are alike in some ways?"

"Maybe," Lauren hesitantly admitted. "I don't spend too much time analyzing myself. I let my actions speak for me."

"Well," Alex chuckled, "Volkov certainly heard you loud and clear." He saw the corners of her mouth curl upwards. She was smiling again. A sheet of scalding heat dove straight into his heart, a warmth filling his chest. That woman's mouth was always tempting to him. Lauren's was like no other Alex had ever encountered. Her upper lip was slightly thinner than her full lower lip. The corners of her mouth were deep and naturally curved upward. When she smiled, she had dimples. Another pleasant surprise about her. And he watched her smile go up into her gray eyes that were, once more, the color of a Mourning Dove's breast. That told him Lauren was at peace. And he desperately wanted her to be given that kind of calm because he sensed her life had been anything but.

"I hope like hell Hunter gives me the thumbs-up to take Volkov out, too. And yes, I know that's a pun and I did it on purpose."

Alex gave her a feral smile. "I liked it. Someday I would like to learn puns. I talked to Gage earlier, after you left. He said he had to talk to his contact in the Defense Department and would get back to us about Volkov."

"If I don't take him out, Special Forces' job is to round the rest of those sick bastards up and haul their asses to the Peruvian Police, where I hope they rot and die in that prison that is at ten thousand feet, and there's no heat any time of the year for them."

"We will see what Hunter's orders are to us. If I ever run into Volkov again, there's going to be serious trouble." Lauren's mouth thinned. "And next time, I'll be packing. I'm not letting that bastard near me again."

"This poses us a problem," Alex said, frowning. "We are going into Petrov's territory. My old stomping-grounds, as Cal would say. No one has seen you except Volkov. If his crew shows up in one of those Quechua villages where we must go to for the orchids, he could identify you."

"As what? An American woman? A tourist," Lauren scoffed. "We're undercover, Alex. They won't have a clue as to why we're here."

Shaking his head, he muttered, "You make a mistake, *Malen 'kaya*. The moves you put on Volkov sent him a very loud, unmistakable message."

"What are you talking about?" Lauren demanded, irritation rising in her tone as she stared at him.

"He KNOWS you are an operator. No one fights CQC except black ops people."

Lauren's brows fell and she stared down at the table and the empty food containers, considering his statement. "Shit, you're right... damn..."

Alex shared a sour grin with her. "If you had fought like a woman, a civilian, we could have felt safe even if they saw us at one of those villages. As it stands, Volkov is going to have a lot of time nursing his injured knee and thumb on ice and he's going to be replaying everything that happened. In detail. It won't escape him, Lauren. He is a smart Russian soldier. He will figure it out."

Thunking the front legs of the chair down, Lauren pushed away from the table and paced the kitchen, scowling. Finally, she stopped and looked at Alex. "You're right. We're screwed."

"At least with Petrov's team. The other teams will not know us. They do not communicate with one another, so far as I know."

Mouth flexing, Lauren muttered, "Dammit. This means we've got to hightail it out of here now. If Volkov spots me or you, he's going to have a field day with us. He'll alert the whole team and then the shit is gonna hit the fan."

"I like that American slang," Alex said, keeping a straight face. "I think I will write this one down."

Lauren rolled her eyes at him. "I'm serious, Alex. We're compromised. We need to get out of here. Tonight."

He took out his notebook and dutifully wrote down the slang words. "Do you want to talk to Gage? Or do you want me to do it?"

She sighed loudly. "I might as well. They've got two other Special Forces teams up in the area where we're going. I think we should meet with the closest one somewhere and have a little confab with them. Their job is to shadow us. Be there, if we get our asses in a sling."

"That is not a very good image," he murmured, rising. "Another slang?"

"Yeah, but it's appropriate," Lauren said, rubbing her brow, a headache coming on. The day had been hell for her. She didn't want to tell Alex how frightened she'd become, how it had pushed every button she had, because Volkov had wanted to rape her. If she told Alex that, Lauren wasn't so sure he wouldn't just go for a visit to that fleabag hotel and shoot all six Russians in their sleep. Ukrainian blood, she was discovering, boiled hot and just below the surface. *All the time.* And it was just as lethal, or worse, than the Russian variety. The saying, "scratch the surface of his skin and you find the savage," applied to Alex in every possible way. The feral, glittering look in his eyes told her that. He'd take Volkov down before she ever got her pistol out of the holster.

Alex started collecting the emptied plates on the table. "Make the call. There is a Night Stalker Black Hawk helo in Cusco on twenty-four-hour stand-by with two Army pilots. I do not envy them if they must fly us out tonight. It will be very dangerous for them and us."

"Why?" Lauren asked, halting at the door to the kitchen.

"Because at night, the winds shift and flow off the Andes toward the Pacific Ocean." He pointed toward the east. "The mountains are covered with snow; the winds are very cold. They meet the warmer air rising from the ocean, it becomes highly unstable air. Commercial airlines refuse to fly at night between Lima and Cusco because of this unique weather situation. There have been too many air crashes due to the clear air turbulence that the weather condition creates. It has been known to tear wings off aircraft."

"Great," Lauren muttered. "How does it affect a helo?"

"Same way," Alex said. "The air pockets are huge. They can drop a chopper a hundred feet in seconds. And this makes it highly unstable to fly in those conditions. I do not know if the Night Stalker pilots will agree to fly up here tonight. Maybe at dawn, when the winds are switching and flowing up from the Pacific toward the Andes. That is much more stable air and no clear air turbulence."

Lauren replied, "Dawn? That could be risky. You said Petrov and his men would probably leave tomorrow morning for their territory? How are they getting up there?"

"There's an old Russian helicopter at the airport," Alex said. "They pay the pilot who owns it to fly them into their territory."

"Then, that means we could accidentally meet them at dawn at that little airport outside of town?"

"Very possible."

"That won't do."

"No, it will not. We need to get the Black Hawk up here tonight. No later than 0300. Usually, when I was with Alexandrov's team, we left in the dark because we wanted no one in town to know we were leaving."

Lauren stared at him for a moment. "You sure aren't leaving many options open for us, Kazak."

"It comes down to two options," he told her, seriously. "Stay here tomorrow and see whether Petrov leaves or not. Volkov's knee may be so bad that they are forced to stay here a few days longer. Or, we hope these two Army Night Stalker pilots are the best of the best and they can negotiate the winds and fly up here to pick us up."

"Will we still encounter CAT from here to up in the highlands?" asked Lauren.

"CAT?"

"Sorry, clear air turbulence."

"Yes, it is a bumpy, dangerous ride all the way with 'CAT'. As Cal would say, the wind will take no prisoners. I have ridden this route many times in a helicopter. You get tossed around like a ball in a fifty-gallon drum. Everyone has bruises all over them. One time, one soldier received a very serious concussion. It is a hard flight."

"Crap."

"I vote you encourage Gage to let us meet the Black Hawk at 0300 tomorrow morning. If the pilots do not want to risk it, then we lay low until we are sure Petrov and his team have left town. Then, we will fly up to our area during the day and avoid CAT."

CHAPTER 9

LAUREN PUT HER back to the Black Hawk coming in for a landing on the large grassy field, that they called an airport, outside of Aguas Calientes at 0300. The eighty-mile-an-hour blasts from its blades might have tumbled her, if not for the sixty-pound canvas gear bag she carried slung across her body. The roar of the twin engines of the Hawk drowned out everything else. Twigs, leaves, hunks of mud, all flew up, splattering against her body like fists, her eyes shielded by safety goggles. Turning toward the bird, she heard the copilot give them the radio order to get on board. Alex gripped her upper arm, pulling her forward, the wind buffeting her to a near standstill. Crouching over, head down and forward, Lauren broke into a trot, the blades whirling swiftly above them.

The night was dark. Alex wore NVG's. She did not, trusting him to get her to the deck lip of the Hawk. They both staggered forward, climbing into the bird on their hands and knees, the tread plate of the hard metal deck biting into their knee joints. An aircrew chief who was standing nearby, pulled them onboard by the scruffs of their necks, dumping them on either side, and quickly shoved the sliding door shut.

Instantly, before Lauren could even roll back over onto her hands and knees, the Hawk was breaking the earth, the upward acceleration shoving her downward. She struggled to move, crawling to the bulkhead and sitting down, drawing her boots up toward her body. Alex sat down next to her. He handed her a helmet and she quickly pulled it on. The shaking and shuddering of the helo vibrated through her. The roar of the twin engines atop the bird were deafening. Quickly, Lauren jerked off her protective glasses and let them dangle around her neck. She strapped on the helmet and found the rail at the top of it. Pulling her NVG's up over her eyes, she flipped them on. Everything in the dark cabin became a grainy green color, her view limited, as if she were looking through two toilet paper rolls. Locating the ICS, "inter-cabin system", radio cord, she inserted it into her helmet and brought the mic close to her lips.

"Welcome aboard, ladies and gentlemen," the pilot drawled in a slow, syrupy Texas accent. "I'm Captain Jake Curtis. Y'all must be wantin' some excitement here in Peru? Callin' us out on a hellacious night like this? Even horny toads wouldn't volunteer to do this…" and he chuckled.

Already, Lauren could feel the helicopter, as it soared to altitude, fighting the controls that the pilot was manning. She looked forward into the cockpit. "Captain, is this going to be a rough flight?"

"Yes ma'am, it's sorta like riding through one of those frog-stranglin' thunderstorms we get in West Texas. Ever been through one?"

Grimacing, Lauren muttered, "Yeah. Once. That was enough."

"Well," Curtis drawled, good-humoredly, "you'd best try and keep your butt nailed to that deck. No seat belts in this girl, as you know, for those in the rear cabin. Yore pardner looks pretty big. You might feel a hankerin' to let him hold onto you. You're liable to bounce around back there in the cargo bay like a BB in a boxcar."

"Great," Lauren muttered.

The air crew chief sat down, his back against the rear of the pilot's seat. He had his knees up, boots heels against his butt, and was hanging onto the door railing with his gloved left hand, his other wrapped tightly around the leg of the pilot's seat. That was not a good sign. Lauren cast around, looking for something to hold onto, the vibration in the Hawk deepening. They'd already gained over two thousand feet of altitude.

The Hawk suddenly sank like a rock.

Lauren gasped. She felt herself rising off the deck and she threw her arms out. Alex caught one of them.

The helo jammed to a midair stop. The g-force was crushing. The engines' noise changed; deepened and growled.

Lauren slammed into the deck, landing on her left hip. She grunted, pain shooting up into her back. Alex had kept ahold of her arm. If he hadn't, she'd have been tossed to the ceiling, and then bounced around the cabin.

"Alex," she panted, struggling to sit up as the Hawk baubled violently again. She heard the blades thunking harder, pulling air. Struggling mightily. It was impossible for the helo to remain stable.

She felt Alex's long arm move around her shoulders.

"Hold onto my waist belt with your left hand," he told her. "Slide your right arm behind me and hold on tight."

Lauren had barely done what Alex had instructed when, suddenly, the Hawk was flung upward like someone had shot it out of a damned cannon. A gasp tore from her. Lauren felt the brutal g-forces crushing her downward. Alex's arm tightened painfully around her.

Curtis cussed in Texan, "Shhheeeeiiiiiittttt…."

The Hawk suddenly stopped its wild elevator ride up into the black sky.

The blades floundered, thudded and flapped at the tips.

The bird suddenly heeled over and fell unnaturally to the left.

Lauren wanted to scream, feeling as if the helicopter was out of control. Alex's arm drew her tight against him. She buried her face into his chest, feeling the g-forces now trying to tear them up off the deck once again. *Holy shit!* Alex hadn't understated how dangerous this flight was going to be!

And then, suddenly, the Hawk was flying straight and normal. Breathing raggedly, Lauren felt Alex draw his hand around her left shoulder, holding her even harder against his chest. It felt good. Safe. Safer than anywhere else at the moment at least. Her bruised hip was throbbing. Alex hadn't overstated getting tossed around like a beanbag, either. Lauren heard the captain talking to his copilot. Their voices were too quiet to overhear what they were saying, but she picked up the strained tones between them.

"How long is this flight?" she demanded unevenly.

"Too long for all of us, ma'am," Curtis drawled in his best good-ole-boy tone.

"God, was it this bad flying up from Cusco?"

"About on par with what we're fightin' right now, ma'am. Y'all jess' kick-back and try to relax now, hear?"

The Night Stalker pilot had the sickest ironic humor Lauren had ever encountered. She'd be shitting her pants if she was up in the cockpit right now. She heard the blades thunking, heard more power being fed to them by the copilot who played intricately with the overhead throttles between the seats. They would be climbing from sixty-five hundred feet to twelve thousand feet. She noticed that, one at a time, the pilots were putting on oxygen masks. So did the air crewman.

"Where's our O2?" Lauren demanded.

"None to give out to you, ma'am. But don't you worry yore pretty little head, though. Hypoxia only begins to occur at ten thousand feet and above. We're climbin' to twelve-five but it's only for twenty minutes. Hypoxia don't really start makin' your brain funny and helpin' you make poor decisions for about thirty minutes. So, you're safe. You might feel a tad dizzy, but that's all. It will wear off fast once we got your boots back on the ground."

She felt Alex laughing. It rumbled through his chest, beneath her ear and cheek.

"Captain, has anyone ever accused you of being a sadist in the air?" Lauren growled.

Chuckling, Curtis said, "Yes, ma'am, many a time. It's just part of the perks you get flyin' with us loco, Texan, Night Stalker types. We're a well-known group among 'em," and he chortled indulgently, enjoying every second of this ride.

Alex laughed again. Lauren didn't think it was funny. How long was this even, straight flight going to last?

"Very funny," she muttered.

"You do know, ma'am? Our Night Stalker motto?"

"No, I'm not aware of it, Captain Curtis. What is it?"

"Death waits in the dark."

Both pilots laughed hilariously and uproariously, as if it were an inside joke.

Alex was howling right along with them.

Lauren scowled. "You're all a bunch of sick bastards," was all she'd mutter.

Her helmet phones erupted with even more roars of hearty, high-hilarity laughter.

And then, the Hawk hit a wall of clear air turbulence. Lauren felt the g-forces shift violently within the bird. It felt as if invisible hands were tearing her out of Alex's arms. It was so powerful that she cried out, her grip loosening from around his waist, fingers ripped away from his belt. She was being flung toward the door.

The bird flailed.

Blades chugged.

Engines roared, and then screamed.

Lauren slammed into the door, nearly knocking herself out. She saw stars behind her tightly-shut eyes.

The helicopter floundered, on its side, sliding sideways through the air. She was pinned against the door. No one could move, the g-forces too much.

She heard the captain grunt, "… great balls of fire…"

They were out of control! The blades were shuddering and chopping. The Hawk was trembling, as if being torn apart by unseen hands out in the darkness.

Suddenly, they were level again!

Giving a cry of relief, Lauren collapsed against the deck, panting for breath. Her pounding heart felt like it was going to tear out of her chest. Adrenaline was surging through her. She had thought the door would give way, and she'd be hurled out into the darkness, falling God only knew how many thousands of feet to her death.

"Lauren."

Alex's quiet, calm voice came in over her helmet phones.

"I'm okay," she rasped, struggling. The air crewman got on his knees, helping her to sit up.

Alex moved forward, dragging her back into his arms, settling her across his lap. "Now, wrap your arms around my waist. Tightly."

She nodded, their helmets against one another. Her breathing was chaotic and she had never been so damned scared in a helo before. She'd ridden in plenty of them. But not like this. This was... hell... it was life and fucking death!

Alex wrapped his arms around her, slipping one hand between her back and the sixty-five-pound gear pack she carried slung across it. He brought up his long, strong legs, pinning her against him completely. She wasn't going anywhere this time. He could feel her trembling, her breathing erratic.

"Did you hurt yourself?" he demanded. Because he could feel her shock. She'd slammed hard into the door. Maybe a concussion? He was in combat medic mode now. "Lauren?"

"I hit my head. The helmet took the hit. I'm okay. Okay..."

Now was not the time to examine her. Cursing to himself, Alex wished to hell this flight was over. Lauren was clinging to him like a shaking leaf in a storm. He couldn't blame her. She didn't weigh as much as a man. And, even wearing that heavy pack, the air pocket they'd first flown into had tossed her around like a feather in the darkened cabin. She'd end up with a concussion at least, or a broken arm or leg if this kept up. And Alex knew it could happen.

The bird suddenly lifted, as if thrown like a baseball at a hundred miles an hour. The surge nearly tore Lauren out of Alex's arms but he held her down, fought the g-forces that wanted to tear her loose. His arms around her hurt like hell. He saw bruises on her. Oh yeah, no question: she was going to be black-and-blue from head to toe IF they ever got back on the ground alive and walked away from this bird.

The Hawk stabilized.

Lauren panted, relief zinging through her tense body. She could tell when the whirling blades were straining. Their heavy beating deepened and it felt like she was being bounced around like a damned yo-yo. Alex's arms finally eased. She felt his hand find her cheek, brush it, as if to sooth her.

Was she upset? Hell, yes! Scared out of her mind? A double HELL, YES!

"Hey," Curtis called, "ma'am? How many helo crashes have you got under your belt?"

Lauren couldn't believe this guy. He was fucking certifiable. "Why?" she snapped.

Laughing, Curtis jawed, "Wal, us good-ole-boys from Texas always like to place a bet with our passengers. My copilot bets you have none. I told him you probably have at least two."

Snorting, Lauren growled, "Five. So, you both lose the bet. What did I win?"

The pilots laughed hilariously.

"Ma'am, you are our first woman black ops we've ever had the privilege of flyin' in this godforsaken CAT here in Peru. I'm gonna give you a Night Stalker patch you can proudly wear and show off to the other operators just to prove you survived this hellacious ride. It's special-made for us crazy bastards who fly this region. It says, "Night Stalkers never quit"

Lauren shook her head. "I would get down on my hands and knees and pray that I get that patch from you, Captain. Because, from where I'm at, I don't think we have a chance in hell of making our destination."

More hilarity burst loudly out of the cockpit.

Lauren shook her head. *Crazy bastards.*

Alex gave a rumbling laugh, joining them.

Black humor always saved everyone's ass on a bad day. Or, in this case: on a bad ride.

The Hawk was clawing and climbing now. Lauren could feel the blades cutting air, hanging on and scrambling like a climber might on the side of a rugged mountain he could fall off from at any moment. The jostling was less. She hoped that lasted. Wearily, she laid her head against Alex's broad shoulder. She liked being in his arms, being sandwiched between his chest and his strong thighs. Closing her eyes, she felt a headache coming on. Probably from her helmet striking that door. If she hadn't been wearing it? She'd be dead now.

More air pockets. But they weren't as severe. And, every time, Alex's arms tightened and held her snugly against him. He was like a huge, human safety belt around her. It felt strangely calming to have her arms around his thick torso, to feel him breathing so slowly; as if nothing were wrong. Operators' blood pressures actually went DOWN during a firefight. And this time was a helluva sky flight.

Finally, she felt the Hawk begin to descend. She lifted her head.

"Are we there?"

"Yes, ma'am, this Night Stalker luxury flight is at the GPS point where you will be meeting an Army Special Forces team. And, if I don't miss my guess, I see their chem-light about a hundred yards out from where we're landin'."

Alex eased his arms from around Lauren and straightened his legs. He helped her scoot down on the deck and turn around, her back to the bulkhead and facing the door. She felt wobbly to him. And there wasn't much he could say or do until they were on the ground. He bet the ground had never looked so good to Lauren as it did right now.

The Hawk landed, the engines idling, the blades turning slower. The air crew chief unlocked and opened the sliding door. Heavy, humid air rushed in. As Lauren took off her helmet and set it on the deck, she moved to the cockpit. Balancing herself on her knees, a hand on the back of each seat, she offered the pilots her gloved right hand. It was something operators did whenever they could. The Texas Captain in the right seat turned and grinned up at her. He shook her hand, gave her two patches, and nodded. She smiled back. Lauren shook the copilot's hand as well. These men and women risked their lives in flying conditions that would scare most anyone else away. But not them. As far as she was concerned, Night Stalker pilots had balls the size of the state of Texas. That was saying something! She was sure the captain would appreciate her thoughts.

The air crew chief got out, extending his hand into the cargo bay for her. Lauren grabbed it, crouched over, shuffling forward, the gear she carried heavy and bulky. Once out of the bird and on the ground, she thanked him, shook his hand and then, breathed a sigh of relief, pulling up her safety goggles and putting them over her eyes. She stepped aside, allowing Alex to get out. She couldn't see anything yet. Her NVG's were in her pocket. As soon as they cleared this bird, she'd swap them out in place of her safety goggles to see where the hell they were going.

Alex guided her away from the Hawk and they crouched and ran, the gusts from the blades still slapping at their backs, making them weave and struggle to stay upright. Finally, they were well away from the idling Black Hawk. Keeping her back to the helo, Lauren removed her safety goggles and pulled on her NVG's and flicked them on. She turned just in time to see the helo lifting off. The rotor wash was brutal and she turned away, dirt, rocks, tree limbs and gravel flying up and brutally striking her from head to toe. Finally, the bird rose high enough into the sky and the chaos stopped. The thick, chopping sounds disappeared rapidly as it headed down the slope to a lower altitude, heading back to Cusco.

"Are you all right?" Alex asked, concerned. With his NVG's on, he could not tell if she was pale or not.

"Yeah, just a little headache. Nothing to write home about. We need to hook up with those spec ops boys."

Alex keyed his mic near his lips. "Dusty One, this is Tower One. Over."

"Dusty One, read you loud and clear. You see our chem-light at twelve o'clock? Over?"

Squinting, Lauren spotted it. The spec ops boys were supposed to be hiding inside the wall of the jungle. The Hawk had dropped them off in what appeared to be a plowed field about two miles wide. There was no moon. Just clouds all around. "I see them," she told Alex.

"We're coming your way, Dusty One. Out," Alex said, clicking off his radio.

The ruts and furrows were huge and Lauren labored. Alex slipped his hand beneath her elbow, steadying her. It took them twenty minutes to reach the jungle. In the distance, Lauren could see a grayish light growing between the peaks of the Andes. The mountain range looked like a sharp, jutting spine rising out of the earth to the east of them. Dawn was coming. She saw three men melt out of the darkness, their weapons in hand, faces painted, big heavy rucks hanging from their broad shoulders. They were the Special Forces team that would support this sniper op.

Lauren stepped forward, extending her hand to a man who was almost as tall and broad as Alex. "Lauren Parker," she said, gripping his gloved hand.

"Sergeant Mason Kilmer, ma'am."

"This is Alex Kazak, my partner and spotter."

Mace released her hand and shook the extended one of the tall Ukrainian. "Seems we've met before, Kazak? In that Quechua village? About five months ago? You were wounded in the left calf? Beat all to shit? Left for dead. Right?"

Alex grinned, eyes fixed on the rugged face of the Special Forces sergeant who was the leader of the three-man team. "Yes, I was. Same person. Thank you, again, for saving my life."

Mace grinned; his teeth white against the camouflage paint of his face. "A good man is hard to keep down, Kazak. Both of you, follow us. We have a little camp deep inside this twisted jungle of theirs…"

Alex urged Lauren ahead of him. She didn't seem strong. He pulled her to a stop. "I'll carry your gear."

"No…"

He patiently began to pull the thick nylon strap off her shoulder. "I'm your partner. When I am strong, let me help?"

Nodding, Lauren reluctantly gave him the sixty-five-pound weapons bag. "Thanks…" She saw how easily Alex hoisted the strap over his free shoulder, now balanced with both bags. Together, that was a hundred and thirty pounds. "I'm a little dizzy."

"I could tell," he told her dryly. "Probably a bit of a concussion when you hit your head on that door."

"Yeah," Lauren muttered, "wouldn't surprise me. I'll be okay," and she turned, following the narrow path between the twisted, wooden vines that climbed eight feet above them on each side. At twelve-thousand five-hundred feet, the jungle, if it could be called that, looked more like a Chinese puzzle of vines twisting, tangling, and looping in among one another. There was little vegetation on the ground at this altitude. They followed the three-man team downward on a steep path for nearly an hour. Lauren sipped water from her CamelBak to remain hydrated. The Special Forces men set a blistering pace and she kept up with it, thanks to Alex who was doing the heavy lifting.

Finally, as gray light filtered through the jungle from the dawn, the vegetation thickening, Lauren realized she was breathing easier. In an hour, they'd probably walked three miles down in elevation. Lauren figured they were at around nine thousand feet. Her legs ached and she knew she was dehydrating, forcing herself to drink more water to stave it off. The high walls and shadows were deep and, without NVG's, she wouldn't have been able to see the thin path between the vine walls. Everyone was quiet. She heard monkeys screaming in the dawn light. Tropical birds were waking up as well, calling back and forth. The humidity was high, her clothes were damp.

Mace Killmer called a halt as they entered a clearing that had been hacked out over time with a lot of brute manpower and machetes. The sergeant pushed his NVG's up onto the rail of his helmet and waited for everyone to gather around him. He relaxed, slinging the strap of his rifle, barrel down, across his left shoulder. "Welcome to our little jungle retreat," he told them with a grin, gesturing toward five huts that had been built out of the available wood, grass and large, flat leaves of the trees above them.

Alex pushed up his NVG's, marveling at the womb-like oval clearing. "You did this?" he asked Killmer.

"Nah. This is a known drug-route rest point," he told them. "We've been timing the crews who come through here." He wiped the sweat off his face with his gloved hand. "No one's coming through here for six days. I imagine you're pretty whipped. Nate here, will make us some breakfast over a fire built in a hole in the ground. Real eggs," he said proudly. "Thanks to the good people of this region who sell them to us."

"Yeah," Sergeant Cale Merrill added, "Mace traded a bunch of our MRE's to a chief and his wife in a neighboring village for an ongoing supply of hens' eggs. Works out real well for us. I don't know what they find appetizing about those MRE's, though. We got the better end of the deal."

"You guys were always scroungers of the first order," Lauren said, amazed at the well-hidden meadow carved out of a jungle that nothing or no one could ever traverse through.

"Thank you, ma'am," Mace said, grinning down at her. "We understand you're our sniper?"

"I am."

"Where'd you pick up that little art?" Mace asked casually, leading them toward the huts. He put his rifle down near one hut and took off his helmet and removed his earpiece and radio mic.

"Oh," Lauren deadpanned, "a little place called Marine Corps Sniper School about eight years ago."

Mace's gray eyes glittered as he glanced down between her collarbones. "See you're wearing the graduation present around your neck: a hog's tooth on a leather thong."

Lauren knew the price of entry. Operators were a tight, small club. Few were accorded entrance into it and their world of danger. Mace Killmer look to be around thirty years old, rugged looking, a hunter of the first order, with black hair and a black beard. He knew his own kind and she saw him give her a nod of respect. Anyone wearing a hog's tooth meant they had graduated from one of the most well-known and respected sniper school in the world. Foreign countries friendly with the USA, sent their best men over there to be trained. She was one of a handful of women who had carved a path into the men's world of sniper ops. The irony was that women were better snipers than men. She'd proven so all the time throughout her schooling. And in the field as well.

Mace rubbed his chin. "Mind sharing with me your final school scores, ma'am?"

Lauren said, "990." She saw Killmer's straight black eyebrows raise. She saw his eyes narrow.

"That's...," and he cleared his throat, "pretty unbelievable. A perfect score is one thousand. Not many men get to 920, and it's just a handful that have made it that high."

Lauren gave him a feral grin. "They were men, Sergeant. I'm a woman."

Alex hid his grin, and saw Nate gesture to the last hut on the left. He took their gear and pushed it inside the hut.

"We've been hearin' the ladies are straight shooters," Mace admitted, dipping his head, giving her the due admiration she deserved.

"We've proved we're the best," Lauren told him calmly. She had no reason to get defensive. Gage Hunter had hired five military women out of a top-secret program, paid them top price as snipers, and the military was crying now because their best had left for a helluva lot more money. Never mind that the military gave them a paltry thirty-thousand dollars a year. With Shield, Lauren was earning a hundred and fifty thousand a year. Because she was that good. She saw Mace grin a little, amusement glittering in his eyes.

"I'm truly looking forward to working with you, ma'am. It's going to be interesting."

Right. Well, Lauren knew that tone of voice, that look. Killmer was like many operators. It didn't matter which branch they came from; they were all eyeballing the women infiltrating their ranks. Snipers were no longer a boys' club as before. There were women trained in combat, the elite of all the women in the military, and they were as good as, or better than, the boys. And Lauren could tell Mace was just dying to see her shooting capabilities. She might wear a hog's tooth but, as always, she would have to prove herself all over again. She nodded and turned, heading for where Alex was standing outside their hut.

And then, it suddenly struck Lauren that she'd be sharing that small, cramped little hut with Alex. And, as she looked through the grayness of the dawn at it, the hut seemed awfully small. Maybe too small…

CHAPTER 10

"COME OVER HERE and let me examine you," Alex urged as Lauren walked up to their hut. He pulled out his medical ruck and opened it up.

Lauren stood waiting while he was crouched over the ruck, selecting what looked like a pen light. "I'm okay, Alex. Just a headache, is all."

Rising, he came over and gently took the hat off her head and handed it to her. "Humor me?" and he met her shocky-looking eyes.

"I'm not smiling, Kazak."

He grinned and tipped her chin up. "Look at my nose? I want to see if both your pupils are equal and responsive to light."

Patiently, Lauren stood. "Thanks for saving my butt in the Hawk. If you hadn't held me, I'm sure I'd be in a helluva lot worse shape than I'm in right now." He moved the small light slowly from one eye to the other and back several times over. Alex was so close and she absorbed his quiet strength. He cupped her cheek with his hand, not wanting her to move while he performed the pupil-check.

"I told you it would be rough."

"You were right."

Alex held aside the pen light and said, "Good, your pupils are responsive and equal."

"And that means?"

He gently eased his fingers through her hair, moving slowly across her scalp, feeling for a cut or a bump. "That you do not have a bad concussion. Probably just a level one, which gives you a miserable headache, maybe some acute dizziness and feeling tired. But it will not last for usually more than a day or two." The pleasure of getting to touch her silky hair, even as damp and flattened as it was by the hat she'd worn, was an internal joy to Alex. Even better, he saw Lauren's eyes droop closed, as if enjoying his examination of her scalp.

"I told you: I'm okay."

"Spoken like a true operator," he teased. Reluctantly, Alex eased his hands out of her hair. "You have a nice egg goose above your left eye. That is probably where your helmet struck the door."

"Alex, it's a goose egg. You got it turned around again." She saw him give her an apologetic grin.

"One day, I will surprise you and I will say all my slang I am collecting correctly."

He saw her give him a slight smile. It felt like a gift to him.

"All I need is some Ibuprofen. Do you have any?"

"First," he said, "tell me what other symptoms you have?"

Lauren could hear the spec ops boys puttering around the camp, and smelled coffee in the air. She was hungry, her stomach growling. "Headache. Slightly dizzy. I have a bad bruise on my hip for sure, but no broken bones."

"Dizzy when? How often?"

Shrugging, she muttered, "It's mostly gone, Alex. Worse when I was in the bird."

"You were not walking well after we left the Hawk."

"No, because of my bruised hip." Lauren shook her head. "You combat medic types are ALL alike. Such mother hens."

"I am a hen mother," Alex agreed equitably, grinning proudly. "Let me feel where your bruise on your hip is located?

"Mother hen, Alex." She heard him chuckle as she pointed to the sore area. His touch was light and, sure enough, it felt swollen like another goose egg under his palm.

"It is a nasty bruise, but that is all." He crouched and found the pills he needed from his medical supplies. Standing, he opened the bottle and took her hand, turning it over and dropping one white capsule into her palm. "Ibuprofen. Take this with the breakfast they are making for us. I will check with you later today and see how you are doing."

Tingles raced up her wrist as he cupped her hand. Lauren could feel his calluses, and her skin skittered with tiny, pleasurable jolts. "Thanks," she murmured, lifting her gaze to his. The grayish dawn was growing into the full light of day as the world was awakening around them. His face was strong, and his morning stubble gave him a decidedly dangerous look. But she was no longer afraid of Alex. "I'm okay with you being a mother hen."

Alex's mouth drew into a wry grin as he released her hand. "Really?"

Lauren placed the capsule in her mouth and sucked water from her CamelBak tube, swallowing it. "Don't let it go to your head," she growled in warning.

Chuckling, Alex turned away and pressed the Velcro closed on his large medical pack.

"Hey," Cale called, walking up to them, "you two ready for some fresh eggs? I'm cooking them right now." He grinned at them. "Better than MRE's, for damned sure."

Lauren thrust her fingers through her hair, trying to get it tamed into place, and said, "I'm more than ready. It's great to have fresh eggs out here in the middle of nowhere. Thanks." She saw Merrill's blue eyes dance with amusement. Wrapping a rubber band, Lauren quickly remade her hair into a fresh ponytail.

"Come on over to our fire pit," Merrill invited, turning and walking quickly back to where his teammates were sitting on some logs placed around the fire.

"Pity," Alex murmured as he closed the ruck and stowed it inside the hut.

Lauren turned. "What?"

"Your hair is beautiful. It looks nice when it is allowed to go free."

She saw the sudden wishful look in his eyes. "My hair would be in my way, Alex. I can't have that."

Sighing, he nodded. "I know. But someone should tell you how beautiful you look even though we are out here," and he walked with her toward the group.

Lauren felt her lower body simmering. He made her feel good about herself. Maybe even beautiful. Usually, a man complimenting her didn't make a dent in the armor she wore around herself because it was always about wanting sex with her, wanting to take something that didn't belong to him. Alex was different, Lauren acknowledged to herself. But maybe that was because she had been around him, gone through a number of experiences with him, and he hadn't made a single stupid move like Volkov had. She didn't see him like all those other men anymore.

Alex chose the last log that was empty by the deep hole in which the fire was burning, sitting down on it. Merrill had a black iron skillet in his hand, and Alex could see a mountain of eggs being scrambled on a metal grate over the fire. The spec ops men had cleaned their faces of paint and were sitting, relaxed, on the logs. Each wore a sidearm, but their rifles and other gear had been tucked away in their individual huts. They smelled of sweat, having had no opportunity to bathe for quite some time. Their cammos were muddy and stiff from weeks of sweat as well. Alex knew the Special Forces teams would often stay in an area for up to three months, reconning the area, learning it. He was hoping their leader, Sergeant Killmer, would have some specific intel on how Petrov was operating in this area.

The 18-Delta combat corpsman, Nate Cunningham, a five-foot ten-inch, lanky sergeant from Montana, handed each of them metal cups with handles, filled with coffee.

"Welcome to our little piece of paradise," he told them with a flash of a grin.

Lauren nodded and took her cup. "Thanks. You guys have all the important jungle hotel amenities one could wish for. I'm impressed."

Alex thanked the corpsman. He sipped the coffee, watching Merrill expertly stirring the eggs with a stick. There were five thin aluminum plates sitting nearby. "Does Petrov know this place?" he asked Killmer.

Mace shook his head. "No, he doesn't seem to. There's an overlapping group of Quechua Indians who work for another Russian team to the south. The Indians know about this place. But, so far, based on all our recon from following Petrov and his team around, we think the Russians don't have a clue about this encampment."

"Hope it stays that way," Merrill said, bringing the plates over to divide the scrambled eggs between the five of them.

"Yeah," Nate said, picking up the first two plates heaped with steaming eggs and handing them to Alex and Lauren. "This is a nice little nest for us to grab some serious sleep in while staying relatively safe."

"Well," Merrill told his teammate, "as safe as it can be, knowing nothing is safe around here."

Lauren said, "I brought a couple of jars of Bacon Bits from the states with me. Would you guys like some sprinkled on your eggs?" She saw every man's face pop up and grin widely at the offer. Setting her plate on her log, she walked back to the hut, opened the weapons bag, and pulled out one of the three jars. It was the least she could do, because now these men had two more mouths to feed and hens' eggs didn't grow on trees. Lauren had felt touched by their sharing of what little they had with her and Alex, but that's the way operators worked with one another.

Bringing the jar back, she twisted off the lid and handed it to Sergeant Killmer first. His gray eyes gleamed as he took the jar from her.

"You're a sniper," he said, one corner of his mouth flexing upward, "you remember the details. Glad you packed this. Thanks."

Lauren nodded. "It's a good habit to get into. Pass it around, Sergeant. Everyone, have all you want."

Alex watched the battle-hardened leader, Killmer, turn soft within the aura of Lauren's presence. The man's hard, weathered face lost its tough edge as she shared the jar with him. Lauren had that effect on everyone. He saw that Merrill and Cunningham were thrilled to have the unexpected gift. Out here, MRE's were the only game in town, and no one liked them. He didn't either, but tolerated them because there was nothing else to eat. As Lauren turned and walked back to Alex, he felt his heart twinge with emotion. She was a team player. And her sharing something this precious, bacon, out in the middle of the Peruvian jungle with men who hadn't seen decent food in nearly three months, had really touched everyone deeply. He was proud of her.

Lauren sat down. By the time the jar of Bacon Bits got back around to her, at the very end of its rounds, there was still enough left in the bottom of the jar for her. She dumped them on her eggs and set the emptied jar at her booted feet, then mixed them in with the aluminum spoon she always carried in her cargo pocket. She figured that the team had probably used every egg they'd been hoarding for a week to make this scrambled feast for everyone this morning. Wishing she could do even more, she decided that she would leave the second jar of Bacon Bits with Merrill, who seemed to be their cook. It was the least she could do for this team.

As they ate, Lauren asked Killmer, "Have you noticed any changes since Alexandrov was killed and Petrov stepped into his place?"

"Insofar as their movement in their area?" Killer asked.

"Yes."

"Same pattern, no changes. They're using the same trails that were cut out of this jungle by ancient Indian people that even archeologist don't know the name of. The ones they used themselves probably a thousand years ago."

"Have you timed their stops at villages in their area?" Alex asked.

"Yeah. We have their itinerary. When we finish up with breakfast, we'll spread out our maps and give you the details." He eyed Lauren. "Got a few suggestions on where you can set up your op, if you're interested."

"I'm always interested in what the people on the ground find, Sergeant Killmer."

"Call me Mace. We don't stand too much on protocol around here with one another. It kinda flies out the door…," and a slight grin leaked out the corner of one side of his mouth.

These were good men. She nodded. "Call me Lauren." She hitched a thumb to her right. "This is Alex."

"Last time I saw him," Mace drawled, "he was looking near death." And then he shifted his gaze to Alex. "You Ukrainians are damned tough hombres. My hat goes off to you for surviving."

Alex nodded. "We can endure anything or we die trying."

Killmer smiled a little, spooning his eggs into his mouth. "Well, you sure as hell came back from the dead. I'm impressed."

Lauren felt her stomach clench. She gave Alex a quick glance. In profile, his broken nose was obvious, a bump at the root of it. It hurt her to think how much he had suffered. And she didn't necessarily like Killmer ragging on Alex, either. She stared across the campfire at the grizzled sergeant. "Just to be clear about this, Sergeant, Alex put his life up for sacrifice to save two of my best friends. They wouldn't be alive today if he hadn't done what he did."

Killmer nodded. "No need to come in hot about this, ma'am. We know what he did."

Anger riffled through Lauren as she stared hard into the sergeant's eyes. "He's a real hero. No one asked him to do it. There were no guarantees that Alexandrov wouldn't drop a round in his head for doing it, either."

She felt Alex's hand on her arm for a moment. Lauren turned to her right, meeting his eyes. He said nothing, but, when he gently squeezed her lower arm and released it, she got the unspoken message.

This action on Alex's part wasn't lost on the team. They said nothing, paying attention to gulping down the hot eggs with the tasty, salty Bacon Bits mixed in. Lauren scowled and dropped the subject, irritated over Killmer's 'so what' attitude. She wasn't sure the reason Killmer even liked Alex was because he was Ukrainian. After all, Alex had been with that Russian mafia team before he'd turned away from them.

"Loyalty is a funny thing," Mace murmured, finishing off his plate of eggs. Rising to his full height, he set the plate near the fire hole. It was Merrill's job to cook and do the housecleaning. He made a point of looking over at Lauren. "But it's not funny when we need to rely completely on one another out here."

Lauren stared at him. What the hell was Killmer suggesting? That Alex might turn on THEM? That she was blind and stupid? That he was not to be trusted? Her lips thinned as she held Killmer's dark, uncompromising gray stare. She felt Alex tense. It was nothing obvious; just something she sensed. He said nothing, but kept on eating, not engaging the American sergeant. "Sergeant," she snapped, "let's get this show on the road. Haul out your maps and intel. I want to get this op moving." Idle hands made mischief.

BY MIDDAY, THE jungle had brightened considerably at the spec ops camp. Lauren had made a call to Hunter on her sat phone, checking in, getting the latest intel and filling him in on what was going on at their end. Lauren stewed silently over Killmer's insinuation that Alex could not be trusted. When she finished the call, she walked up to Killmer who was sitting on the ground outside his hut with his cover spread, cleaning his weapon.

"Sergeant? You got a moment? I need to talk privately with you."

Killmer glanced up. "Sure thing," he murmured. He placed his rifle aside, wiped the oil off his hands with another cloth, and unwound upwards like the lithe, dangerous jaguar that he was.

Lauren walked with him to the other end of the clearing. The rest on the men were cleaning their weapons. Alex, who was at the furthest end of the camp from the pair, was doing the same. The sergeant halted, his large hands on his narrow hips, looking down at her. She kept her voice low so no one else could hear. "You got a problem with Kazak, Sergeant?"

Shrugging, he gave her an amused look. "It's my responsibility to keep an eye on him, is all."

Anger surged through her. "You don't know him. You haven't seen him since you discovered him slowly bleeding to death at that Indian village, Sergeant. I've been working with him the last three months."

Killmer gave a negligent shrug. "He was in the Russian mafia, ma'am. You ought to be taking that into consideration."

"What?!" Lauren gritted out between clenched teeth, "That it's possible Kazak will turn on me during this op? Go back to Petrov's team? Become one of them again? Because that was obviously what you were implying, Sergeant." She glared up into his hard face. Killmer's eyes flickered as he considered her harshly-spoken words.

"Ma'am, have you seen what these Russian boys do to the local populace? They're worse than animals. A lot of innocent men, women and children are suffering hard under their rule out here."

Lauren tried to rein in her anger. She couldn't fault Killmer on his perspective. He didn't know Alex. His story. His life, or that he was a kind and caring man. "Alex is a combat medic. Are you aware that he and Nik Morozov, another medic, have helped these Indian villages for the last two years they were out here? They've saved a lot of lives."

"No ma'am," he drawled. "We boys don't get backstory on traitors out here."

Traitor? Her eyes narrowed on the sergeant's face in fury. "He has my back, Sergeant."

Killmer gave her a hard, studied look. Finally, he said, "Ma'am, we have your back, too. Just don't forget that if things start to go south for you at some point."

He started to walk away. Lauren reached out, grabbed his arm, halting him. Her voice was low with fury. "You're WRONG about him, Sergeant!"

Mace gave her a slight shrug. "We'll see. I'll be watching him, though." He pulled his arm from her grasp. "And so should you."

Lauren watched the tall sergeant walk away, his gait rolling as if he didn't have a care in the world. Cursing softly under her breath, Lauren glared at his broad back. Well? What did she expect? Really? Killmer and his team didn't know Alex at all. Only that he'd turned on his own comrades to save two Americans in deep trouble. Her own gait was stiff as she walked across the camp and sat down opposite Alex to clean her sniper rifle. He glanced up, met and held her eyes for a moment, saying nothing. She knew he sensed her anger, the question already in his eyes. She was too pissed to say anything, afraid their conversation would be overheard.

"Sergeant Merrill just left," Alex told her, wiping down the short barrel of his AK-47.

"Where was he going? Do you know?"

"No. He did not stop to tell me."

Lauren glared over at Killmer, who had sat back down and resumed oiling his own weapon. Daily care of their equipment in this high humidity and daily rain was crucial. If rust collected within the gun barrel it could throw off a shot and make it go wide. "I'll find out later," she said, her voice tight.

Alex glanced at her. "He does not trust me. And it is all right, Lauren. I expected this."

Mouth quirking, she muttered angrily, "Well, I sure as hell didn't! They don't know you Alex, like I do. You'd NEVER turn on me. I know that in my heart."

His hands stilled over his weapon for a moment. Lauren's cheeks were flushed red. Her eyes were angry.

"Killmer has to take that stance. You know that. I am an unknown quantity to him. And he is charged with keeping you safe, Lauren. Even from me."

Snorting, she growled under her breath, "I'm not feeling very grateful to the bastard right now."

"Do not try to change his mind, *Malen 'kaya*. He has a job to do. We can use his knowledge of Petrov's movements, take in his suggestions as to where you might set up your sniper op." He met and held her furious gaze. "It is nice for you to defend me, but I can handle this on my own. Okay?"

"He pisses the hell out of me!" Lauren grabbed the can of oil. "I didn't expect this kind of reaction from him, Alex."

"Killmer is walking fine lines," he soothed. "We are not military any longer. We are civilians acting under DOD orders. He cannot order us around. We do not have rank or position. So, his hands are tied. He does not trust me. His team will always watch me." Shrugging, Alex added, "So long as they do not interfere in our op, I do not care how they think of me."

"It just gripes me," Lauren rasped, rubbing the oiled cloth along the barrel of her favorite sniper rifle. "I didn't expect it, was all. Killmer, of all people, found you in that hut. He saw the shape you were in. I mean," and Lauren released an explosive sigh, "how many people would have done what you did to save Sky and Cal? Take a shot to the leg? Get the hell beat out of them? I'm really upset, Alex."

He grinned a little. "I can see that." He wished they were alone. Wished no prying eyes were around, but he knew this American team would be watching him. Their loyalty lay with Lauren. She was American. One of them. He was not. "I am unknown quantity to them. I will prove my loyalty to them over time, *malen 'kaya*, so let your anger go." His voice grew warm. "I appreciate you would stand up for me. Fight for me."

She flashed him an irritated look. "They don't know you! I do."

He chuckled a little and said, "You are a fierce warrior when you want to be, Lauren. I could not have gotten a better partner on this mission."

"Well," she said, "I told Killmer you had my back. He KNOWS that I trust you whether him and his team do or not." Her nostrils flared and Lauren tossed a glare across the camp at Killmer, who continued to clean his weapons.

"Such a fierce little jaguar warrior you are."

Lauren felt her anger dissolving beneath his warm teasing. The look in Alex's eyes was for her alone. "You would NEVER turn on me. I KNOW that."

Raising his brow, Alex wanted to say, *the only way I want one of us to turn is you, into my arms. Where you belong. Where you can stay the rest of your life.* But he said nothing, paying attention to cleaning his rifle. Around them, the tropical birds sang their different melodies. The humidity was heavy and wet. In the distance, Alex heard a thunderstorm booming and rumbling. It rained every day in the jungle. Thunderstorms were frequent and long. He absorbed Lauren's face. Tendrils of red hair curled in the humidity at her temples. Recalling how elegant she'd looked in her gray pantsuit walking through the door of the Shield lobby, he smiled to himself. She was complex. He delighted in each layer he discovered within her. Now, she was a ferocious advocate on his behalf. Alex would have given anything to have been somewhere within earshot to eavesdrop on her conversation with Killmer. Lauren took no prisoners.

NEAR DUSK, MERRILL returned, wet, muddy and exhausted-looking. He walked into the camp, rifle over his right shoulder. Lauren was studying the rain-resistant maps that Killmer had given her. She was sitting on a log near the fire pit when Merrill came back into the clearing. He went straight to Killmer who had his ruck spread out in front of his hut. Frowning, Lauren wondered what was going on. It were as if Killmer were keeping her in the dark. Why? Because he didn't want Alex to know anything? Or as little as possible? Bristling inwardly, Lauren didn't like the situation at all. Killmer was being damned cagey and she felt as if he were trying to protect her from Alex. That was crazy! But the sergeant was a mature operator and, she was sure, probably had at least a decade of experience under his belt. He was a man who made up his mind and no one was going to change it. She gritted her teeth, unable to hear the conversation going on between Merrill and Killmer.

Killmer rose after Merrill finished with his report. He walked over to where Lauren was and sat down next to her.

"My man tells me that Petrov has arrived. He's at an Indian village in the highlands, about four clicks from where we met you this morning: Tinti Kaballu. That's Quechua for 'dragonfly'. They got a lot of 'em up in that area. Don't know why, but they have 'em." He opened his hands and gave her a measured look. "We know this team on sight, have their names, ranks and backgrounds committed to memory. Merrill was saying that Volkov, the second-in-command, was limping badly. Saw a tight wrap around his knee. You wouldn't know anything about that, would you, ma'am?"

"So, he came with them," Lauren muttered darkly. She told the sergeant about running into Volkov in Aguas Calientes. His chiseled mouth drew into a tight grin as she finished her story.

"So, you took out their CQC expert?" He gave her a respectful look. "Not bad, ma'am." And then he added wryly, "Remind me not to piss you off in a fight."

Lauren wanted to like the sergeant. He had a dry sense of humor. And with her, he was forthcoming, which was absolutely essential to this op being successful. "I don't think Volkov knew I'd been trained in Krav Maga," she said, shrugging off his compliment.

"Oh? You know that Israeli style of fighting?"

She heard the admiration increase in Killmer's voice. The surprise. Giving him a bored look, Lauren growled, "I'm an instructor of it. You know something, Sergeant? Men, for whatever reason, just tend to take us women for granted. They think that we're the poor, helpless females who always needs protection. That we can't stand up and fight for ourselves."

Killmer rubbed his hand through his beard in thought for a moment. "You're right," he finally acknowledged. "It's a generational thing. We know Secretary of Defense Panetta threw open the doors to all women in the military who wanted to volunteer for combat duty. I just find that hard to accept, is all."

"At least you're honest," Lauren growled, giving him a hard look. She saw him give her a feral grin.

"Ma'am, as much as I think about you as a poor, helpless female in one sense, don't think I don't respect your skills. It's my problem. If I want to be a little overprotective about you, that's on me."

"Well," Lauren snapped, "I have enough to contend with right now. I don't need four men thinking I'm incapable of protecting MYSELF."

He chuckled a little. "I've observed the same in your partner. He's a lot like me in that regard."

Heat nettled Lauren's cheeks. She wished she would stop blushing! Killmer's gray eyes danced with amusement. "He's a good man, Sergeant." She rose. "And you're going to find that out soon enough. I've chosen some potential sniper sites. I need to sit down with you and Alex to discuss the pros and cons of each of them." And Lauren made sure her voice was authoritative and that the Army sergeant didn't *begin* to even *start* to protest about Alex being a part of this strategy session. *Not even.*

CHAPTER 11

"**I**'M WHIPPED," LAUREN muttered as she pushed off her combat boots within the hut. Night had fallen, the sound of insects singing in the jungle surrounded them. Another thunderstorm was rolling in across the sky, the sound like drums reverberating throughout the area as it approached. Although the huts looked ugly and piecemeal, she'd found they were at least dry, and that was a godsend for the both of them and their equipment. Special Forces teams knew how to survive off the land where few others ever would. She was grateful for their wealth of experience as she laid down on one of her two silver-foil blankets. They reflected heat back into her body.

Alex kept his boots on as he also lay down to sleep. Although Killmer had sent Cunningham a mile up the trail that led into this meadow to keep watch, Alex knew that anything could happen. His MP-445 pistol lay near his head, unsafed, a bullet in the chamber. Just in case they were compromised by Petrov's team. "It has been a stressful day," he agreed. The hut was so small that they had to lay within a foot of one another. Their equipment took up most of the rest of the space, leaving them little available room left over. He worried that Lauren might feel awkward by his nearness. Alex certainly liked her close, but he wasn't about to tell her that.

Lauren laid down, facing him. It was utterly dark. Only brief flashes of lightning would illuminate the hut for a moment and then she could see him stretched out on his side, his gaze on her. She didn't feel threatened. Rather, she could sense his concern. "I'm just tired."

"And your headache?"

"Gone. The Ibuprofen did the trick this morning. My hip is feeling much better, too."

Alex closed his eyes, one arm beneath the blanket that was his pillow. He had his reflective cover beneath him as well. Although this was the jungle, it could drop to fifty degrees at night. With the high, constant humidity, it was cold. He worried that Lauren would get chilled. She'd brought along her alpaca poncho and had pulled it on over her uniform. That made him feel good. He would never forget the memory of her eyes turning suddenly emotional when he'd stopped at that shop in Aguas Calientes and insisted she buy something to keep her warm.

The hut became silent and Alex listened to the rising wind flowing through the jungle, ahead of the storm coming their way. He could smell the fresh fragrance of Lauren's skin even though they'd had no place to wash up. Stopping himself from reaching out to caress her cheek, a new flash of lightning revealed that she had closed her eyes. She had pulled the poncho hood up over her head, knowing that most of the body's heat was lost there. Her hands were tucked beneath her cheek. She looked like an angel to him: innocent. Beautiful. *Untouchable.*

Alex closed his eyes, absorbing Lauren's nearness. His mind rat-trapped over everything that had happened today. The fact that Sergeant Killmer didn't trust him had placed an extra weight upon her shoulders. Lauren was the head of this op. And that was enough responsibility, even without this side issue. He'd known something like this would probably occur. He had to prove himself trustworthy to this Special Forces team. When he'd volunteered earlier to take a four-hour sentry watch to help them spell one another so they could all get some more sleep, Killmer had nixed the idea. It stung that the sergeant thought he might turn against them. Against Lauren. But there was nothing he could do about it.

He listened to Lauren's softened breathing. It became shallow and slow. He knew she had spiraled deeply into what, he hoped, was a healing sleep for her. This whole mission rested on her shoulders. He smiled a little, thinking about Volkov limping along with Petrov's team. When Lauren had shared that intel with him, he had felt nothing but pride for her. She was right: she could take care of herself. She had many years in the Marine Corps under her belt, working with black ops teams, and she'd emerged alive, unwounded and unscathed. He wondered if Volkov had told Petrov the truth about his injury. If he had, then the whole team would know that Lauren was an operator. If Volkov's pride hadn't allowed him to tell them, then only he knew. That could mean a difference. An important one. And soon, Alex drifted off, the lull of wind and rolling thunder headed their way providing nature's music to fall asleep to.

THE NIGHTMARE BEGAN insidiously, as always, for Lauren. The door to her bedroom would creak open sometime after midnight. She'd wake up scared and paralyzed, her heart beating wildly with fear in her chest. Her foster father's body would be illuminated and outlined by the light behind him in the hallway. She'd whimper, scoot down beneath her covers, pulling the blanket over her head. If she lay still enough, he might not think she was there in the bed. Drawing her thin legs up toward her body, her cotton nightgown tangling between them, she barely breathed. His footsteps were soft, almost silent. But she could hear him coming. Her heartbeat thudded so loud in her head that she could barely hear him approaching her bed.

Lauren froze as the sound stopped. She knew he was looking down. Looking at her. She began to shake in earnest, unable to remain absolutely still.

"Lauren... sweetie... it's Daddy..."

She felt his hand move across her shoulder, the blankets her only shield. A little whimper tore from her. "Go away!" she cried out, her voice muffled by the blankets. Lauren heard him laugh softly.

"You don't mean that, sweetie. Come on, I have candy waiting for you down in the basement. Your favorite. I know you like it..."

"N-no!" she cried out, trying to wriggle away from the hand slowly moving across her shoulders. She hated his touch. She knew what was coming. He would hurt her again. Lauren tried to wriggle to the side of the bed to escape his large hand. Terror sped through her.

"Come here...," he soothed, "...come to Daddy... he won't hurt you..."

Lauren felt him grip her, pull the covers back, revealing her. Raw terror roared through her as he leaned over, smiling down at her, his hands brushing her shoulders, as if to sooth her. At nine years old, she stared up at him, paralyzed as he pulled her toward him. His smile was fixed, and his eyes glittered, never leaving her face.

"N-no... I don't want to go with you!" she whined, struggling to get out of his grasp.

"Shhhhh, sweetie, don't wake Mommie. Don't cry. Everything's going to be all right. You'll see..." and he lifted her easily into his arms, carrying her toward the partly-opened door.

Tears flowed down Lauren's cheeks as she kicked, struggling, trying to break free. But her foster father's arms tightened, holding her captive, and there was no way she could escape. She was breathing hard, her heart pounding as if it would leap out of her tiny chest. He carried her swiftly down the carpeted stairs to the first floor. She sobbed, unable to move her hands to strike out at him. He would take her to that dark basement. It was going to happen again and she cried and tried to scream but he pressed her small face against his massive chest to drown out her wailing. He stopped to open the door that led to the basement.

Lauren sat up, screaming, lashing out with her hands into the darkness. The sound of thunder crashing down, the hut vibrating, scared her even more. It was dark. So dark. Dark like the basement. For a moment, caught in the grip of the nightmare, she thought she was back in that basement, that she was being carried down its stairs by her foster father.

"*Malen 'kaya?*"

The words were different. Foreign. Lauren jerked, pushing away from the sound in the utter darkness. She whimpered, tears blinding her, her heart racing as she gasped for air. Her back hit the wall of the hut. Trapped! She was trapped! *Again. Always.* A small whimper tore from her contorted lips.

"Lauren? Lauren? It is all right. It is Alex. Please… it is all right…"

It wasn't the voice of her foster father. Who was it? She shut her eyes, sobbing, her legs drawn up against her, her hands covering her face, terrified. And then, lightning flashed, illuminating the hut. Her hands jerked away from her face. She saw a man's face, concerned, staring at her. It wasn't her foster father! Her mind twisted and canted. Lauren moaned, trying to reorient herself. The thunder boomed shortly after the bolt of lightning had sizzled overhead. The hut trembled. Lauren found herself shaking, coming out of the nightmare, finally realizing where she was. She tried to stop sobbing, tried to control the rampant terror leaching through her, eating away at her control.

"*Malen 'kaya,*" Alex rasped, "you are safe. You are here, with me. Listen to my voice? You are not there. You are here." Desperately, Alex wanted to reach out but he didn't dare touch Lauren. He knew from experience, when he'd tried to hold Kira one time after she'd awakened screaming during a nightmare, that it didn't work. It had terrified his sister even more and she'd fought like a wild-woman, scratching his face, striking him with her fists, blackening one of his eyes. No, he would not touch Lauren, no matter how badly he wanted to. Hearing her sob ripped him apart.

He had been jerked awake by her screams. Her shrieks had torn through him, and he had sat up, twisting toward the sound, realizing Lauren was trapped in a PTSD flashback.

And then, the impossible happened. He heard Lauren whimper and he felt her trembling hands on his arms, reaching out… reaching for him. It was painful to hear her crying, unable to stop. "It is all right, *Malen 'kaya,*" he soothed, his own voice unsteady. "I will hold you safe. Come here if you want me to hold you…"

Lauren crawled into his arms, her face pressed against his neck and shoulder, quivering like a frightened rabbit. He wrapped his arms around her gently, speaking to her softly, pushing the hood off from her head and running his fingers through her unbrushed hair. He felt the depth of her terror.

She'd wrapped herself up against him in an almost fetal position, trying to hide, seeking protection. Alex settled against the wall of the hut, holding her, allowing her to shake and cry. The rains came down with the lightning, followed by pounding, drum-like thunder. It was a hard, sudden, deluging rain that blotted out every other sound in the camp.

Smoothing her hair, he rasped, "You are safe, Lauren. You are here, with me, Alex. I will not let anything hurt you, *Malen 'kaya*. You are safe..." and he kept up the low, thick words in English so she would understand him. His heart twisted in agony for her. He felt so damned helpless as she wept wildly in his arms. He felt her tears through the thick material of the t-shirt he wore. It soaked in her warm tears. Lauren trusted him. It was such a powerful realization, one that Alex had thought would never happen. He tried to wrap his mind around it and could not.

Gradually, Lauren stopped shaking. Stopped crying. The sky was weeping openly with her, Alex thought, as the wind-whipped rain continued down in torrents. Luckily, the spec ops boys had known to dig a ditch around these huts so that the rainwater was diverted away from them, flowing behind the huts so that they remained high-and-dry during these fierce equatorial storms. He felt Lauren hiccup, and reach up to dry her eyes. He pressed his cheek against her hair. "Better now?"

He felt her give a jerky nod, her hand sliding around his torso, laying her brow against his jaw, seeking his closeness. He represented safety to her. Alex felt tears burning under his tightly-shut eyelids. Lauren trusted him, and she wanted to be held. Tight. Close. It reminded him of the ride in the Black Hawk yesterday. The way he'd bracketed her body against his own bigger one. She'd felt safe then. He gently moved his hand slowly up and down her long back. With each stroke, he felt her gradually begin to relax, to lean fully more and more against him.

"You trusted me, Lauren," he whispered near her ear, stroking her head gently, "you allowed me to unburden myself about my family, about the pain I hold for my sister Kira." Voice softening, he whispered, "Unburden yourself to me? I am here. My heart has ears, *Malen 'kaya*... please... talk to me. What was your nightmare about?"

Shutting her eyes tightly, Lauren felt raw emotions shearing through her. The only place she could bear to be right now was within Alex's arms. For whatever reason, she knew that he would keep her safe. It was crazy, but her instincts had never led her wrong. She started speaking in raw, halting tones. The more she told Alex, the faster the words came tearing out of her. Sometimes stuttering. Sometimes anguished. And, through it all, he gently held her. There were times when his arms would tighten a little more around her, but then he would soon relax them once again. Through the whole thing, Alex listened and never interrupted her, simply stroking her hair, the palm of his free hand moving up and down her spine, making her feel calm in a world that had never been calm like this for her before. Lauren choked out, "That's it...

that's all of it..." She felt Alex take in a slow, deep breath, his hand halting over her head, caressing her hair.

"What of your mother?" he asked her quietly, using his thumb to remove fresh tears from her cheek. "Where was she? She was supposed to protect you."

"M-my mother was lost without my real father. When he was killed, when I was eight, she fell apart. Looking back on it, she was a very weak person, Alex. She'd leaned on my father, having no strength of her own. When he died, she immediately went out and found another man to lean on. My foster father..."

"I see," he murmured, holding her close. "Tell me about your real father?"

"My father was an honest-to-God hero, Alex. He was an officer in the Marine Corps. He was a sniper. H-he had earned two silver stars, two bronze stars with a "V" for valor, two purple hearts. He was... he loved me. Every time he came home, we'd do stuff together. I was always so happy when he was home...," and her voice cracked. Another roar of thunder rumbled across the jungle, further to the east of them now. The wind was still gusting, but not as strongly as before.

The rain splattering noisily across the top of the hut, striking the wide leaves, was lessening in intensity. The storm was moving past them and Lauren saw the symbology in that, too. She swallowed hard, pressed her face against Alex's chest, finding solace for the first time in her life since her real father had held her. Alex never made a move to do anything but be there for her. He did not take advantage of her. Lauren's trust deepened toward him. She could feel his care radiating outward, cradling her.

"Your mother never believed you?"

Shaking her head, pain gutting her, Lauren whispered, "No... she never did."

"Because," Alex wondered aloud, "if she had confronted your foster father, he may have left her? Left both of you? Would your mother be so afraid of standing on her own in life, that she allowed him to do whatever he wanted to you, instead?"

It sounded so cold and brutal coming from Alex. Squeezing her eyes shut, hot tears rushing into her eyes again, Lauren whispered unsteadily, "That's what I always thought years later, after I grew up."

"Where is your mother now?"

"Dead. She died of a heart attack when I was nineteen." Her voice sounded flat, unemotional, even for her.

"But you ran away when you were twelve? Yes? You went to your grandparents' house? Your real father's parents? Asking for help?"

Her throat tightened. "Yes, I fought off my foster father one night. I managed to get out of his arms as he tried to pull me down into that damned basement. I ran and got a huge iron skillet from the stove and, when he came after me, I swung it at him. I hit him in the head and knocked him out. I was so scared, Alex. I-I thought I'd killed him. I panicked. I ran upstairs, grabbed the suitcase I always had packed from the closet and I ran out into the night. I'd taken my mother's cell phone she kept in the living room. I called my grandparents." She wiped her cheek. "They drove over immediately, found me along the dirt road, and they took me to their home." Her voice thickened. "A real home... they loved me. I told them what had happened. And they cried with me. My grandmother called the police." She shrugged wearily. "It was ugly and stressful on me... on my mother... him..."

"And your foster father was placed in prison? Yes?"

Nodding, Lauren muttered, "Yeah, to this day, the bastard's in a prison in California. He got life with no parole. It made me happy."

Alex heard the gritty anger in her voice. "And your mother? What happened to her after he was sent to prison?"

"She lost it. Went crazy, I guess. I didn't want to see her, and the court ordered her to stay away from me. My grandparents took full custody of me and they were like big, bad guard dogs. They kept me safe. They helped me so much... so much..."

"And then, you decided to follow in your real father's footsteps? You joined the Marines Corps?"

Nodding, Lauren closed her eyes, feeling her heart settling down. She was beginning to breathe easier, the terror within her dissolving. "I love him so much, Alex. My father is a REAL hero. I-I wanted him to be proud of me. I wanted to be like him. He would take me fishing and he'd tell me stories about how he and his men helped save Afghan villagers from the Taliban. I could listen to his stories forever. He said it was important that every American give something back and be held accountable. That we should help pay for the freedom we have. He inspired me, Alex."

"Yes, he did, in the best of ways, *Malen 'kaya...* in the best of ways. You have helped earn the freedom your country has, and I know you have made him proud. How could he not be?" and he eased her away, just enough to see her luminous eyes lit by a bolt of lightning flashing in the distance. Her face was haunted by the past, her eyes so large and vulnerable. Alex tucked her head beneath his chin, holding her.

"I fought to get into sniper school. I was the first woman to break down those doors to the good-ole-boys club." Her voice became firmer. "They had to take me. My father's name, who he was, preceded me and they knew him.

And I was given a chance. And I took it. I graduated at the head of my class. The only woman. And I had the highest score any sniper student ever held at graduation."

"I am sure your father was standing there the day they awarded you the hog's tooth," and he smiled faintly, sliding his fingers slowly through her loosened hair. Sometime during the night, the rubber band had broken, releasing the silky strands. "So very proud of his beautiful, brave daughter."

"I felt him," she whispered. "I felt my father's presence there. I felt how proud he was of me. But the truth is, he was with me every day I was there, Alex. I felt him with me. It was so real. And I know he was silently helping me, supporting me."

"And now? Is he here with you now?"

"No... not usually. I always felt him come to me when I'm scared." Lauren pulled slightly out of Alex's arms, just enough to look up at him. "That's funny," she croaked, giving him a confused look. "When I met you, my father left my side. He hasn't been back since... well... since I first met you." She saw Alex's somber expression as the lightning flashed again. Saw the anguish in his eyes—for her. Feeling absorbed in his arms around her, she saw a faint smile cross his mouth. "Why are you smiling?"

Alex's arms urged her gently back into their full circle around her. She felt so right. She fitted against him as if they'd been waiting their entire lives for this moment. "Perhaps your father sees in me a man who will not only care for you, but protect you, *Malen 'kaya*. Your father always comes when you feel unsafe? Yes?"

Lauren nodded. "Yes." She closed her eyes, feeling utterly exhausted. "Alex... I'm so tired..."

"I know you are," he rasped. "Would you like me to lay down and you lay in my arms beside me? I will hold you, Lauren, nothing more. I think you need to feel safe right now?"

His simple words summed up how she felt. Nodding, Lauren whispered, "Yes... I'd like that..."

Alex eased her out of his arms, lay down on his side, and then slid his hand into hers, guiding Lauren down next to him. She trusted him. There was no hesitation. He drew her into his arms once again, settling her back against his front, and then found the corner of the other reflective blanket, drawing it up over them to keep them warm. The passing thunderstorm had made it feel much cooler; even cold.

As Lauren relaxed against him, resting her head into the crook of his shoulder, he felt her hand reach hesitantly across his chest. Was she worried he might try to kiss her? Behave as her foster father had toward her? His intuition told him to give her a harbor of solace and that was all. Even though he wanted to kiss her, make love to her, show her that a man could give her a world of wonder and pleasure, he enforced tight control over himself, over his body. He heard a soft, broken sigh whisper from her parted lips, felt her relax utterly in his arms, against him. It nearly broke Alex emotionally because he realized how much stronger Lauren was than Kira had managed to be up to this point. Lauren had endured four long years of constant sexual abuse. Kira had been gang-raped once. Yet, the startling difference made him understand just how resilient Lauren really was. He was humbled by her quiet, ongoing bravery.

"My mother," he told her in a rasp," when she put me and Kira to bed at night, would sit down on the edge of the bed. She would tuck us in, touch our hair, our cheeks, kiss us and tell us that now our guardian angels would come. And when they flew into our room, they would lovingly embrace each of us within their wings. And as they did, we would fall to sleep and we would have only good dreams. Go to sleep, Lauren. As you close your eyes, your guardian angel will come to you, enfold you in her wings and she will carry you off to a healing sleep. Where there are no bad dreams to chase you…"

Alex felt her sag against him, her breath softening, becoming shallow, telling him that she was sleeping within the wings of her guardian angel. And perhaps, on some level of herself, she might realize he too, was her guardian. Certainly not an angel, but someone on this side of the veil where humans lived, who would protect her. *Always. Forever.*

He continued to lightly stroke her hair, thick and silky strands between his fingers. Lauren had always responded positively to his touch since they'd made peace with one another. Could he dare hope that she had the courage to reach out and love him someday? She hadn't said anything about past relationships but, given what had happened to her, Alex could not imagine Lauren had ever slept with a man consensually. He winced as he thought of Kira, of her crying and telling him she never, ever wanted to have sex again. Never be touched by another man. It broke him in ways he never realized he could be broken.

And yet, as he held Lauren, gave her that harbor of safety, he felt her internal strength, perhaps even an inner-knowing that he would not hurt her. Finally, she had been able to separate him from her foster father. The relief was huge, and he openly wondered if Lauren could take the next step? Did she realize how much he was falling helplessly in love with her? That he saw every day they were together as an incredible gift? That she was his earth-angel? That he would be her wings? Those wings that kept her safe at night?

If Lauren had no experience with relationships, Alex knew she would not pick up on his subtle signals that should have told her, long before now, that he was very interested in being involved with her. She hadn't. Instead, she had interpreted his signals as those of a man threatening to her. And she'd walled him off to protect herself from what she perceived was her foster father coming to get her all over again.

Damn. Alex kept in check his simmering rage over how that man could have harmed an innocent child. How could he? What kind of monster was he that he could have done this to Lauren? All children, his mother had told him, were born innocent. God did not make monsters and murderers. Bad parents made bad children, she'd told him when he was in his mid-teens. She used to shake her finger in Alex's face and tell him good parents loved their children, cared for them, protected them but allowed them to be wild and free. She'd warned him that he was growing to be as tall, or even taller, than his father. That he would be a giant. And, as a giant, he must realize that he might scare girls and women. That he must conduct himself with care around them. Oh, the lessons his wise mother had given him! As Alex drew some of Lauren's hair close to his face and pressed the silky strands to his nose, inhaling the scent of her on them, he silently thanked his mother. She'd taught him respect of women. Patience with them. That they were his equal. *Always.*

Now, as he listened to the last of the storm rolling far away from them, he told himself to use every last bit of his experience, all of his mother's teachings, to try and take the next step with Lauren. The real question was: Did she like him? Even a little bit? And, if she did, could she find herself loving him? Alex didn't have a clue. He couldn't read Lauren like other women. She wouldn't interpret his glances, his subtle body signals, or his voice, in the same way a woman experienced in relationships would. He lay awake for some time, pondering this Chinese-puzzle of a dilemma.

CHAPTER 12

LAUREN AWOKE SLOWLY at dawn. She was warm, Alex's arms around her.
Alex wasn't like other men, and the nightmare made Lauren glad she'd gone through those times in order to appreciate him on an entirely new and different level. She shifted her head enough to gaze up into Alex's sleeping face, resting her cheek on the edge of his shoulder. His breath felt moist as it flowed across her. His black lashes were thick and spiky. His broad brow had furrowed lines etched horizontally across it. She hurt for him as her gaze dropped past his straight black eyebrows, down to his nose that had that bump in it. He'd taken Vlad's fists, sacrificing himself so that Sky and Cal could escape the Russian mafia team. Alex had let the bastard beat him nearly to death. What kind of courage did it take to do that, Lauren wondered. Because if someone was beating on her, she'd have fought back. She would not have laid on that hut floor and let Vlad kick her repeatedly in the ribs, fracturing two of them, breaking her nose, her jaw, and afterward leaving her to slowly bleed to death from that leg wound. A bolt of anguish tore through her heart.

Alex had a hard face. Even in sleep, there was raw strength in it. His cheeks were high and broad and her gaze moved to her favorite part of his face: his wonderfully-shaped mouth.

Lauren moved slowly as she eased out of his embrace, but it woke him up instantly. Operators were always on guard, and she sat up next to him. "Sorry to wake you," she managed in a husky tone. It was barely dawn and she heard no movement outside their hut. More than likely, the spec ops team was sleeping hard.

He sat up, taking the space blanket and slowly folding it up. "You had a very bad nightmare last night. How are you this morning?"

"I'm okay. I'm sorry it happened—"

"I am not," he rasped, easing his large body around so that he could face her and still leave her what little room was available. "I am glad I could be there for you."

She grimaced. "It's my past, Alex. I don't know why it decided to happen out here. I'm so glad you were here for me," and she managed to give him a grateful look, still sleep-ridden and waking up.

"Those kind of nightmares are the worst kind," he agreed, looking at his watch. Leaning forward, he pushed the fabric that hung across the doorway open and peered out. "Everyone is still asleep."

Nodding, Lauren whispered, "It's cold out there."

"Peru's jungle in this region does get cold. It is not like northern Peru, where it is closer to the equator." He studied her. "Are you warm enough? I can give you the space blanket."

Touched by his concern, she shook her head. "I'm going to use our collective latrine. I'll be right back," and she crawled out of the hut on her hands and knees. Looking around through the dark grayness, she stood up and absorbed the energy of the area. The birds were awakening and she appreciated their songs. Knowing that one of the men was stationed out at the entrance to the encampment, she walked across the oval-shaped clearing to do her business.

SHE MET ALEX on her way back to their hut from the latrine. He was making a fire in the pit from wood that had been kept dry within the hut. A slight curl of smoke drifted upward but, otherwise, the surroundings remained still. She helped him get out the grate and place it over the fire. Merrill appeared out of his hut and wandered toward them, rubbing his face and eyes.

"Ready for some coffee?" he asked them.

"Absolutely," Lauren said in a quiet voice. "Where do you keep it?"

"Come with me. I'll show you where I stash all that stuff," and he turned back toward his hut.

In no time, coffee was percolating and the fragrance of it made Lauren salivate. The one thing she missed the most when on an op, was her coffee. In the meantime, Alex had gone to the latrine, followed by Merrill. She figured either Nate or Killmer were on guard duty. The world was awakening. More light, gauzy clouds, hung above the tops of the jungle trees. It hit her that she felt like she was in some other dimension or world, never having done much work in jungle areas before. Putting her sniper persona to one side, she watched the slow, twisting, silent fingers of mist above them. It was magical, if she let herself view it like a child full of awe at the beauty of Nature. It was mesmerizing to her.

She arranged the cups that Merrill had brought out earlier on the logs that surrounded the fire hole. Alex came over and poured coffee into each of them, and took one with him, heading off down the trail.

"Where are you going?" Lauren asked.

"To give Sargent Killmer a cup. He's on duty at the entrance. I am sure he would appreciate this. I will be right back."

Why hadn't she been as thoughtful? Alex disappeared and she sat on the damp log facing Merrill. "I don't know that I could live like you do," she said between grateful sips of the coffee.

"It's a calling," Merrill agreed.

"You stay out here three months at a time, get some time off, and come back for another three months?"

"Yes. How about you, Lauren? How often are you out on a mission like this?"

"Depending upon where in the world and the op, it could be days or weeks." She looked at the wall of the jungle surrounding them. "Most of my work has been in the Middle East."

"Oh, yes, the Sand Box," and Merrill smiled a little. "So? This op is wet instead of being hot and dry? Right?"

She grinned a little. "You could say that. Have you spent your time only in jungle areas?"

"Pretty much. Spec ops for us is about familiarization of an area. Once we get assigned, it's pretty much the same area because we have built up an amount of information on the players, their tactics and such." He gave the jungle an appreciative look. "When I was a kid in elementary school, I was diagnosed with ADD. I could never sit still, I had to be outside, restless, curious and such. I didn't do well in school, but after I joined the Army and got a chance as Special Forces, I jumped at it." He smiled a little. "It suits my ADD. I'm constantly on the move, I'm outside in Nature where I want to be, and my curiosity is always alive and well because there's so many things about the jungle that are new to me. I like learning."

"It's a good fit," Lauren agreed, appreciating his openness.

"I heard you scream last night," he offered quietly, giving her a concerned look.

"Oh... that... a flashback revisited me," she grumped. "I'm sorry if I woke you. I didn't think anyone would hear my scream as I woke up with all the thunder booming around the area."

"Wolf ears," Merrill said, smiling a bit. "PTSD from combat engagements?"

"Yes." Lauren didn't like to lie to the soldier, but she didn't want to drag her childhood into it.

"We all have PTSD," he said. "There's been times when one of the three of us would wake the others up over the same kind of thing: a nightmare or a repeat flashback. How are you feeling this morning?"

Appreciating his care, she said, "I'm okay. Alex woke up and walked me back from it. He's no stranger to PTSD, either."

Nodding, Merrill sipped his coffee. "Anyone in our business is going to get nightmares like that. I'm glad you're feeling okay this morning, though. Sometimes, it hangs around for a day. I hate those kind."

"I'm over it," she assured him. She saw Alex return. Like everyone else, he was armed, a pistol on his hip.

Merrill looked at his watch. "Time for me to relieve Killmer. My turn for standing duty," and he got up, placing his emptied cup on the log.

As Alex came over and retrieved his cup that sat on the log by Lauren, he nodded to Merrill as the younger man headed to his hut to retrieve his rifle.

"So, did Killmer appreciate your thoughtfulness?" Lauren asked Alex as he sat down on the log, coffee in hand.

"Surprised, perhaps," he said. "He does not trust me, and I'm fine with that."

"He's a throwback," Lauren growled under breath, holding the tin cup between her hands to warm up her fingers.

"Yes, but his experience has been built on everything he knows or does not know, and that is a good way for an operator to be. Personally? I like him. He and Nate saved my life at that village. I owe them."

Her mouth tightened and she said nothing, each of them drinking their coffee. Finally, after Merrill had headed up the trail, she said, "We need to talk, Alex."

He sat on the log, the cup between his large hands. "About last night?"

"You have the patience of Job," she began. "You never got angry with me for waking you out of a dead sleep last night. You were never defensive... Instead? You helped me."

He smiled a little. "You are true alpha female wolf, there is no question. You were disoriented, you were panicked and did not know where you were. I knew it had to be PTSD of some sort that had entrapped you." He gave her a warm look. "I always looked beyond the walls you put up. Despite that, I saw the real you. The woman who sits with me right now. We shared that terrible moment together, last night."

Shaking her head, touched by his simple words, her throat tightening, Lauren said shakily, "You're a far better human being than I'll ever be, Alex. You put up with such shit from me. And you can honestly sit here and tell me that you're okay with how I treated you when I first met you? How I made you suffer?"

"I am no saint, either, *malen 'kaya*. For example," and Alex gave her a shy glance, "I always liked you from the moment I saw you."

"Well," Lauren said grimly, giving him a look of disbelief, "you sure did suffer in that hell I put you through at the office. I was really mean and ugly toward you and I shouldn't have been. You must have seen something in me that I'm completely unaware of, because I feel guilty now over my treatment toward you."

He gave her gentle look. "That is the past and it is done and gone. If you would allow me to introduce you to your own beauty, your heart that is so innocent and beautiful within you, Lauren, that it is all I would ever want." Alex held her widening eyes as his words sank in and he saw understanding in them. They were a beautiful dove-gray, her pupils huge and black. "Is that possible? Do I dare to dream of such a time in the future with you? After we finish this mission? Perhaps we can start over?"

Swallowing against a lump, Lauren felt the full brunt of his raw emotions toward her. She had never been in love. She'd seen other people in love. Had wished she could have what Sky and Cal shared. Their love was so touching to Lauren. Deep, broad and forever. "I guess," she admitted quietly, "I never dreamed of trusting another man who would... who would make me want to be in his company, to laugh and cry together. Does that make sense to you, Alex?"

"Yes, *malen 'kaya*, it does. I know you have already given me a certain amount of your trust. Here is what I can promise you going forward: I will ALWAYS hold your heart gently in my hands. You will never have a reason to fear me. What I hold in my heart," and he pressed his hand against his chest, "is that you are an angel who has come down to earth to rescue this poor, sorry-looking Ukrainian peasant. That he does not deserve you, but that you fill his heart to overflowing. That you fulfill every dream, every wish he has ever had."

Tears came to her eyes. His words were low, rich with emotion, and flowed into her heart. Alex's expression was so readable. Lauren was struck again by how easy it was for him to be fully honest and vulnerable with her. And it was so hard for her to be that way with anyone. Except with Alex. "It won't be easy," Lauren warned him. "I'm not perfect, Alex. I-I have so many issues... shadows in my life that rise up at sudden times and I have no control over them..."

"Then," he rumbled, sharing a gentle smile with her, "we will walk through these shadow times together. We will talk. We will dream a better and new life for you, together. We will be a team just as we are right now, Lauren."

She drew in a ragged breath. "Okay," she said, "a day at a time?"

"Always. Dreams are built on the bricks of the day beneath our feet."

Dreams. She'd never had any. And Alex had so many. Maybe he had dreamed for both of them? She drowned in his hazel eyes, feeling the utter warmth, the fierce love he held for her. Lauren thought it was love, but wasn't sure. But it was something that felt so incredibly wonderful, so life-affirming, so hopeful, that she wanted more of it. And Alex wanted to give it to her. And she would accept it from him. "I don't know what happiness is," she admitted with a half shrug.

"It is right now. Do you feel it here?" and Alex touched his chest. "Here?" and he grinned and touched his head. "Does it not make you feel light. Floating? Hopeful?"

"All of those feelings. Yes."

"It is a special gift a man and woman share when their hearts are in agreement."

She gave him a look of awe. "Do you always say the right things, Alex?"

He gave her a wry look. "English is a second language for me, *malen 'kaya.* I am a country bumpkin at best. I am grateful you do not peel me alive in my skin."

Choking on a sudden laugh, Lauren gripped his lower arm. She pressed her other hand to her throat, laughing quietly. She managed, "It's 'skin me alive', Alex." She saw his eyebrows raise and that goofy grin of his spread across his face.

"See? And you say I have a way with words that touch you."

Her smile deepened. Lauren clasped his hand. "You do. Trust me. You do."

Alex looked at his watch. "We must end this conversation. I do not want other ears hearing it. Sergeant Killmer will be returning any minute now."

Glumly, Lauren agreed. It was still gray out, the dawn at least an hour away. "They don't need to know anything about how we feel toward one another," she told Alex. She saw him become serious and nod. Their personal lives were just that. Private.

It was 0500. The hooting of monkeys was growing by the minute. No one could sleep through that except bone-tired operators who always lived on too little sleep. They had all learned a long time ago to cat nap anywhere. Anytime. Any place. Their life-affirming conversation had softened her, had opened up her trust toward Alex. Lauren turned, appreciating him in new ways. *Possibilities. Dreams.* All of a sudden, she was being handed them. To her, Alex was a stalwart warrior who, while looking hard on the outside, carried such a huge, loving heart within him. The fact that he not only understood her, but was patient with her, staggered Lauren.

She stood, placing her empty tin mug on the log. Lauren wished for some water just to clean herself up a bit. She knew Killmer collected water in large green tarps that funneled into several large five-gallon cans. That was their drinking water.

It wasn't the first time Lauren was going to have to go without bathing. She'd been out on sniper ops lasting weeks, with her spotter. They'd reeked when they'd finally come in after completing the mission. Her heart and mind turned gently to Alex as he replenished the fire, and placed the grate back over the hole. He was a team player and she hoped that this spec ops team would trust him as much as she did. Time would tell.

FOR THE NEXT three days, they checked out two of the five possible sniper op sites. This entailed hours of hiking through the known trails, avoiding the ones Killmer knew Indians hired by the Russian mafia were carrying sacks of cocoa leaves along to be distilled into cocaine. There were ten villages that comprised Petrov's area, where he manipulated the people, threatening them and forcing their men to carry drugs, or the cocoa leaves, to specific spots for production and transportation.

At one site, there was a hill above the village. Lauren didn't like it because the only exfil route was a path leading through the village. If Petrov's team engaged, and they had to run, they would put all the villagers at risk. Killmer agreed. On another site, there was no exfil. They'd have to stand and fight if the Russian team decided to stay, hunt and then engage them. Three days and two sites that wouldn't work.

On the evening of that day, their last night in the meadow before they had to move out, because a mafia team would be using it tomorrow night, Alex and Lauren poured over the other three sites that Killmer had marked on the waterproof map. They sat on a log together, the map spread between their laps. The day was waning and, soon, there wouldn't be enough light. Alex pulled out a topical map he'd brought and opened it up. Elevation was important. A sniper took the high ground every time if they could.

"Look," Lauren said, tracing a trail in the jungle with her index finger, "there's a village here, and there's a small hill about half a mile away from it." She peered closer, looking at thin, light lines on the map. "Are those feeder trails?"

Alex studied it, frowning. "Looks like." He tapped the light lines radiating out from the hill. "These may be pig or jaguar trails."

"Oh?" Lauren lifted her head, drowning in his hazel eyes, absorbing his nearness. At night, she slept near Alex and, sometimes, she would awaken in the morning and find herself curled around his back and legs, seeking his warmth. Never once did he make a move to take advantage of her or the situation. This increased the trust of him with the fragile self she kept buried deep inside her.

"Feeder trails are not made by humans," he explained. "Wild pigs make them by rooting out the vine roots, looking for grubs and worms to eat. Over thousands of years, they have created hundreds of feeder lines in the jungle that they traverse as a result." He frowned. "The only problem is, jaguars know about these pig lines, too. So, they are often sitting in a tree, or waiting on the ground or a hill, for the pig families to pass by at night. Pigs and jaguars are nocturnal, Lauren."

"Great," she muttered. "Does this mean then that if I like this hill site, there could be a resident jaguar around? Maybe who OWNS that real estate and won't like me encroaching upon it?"

Alex grinned a little. "I have run into wild pig families many times at night. The boar males are dangerous because of their curved tusks. They have very poor eyesight and rely on their sense of smell. So, what they cannot see, if they are threatened, they lower their heads and charge. One of our team had his lower leg sliced open to the bone by one of those tuskers. He nearly died. I had a time stopping the bleeding. He had several torn arteries. I had sewn nearly a hundred stitches into his leg."

"Have you crossed the paths of any jaguars?"

"Not that I know of, but I have seen their spore often enough."

Mouth flexing, Lauren glanced over at the three Special Forces men. They were getting MRE's out to eat. "Hold on, let me go talk to Killmer."

Nodding, Alex was fine with Lauren being the connection between himself and the soldiers. None of them ignored him, glared at him, or were disrespectful toward him, but he also sensed that none of them fully trusted him, either.

Lauren handed Killmer the map and sat down next to him. He set his MRE aside.

"You've been here how long, Mace?"

"Five months."

"Have you seen any jaguars around?"

He pursed his lips and thought. "A couple of times, me and my team have run into them at night when we're doing recon."

"On what kind of trails."

"Pig trails. Why?"

"Because the sniper site that seems the best out of the last three has a hill with three feeder lines around it."

Killmer grunted. "I know which one you're talking about." He picked up his MRE, opening the foil package. "It's a good site. Village is about half a mile away."

"That's what I like about it."

"We can head that way tomorrow morning. We need to set up the shot away from this area, anyway."

"Well," Lauren muttered, sitting up and brushing off her pants, "is there a jaguar around there?"

"Sure is. Jags are everywhere. They own this place as the A predator. Matter of fact, two weeks ago we stumbled upon a mom and her kittens."

She gulped, eyeing him. He seemed to be smiling but she couldn't tell because of his unkempt black beard. "They're everywhere?"

"Yeah, this one was a female. Nice one. We saw her with two cubs in tow. They are beautiful animals."

"Are they dangerous to us?"

Killmer shrugged. "If she's hungry, I guess. But she lives somewhere near that hill and we've found all kind of pig bones scattered around it. Cunningham, who's our tracker, seems to think she's got a den about a tenth of a mile from the hill."

"And she goes up on the hill to watch at night for pigs to walk by?"

"Yeah, something like that."

"But, if I'm up there with Alex—"

"She'll smell you if she's downwind of you. No worries. She will avoid humans at all cost."

"Even at her dinner table?"

Killmer's mouth stretched. "She may try to skirt the hill, walk down below it. Might get the bejesus scared out of you some night when you're working that scope, watching the trail and you suddenly spot her." He chuckled darkly.

Lauren didn't think it was funny at all. "But you're sure she will avoid humans if she smells us?"

"Smells or hears you. Yes. Did you ask your partner about it?"

"Yes. He hadn't seen any in two years of working in the Highlands area, but he did see spore every once in a while."

Grunting, Killmer nodded. "Well, we're heading that direction bright and early tomorrow morning. Be ready to saddle up at 0500."

Nodding, Lauren picked up her map and walked across the oval-shaped clearing. Alex had his penlight out, studying a terrain map. No one said this would be easy. She hadn't counted on another danger: a jaguar. Men were bad enough. Now a cat was thrown, potentially, into the mix.

She sat down and told Alex what Killmer had said.

"It sounds like a good sniper site," he agreed.

Giving him a brooding look, Lauren said, "I'm real uneasy about a jaguar living in the vicinity."

Alex grinned and folded up the map. He leaned down and handed her one of two MRE's sitting on the log beside him. "Well, we could always kill a pig, put it on one of those other feeder trails, and she'd drag it off. She and her cubs would be well-fed for at least three days. She would just lay around and sleep most of the time, not hunting on her part and she will not bother us."

That sounded like a good plan to Lauren. She thanked him for the MRE, seeing it was spaghetti tonight. Merrill had the fire going and was making everyone real coffee. She'd found out he carried Peruvian coffee beans in a big sack in his ruck. He was a coffee-hound of the first order and hated the freeze-dried packets that came in military rations, turning up his nose at them. They all benefited from his love of real coffee. By the time they ate, night had fallen.

"I miss the stars," Lauren told Alex in a quiet voice later, a tin cup of coffee in her hand. She looked up to see the nightly, white, fog-like clouds stealing silently over the top of the jungle canopy.

"I miss them, too," he confided. Tonight would be the last night he would be near Lauren. They were leaving tomorrow, and they would not be afforded the luxury of huts. It would be open camping. Watches would be set. Killmer didn't want Alex or her on the roster. That was fine. They'd be doing sentry duty soon enough after they set up an op location. One person would sleep while the other stayed awake and alert. It was a test he wasn't looking forward to.

"Coming to the hut?" Lauren asked, finishing off her coffee. She stood, going over to where the dirty dishes were stacked. Lauren had asked Merrill if she could contribute by washing them, but he'd smiled and declined her offer.

"I will be there shortly."

Alex watched the sway of Lauren's hips as she headed in his direction. It was getting dark, as if someone had suddenly pulled a black blanket across the sky. He got up and accompanied her to the hut. Never making the mistake of walking too close to her, touching her, Alex wanted it to look like they were a working team, not personally invested in one another.

The roll of thunder began to the west of them. Nearly every night at least one cell, maybe two or three, would drench the area. Already, the wind was starting to pick up. Lauren knelt down and crawled into the hut. He followed and pulled the waterproof tarp down behind him.

She unlaced her boots after she sat down. "I wonder," she said in a very low tone, "if they suspect anything?"

Earlier, Alex had realized that he could see through some of the vines that created the main structure for the hut. There was a loose array of long, thin grass woven between them, along with leaves. He'd brought out another waterproof tarp, a much larger one, thrown it over their hut, and anchored it down so that they would remain dry during the night hours. "I do not think so. Why?"

"Guilt."

Alex saw a flash of lightning off in the distance. It looked like they were going to get hit squarely by a series of storms tonight. "Guilt about what?"

"That we have each other. Their loved ones are back home in the States."

Alex could hear Lauren getting out of her boots, a damp, soaked tee, and stripping down to her panties and her silk camisole. She had two of them and, every morning, she would wash one out carefully with a bit of rain water, hang it inside the hut and let it dry somewhat. Nothing ever dried completely in a nearly one-hundred-percent humid jungle. "It is the fortunes of war," he told her, undressing. Lauren had devised what she called a 'spit bath' for them. They both had Baby Wipes, which were a godsend in a place like this where they couldn't bathe. But she'd gotten hold of an old aluminum pot. She grabbed her bar of unscented soap and her washcloth and, over it, cleaned herself up. Then, he would use the water. Being clean was important in a jungle. Bacteria from a scratch could be life-threatening. The bugs were also deadly, and some of their bites could put a person in hospital.

Lauren pulled off her camisole and panties without care because they were in utter darkness together. She quickly began to wash herself, starting with her face and working downward. She felt, or perhaps heard, Alex lay down nearby.

"Can you see me in the dark?" she wondered, the soap feeling wonderful against her sweaty skin.

"No. Why?"

"I feel you looking at me."

There was humor in his voice. "I can imagine in my mind and heart what you look like naked, *malen 'kaya.*"

His words fueled her lower body to glowing life.

Just then, there was a flash of lightning not far away. Lauren hesitated, the light flashing through the hut. She realized she Alex could see her. For a moment, Lauren froze. And then, she gave a short, quiet laugh. "Well, I guess you don't have to imagine anymore, do you, Kazak?"

"Not any more. You are beautiful, Lauren. Even more than I dared to dream and imagine."

Lauren took a steady breath and forced herself to focus on getting clean.

"Does it bother you that I saw you?"

"I guess not... no... not really. It was just... well... unexpected."

"You have a beautiful body, Lauren. You should be proud of it. Not hide it."

"I've been hiding all my life, Alex. I don't think I'll ever wear clothes that make me feel uncomfortable or bare too much of my skin." Because it drew the unwelcome attention of men who wanted sex with her.

"That is because you are afraid to be vulnerable. You fear being hurt once again."

She continuing washing, scrubbing, and rinsing the cloth out in the bowl. Taking a towel, she patted her clean body off. "Yes, you're right." Lauren hesitated and then said, "Alex?"

"Yes?"

Donning her clean t-shirt, trousers, socks and boots once more, she gently slid the aluminum pot, with the soap and washcloth inside it, over to where he sat waiting patiently. "I'm finding," she said, "that I am trusting you more than I've ever trusted another man, Alex."

"I would guess you did not have any relationships after your experience with your foster father. Is this true?"

She listened to the splash of water, knowing he was semi-naked. "Yes. I've never wanted sex again."

"I understand. I like that you want to curl around me. That is a sign you are trusting me a little more."

"I don't know where this is leading."

He laughed a little. "Neither of us do, Lauren. But this is all in your hands and your decisions. I am here for you, no matter what. I want to earn your trust. It is up to you to tell me what you do or not want to do where we are concerned. Okay?"

She compressed her lips, hearing the thunder in the distance. "Yes, and thank you for having the patience you have with me. I need to earn your trust, too."

"*Malen 'kaya*, do not worry. Good things in one's life often take time. We are on a journey of discovery with one another and I am grateful you are at my side in whatever way is comfortable for you."

She felt tears burn in her eyes, wiping them away. "Okay… you are a type of man I've never met in my life."

A rumble of a chuckle reverberated in his chest as he washed himself. "We are on an exploration adventure with one another. There is no hurry, no demands. I like building our trust with one another. It is a good way to be with a person."

CHAPTER 13

I T WAS STILL raining the next morning when they broke camp and started down a major trail that would lead them to the village called Kurmi. Its Quechua name meant 'rainbow' in English. It was also a village that the American charity, Helping Hands, supported with a new well that had just recently been dug so they could have clean, safe drinking water. Lauren was number three in the line, hefting her ruck and carrying all of her own gear. The rain was light, but by the time they'd established a twenty-minute-mile pace she was soaked, grateful for her camouflage floppy brimmed hat, for the way the rain dripped off it and not down her face or into her eyes. She felt Alex behind her. Killmer was in the lead as point man, a good tenth of a mile ahead of the main group, keeping watch for tangos, enemies. Cale Merrill brought up the rear. The Special Forces operators all carried their rifles, barrels down toward the ground. If they were really expecting trouble, Lauren knew they'd have those barrels up toward the sky. It made it quicker to lower them and fire. Split seconds could determine life and death.

The path was slippery red clay, and she knew the village of Kurmi could be reached by two different paths. They had chosen a gentle slope that took them down to six thousand feet in order to check out what Killmer termed 'Jaguar Hill', and possibly set up an op. They were operating in Petrov's territory. Although Killmer couldn't be a hundred percent sure if the Russian mafia team was or wasn't in the area. They had followed the Russians enough in the past to have cause to hope they were on another trail, headed for another village. But no one really knew for sure, which was why she was alert, on guard and listening to the sounds ahead of her up the trail. The rain effectively acted like a muffler, muting noises to a high degree. And since Petrov and his men were ex-Spetsnaz, they weren't going to give their whereabouts away by talking any more than necessary.

Lauren knew it was a game of chicken. Killmer had gone over egress routes in case they ran into the Russians. There were always contingency plans in case they got scattered and had to regroup at the rally point. Worst case scenario, Lauren knew, was to unexpectedly run up on Petrov and his men and have a firefight ensue. Bullets would be flying and there weren't a hell of a lot of places to hide if that happened. Today, as on every other day, she and Alex wore their concealed Dragon Skin vests beneath their cammo blouses. She silently thanked Jack Driscoll, CEO of Shield, who had put out thousands of dollars on each one of these lightweight, bullet-stopping vests for his people. They weighed three pounds each, compared to the thirty- to-sixty-pound Kevlar vests that the military had to use with black ops teams. The weight of those vests took a tremendous physical toll on anyone who was on patrol or had to march any distance. With Dragon Skin, Lauren felt as if she weren't even wearing one, and she could maintain the blistering pace Killmer had set for them, raining or not.

They arrived at the village of Kurmi at noon. The rain had stopped for now, the ragged white clouds hanging over the top of the canopy. This was a small village of about seventy people. Killmer had briefed them on it earlier. The huts were made of grass, vines and leaves and were set in neat rows, mud puddles in the streets between them. The children were out playing in those, splashing barefoot, nearly naked except for colorful shorts that looked threadbare to Lauren. The women were busy at metal tripods that suspended black iron kettles over sheltered areas where a fire could burn despite the daily rain, and where food could be cooked.

Killmer strode into the village, heading directly for the chief's house. Alex knew the routine. The sergeant spoke Quechua, the native language. Among the important things Army Special Forces had to do were know the people of the villages, the leaders, and speak the local language. Most other black ops groups didn't, and Killmer found the Special Forces way a far better resource to get the people on their side. Or at least, to gain their trust enough so they would give them vital, perishable intel.

Cale Merrill jogged up to them. "There's an empty hut over there," and he pointed down the most major street in the village. "We'll put all our gear in there. Come on, follow me."

Lauren was looking around. She had spotted what they called 'Jaguar Hill', half a mile back on the trail. It wasn't much of a hill, maybe a hundred feet higher than the trail that wound past it. What was important, from her perspective as a sniper, was that the trail before the hill was straight for nearly five hundred yards. That would give her a clear, unobstructed shot in the event the Russian team rounded that corner before coming down the straightaway. Despite her discomfort about the local jaguar with cubs, she felt Killmer had hit paydirt with this site.

Her clothing was wet, chaffing against her flesh. As they put their gear inside the large, empty and dry hut, Lauren felt the cramps in her lower legs. She pulled her CamelBak hose and stuck it in her mouth, hydrating as she waited outside for Alex. Looking around, she saw a small group of brown-skinned, black-haired children standing shyly nearby, watching her intently. It must be her red hair that they were fascinated with. Their dark brown eyes shined with curiosity. When Lauren removed her wet hat, slapping it against her leg to get rid of some of the water soaked into it, the children, as a group, drew closer, all gazes on her hair.

Alex came to her side. "They are entranced with the color of your hair," he told her. "They do not see blond or red hair out here."

Lauren looked up. Alex was fully in operator mode. His game face was in place. "They're beautiful children," she murmured.

"They like candy," and he smiled a little, watching them creep a little closer, their inquisitiveness stronger than their fear.

"I've brought some," Lauren murmured, opening up the cargo pocket on her right thigh. "What's the protocol here? Will the chief of the village get upset if I give them some or not?" She saw his strong mouth draw up into a slight smile, his gaze ranging around the area where the village sat.

"The chief will not mind. Kids are the same everywhere," he told her. "Just slowly approach them. When you get about ten feet away from them, kneel or crouch down. You are very tall in their eyes and that makes them unsure of you. To them, you are a giant. If you crouch, they will surround you. Do not be surprised if they want to reach out and touch your head or your horse tail."

He saw the amusement glitter in her eyes. "Pony tail, Alex."

He had the good grace to blush. "Slang has shot off my foot, again… yes, pony tail, thank you. I will put this in my notebook later."

She grinned and didn't' have the heart to correct him on shooting himself in the foot, instead. "No worries."

She didn't have the heart to tell him about the foot shot versus shooting one's self in the foot. "We have nothing to do until Killmer gets back after talking with the chief," and Lauren saw him nod, as if to tell her to go ahead and engage with the excited children.

Alex watched Lauren walk slowly in their direction. The children were wary because of their encounters with the Russians. They weren't sure if this group were Russians or someone else. He knew, from two years of first-hand experience, that Vlad Alexandrov hated children. He would kick at them, curse them and threaten to hit them. Any time they had gone into a Quechua village, the women and children had run away and hidden in their huts, afraid of them. And they had good reason for that fear.

His heart opened as Lauren smiled and called hello in Spanish. The children didn't understand what she said, but that didn't matter. Alex could see that her warm, engaging smile, and her soft, husky voice had already won them over. There were five little girls in the group and six boys. They clung together like a ragged, colorful wall of fabrics until Lauren knelt down on one knee, extending her hand out toward them with red-wrapped hard candy in her palm. Then, the children surged forward, surrounding her. He chuckled, watching the little girls swarming behind her, eagerly touching her hair, running their small fingers through the damp strands. They lifted her hair, amazement on their tiny faces. The boys, on the other hand, went straight for the candy.

Merrill came up beside Alex and chuckled. "She's got a way with those kids."

"Yes."

"We can't hardly get them to come anywhere near us." Cale scowled. "Damned Russians have made them fearful of everyone."

Alex nodded. "The Russian mafia is a cruel place. They have no heart."

"Got that right," Merrill muttered. His face lightened as the little girls continued to touch Lauren's hair, her shoulder and then her face. They were shy, mesmerized by the white-skinned American woman with red hair.

"How is your good will with this village?" Alex asked him.

"Killmer has been slowly winning over the chief. But, as you know, Alexandrov turned at least ten of the village men into cocaine mules. They work for Petrov now, and the chief is furious about that. Those men were the hunters for the village and without them now, they are near starvation."

Alex nodded. He knew the chief, Juan Zavas, an older man in his fifties. "Zavas hated Alexandrov and the rest of us, with good reason," he murmured, continuing to look around. The village had been cleared out of the jungle, the walls of which were about fifty feet away on all sides from the huts. "I am sure Sergeant Killmer had problems getting Zavas to trust him."

"Yeah, it's been pretty tough earning the chief's loyalty." Merrill motioned to the children who were now laughing and smiling around Lauren. She was pulling more candy out of her pocket to give one piece to each of the little girls first, making the boys wait. "He's agreed to let us sometimes stay in that empty hut, but not for any length of time. And he's stingy with what he knows. He's afraid Petrov will find out and punish his people by killing them."

Alex felt badly for the villagers, and said nothing. He kept one eye on Lauren and the children, but continued his perusal of the area. "I know there are small feeder trails that lead from that hill to this village."

"Yeah, there's three."

"We saw them on the map the other day. I was looking at those feeder paths surrounding the hill when we hiked by it earlier. The map wasn't clear about how many egress routes there really were." Being able to egress or escape, was vital for a sniper and his or her partner if everything went to hell in a handbag and they were outnumbered and outgunned.

Merrill rubbed his bearded face. "There's one trail that leads to the village, but the other two swing back on this same major trail," and Cale pointed in the direction of the hill. "There are three smaller paths made by peccary, but two, further down off the hill, merge back into the one main feeder trail below it and it goes back into the jungle."

Nodding, Alex looked up and saw that the whitish clouds were beginning to lift. He figured a front had passed through the area last night. It would be good to be able to dry out a little. He spotted Killmer coming around the edge of a hut further down the same street where Lauren was with the excited children.

He didn't seem happy, despite the game face that Alex knew the sergeant had on. It was more a sense than any expression in the operator's gray eyes. The children saw the big, tall soldier coming and they scattered like a flock of startled birds, running toward their families' huts and disappearing. Alex felt badly for them. The children were frightened of any white men they saw, most likely thinking they were the violent, murderous Russians. He watched Lauren get to her feet, and wipe some of the worst of the mud off her right knee. Killmer slowed down as he approached them. Alex saw happiness in Lauren's eyes. Her gaze met his, and he felt warmth spread across his chest. She looked so beautiful to him, his gaze flickering momentarily to her smiling mouth. There was a new softness to her this morning. He saw it. He wondered if the others did, too. Her cheeks were flushed and she was radiant.

There was such a powerful, invisible bond growing strong and unbreakable between them. He ached to see happiness like this in her eyes and face. She was smiling. And it moved deeply through Alex.

Killmer halted as his group moved in to hear what he had to say. Lauren joined the group.

"We have some Band-Aids to put into place," he growled. Lifting his chin, he moved it in the direction of the trail outside the village. "Petrov came through here two days ago."

"Shit," Cale said, "he's off schedule, then."

Frowning, Lauren said, "How reliable is Petrov with his schedule around his region?"

Rubbing his beard, Killmer said, "Not at all reliable." He scowled. "We think things are changing, but we don't know why. Petrov may be responding to something I'm not aware of. Could be firefights with the local drug lords."

Alex said, "It could be that Petrov is getting pressured from above. His boss may be wanting more production of cocaine being made."

Nodding, Killmer said, "My thoughts, too." He studied Alex for a moment. "When you were here with Alexandrov, was he consistent in his visits to all the villages under his command?"

"Yes, very. He gave each chief a demand for exactly so many pounds of cocaine that they had to produce. If those quotas were not met, well," and he shrugged. "Things went badly for the chief's villagers."

"So," Killmer growled, always looking around, always assessing the area, "you knew Petrov?"

"Yes."

"Was he disciplined, like your boss?"

"Yes."

"Then what the hell is going on?" Killmer growled more to himself than them.

"What did Chief Zavas say to you?" Alex asked mildly. He saw the wariness in Killmer's eyes, weighing whether or not he wanted to tell him anything.

"Petrov came through here unannounced. He was supposed to be here in seven days. He took all their cocaine they'd made. And he wasn't happy because the chief didn't meet the quota."

"Why did he arrive early?" Alex wondered.

"I don't know. Zavas was surprised, too."

"Had Petrov been consistent in his visits before this time?" Alex pressed.

"Yeah," Killmer grumbled. "Which leads me to think that something we don't know about, something we can't put our finger on, is happening. There's change, and damned if I can figure out what it is, but it's sure-as-hell affecting their schedules."

"I'm going to call Gage Hunter of Mission Planning at Shield," Lauren told him. "He's got carte blanche with the CIA. Maybe he can shake something loose for us. Or," and she frowned, "at least give us a hint as to what's causing Petrov to break his normal pattern of movement."

"Well, one thing for sure," Killmer said, giving them a hard look, "it means your op has suddenly become a helluva lot tougher to accomplish. If Petrov is going to start being erratic, you could sit on that hill for a week or two and never have him come down the trail. Before, I could have timed it to the day and hour for you but now," and he shook his head, "all bets are off."

"Did Chief Zavas say where Petrov was going next?" Alex asked.

"Didn't say."

"There are two trails that meet about a mile from here," Alex told them, pointing to the western jungle. "One leads to the upper village of Wayra in the jungle and the other, Tuyur, and that is about six miles further and it's on the edge of the Highlands. Both are in Petrov's territory." Alex knew the trails at least as well as, and probably better than, Killmer and his team did. "Neither of those trails led back directly to La Paloma, the village where Petrov and his men have their base of operation," he added, continuing to think aloud. "Either way," and he looked down at Lauren, "Petrov is going to HAVE to take this trail we just came down to get back to his base at La Paloma. Wayra and Tuyur are dead ends, trail-speaking-wise. Petrov has to turn around and come back through here."

Killmer agreed. "And he usually stays overnight in a village and then moves on."

"Yes, that is how we operated when I was with Alexandrov," Alex said.

Lauren said, "Then, the only thing I want to do right now is get back to that hill, check it out, and see if it's viable."

"We'll take a hike up to it," Killmer told her, "After we grab chow and rest a bit."

Lauren made the call on the sat phone as she sat in the unused hut, while the rest set about getting the group something to eat. Alex remained nearby, listening to the conversation. When she clicked it off, she gave him a dark look. "Apparently, from what Jack's people could find out? There's a fight underway for who is going to control the Russian Mafia out of New York City. Rolan Pavlovich has taken over, and he's scourging the old guard from his ranks who were working with Yerik Alexandrov. Jack believes Pavlovich is weeding out Alexandrov loyalists from the ranks right down to these Russian teams that are here on the ground. He's apparently replacing some of them with his own hand-picked people."

"That would answer why Petrov may be changing his habits."

Nodding, she said, "I'm taking this intel to Mace. I think he'll agree with us about what's upsetting all their schedules and blowing them to hell."

"And," Alex added, "this is going to throw everything these three Special Forces groups know off-balance and they won't know who is where, anymore. At least, until Pavlovich cleans the ranks out of Alexandrov loyalists."

"What a friggin' mess," she muttered, shaking her head, leaving the hut, the sat phone in hand.

A LIGHT MIST began as Lauren and Alex carefully moved up the nob of the small hill. Down below, the red clay trail, pitted with mud puddles, curved around one flank of the hill and then continued in a westerly direction toward Kurmi. The bump, as Lauren referred to it, was littered with fallen trees, cracked logs, and orchids that had been blown out of the trees that surrounded the hill by the gusts of wind that came with the violent, daily or nightly thunderstorms. There was a layer of leaf debris about six inches deep, making the surface springy as well as soggy, their boots sinking into it. They carried their rifles as they reconned the area. Killmer and his group had remained behind at the village where he was trying to find out more from the chief about Petrov's untimely appearance.

Lauren liked the stacked logs that looked like gigantic toothpicks that had been haphazardly scattered about on the hill. She stood atop the center of it, eyes narrowing as she studied the straight length of trail that led up to, and past, where they were at. Alex was looking around, lifting and peering through some branches, checking out the strength of the logs piled on top of one another. "This is ideal," she told him, gesturing toward the trail. "Five hundred yards, if I don't miss my guess."

Alex joined her. "It is an easy shot. Once Petrov and his men round that corner down there," and he gestured toward it, "there is no place for them to run and hide. All the feeder lines are here, at the hill. They are walled-in on both sides of that trail, with no place to run and hide. They cannot escape into those thick, woody vine walls. It is impossible to do."

"The only thing they can do is lay down a wall of fire and back out," Lauren agreed. She was glad to be alone with Alex. She could relax to a degree. "Let's go check out those two feeder lines? Because we can't use the one that curves around through the jungle and ends up back at that village. There's no way I'm leading Petrov, and what's left of his gang, into it. I want to keep the villagers safe and out of the line of fire."

Nodding, Alex said, "This way, then," and he moved gingerly down the knoll. At the bottom, he took the trail to the farthest left. "These pig feeders are narrower," he warned her.

Lauren moved ahead of him, seeing the wall of tropical plants and vines rising at least eight feet high above them on either side of the red, muddy path. "If we need to egress because Petrov's men fight back, we need to be sure they can't see us when we slide down the other side of this hill."

"They will know these feeders, also," he warned, following her onto the trail. It got considerably darker because of the thick, continuous cloud cover over them, and also due to the jungle absorbing the light above, not letting much of it reach the ground.

They walked down the slope until the point trail flattened out and ran straight from there. That stretch was at least a mile long and when Lauren emerged back onto the main trail she was feeling her calves begin to knot again. A sign that she had to hydrate. Alex pulled out a waterproof map, leaned in near to her, and opened it. "Here's where this feeder comes out on this path."

Lauren sucked a lot of water out of her CamelBak and fixed the tube beneath the Velcro tab on her shoulder that kept it in place. "I keep worrying about something though, Alex." She looked over at him. "What if we take out Petrov and Volkov decides to fight? He could send one of his men back to hide and take us out right here." They had not been given approval to snuff out Volkov according to Gage Hunter when she'd spoken with him on the sat phone earlier.

"There is only five men left once you kill Petrov. Knowing Volkov, he will probably retreat. He will not know how many people are on that hill. I do not think he will risk it."

"What? Then retreat the way they came in? Get out of Dodge?"

Nodding, Alex added, "Look at it this way, Lauren. With Petrov dead, Volkov will be leader. He wants to live. Not stay and fight an unknown size of force hidden on this hill."

"We still need an egress point even if he retreats," Lauren said.

"Absolutely."

"You look worried."

"Petrov is behaving erratically. This worries me greatly. We do not know if he's an Alexandrov loyalist or if he's on Rolan's side, yet. Until we know, everything is unknown."

"Doesn't matter," Lauren said grimly, hands on her hips as she looked back up the feeder path they'd just emerged from. "He's got to come by this hill sooner or later. And we'll be there to stop the sonofabitch." She snorted. "I just wish DOD had given me the green flag to take out Volkov, too."

Alex nodded. "Their decision does not make sense to me, either." He took her elbow and led her back onto the feeder path just enough so that they were hidden from possible people coming down the trail. Brushing her cheek with his fingertips, he rasped, "We have something good between us. I would wish this op was finished and we were flying home. I want the time so we can explore and know one another without danger all around us. I have many dreams for you, *malen 'kaya*, that I want to share with you."

Lauren held his sincere gaze. "That makes two of us," she whispered, sliding her fingertips across his stubbled jaw. It felt so good to not only be honest with this man she trusted, but also for her to give voice to how she felt.

Alex nodded. "Let us take the feeder back to the hill. We will check out the other one to determine which will be best for us in case we have to egress."

CHAPTER 14

THE CHILDREN WERE waiting and watching for Lauren to arrive back at their village. Alex and her had finished their inspection of the two feeder trails and it was late afternoon. The rain had stopped and Lauren was glad. She carried an M4 rifle, a favorite of Navy SEALs, having found it the perfect weapon for her. It had a short eight-inch barrel and fit well for her size and height. Alex walked slightly behind her, always watchful, his AK-47 hanging off a strap across his chest. She sucked down more water, feeling hungry. They had worked hard all day scouting out the potential site.

"I think you are going to be the most popular person here," he teased, walking up by her shoulder, grinning. The waiting children were twice as many as Lauren had gathered before. Alex was sure word had spread like wildfire through the village that they had each gotten sweet candy from this beautiful red-haired white woman. His heart expanded fiercely with love for Lauren. The children swarmed her, jumping up, calling their name for her, *La Mujer Roja*, "The Red Woman", because of her hair.

They were grabbing at her hand, tugging at her to come with them, to somewhere else in the village. Alex heard her laugh as she reached out, caressing their heads, leaning down to kiss a little girl who was begging to be carried. She was mobbed, but took it in good stride.

"They're taking me somewhere," she called over her shoulder, laughing.

Alex nodded and said, "Go play, *malen 'kaya*." He saw the radiance in her face, the flush of pink in her cheeks as he held her warm gaze. He knew Lauren loved him although she had never brought up the topic or spoken to him about it. He felt it in every cell of his body. "See you later?"

Lauren nodded. "Yeah, let me see where the kids want me to go. I still have some candy in my pocket. They must know that?"

His grin deepened. "All children have candy radar." Her returning laughter made his chest swell with love for her. Children clearly loved her, too. They saw her heart. So did he. He watched as Lauren grabbed her M4 rifle and pulled it off over her shoulder. As routine, she'd always had it on her but he could see she was worried about the powerful military weapon being around the children.

"Here," she said, lifting it up over the children's heads toward him. "Take it to the hut? I'll be back in a few minutes. I won't be long."

Alex took the weapon from her hands. Up ahead, he saw Merrill with his own rifle, walking slow, keeping watch. Lauren would be safe enough. "Okay, do not be long?" Because it looked like it was going to rain again, darker clouds in the west churning rapidly toward the village once more.

"Promise," she said, turning and placing her hand on the shoulder of a thin, tall boy who was smiling up at her, begging her to walk faster with him.

Alex watched the children drag Lauren off between two huts and onto another street. He saw that, finally, they had brought out her own childlike side. It made him wonder that if, someday, she would desire children of her own. As Alex walked down the muddy street, adult villagers out and about their daily business all around him, he pondered that possibility. His heart swelled even more. One of his secret dreams was to one day have a family. He missed his extended family so much that, sometimes, a different kind of ache would arise within his soul. Alex felt lonely without them. Maybe, he thought, it was in his genes to be surrounded by a loving, supportive family like he'd grown up in. Was Lauren even open to the possibility? Alex thought so, judging by how quickly she'd opened up and smiled and cared for her young charges with such focus and tenderness.

He saw Killmer coming up from another street below the one he was walking along. Alex decided to meet him at their vacant hut where their gear was stored, to go over the intel they'd gathered earlier. He'd like the Special Forces sergeant's feedback. Killmer might not trust him, but would fully help them in the setting-up phase of the op.

LAUREN WAS SWEPT up in the joy, laughter and playfulness of the fifteen or so children. They were all barefoot, red mud splattered all over their short twig-like legs and calloused bare feet as they tugged and pulled at her hand. First, she stopped and gave each of them a piece of candy, delighting in their eyes shining back with thanks. And then, the two oldest boys, probably ten and twelve, grabbed her hands, tugging her forward, pointing excitedly toward the edge of the village.

Where were they going? What did they want to show her? Lauren saw a number of women by their huts. They smiled and waved to her. It felt good to be welcomed and Lauren pulled her hand free from one boy and waved back. She turned her attention back to the children, and saw that they were leading her behind a large family-sized hut. There was a path there that led into the jungle. It had to be the other feeder line. The one they had not walked today.

Several children raced ahead, their hair flying, calling out to her in their Quechua language that Lauren couldn't understand. They went up a steep slope, everyone sliding and slipping in the red mud. The children laughed. Three of the girls got behind Lauren, pushing on her butt to help her up the steep hill. The boys tugged even harder on her hands, helping her to make the ascent. At the top, they were all looking very excited. The trio of girls who stood on the flat path, gestured for Lauren to hurry forward. She nodded and grinned. These kids were up to something, their excitement infectious.

Lauren noticed that the woody vines that normally didn't allow anyone to walk through the jungle were non-existent in this area. She could see into the dark jungle full of trees, most of the ground free of bushes. Wondering if the villagers had removed the ground cover over time, Lauren realized that one could move quite easily across this litter-free jungle floor. Because not much sunlight could reach the ground of the jungle, few plants grew there. Instead, the earth was covered with decaying leaves, much like the hill they would put up the sniper hide on tomorrow morning.

The children became very enthused, their little voices reaching high pitches as they called to her. They rounded a slight curve. There, on the path, was several blooming orchids that had been blown out of overhanging trees last night by the gusty winds from the thunderstorms that had rolled through the area. One little girl knelt, gesturing for Lauren to stop and come look at them.

"Ohhhh," Lauren said, smiling as she halted, kneeling down, "these are beautiful!" and she scooped one orchid in bloom up into her hands. The children surrounded her, wriggling like happy puppies, their faces alight and beaming. Lauren looked at the huge white orchid with its long, leathery, oval leaves. She saw a lot of roots still gripping onto what looked like bark and moss from where it had lived on a branch of a tree above them. Looking up, because the children were pointing that way, she saw several more of the same type of orchid still clinging onto the tree by the path.

One child took her hand and pushed it toward her. Another kept pointing at her nose, trying to tell Lauren to smell the flower she held.

"Okay," she told them, laughing, "I get it." And she lifted the huge white orchid with its purple lip up to her nose. The fragrance reminded Lauren of a heavy vanilla scent. Closing her eyes, she sighed, inhaling the scent deep into her lungs.

Suddenly, Lauren felt the grip of man's hand on her shoulder, fingers digging in, holding her right where she was.

The children all gasped. Some cried out. They scattered away from Lauren.

Dropping the orchid, Lauren jerked her head up. Her heart plunged. Tamryn Volkov had his pistol pointed at her temple, grinning down at her.

"So," he whispered triumphantly, "we meet again, eh? Stand up!"

The children ran screaming back down the path toward the village.

A second man appeared out of the dark jungle, short brown hair, as tall as Alex, with his dark blue eyes narrowed on her. He quickly removed the pistol from her belt and frisked her roughly for any other weapons.

"Hurry, Morozov!" Volkov snapped. He jerked a look over his shoulder. "Those brats will alert everyone."

Lauren gasped, her heart pounding in her breast. How? How did they find her? She felt Volkov's hand dig painfully into her shoulder. "Scream and you die," he snarled.

Morozov pulled out a pair of plastic flex cuffs, quickly binding her hands in front of her. Next, he took out a dirty green rag and pushed it into her mouth, tying its corners behind her head. "Let's go," he snapped, gripping her arm, jerking her forward.

No! God, no! Lauren wasn't going down easily. The instant Volkov lowered his pistol, she whirled on her left boot, her right leg arcing up, catching him in the chest, flinging him backward off his feet. He grunted. The pistol flew out of his hand.

She head Morozov curse and swung around. He lunged at her. She snapped her booted foot upward, slamming it into his chest. He let out a loud, "oofff," and staggered backward, falling.

Now! Lauren turned, racing, slipping and sliding down the trail, heading back toward the village. Her nostrils flared as they drank in huge draughts of air. The mud slowed her. She heard pounding boots coming up behind her, catching up with her. *No! No!* One of them tackled her from behind. Lauren slammed into the ground, striking her head on an exposed root. It was the last thing she remembered.

ALEX HEARD THE children screaming. He knew Quechua. They were calling out for help. He lowered the map he was showing Killmer.

"What the hell?" Killmer growled, picking up his rifle.

Alex saw the first child flying between the huts, running toward them, her face etched with panic and fear. He snapped up his AK-47, hearing the girl screaming, "Bad men! Bad men!"

The rest of the children were flooding down across the other street, moving between the huts, racing toward them for safety's sake.

Alex leaned down to the first little girl, her eyes wide with fear, crying. Quickly, he spoke to her in her language. "Where is the red-haired woman? Where is she?"

The little girl sobbed. "Bad men have her! Hurry! She will die! She will die!"

Alex's mouth thinned. "Where? Where did this happen? Show us! Quick-ly!"

The rest of the children arrived, panting, scared, looking over their shoul-ders, panicked. They all pointed toward where they had just come from up on the hill.

"Dammit," Killmer growled, "she's been kidnapped by Petrov!" He got on his radio, calling his other two team mates, ordering them back to the empty hut immediately.

Alex caressed the little girl's muddy cheek, keeping his voice soft and low. "Tell me where they went? Where did the bad men take Lauren?"

The girl sniffed and turned her face up, "The trail. We took her up there to show her orchids that had fallen from the trees. T-they grabbed her. We ran…"

Alex didn't wait for any of them. He knew where the trail was. Remem-bered it well. Digging in the toes of his boots, mud flying behind him, he dashed away. *Petrov!* The bastard must have shadowed them. His mind was working like a steel trap. He heard Killmer yell at him, but he refused to stop.

With his AK-47 in hand, he unsafed it as he ran, ramming a bullet into the chamber. Alex hit the trail hard, slipping, damn near falling. He righted himself, taking the steep slope with huge strides, urgency thrumming through him. It began to rain. Heavily. The jungle was dark and, as he crested the hill, he saw nothing. Running forward, his heart bursting with agony, with fear for Lauren, he rounded a small curve.

There, on the ground, were several scattered orchids. He slid to a stop, breathing hard, forcing himself to listen. To see if he could hear his old team. Turning, eyes narrowed, he peered into the grayish veil falling into the jungle. It was easy for the Russians to move through this area and make a quick escape because there was no brush or other impediments to slow them down. Looking around, he spotted muddy tracks. He'd recognize Russian combat boot prints anywhere, and saw two sets of them. And then, he recognized Lauren's boot prints. Wiping his mouth, sobbing for breath, he wanted to scream out her name. But, if he did, Petrov would hear him… know he was being pursued. The rain fell hard, blocking his view of most of the jungle. The tracks were already being washed out. What were they going to do with Lauren? Alex didn't even dare go there. Oh, God, this could not be happening! He'd just found her! And she was in the hands of ex-Spetsnaz soldiers who knew how to torture. To rape. To kill. The only hope they had was that his friend, their combat medic, was with the Russian team. Nik Morozov could protect Lauren. Alex knew that Nik's protective side toward children and women was just as strong as his was. If only Nik was with them… Alex was unsure, but he prayed that his friend was present.

Killmer and his team raced down the path, their faces hard. Sliding to a halt, they did the same thing Alex had: look for tracks. Look for the direction their enemy went.

Wiping his face, Alex said, "They're taking her through the jungle," and he pointed to some prints he'd found in the soft, soggy, decomposed soil.

"Yeah," Killmer growled. He looked around. "Petrov's team."

"For sure," Alex rasped, wiping his face. He pulled out his black baseball cap, settling it on his head. "I'm going after them."

"Not without us, you aren't," Killmer said.

Alex gave them a hard stare. "I know them. I know where they could be taking Lauren."

"Then we'll follow. But first, we need to get our rucks, get ready to go after them."

"Lend me one of your radios and ear pieces," Alex demanded, holding out his hand. Every second counted. If he ran hard enough, had a good enough trail to follow, he could catch Petrov before they could do anything to Lauren.

Killmer hesitated, thought better of it for an instant, but then sharply gestured to Cunningham to hand over his radio equipment.

Alex thanked him, quickly shoving the earpiece into his ear and the waterproof radio into his cammie blouse pocket. "What is the range?"

"Five miles," Killmer said. "All right, you take off, follow them. We'll saddle up as quickly as we can. Leave us trail markers. They will help us get to you sooner. We'll bring your ruck with us."

"I will find her," Alex gritted out. "And I will kill all of them. You need to know they MAY have a combat medic with them. He is a good friend of mine, Nik Morozov." Alex pulled out his iPhone, protecting it from the rain as he thumbed through his photo gallery. Turning it, he showed the three men a photo of Nik. "Under NO circumstances do you kill or wound him. He is working undercover for the DOD and CIA. He is a plant in Petrov's team and he feeds the US government with vital information. Do NOT KILL HIM."

Mace's eyebrows rose as he intently studied the color photo of the Russian ex-Spetsnaz soldier. "I'm going to have to take your word on this," he growled over at Alex. "No one has told us anything of the sort."

Grimacing, Alex said, "You will have to trust me on this. I can prove it to you later, after we find Lauren." He snapped off the iPhone, tucking it deep within his jacket to keep it safe from getting wet.

Gripping Alex's arm, Killmer growled, "Don't do anything stupid out there, Kazak. You can't go off half-cocked. I know you and that woman have a relationship, but you're not going to do her ANY good if you let your emotions get the better of you."

Alex didn't care if Killmer knew about them. "My focus is on saving her life. You just get your ass on my trail, and I'll leave signs so you can follow me." He turned, trotting into the jungle, the rumble of thunder reverberating through the heavy, ongoing rain.

Quickly, Alex was swallowed up by the gloom of the jungle. The downpour stopped him from hearing anything because the drops of rain sounded like nails being dropped onto a taut drumhead. It was the wide, thick leaves at the top of the rainforest canopy making those noisy, constant sounds. More than likely, they had gagged Lauren and flex-cuffed her. That was SOP, standard operating procedure, when kidnapping a victim. His heart kept tearing open with grief. He followed the boot prints, counting five men. He could not find Lauren's boot prints, however. Kneeling down a half mile in, where the jungle opened up a little to allow more light to penetrate, Alex knelt down, studying the prints closely. One set of boot prints was going deeper into the soil than the other sets. Looking up, rain dripping off his hard jaw, he knew Lauren was being carried by one of the soldiers. Had they shot her up with a drug to render her unconscious? Knocked her out? Broken her jaw? These men were rough. They wouldn't think twice about hitting a woman.

He continued on, feeling a little relief because the soggy ground made it easier for him to tag the group. They were moving out. Trotting steadily. Where were they going? Alex searched his memory frantically. He knew of this feeder trail, but little else. This was off the beaten path of his experience. Vlad had never cut cross-country like this. Petrov had a destination in mind, that was for sure. And Alex had no earlier recollection of this area or this particular path; it was all new to him. Even the topo map Killmer had, showed this particular feeder dissolving as a trail above the village. As a consequence, he couldn't tell Killmer where the Russian team was going, or what their endgame was. That made this even more dangerous for Lauren. For all of them. He'd have to watch for places where a trap could be set up and they could all be shot and killed.

LAUREN MOANED. THE sound reverberated in her ears. She was curved across the man's thick, broad shoulders, in a fireman's carry. And he was jogging. And it was creating pain in her head so excruciating that she cried out. But the dirty rag in her mouth stopped most of the sound from escaping. The Russian who carried her was gripping her wrists with one hand, his other around one of her ankles, keeping her positioned against his neck, shoulders and back. Branches swatted at her, slapping her in the face. Rain poured down and she blinked, trying to see, her vision blurring.

Whoever was carrying her was panting, straining as they moved up an incline she couldn't see, only feel. She tried to see where they were at. Dark jungle surrounded them. Rain was leaking in off the canopy, soaking them. She heard the man's deep panting, laboring as he was under her bulk. She was no lightweight. Her mind spun and she closed her eyes, trying to think. There were sharp orders in Russian. They changed course. Lauren groaned, feeling nauseous, her stomach rolling. Warm blood trickled down her temple and ear. She vaguely remembered hitting something when she'd tried to make her escape.

Her hands were free! They'd flex-cuffed her before. But the Russian who was carrying her had big hands, the long, spare fingers of which easily spanned around and gripped both her slender wrists. She was pinned against him, no way to escape. Terror worked through her. Lauren gulped. She couldn't let fear overwhelm her. She had to think! She knew Alex and the Special Forces team would have been alerted to what had happened to her by the frightened children. She remembered their shrieks and screams of terror as they ran down the slope to the comparative safety of the village below.

They changed course again. This time, they were going down a slope. The rain was constant. Cold. She shivered, her clothes wet, chaffing against her skin. The man carrying her was gasping for breath. She felt him shift her, as if to make it easier on himself. Her head kept banging against his shoulder, increasing the pain in it from the fall. Where were they going? What was out here? She tried to imagine the map behind her tightly shut eyes. She recalled nothing, the pain making her gasp.

Suddenly, the man stopped. His chest heaved with exertion. Lauren opened her eyes, partially glimpsing another Russian soldier on her left. She saw the AK-47 he carried. Then, they were on the move again. Miraculously, the rain stopped. Lauren realized they had entered into a cave of some sort and that was why the rain had ceased. She heard murmurs in Russian ahead of her, the voices echoing. Lauren closed her eyes, feeling her stomach roll strongly. She fought not to vomit.

Nik Morozov halted. He saw his leader, Anton Petrov, waiting for them. Nik was the shortest man of the group, about five foot ten inches tall, and he'd often been teased that the team saw him as a lean, starving, Russian wolf. Petrov was smiling as Nik approached him. They'd entered a second cavern, dry and filled with dim light from a hole above, making the area look grayish.

"You got her?" Petrov murmured, pleased, giving Volkov a nod.

"Little bitch. I'm telling you, Anton, she's an operator!" Volkov said, making a sharp gesture for Morozov to drop her from his shoulders to the ground.

Snickering, Anton said, "Well, we are going to find out."

Morozov knelt down and carefully pulled the woman off his shoulders. He saw no need to hurt her any more than she was already injured. He heard her groan as he cupped her neck and head, allowing the rest of her body to ease to the dirt floor. Her head was bloody. And he worried, but said nothing, laying her out on the ground and then backing away.

Dizziness assailed Lauren. She'd felt the man leave her on the ground, and then the world tilted. At first, she had thought to get up and run but, as she opened her eyes, the cave around her spun. Groaning, she shut her eyes. She heard low Russian voices. They were standing around her, talking about her, she was sure. Lauren forced her eyes open again. Five men stood in a half-circle around her. Watching her. Their faces were deeply shadowed in the cave's low light.

"She's bleeding," Petrov said. "What happened? I told you; I wanted her unharmed."

Volkov made a face. "She tried to escape. I had to tackle her. She hit her head on a tree root. She'll be fine."

Lauren felt her stomach revolt. She rolled onto her side, her knees coming up toward her body, retching violently.

Petrov snorted. "So much for being fine!" He jerked a look over at Morozov. "You're our medic. Take a look at her! Fix her!"

Nik nodded. He went to his gear, opened his ruck and drew out a large medical pack. The woman kept retching. It was a bad sign, but he said nothing. Grabbing a canteen of water and a washcloth, he stood and walked to her side. She was pale, gasping, and blood was still flowing freely from where she'd hit her head.

Petrov glared at Volkov. "You fool!" He walked over to where Morozov was kneeling. "You are in charge of her. We need to go out and create a false trail to lead that Special Forces team away from here. We'll be back in four hours."

"Yes, sir," Nik said.

"Let's go!" Petrov growled, waving the other three soldiers toward the tunnel that would lead them to the first cavern and then outside.

Nik leaned over the woman who lay on her side, eyes tightly shut, her hands pressed against her stomach. He touched her shoulder lightly. "I need to get you sitting up," he told her in English.

Lauren's eyes snapped open. The man looming over her was lean, but just as tall as Alex. She recognized him, but her mind was scrambled and she couldn't identify him. He looked awfully familiar to her. She felt his hand, tentative on her shoulder. He was dark-haired, his blue eyes narrowed upon her, his mouth thinned. "Y-you know English?" Her voice was raspy.

"I do. I'm Nik. Come, I must sit you up in order to help you," and he gently eased her into a sitting position. The woman weakly tried to sit up but he saw her blanch and then she started to pitch to the left. This wouldn't do. He stood up and hooked his elbows beneath her armpits and dragged her against the cave wall so it would support her. She grimaced and bit back a groan as he released her.

It helped for Lauren to close her eyes. Less dizziness. She felt his hand on her shoulder and cringed, trying to pull away.

"Open your eyes," he commanded. "I'm not going to hurt you. I need to you to drink some of this water. Slosh it around in your mouth and then spit it out to the left."

Lauren opened her eyes and saw him holding out a canteen toward her. She lifted her hands, wrapping them around the aluminum canteen. Her hands were shaky but she followed his directions, spitting out the water several times before her mouth felt clean. "Th-thank you," she whispered.

"Drink some," Morozov ordered, quickly daubing away the blood running down the right side of her face. His shoulders ached like fire from carrying her a good three miles at a constant trot through the jungle. Speed was of the essence. He knew the Special Forces Army team would quickly follow them. This was a risky venture in his mind. If Volkov had stopped talking about the woman in Aguas Calientes who had kicked his knee in and broke his thumb, Petrov would have ignored his limping. But Volkov's considerable ego had been deflated. By a woman. *Her.* Nik studied her. She was beautiful. She didn't look like an operator, but Volkov swore she was one. That was why Petrov, who had spotted her earlier today from their hiding place, had wanted to grab her. Was she a new breed of operator? Was the US sending women to do a man's job? Set traps for sex-hungry men who would never suspect them of being deadly agents?

Lauren handed the man his canteen back with a whispered thank you. She closed her eyes, feeling his gentle touch. Her mind refused to work. Why did he seem so familiar to her? Was he a combat medic like Alex? Did Alex know this man? She didn't know who else had been on his team. She tried to think. Tried to plan, but it was impossible. Every time she opened her eyes, the dizziness made her stomach roll.

"You hit your head badly," he informed her. Pulling on a pair of latex gloves, Morozov separated her hair, finding a good one-inch gash in her scalp. Scalp wounds always bled heavily. "I'm going to have to put stitching tape along it to stop the bleeding." He released her hair and crouched back on his heels, staring intently at her. "What is your name?"

"Lauren," she whispered. "I'm a botanist. I'm an American citizen." She turned her gaze up to his. "Please, let me go. I've done nothing to you. I don't even know why you did this." She had to play her role as a botanist. Just an American tourist on vacation. Morozov's lean, oval face softened a little. His eyes were well-spaced, intelligent-looking.

"It's not for me to decide anything," he told her gruffly. "Now, I'm going to give you a choice. I have to clean and tape-up your wound. If you promise to sit quietly while I do it, I will not cuff you again. But if you fight me, I will cuff your hands and your ankles. You're dangerous with those feet of yours."

"I'm so dizzy I couldn't move if I wanted," Lauren muttered, her voice low from the pain throbbing through her skull.

"Your word, Lauren?"

"Y-yes. My word…"

Morozov nodded. "You're a smart woman. Now, sit very still. I'm going to give you a shot of lydocaine around the cut so I can tape it up without causing you a lot more pain."

Lauren sat there feeling terror. It alternated with hope. She knew Alex would find her. He was a tracker. He knew his own kind. And, from what she could tell, there was no one but her and this man around. Where had the others gone? Would they come back? What were they going to do with her? Why had they captured her and not just killed her at pointblank range? Petrov must have a reason and that scared her even more.

CHAPTER 15

THE RAIN CONTINUED to fall. Alex was moving at a slow trot, water streaming down his face. He had his AK-47 gripped in his right hand. Behind him were Killmer, Cunningham and Merrill. It was close to dark, but he had his NVG's that they'd picked up for him. Alex knew he was a fast mover, but the Army operators caught up with him nonetheless, giving him his ruck and the rest of his gear to carry. It showed their toughness and how good a shape they were in. They were moving out with a hundred and twenty pounds on each of them. They didn't know how long they would be out here, but it didn't matter. All he could think of was Lauren. *Where was she? Alive? Dead? Being tortured? God, raped? No...* He went over in his mind who was still in Petrov's group. The ONLY possible aid that Lauren might get would be from his best friend in the team, Nik Morozov, IF he was with the group. The rest were animals. They would hurt Lauren without a second thought.

But why kidnap her? Why? His mind churned over the issue as his wet boots sunk into the squishy, soft leaves. They had risked a lot capturing her in broad daylight. Petrov wanted her for something. What?

"Let's take five," Killmer told him over the earphone.

Alex didn't want to slow down, but he knew from long experience that a body could recoup in five to ten minutes. He hadn't been drinking enough water, either. Turning back, he went to where the operators crowded in under a gigantic fallen log, sitting down to rest. They were all sucking water like camels. He did the same. With the AK-47 wet and gleaming across his thighs, Alex pushed up the bill of his baseball cap, the overhead log shielding them from getting even wetter.

Killmer shot him a look. "I've been wanting to know WHY they took Lauren."

Alex shook his head. "I do not know. The only thing I can think was that Lauren accidentally ran into Volkov in the grocery store in Aguas Calientes. He pinned her and she swung at him. She grabbed his thumb, breaking his hold on her, and then kicked his knee out from under him with her boot. He fell and she ran. That is why we left the town sooner than we wanted. I knew Petrov or any of his team could identify me on sight. And then, Volkov had to know she was not a tourist. If they saw either of us, we were marked. We left that night to hook up with you."

Rubbing his beard, Killmer muttered, "Volkov put it together, then. He figured out from the way she fought back that she was an operator. Not a civilian."

"That is what I think," Alex said, popping two salt tablets. Already, his calves were tight. Next would come cramps, so nasty that he wouldn't be able to walk. He looked around through the dusk.

"Why?" Killmer demanded. "To teach her a lesson? Torture her for information on why she's with us?"

"Possibly," Alex agreed, wanting to deny that any of that could happen, but could not.

"Well," Killmer grouched, "they made us. They were here and they could see all of us." He shook his head, angry with himself.

"They laid in wait," Alex agreed, drinking more water. He pulled a protein bar out of his cargo pants pocket. He had no intention of quitting this hunt until he found Lauren. If he had to track through the night alone, he'd do it.

"Look," Cale Merrill said. "maybe we're approaching this sideways? What if they grabbed Lauren to trap *us*? You know... they're leaving very easy tracks for us to follow."

"Yeah," Cunningham piped up. "I was thinking they could be setting up an ambush further ahead for us." He looked around. "We've never been in this area. We know nothing about this part of the jungle." He looked up at Alex. "Do you?"

"No. I have never been beyond this village. We always stuck to the known trails when I was with Alexandrov."

"Shit," Killmer growled. He downed two salt tablets, chewing on them, thinking. "There's five of them and four of us."

"Good odds," Alex said.

"But they have surprise on their side."

"Do you think they want to capture some of us?" Merrill posed.

"Yeah," Nate said. "Maybe they see us as trying to take their territory away from them? Make examples of us? Scare the U.S. into not sending more Army teams down here after they greet us, hang us in some tree limbs, strip us naked, take cell phone photos and post it all on YouTube?"

Alex looked around at their dirty, sweaty faces. "None of us want to be caught alive by them."

The heaviness and warning in his tone made all the operators grimace.

"I think they're setting a trap for the bigger prey: *us*," Killmer said. "They knew we'd come after Lauren. And they're hoping we'll go off half-cocked, over-emotional, and become distracted."

Alex said nothing, unable right now to control his own emotions where Lauren was concerned. The sergeant was right. Dead right.

Killmer looked at him. "What kind of ambushes do Spetsnaz like to set up?"

"Like the SEALs," he told the sergeant. "L-shape or Diamond. My bet is they will lay an L-shape ambush for us, if possible."

"That means it has to be in an area where they have one shooter looking straight at us and the other three on one side or the other of where we're coming in."

Alex nodded. "The land shape determines the place they chose."

"Then," Killmer grunted, pushing to his feet and shifting his ruck into a more comfortable position, "I need you on point. You're the only man here who is familiar with their ambush tactics. You know the kind of land they'd choose to set one up."

"Night is coming," Alex warned. "We will be moving slower. And I am going to have to stop if I see an area ahead that I think might be a trap." He didn't want to slow down. But he knew Petrov was a wily fox. It made more sense to him, now that they'd taken Lauren, that they would lay a trap for a larger prey: *them*.

"Fine, take your time," Killmer said.

"I WISH we had a map of this area," Cale bitched.

Killmer nodded. "Put a sock in it, Merrill. Let's saddle up," he growled.

VOLKOV LAY NEXT to Burak and Laskin in an L-shaped ambush. There was a small, rocky cliff rising out of the soggy ground to his left where Petrov sat dry beneath an overhang with his AK-47. The rain had stopped. They were lying on their bellies on dry, waterproof tarps, but their clothes were soaking wet. His skin was goose-bumped, the temperature dropping. He thought about the red-haired bitch in the cave. Morozov had better patch her up good because he had plans for her. Smiling in the dark, Volkov thought about how he was going to claim her, rape her in front of everyone. He would teach her to kick him in the knee and break this thumb, and embarrass him in front of his team. Chances were, though, Petrov would trump him and claim his right as leader, to take her first. He wanted to feel her soft flesh in his hands, spread her legs, and then take her hard, hear her cry out in pain. Petrov liked doing the same thing, dammit. If only their leader would let him have this woman first! Perhaps he could make the argument to Petrov that it was revenge and, therefore, that first claim belonged to him. She had injured his pride. His reputation. And he had a right to extract his revenge on her as a result. Would Petrov buy his reason? He was still limping a little on his knee. He'd been lucky the bitch hadn't cracked his knee cap.

Wiping his wet face, Volkov wondered how long it would be until that traitor, Kazak, and those three Special Forces soldiers would fall stupidly into their trap. They knew how to track at night. And Petrov had left plenty of easy tracks for them to follow. Sooner or later, they'd stumble into their ambush. It was dark and miserable out. They'd be humping a lot of weight, and the jungle humidity always wrung a man dry in a hurry. Dehydration played tricks on the mind, on perception, on visual acuity. Especially at night.

It had been a shock to Volkov to have discovered Kazak among the American black ops team. He was a traitor. Volkov had wanted to put a bullet through his head right then and there but Petrov, the cooler head, had prevailed. He'd come up with this scheme. Petrov had been ordered by Yerik Alexandrov, while in mourning over his son's death, to put a hit out on Kazak. And whoever made that hit would receive a million U.S. dollars. Sadly, Yerik had been killed in Costa Rica by an American black ops hunter-killer team. Volkov had heard that Alexandrov's empire was in disarray in New York City. That four top mafia leaders, all Georgians, were fighting among themselves, to become the new leader. Petrov was Georgian. He felt he stood a good chance that, if he took out Kazak, and brought photos of the kill to the new leader, he would be paid well for his efforts. Russian or Georgian, it didn't matter. Traitors were hated by all of them. They were killed. But first, they were tortured. And Volkov couldn't wait to get his hands on that bastard: Kazak. Who would regret the day he was born.

LAUREN SLEPT DESPITE her predicament. As she slowly awoke, she realized the cave was dark and she couldn't see anything. Morozov had given her a low dose of morphine because she had been in agony, the pain in her head so bad that she couldn't speak. Now, as she lay still, listening, sensing, Lauren had a dull headache, but that was all. Morozov had been gentle with her. He'd expertly taped shut the cut on her scalp. The bleeding had stopped. Lauren slowly lifted a hand toward her tender scalp, feeling the gauze dressing over it, the bandage wrapped firmly around her head.

She finally remembered who Morozov was, her mind starting to work once more. Alex and Nik were best friends. She remembered Alex telling her once that they had both grown up on nearby farms. Alex didn't have a brother, but had confided to her that, if he could have chosen one, then Nik would have been his younger brother. There was a year's difference in age between them. Did she dare tell Nik about Alex? Did they see him at the village, too? She had no idea how long they had been lying in wait, watching them. Lauren shivered, her clothes damp.

Something moved nearby. She froze.

"It's only me, Nik," he told her gruffly. "How do you feel?"

Relief sped through Lauren. "I don't know yet." She felt him close, still unable to see him. He had to be wearing NVG's. She heard a match being struck, the light suddenly illuminating the area. She saw Morozov kneeling nearby, lighting a kerosene lamp sitting near the wall. The cave slowly revealed itself and she blinked, realizing her vision had cleared. Morozov's face was deeply shadowed. He sported a beard, making his lean face look stony. He looked exhausted. She watched him rise with the same male grace that Alex possessed. Much leaner than Alex, but he still had Alex's height. She watched him come over and kneel next to her.

Picking up her wrist, Nik felt her pulse, avoiding her gaze, looking down at the ground.

"Good, your pulse is returning to normal." He pulled something out of his cammo jacket. "Can you sit up? I need to see how your pupils are reacting."

Lauren slowly pushed up into a sitting position, feeling a lot stronger than before. "What time is it?"

"Ten p.m."

"I slept a long time…"

He put his fingers beneath her chin, holding her still. "Stare at my nose."

Lauren almost smiled, remembering Alex speaking nearly these same exact words to her. His touch wasn't harsh, but gentle instead. His straight eyebrows drew down, his shadowed, blue eyes intent under them as he moved the light slowly back and forth across her eyes. His mouth pursed and he released her chin, getting up, stepping away from her.

"You have a level-two concussion," he said, his voice flat.

Lauren watched him walk away, to one end of the huge, oval cave. She felt a breeze moving through it and shivered. She laid her back against the cave wall, bringing her knees up against herself. Morozov opened up a large green canvas bag. He drew out what appeared to be two blankets.

"Now," he said, tossing them down next to her, "get warm."

Grateful, she whispered, "Thank you." Dizziness overtook her and Lauren closed her eyes, not moving for a moment.

"There's no need to tie you up," he remarked, going back to the same bag. "You couldn't take two steps without falling over. If I were you, I wouldn't think about trying it."

Lauren had to keep her cover. Pulling one blanket across her shoulder, and draping the other over her drawn-up legs, she felt warmer immediately.

"Please, I'm an American. I'm here on vacation—"

Morozov gave a harsh laugh. "Really?" He stood and walked back toward her, something in his hands. Crouching down near her, eyeing her with amusement, he said, "Then why are you wearing a hog's tooth? I don't think many civilians go around with one. Do you?"

Her heart squeezed with fear. Lauren stared at him. Morozov was grinning and he shook his head.

"You are a sniper, Lauren. A Marine Corps Recon sniper if I don't miss my guess. What? You think we're stupid? I was Spetsnaz black ops. It takes one to know one." His smile disappeared.

"Who else knows?" Lauren asked, her voice low and urgent.

Shrugging, Morozov said, "Only me. I saw it as I was taping up your scalp wound."

"What are you going to do with this information?"

He shook his head. "I don't know. Not yet." He handed her a half a loaf of bread and took out his knife and cut a block of cheese in half. "Here, you need to eat. Keep up your strength."

Lauren gratefully accepted his food. "Thank you…"

Morozov sat down, cross-legged, near her feet. "You don't look like an operator, but from what Volkov told us, you are one." He grinned a little. "You're the first person I've ever known to take him down. He's a CQC, close quarters combat, specialist." His grin widened as he tore off a piece of the bread with his teeth. "Couldn't have happened to a better person. And then, to make this even better, you, a woman, did it to Volkov," and he laughed quietly, enjoying the joke.

Lauren found herself ravenous. The cheese was salty. Pure fat and protein; something that would fuel her body, pour strength back into her. The bread was old and very dry, but it would fill her up. She watched the Ukrainian eat, his gaze never in one place too long, listening, sensing, like all operators always did. She felt that Morozov was basically a kind person. For whatever reason she wasn't afraid of him. Maybe because Alex had spoken so warmly and fondly about him.

"So, I know," Nik murmured, "you won't admit to anything to me about that hog's tooth." His brow fell. "They will torture you, rape you, and you will die, Lauren. It will not be a pleasant death for you."

Her throat tightened and she stared into his bleak gaze. He seemed upset by this outcome. Did he have that much conscience left within him to feel sympathy for her? An ounce of humanity still left within Morozov? Hope flared in her. She finished off the cheese, rubbing her hands against the wool blanket. "Then let me go."

"And be killed by them for letting you escape?" he scoffed.

"I think you care, Nik," Lauren began softly, holding his stare. "I don't think you want to see me hurt by your team. Do you?" She held her breath, watching his eyes come alive with confusion, anger and frustration.

"It cannot be."

"Where did your team go?"

He shook his head. "You have balls. You're the one who is the prisoner. You're not to ask questions. You are to answer them."

She felt that he was just waffling. It wasn't anything obvious. Just the tone in his voice. Lauren wasn't sure what to do. If the rest of the Russian team came back, she knew she was going to die. It was only a question of when, not if. And did Alex or Killmer know where she was? Were they tracking her?

Looking at him, she whispered, "If you saw me in the village, then you saw Alex Kazak. Didn't you?"

He twitched uncomfortably, glared at her and then got up, moving back to the same opened canvas bag across the cave.

Licking her lips, Lauren felt thirsty, her throat dry. Her heart was pounding. The urgency to try and convince Morozov that he should help her had never been as real as it was in this moment. He walked back, a bottle of water in each hand.

"Here, drink this."

She took it. "Why are you helping me? If they're coming back to kill me, why did you tape me up? Why are you feeding me? Giving me blankets to keep me warm? Tell me why, Nik?"

He sat down, considering her low, urgent questions. He opened one bottle of water and drank deeply, his adam's apple bobbing. When he finished it off, he wiped his mouth with the back of his sleeve. "It's my duty. I'm a medic. I give comfort and help to friend and enemy alike."

He sounded so much like Alex that it drove unexpected tears to Lauren's eyes. She was embarrassed, quickly wiping them away. When she looked up, Morozov's face was shockingly readable. He looked upset. Uncertain. He pushed his long fingers through his short hair in an aggravated motion. "You know Alex?"

She gave a bare nod, unsure of where this conversation was going to lead. Nik stared at her, as if trying to read her mind. Or at least, that is what it felt like. Lauren also didn't want to give away any intel to him. Morozov was potentially her enemy despite his friendship with Alex. She knew he was undercover with the CIA. Would he protect her? Help her escape if she told him more?

"Alex and I grew up together," he told her in a low tone, shaking his head.

"He is… was… like a brother to me. We were best of friends. He always had my back when we worked together." His mouth turned into a slash and he lifted his head, his voice roughening. "I deeply miss him to this day."

The heart-rending emotion she heard in his raw voice startled Lauren. She folded her hands, feeling sympathy for the man. Nik's eyes were alive with strife, indecision and grief. Taking a huge leap of faith, Lauren whispered, "He joined the Russian mafia to make money so his sister, Kira, could get psychological help after she'd been gang-raped, Nik. He didn't like doing it, but he felt a love and loyalty to his sister. He did it for her."

Jerking his chin up, Nik's eyes widened. "How could you know this?"

Fear snaked through her. How much to say? Or not? But there was something about Nik that made Lauren believe he could help her escape. She strengthened her voice. "Because Alex told me."

Blinking, Nik looked away, the silence deepening between them. He rubbed his wrinkled brow. "Then you know him?"

"Alex saved two of my best friends' lives, Nik," she told him quietly. "Do you remember a young, blond-haired woman named Sky?"

He reared back. "Why yes. She was an American! My commander, Vlad Alexandrov, was deeply in love with her. Or so he said. He had an obsession with her."

Lauren tried to keep her face neutral. "Vlad captured her."

"Yes, I was there later, at the village. Alex and I rescued her."

"Then you know, after her capture, that Sky fell ill with malaria? Alex said you helped care for her."

'Yes, yes of course. I got the IV's for Alex while he cared for Sky in that hut. I went and got him the chicken soup that he asked me to get for her. We tried to protect her from Vlad, who wanted to rape her whether she was sick or not. Alex stopped him from doing it."

Her fingers tightened. "Alex said you played an equal part in helping care for Sky. You did a good thing, Nik. You're a hero in my eyes." She saw Nik's eyes widen with disbelief. And then Lauren saw him grow confused.

With a curse, Nik leaped up, pacing the cave. His hands were behind his back, his head down.

Lauren felt shaky with urgency to turn Nik so he would help her escape. She wasn't dizzy any longer. Watching him pace for a few minutes, she could see the struggle, the anger and questions in his face. Finally, Nik halted, and stared across the grayness of the cavern toward her. He stalked like a predator toward her, his eyes slit.

Lauren tensed, feeling the intensity in him as he came close, kneeling down on one knee, right up in her face. He was breathing unevenly.

"You tell me the TRUTH. Now! Don't lie. If you do, I swear, I'll stand aside and let Petrov have his way with you."

"What do you want to know?" Lauren demanded, her voice husky with emotion.

"How could you know so much about Kira? I know Alex well. He told NO ONE about his sister being gang-raped! I had to pull the story out of him. He was that grief-stricken when he returned to our team."

Lauren held his agitated gaze. "Because I love him, Nik. We love one another. He told me everything." She waited, expecting him to curse once more. He froze, his eyes widening, the emotions flowing within them so many that she couldn't possibly begin to interpret them. Then, slowly, he rocked back on his heels, covering his face, rubbing it savagely with his hands.

This information she'd just shared with him could damn her to certain death. Morozov could tell Petrov everything she'd just confided in him. It would make the Russians hate her even more, if that was possible. Nik knew about her hog's tooth, that she was a sniper, and that she was part of a black ops team. And, with that last piece of information, her life was completely in his hands. Lauren had to risk it, had to hope Nik was still enough of a friend of Alex's to help her.

"Tell me why," Nik gritted out between clenched teeth, "that I should help you escape?"

Lauren didn't waver her eye contact with him. "Because Alex is your best friend. He talks of you often, Nik. He knows you're undercover with the DOD and the CIA. You were tired of your team raping women, hurting children, as he was. It sickened both of you, Nik. It would sicken anyone who had half a heart, *don't you think?*" Lauren hurled the last three words in a low, emotional tone.

Morozov winced. He released a ragged sigh, hanging his head, looking down at his hands. "What is the truth here?" he muttered. He jerked his head up and stared at her. "You know things about Alex and myself that no one else but we know."

"You helped save two people's lives in that village, Nik. Alex and you worked together as a team to make it happen."

"That is the truth. Alex knew if Sky remained there after she got over her malaria attack, that Vlad would rape her."

"And so, Alex was a part of a very strategic plan, that included you, to get Sky to safety." She saw weariness fade into Nik's eyes, his mouth thinning.

"Who shot Alex in the calf, then?"

"An American operator." Lauren wasn't about to give out Cal's name. She would protect her team no matter what.

Nik thought this over. "Alex sent me and the team north of the village, saying the American woman had escaped that way."

"And when you couldn't find her," Lauren said, "Alexandrov came back and nearly beat Alex to death. He was left lying on that hut floor, Nik, bleeding out. No one, not even YOU, could help him. If an American Special Forces team hadn't arrived later...," and her voice cracked, her hands curling into fists. "They stopped the bleeding. If they hadn't been there, he'd have died. They saved his life."

Wincing, Nik whispered, "I WANTED to help him," he growled. "But my commander was angry. He had a gun held to Alex's head. Did you know that? Alex was unconscious. I was the one who distracted my commander. I came forward, took a great chance with my own life, and told him to let him die of that slow bleed. That Alex was bleeding out at such a rate, that he would die anyway." Breathing hard, Morozov added, "I lied to save his life! Alex was bleeding, there was no question. But I was praying... hoping... that he would regain consciousness and would know what to do to stop the loss." His voice cracked. "I did what I could. If I'd begged my commander to help him, he'd have turned around, shot me in the head and then shot Alex. He was that angry. I did what I could for my friend, hoping against hope that there was an American team somewhere in the area searching for Sky."

"I didn't know that... Alex didn't either..."

"He was unconscious at the time, so he couldn't know," Nik breathed, his hand knotted on his thigh. "I found out later. When the CIA agent contacted me in Aguas Calientes and asked me to become a mole in Petrov's Russian team, he answered some of my questions about Alex. Until that day, I didn't know that he'd survived." He stared morosely around the dark, shadowy cave. His voice grew hoarse. "Petrov blames Alex for everything." He wiped his furrowed brow and muttered, "Right now they lay in an ambush, waiting to lure Alex into it. Your kidnapping was a ruse, Lauren. You were bait. Petrov wants Kazak. Not you..."

Lauren gave a little cry, her eyes locked on Morozov's dark, grief-stricken stare. His mouth was twisted, as if trying to hold back a barrage of terrible emotions. Nik was Alex's best friend. She could see he still cared deeply for him. That he didn't want this terrible ambush to go down. Oh, God, what was he going to do? What could SHE do?

CHAPTER 16

MOROZOV HAD TO think. He stared down at Lauren. "I'll be back. Don't try to escape because you won't be able to." He stalked out of the cave, moving swiftly down another tunnel. His emotions were being torn apart. The look on the woman's face had been abject terror. People undercover could frequently be good actors, but Nik had ten years' experience as an operator and was able to discern play-acting from real-time visceral actions and reactions. And Lauren was as real as they got. Pushing his hand roughly through his short hair, he pulled up the NVG's over his eyes as he stalked down the breezy tunnel between the two caves.

He walked out of the smaller cave, and could smell the dank humidity and hear the plopping of drops on the wide canopy leaves far above him. It had stopped raining, at least for the moment. He stood at the cave mouth, hands on his hips, his mind whirling with options. Alex was in love with Lauren. Before today, he had had no idea that Alex had finally found the woman who held his heart. Nik felt relief. Maybe even joy for him. He and Alex had worked side-by-side for seven years in Spetsnaz. And, growing up, Alex had always been like a brother to him.

Looking up into the darkness, Nik dragged in a deep breath. He knew where Petrov was setting up the ambush. It would only be a matter of time until Alex, and the Special Forces men with him, would fall into it. Rubbing his jaw, he paced. If he threw in his lot with Alex, tried to find him on this wet night, to warn him off, then he would be considered a traitor by his Russian team. His undercover job would be finished. Blown. His loyalty for the CIA warred with his concern for Alex and, now, Lauren. Petrov had never forgiven Kazak for abandoning them. And his leader had nearly revealed their recon position within the jungle earlier today as they overlooked Kurmi. They hadn't expected American black ops coming into the village. It had merely been a recon to watch and see what the villagers were doing. Petrov wanted the stubborn chief to work with him and, so far, he'd resisted. And that had pissed Petrov off. They had hidden and watched silently to learn more.

Morozov remembered the shock he'd felt, looking through a spotter scope as the Americans had come off the trail and walked into the village. He'd heard Petrov snarl a low curse, vowing to get Alex, one way or another. Their entire objective had changed in those moments when Kazak had been spotted.

What was he going to do now?

This woman was in LOVE with Alex. Her tears were real. The look in her eyes ripped at him. Nik didn't question she had fallen in love with his friend. So much had happened in the last six months.

If he threw caution away, decided to try and find Alex before Petrov found him, he'd be seen as a traitor. The money he was earning would be gone.

And yet, as he stood there, feeling as if his whole life had shattered apart moments ago, his conscience wouldn't allow him to sit idly by, either. God, there were so many variables in play! He could end up getting shot by Kazak and his men. They'd shoot first and ask questions later. Lifting his chin, Nik thought about the woman in the cave. Was she ambulatory? Could she walk? He couldn't leave her alone in the cave, prey to Petrov and his men. IF they survived the firefight, they would naturally come back to the cave where all their food supplies and weapons caches were stored. And they'd find Lauren and rape and torture her.

Shaking his head, Nik realized he'd already made his decision. But, until he went back to see if Lauren could walk, could leave this cave, he wasn't sure of anything. He turned, trotting through the cave system and down the tunnel. Pulling down his NVG's, unneeded due to the lamp light flooding the second cave, his gaze moved to Lauren. She was sitting there, wiping her eyes, trying to stop crying.

Lauren jerked her head up, hearing a noise to her left. She saw Nik Morozov stalk grimly into the cave. His eyes were alive with raw emotion. His face unreadable, mouth set. She tried to think. To plead for Alex's life. Morozov came over, thrusting out his hand toward her.

"Get up!"

Lauren pulled the blanket off her legs. She struggled to her feet, a little wobbly, her hand moving to the cave wall to steady herself as she straightened up. He was glaring at her.

"Walk! Now!"

She pulled the blanket around her shoulders and took a few steps. Miraculously, she wasn't dizzy. She walked halfway across the cave.

"Halt!"

Turning, she stared at him. "What are you doing?" she demanded. He looked as if he were going to explode, his narrowed eyes flashing, his mouth a hard line. He suddenly moved toward her.

"We must hurry," Nik growled. "Get rid of the blanket. You're coming with me." He hurried over to the weapons bag, hauling on his bulletproof vest, grabbing a second set of NVG's and tossing them in her direction. "Wear these. I'm sure you know how to use them."

Lauren caught the NVG's. "What are you doing?" she whispered, hope rising with her fear. He pulled out the pistol he'd taken from her earlier along with an AK-47.

"I'm going to TRY and find Kazak before he steps into Petrov's trap," Morozov muttered. He gave her a stripping glance. "And you are going to have to keep up with me. I can't leave you here. Petrov will come back here sooner or later. He'll rape and then kill you."

Her heart jammed in her throat. Tears blinded her as she quavered, "You're going to help warn Alex?"

Morozov shook his head. "It's probably too late. But I have to try…" He had not been expecting the woman to throw her arms around him, hugging him. If he'd had any doubts as to where her loyalty lay, he knew now, unquestionably, it was with Alex. Technically, they were enemies. And enemies didn't hug one another. He gripped her arms, pulling her away, seeing tears streak down her face. "I will do what I can," he rasped, giving her a small shake. "It's a hard run, two miles from here. Do you think you can make it? Keep up with me?"

"I'll die trying," Lauren whispered, taking the pistol. She swallowed hard, holding his glittering gaze. "Thank you for trusting me, Nik. I hope Alex will know of your loyalty to him. He loves you very much. He never stopped loving you as a brother. You need to know that." She quickly unsafed the pistol, and checked the chamber to make sure a bullet was in it.

"He deserves you, he deserves to live and have a happy life," Nik muttered. He tossed her a jacket. "Put this on. It's Russian. I need to make you look like one of us so Petrov and his men won't shoot at you."

It was a smart idea. Lauren quickly hauled the too-big cammo jacket over her shoulders.

"Do you have a vest?" Nik demanded, shrugging into his own cammo jacket.

"Yes. You?"

"Always."

The urgency thrummed through Lauren. She felt okay, but not great. Her head ached a little. She watched him quickly gather up a bunch of AK-47 magazines, stuffing them into the pockets of his jacket. His face was set, he was gearing up for battle. He threw her a black balaclava.

"Wear it as soon as we leave this cave. Your white face will stand out and get noticed."

Tearing through the gear, Nik located a dark green baseball cap, throwing it in her direction. "Spetsnaz cap," he muttered, digging some more.

Lauren said nothing, standing and letting him dress her up like a Russian soldier. "What's your plan?" she demanded.

Morozov tossed her a pair of gloves. "Wear them."

Lauren pulled them on, fitting her hands. Morozov leaned down, pulling out another AK-47. He handed it to her.

"Have you ever used one?"

"I'm familiar with them." Lauren hefted the dark green metal rifle. It was one of the toughest, most reliable rifles of the last sixty years. It would not jam in rain, snow, or desert heat. She quickly went through the motions of making sure the selector was set for single shot, not semi-automatic or automatic. The curved metal clip held a lot of bullets, but Morozov handed her six more magazines which she stuffed into the pockets of her baggy cammo jacket.

Nik straightened up; his face taut. "Here's the plan," he told her. "I'm dousing the kerosene lamp. We'll put on NVG's. Once we're outside, you need to hold onto my belt: here," and he lifted his jacket, pointing to the dark green nylon belt around his waist. "You're going to shadow me by holding onto my belt. We won't talk." He latched a radio onto the inside of her jacket lapel and handed her the earpiece. "Well, we could, but I prefer you click your radio instead. That way, no one will hear us."

"Is this radio tuned to Petrov's frequency?" Lauren asked, worried.

Nik snorted. "Good question." And then he gave her a look of admiration. "You know your business." He had forgotten that detail. A detail that could have alerted Petrov to their escape, thereby blowing their cover.

Lauren unlatched the radio, handing it back to him to reprogram. Morozov would know what frequency to put it on. "I won't let you down," she promised him quietly, meeting his eyes. She could feel the adrenaline starting to leak into her bloodstream. It made her restless, wanting to move, to get on with it. Every minute they wasted could possibly be putting Alex and the spec ops team in greater danger.

Morozov gave a nod, and replaced the radio, making sure it was secure inside her jacket. "Put the earpiece in," he ordered. He made several clicks to test their connection.

"Hear them?"

"Yes," Lauren said. "What else in your plan?"

"We have no way of knowing where Alex or the others are at." He pulled up a sniper scope. "This one has infrared capability." He handed it to her. "Every once in a while, when we can find higher elevation, I'll want you to scan the area for body heat. It's the only way we'll know who is around and where they are located."

"Brilliant," Lauren murmured. She tucked the scope into a pocket of her cammo jacket and then buttoned it closed to protect it from the rain she was sure would come, sooner or later. She watched him gear-up. The last thing Morozov strapped on was a knife sheath, on his right lower leg. "Do you have another knife?" she wondered.

"Yes," and he dug into the gear bag, produced one with a sheath, and handed it to her.

Quickly, Lauren strapped it on her left lower leg. It was a Russian knife and she wasn't familiar with it, but it was better than nothing. "What are you planning on doing once you reach their ambush site?"

"Nothing," he said flatly. "I want to angle away from it and try to find your friends on the only feeder trail that leads to the caves. They will be on it, no question. We need to try and stop them from walking into the trap."

Lauren nodded. She could sense that if he didn't have to kill anyone, he wouldn't. Maybe it was a medic thing. He could be friends with some of the other Russians, too. Morozov was trying to avert a bloodbath. "Then you're going to backtrack? Because I know Alex is a tracker. He'll be following those tracks."

"Exactly," Nik breathed, rolling his shoulders. "But he's not stupid. He'll know there's the possibility of an ambush, too. I hope we can locate them before it's too late…"

"I do too," Lauren whispered.

"Ready?"

"Yes."

Giving her a brisk nod, Nik swept past her. The AK-47 was in his gloved hand. Lauren put on her NVG's and waited until the kerosene lamp was turned off. She flicked them on, everything becoming green, grainy and very dark. NVG's work through ambient light, and there wasn't much in the cave.

"Nik?"

"Yes?"

"I'm ready." Lauren heard him approaching her. He found her gloved hand and placed it on his belt. She wrapped her fingers around it.

"Let's go," he said.

He had a damn long stride and Lauren had to nearly trot to keep up with him. She wasn't about to ask him to slow down. They had to save Alex and the Special Forces soldiers. Were they too late? That urgency she'd heard in Nik's gruff voice filtered through her. Once they were outside, her NVG's suddenly lit up and she could easily see everything around them.

"Stay close," Nik growled. "Try to keep my rhythm," and he took off at a fast trot across the wet, soggy ground outside the cave.

Carrying the AK-47 with her left hand, Lauren clung to the nylon belt with her right. Morozov moved like a shadow, making absolutely no sound as he stretched his stride out, locating the original tracks and trail. She nearly stumbled on an exposed root, and gripped his belt tighter. He slowed down, allowing her to get her feet under her once more.

"How are you doing?" he demanded after switching to a private frequency over the radio.

"Okay," she huffed, following him up a slight incline before it leveled off and they were once again dodging in and out around tree trunks.

"Your head? Dizzy? Headache?"

"No... I'm fine..." And then, she heard the dark humor in his returning growl.

"Adrenaline works wonders...."

She nearly laughed; nerves taut. It wasn't funny, but it was typical military black humor. Now on level ground, the medic set a blistering pace. She was running, not jogging. He was jogging easily, like a long-distance marathon runner. The terror of losing Alex fueled her and Lauren maintained the pace, her breath starting to come in gasps, but she didn't ask Morozov to slow down. They HAD to reach Alex and the Special Forces team in time!

Lauren didn't want to think about the possible outcome facing them. She would be forever grateful to Nik for believing her. For still having loyalty to Alex.

They moved silently, backtracking, their boots wet, squishiness with each step. Lauren felt the loping stride of Morozov, who was in extraordinarily top shape; a warrior athlete. She, more than most, knew what it took to be in this kind of condition. The longer they jogged, the more she was able to create an in-sync rhythm with him. She felt Morozov slow down. Unable to keep looking around, she kept her gaze fixed on the earth in front of her. She couldn't risk stumbling or falling. The noise could attract the wrong people.

They breasted a slope forested with the thin trunks of many trees. It hid them. She felt Nik grip her shoulder as she released his belt, panting, mouth wide, trying to lessen the sounds.

"Lay down," he ordered her over the radio. "Get out the scope."

Lauren knelt on the spongy ground, her knees instantly becoming wet and muddy. She tore off one glove with her teeth as she pulled out the scope and fumbled, finding where the switch was at to turn it on. It was a Russian scope and she wasn't familiar with their operation.

"Start left, pan right."

"Roger." Lauren grimaced. It was like they were a team. An odd couple, for sure, but they were both military-trained and the jargon came as easy as breathing. She tried to slow down her pounding heart. Heard Morozov sucking on his CamelBak, hydrating himself. Holding the scope up, the green cross-hairs in the circle, she found another dial and lowered the intensity of the brightness. Lauren placed the scope against a tree trunk to steady it and began to slowly pan.

As she did, her mind spiraled into doubts. What if Nik was leading her directly to Petrov? Was this a way to get her killed along with the ambush they'd set for the others?

No. She either trusted the medic or she didn't. And she had no way of knowing the truth. A small voice within told her he would never have given her weapons she could use against him if this was all a trap. Lauren knew that, and steadied her breathing, panning, hoping against hope she'd locate the four heat signatures that would indicate Alex and the soldiers.

"Nothing," she rasped, lowering the scope.

"We should have run into them by now," Morozov rasped, concerned.

"Did Petrov create another trail that would have led them toward the ambush?"

"Yes," Morozov admitted, his voice tight with tension.

"What does this mean?" Lauren demanded, feeling fear clutch her heart. "That they've already peeled off on that trail and they're moving toward the ambush?"

"Yes," he said, frustration in his tone. He slowly stood up. "Now we must run half a mile back, the same way. There's the ambush trail at that point. We will follow that and pray we are not too late to warn them..."

Lauren stowed the scope inside her cammo jacket and buttoned it up, her fingers trembling as she pulled on the glove. "We'll be coming up behind them. That could make them think they're being attacked from their six. They could turn and fire on us."

"I've thought of that." Morozov shrugged. "There's nothing we can do. We must hurry. You must give this your all. Run as hard as you can..."

"Do Petrov and his men have any infrared scopes among them?"

"Yes. Do you know if the Special Forces has one?"

"I don't know," Lauren lamented. She rearranged the balaclava. It had shifted as she'd ran.

"Come. No time to waste."

"How long is that trail to the ambush site?"

"Only half a mile," he said grimly.

Lauren gripped his belt, and turned swiftly. He nearly flew down the small slope, no longer trying to cut his stride for her sake. Alex and the Army team were on the ambush trail!

They tore down the slope. They had half a mile before they could branch off to the real trail to try and catch up with them. Lauren stumbled, nearly fell, crashing into Morozov's back. He slowed, grabbing her by the arm, preventing her from going down. She bit back a cry, feeling his strong arms lift her to her feet.

Gasping, Lauren gripped his arm. "Go! You're faster than I am! You HAVE to get to them! You won't make it with me along." She felt him tense.

"Very well. Come as fast as you can. The trail is easy to find. Bear left."

Nodding, Lauren whispered raggedly as she thrust the scope into his hands. "Just go! Hurry!"

Without another word, Morozov whirled around, running swiftly down the trail. Lauren dug her boots into the soft leaves, racing after him. She didn't have the stride of a man who was taller than her, but she wasn't weak, either. Wind tore past her as she kept her eyes on the path. Soon enough, she lost sight of Morozov as the land dipped and sloped downward.

Hurry! Hurry! Lauren gulped draughts of air into her burning lungs, pushing herself. If they didn't arrive in time, Alex and the soldiers would be ambushed and killed.

Lauren tried to brace herself for gunfire. She knew what an ambush was designed to do. And these were Spetsnaz-trained men who aimed and killed for target mass. And they didn't miss. She grabbed the AK-47 into both hands, unsafing it, knowing there was a round in the chamber, worrying that if Morozov moved silently up behind Alex and the soldiers, they might become startled, turn and shoot him. He was dressed as a Russian. They wouldn't hesitate. Oh, God, this was a mess!

Lauren spotted the path off to the left and she sped up, digging her boots in, unable to see anyone ahead of her. The land dipped again into a series of rolling slopes. If the firing began, none of the AK-47's had muzzle suppressors. The flashes of fire from the bullets ripping out of the barrel would be easy to spot. It would show the position of the shooter. She knew Alex also carried an AK-47. The Special Forces might have muzzle suppressors on their rifles. She didn't know. It made them much less of a target to find, unlike a rifle with no suppressor. It was practically like waving a flashlight and saying, "Over here! I'm over here!" She groaned inwardly, breath tearing in and out of her mouth. Her body was dripping with sweat, the canvas clothing rubbing her raw here and there. Adrenaline pushed her ahead. The terror of losing Alex, him being killed, made Lauren want to call out for him.

If he heard her voice, he'd stop.

But then, if they were too close to the ambush, Petrov would hear her too.

Lauren realized, with a sinking feeling, that if she yelled out, it would only draw attention their attention to her. And then bullets from both friendlies and enemy, would come her way. All it would do was set off the firefight. And she wouldn't live to see who won.

For a second, Lauren glimpsed Morozov cresting another hill. He was running hard, running straight into the fray without regard for his own safety. She was gasping for breath, burning in her leg muscles as she pushed herself beyond her limits. If only Alex knew his best friend was coming to try and rescue him. *Again.* She would never forget Nik Morozov. Not ever. He was a brave man in a terrible dilemma. And yet, his heart remained true and utterly loyal to his friend. Despite everything, Morozov was heroic. Years of combat had not killed his morals, integrity or values. He'd retained them just as Alex had. She wanted everyone to survive. No one to get hurt. But she knew that was idealism, not reality. They were racing head-on into a firefight that would take lives, tear men's bodies apart and there would be death.

As she ran, Lauren ripped off the dark gloves, needing her fingers free. She reached down as she ran, slipping off the safety strap across her Glock 19. She wanted that pistol free so she could reach down and pull it swiftly out of the drop holster. The downward slope speeded her up. One more hill! She was slowly catching up to Morozov. How much time had elapsed? Had they run half a mile yet? She had no idea, feeling as if the world were holding its breath. Waiting. Waiting…

CHAPTER 17

I T WAS ABOUT to become a deadly game of chess. Alex lay next to Killmer, an infrared scope on his sniper rifle. They lay on a slight slope thirty feet above the rest of the land below, between two spindly jungle trees. The ground was soft and wet. Alex sensed Petrov was near. It wasn't anything factual he could point to. Just a feeling. And he'd never not pay attention to such an instinct.

"There they are," Killmer said in a low voice over the radio. The other two operators were covering opposite directions, making sure no one could sneak up on their position. "Four tangos." Killmer handed Alex the rifle. "Take a look. Pan left to right. First tango is sitting under a rock overhang."

Alex pulled down his NVG's. He settled the butt of the .300 Win-Mag rifle against his shoulder, he was glad he'd been working with American weapons the last three months. They were different in small, but important, ways from Russian weapons. Placing his eye about an inch away from the Night Force scope, Alex could see heat signature on a man who was sitting down. The scope couldn't show fine details, so Alex couldn't identify him. What he could see was that the man's hands were resting on something across his thighs. A rifle gave off no heat unless it was fired and the barrel was hot. Nonetheless, Alex was sure it was an AK-47 resting across the man's lap. He then scanned slowly to the right and picked up three more heat signatures. It was a classic L-shape ambush.

"It's them," he confirmed lowly. They were only three hundred yards away from the ambush point. Whispers could be picked up far more easily than a person speaking in a low tone of voice. "Four. Not five." Where was the fifth man?

"Might be with Lauren?" Killmer suggested. "Holding her prisoner?"

Alex grimaced. In one way, it was a good sign that Lauren was still alive. One of the soldiers had sentry duty over her. "Yes. My friend, Nik Morozov, is the medic for this team. He could be with her." He couldn't afford to allow his writhing emotions to rise within him. It would distract him. If it was Nik, that could mean Lauren was safe. Or injured. All Alex could do was hope his friend had the woman he loved with him.

"Would he bring her out to the ambush?" the sergeant asked.

"Doubtful. It is a gun-and-run situation. They cannot move fast with a captive."

"Would Morozov help Lauren to escape?" Mace demanded.

"If he could, he would," Alex confirmed. "But we do not know her condition. She could be injured and non-ambulatory." He hated admitting that as a possibility.

Grunting softly, Killmer nodded. The humidity was heavy. The breeze sluggish. He wiped his camouflaged face lightly, trying to stop the worst of the sweat from dripping down into his eyes.

Alex continued to pan right, wanting to make sure no more heat signatures were in the area. Would Petrov use Lauren as a decoy, possibly? Tied to a tree somewhere? Lure them in and then hammer them? He put nothing past the wily Russian leader. But if that was so? Then where was Nik? Petrov knew they would come for Lauren. Was she hurt? Suffering? Beaten by them? He closed his eyes, battling his anguish and worry. Such emotions had no place here. *Not now.* He had to think clearly. Killmer was relying on his knowledge of Russian ambush tactics. Alex couldn't screw this up and get them in trouble.

Suddenly, he halted his pan. There was another heat signature! And it was moving slowly forward, toward the ambush site.

"What?" Killmer asked.

"A fifth person." His heart sank. Oh, God, no. It meant… he didn't want to go there.

"Russian?"

"Yes, must be. He is moving quickly toward the ambush site." His throat tightened and he forced back unexpected tears.

"That means…," and Killmer didn't finish the sentence. "Son-of-a-bitch!" he snarled.

Alex continued to pan, battling the possibility Lauren was either dead or tied up somewhere else. There was no one else out here other than these predators. He wanted to scream. He wanted to sob. It meant that the fifth man was Nik Morozov, returning to take part in the ambush, or… and he held onto a thread of hope, that perhaps Nik had hidden Lauren somewhere. But then why was he coming back to this ambush site?

"They might have Lauren detained elsewhere," Killmer said.

Alex didn't think Killmer believed what he said. Lauren had been bait, just as Alex had accurately foreseen. They didn't really want her. They wanted him. God, had she paid that price? For him? He flinched inwardly, barely able to contain his raw, grief-stricken emotions.

Alex froze. "Wait…"

"What?" Killmer demanded.

Blinking several times to refresh his eyesight, Alex stared through the scope. A SIXTH body-heat signature? He stared hard through the scope, his heart starting to pound harder in his chest. His throat closed up. He rasped, "Sixth body-heat signature."

"What the fuck?" Killmer snarled.

"The signature is running toward the fifth signature. There's some distance between them," he murmured.

"Who the hell are they, then?" Killmer rasped, tense.

"I don't know."

"Could Petrov have six in his team now? Not five?"

"I don't know," Alex wished the hell he did. The person was running. He lost sight of number six for a few moments, and then the heat signature reappeared. There were small hills everywhere around this area that intermittently blocked his view. He moved the scope back to number five. The figure had slowed down and stopped. Waiting. For what?

"Something is not right," Alex said, and then quickly described the situation to Killmer.

"If he's part of that team, he would be moving toward it," Killmer replied. "What's number six doing?"

Panning, Alex picked up number six. "Still running. Fast. Heading straight for number five's position."

"Shit. This makes no tactical sense. Does the other group of four know they are nearby?"

Panning, Alex said, "No. There would be no hesitation for number five if he was part of the team. I do not know why he has stopped."

"What's six doing?"

Alex picked up on the sixth person. "Slowing down. I think he sees number five…"

This was utterly confusing to Alex. The chief of the village had reported FIVE Russians had come through there two days earlier. Now, there are six of them? Where did the sixth come from?

"Their signatures have merged," Alex reported. "They must be standing together."

"Not moving?"

"No."

"Shit, this is getting nuts."

Alex saw six pull up something to his head, aiming it toward the group of four Russians. "Six is… doing something… I cannot make it out… holding…

I cannot see."

"Are they moving?"

"No. Stationary. About two hundred yards from the ambush."

"Are you SURE there are no rival mafia teams in this area?" Killmer gritted out.

"Positive."

"Then how the hell do you explain what you're seeing? And WHO are they?"

LAUREN BREATHED THROUGH her wide-open mouth so she couldn't be heard. She'd run up on Morozov, who'd made a sharp signal for her to stop and wait with him. Somewhere ahead, was the ambush. He leaned down, mouth near her ear, and breathed out, "Scope."

Nodding, Lauren pulled her NVGs down over her eyes and turned them on. Gulping, she rapidly spotted three men about fifty feet apart, a fourth man in another position: the L-shaped ambush. And they were close. Almost too close. She slowly, very slowly, crouched down. To do so rapidly could mean they'd spot the fast movement. Lauren knew they had NVGs as well. If either of them made one wrong move, they'd be in a firefight. Morozov crouched down slowly in unison.

They squatted in back of a large tree with a wide girth. Lauren pressed the scope into his hands and waited. Her heart was thudding slower due to this chance to rest. She knew the enemy had an infrared scope, too. Had they spotted them? Or had they been looking a different way when Nik and her had crouched down to hide? Or not using theirs at all? No, they were ex-Spetsnaz. Someone in that group would be responsible for scanning constantly with that infrared scope. To rest, to not scan for even a single moment, meant they could be attacked. With her NVGs in place, she saw Morozov slowly scanning. He swept the entire area around them, three hundred and sixty degrees. She knew he was hunting for Alex and the soldiers. Holding her breath, she hoped he picked up some heat signatures.

Moving the scope slowly downward, Nik turned, pulling Lauren close, his lips near her ear. "No sign."

"Where?"

"Unknown."

Lauren sat still, her mind skipping over possibilities. Had Alex not looked for her? She couldn't believe that. He loved her. He'd come after her. Had they gotten lost? Missed their tracks? Were somewhere else as a result? That could happen, especially on a black, moonless night like this with the intermittent rain washing out boot treads. Had Alex somehow, out of sheer luck, avoided this ambush?

She could feel Nik thinking, always alert, watching, listening. She felt safe with the man. Now, more than ever, she understood why Alex liked Morozov so much. They were like two peas from the same pod, and she smiled faintly.

There was the soggy snap of a twig behind them.

Lauren instantly jerked around. Her heart slammed into her ribs. It was a Russian!

She didn't have time to do anything. The hulking soldier rushed forward, his long wicked blade in his hand. He slashed out at Morozov, trying to slit his throat.

Lauren gasped, watching the two men roll and start fighting one another. Morozov grunted and knocked the knife out of the soldier's hand. They had been spotted! Where were the others? It didn't matter. She had to help Nik! The men had rolled down the slope, trading lethal punches; each trying to kill the other. Racing and slipping, nearly losing her footing, Lauren carefully timed lifting the butt of her AK-47. As the enemy soldier rolled back around on top, she jammed the butt down as hard as she could on the base of the man's skull.

The soldier grunted, suddenly going limp, falling on top of Morozov.

Breathing hard, Lauren saw black flowing across Morozov brow and down the side of his face. With NVGs on, blood appeared black. As she crouched, sliding her arm beneath his shoulders, helping him sit up, she gasped. The knife had been sliced down his upper arm, flaying open his cammo jacket. Blood was spurting out of the tear. An artery had been cut! Morozov was breathing roughly, slapping his hand over his bicep, trying to stanch the flow of blood.

Lauren placed her AK-47 down, pulled out a pair of the plastic flex cuffs he'd given her in the cave and leaped up, quickly hauling the unconscious soldier's hands behind his back. His wrists were thick and large. She fumbled at first, but finally got the cuffs on him, tightening them. Looking up, she saw Morozov grimace, pushing his back up against the tree. In her cargo pocket she carried a blowout kit; the medical items needed to save a life. With a trembling hand, the adrenaline surging through her, she found the nylon tourniquet.

Jerking it out of her pocket, she leaped over to Nik's side, crouched, and slipped the loop up his arm. "This will hurt," she warned.

Morozov winced, clenching his teeth. Not a sound came from him as Lauren tightened the tourniquet down and locked it into position so it would hold. He took his hand off his sliced arm. The spurting had stopped.

"No time," he rasped. "They know we're here. Get up! Follow me!" and he lurched to his feet, stumbling but quickly righting himself.

Lauren picked up his AK-47, shoving it into his hands. Morozov was weak from loss of blood. And now, they were being hunted by three other lethal, silent operators.

ALEX CURSED. "FIVE and six are NOT tangos!" He got up on one knee, pulling his AK-47 up, unsafing it.

Killmer grunted, ordering his men to his side. "Who the fuck are they?" he growled, staring down the hill.

"I do not know. But they are running away from the ambush."

Suddenly, the night lit up with flashes of muzzle fire. The roar of rifles being fired shattered the silence. Alex dove for the ground. So did the soldiers. He looked up. Petrov and his men were not firing up at them! They were firing at five and six!

"We need to help them," Alex snarled.

"Petrov hasn't spotted us yet," Killmer said. He gave hand signals, spreading out his other men. The closer they were grouped together, the more likely a grenade could kill all of them in one toss.

More gunfire.

Alex watched as five and six returned fire. They were spread apart by about ten feet, presenting less of a target. Both were firing slow and careful. Like operators. Could they be rival mafia gang members? It just didn't seem possible to him.

"They're on the move!" Killmer hissed, jabbing a finger toward the ambush site.

Alex followed the muzzle fire as the three Russians ran after five and six.

"Where's four?" Killmer demanded, getting up on one knee, rifle ready.

Alex followed him. Where was four? What had happened to him? Was that four who fought with five and six? Confused, he followed Killmer as he crouched and ran at a slant, almost paralleling the three Russians who were now chasing down five and six. The Special Forces sergeant wanted to get closer; make sure that when he fired, he'd hit his target. They were closing the distance rapidly, slipping and sliding through the muck, rain puddles and spongy earth. The smell of rifle fire met and stung his flared nostrils. The night was in chaos. And Petrov still had not made them. The Russians were focused on the other two who were rapidly putting distance between themselves and Petrov.

Alex surged forward in a crouch, grabbing Killmer's arm, halting him. They both knelt, lowering their profile. Killmer turned to him, his eyes slits, glittering with intensity. "We need one of those Russians alive," Alex rasped. "We need to find out where they have Lauren."

Killmer nodded. "We'll make sure," he promised roughly. "Let's go!"

Alex kept distance between himself and Killmer. He kept the last man in his sights. He was close enough now to see it was Petrov. Two hundred yards separated them. The Russians were so focused on five and six that they didn't even realize how quickly Alex and the rest were closing in on them. Rage swept through Alex. He wanted Petrov. *That bastard was HIS!*

Suddenly, another firefight broke out. He saw muzzle flashes lighting up the night. Five and six were making a stand. And all three Russians were rushing them, firing slow but consistently, trying to kill them. To make matters even worse, the bullets being fired by five and six were snapping around Alex's own position! He felt the heat of a bullet passing so close by his cheek that it burned the skin. He saw Killmer hit the ground. So did he.

LAUREN ALMOST CRIED out when Morozov suddenly crumpled ten feet away from her. He'd passed out from loss of blood. She leapt to her feet, eyes on him and the two other Russians stalking them. Dropping to her knees, she hauled the heavy medic around the side of a low boulder about four feet high and ten feet wide. She knelt, aiming her AK-47 at the first Russian. She fired once. Twice. The man screamed. He tumbled backward, his rifle flying out of his hands.

Sweat ran down into her eyes. Her breathing was chaotic from the effort. Her cool sniper control took over. She couldn't aim well if her chest were heaving up and down. She saw another Russian race behind a tree, fifty yards to her right, trying to skirt behind her. Twisting around, she fired three times. Wood and bark splinters exploded from the tree the Russian was crouching behind. He ran.

Bullets started flying by her head, coming from another direction. They hit the boulder protecting her. Sparks and chips of rock went flying everywhere. Lauren felt the shards striking her face and neck. She didn't even notice the sting of them, the adrenaline making her impervious to pain. More fire poured into her position and she had to duck behind the rock, covering her head.

Just then, she sensed danger coming from behind her. Jerking her chin up, she saw the other Russian raising his AK-47 directly at her, no more than twenty feet away. He was grinning.

Snapping up her rifle, she twisted and grunted, throwing herself protectively across Morozov, firing as she moved. The Russian fired twice.

The bullets struck her in the chest. Lauren was slammed backward into the rock, her chest on fire. She couldn't breathe. She felt pain radiate throughout her and she felt her rifle falling from her hand. *No! Oh, God, no!* The Russian was grinning, moving slowly toward her, the barrel of his AK-47 pointed at her head.

She jerked the Glock 19 out of her drop holster. Everything slowed down to single motion frames like in a movie. The look of glee in the Russian's eyes burned into her. He fired.

The Glock spun out of her hand. Lauren cried out, feeling her hand go numb and useless. She tried to scramble to get her sidearm back. The Russian was almost on top of her, still smiling. Barely able to breathe, sobbing for breath, she watched him, knowing he was going to go for a headshot. She saw his confidence. He wasn't afraid of her. But she had a balaclava on. He didn't know she was a woman. It wouldn't have made any difference.

Just as the Russian strode the last few feet between them, she saw a flash of movement from behind her. A knife glinted through the air. Right at the Russian.

Gasping, Lauren saw the knife stick through the throat of the Russian. He gurgled and stopped, his eyes bulging. He dropped the AK-47, his thick, meaty hands going for the blade. Blood was spurting out of his neck as he staggered around. And then, he toppled over backward, jerking and rolling away from them.

Morozov sat up, giving her a look. "Get the rifle!"

Lauren realized Nik had regained consciousness, and he'd had just enough strength left to pull the knife from his left calf sheath and throw it with deadly ease. But he slumped onto his back again, his effort spent for now. She looked down at her right hand. It was bloody. She couldn't feel it. Frantically, she turned around in a crouch, diving for her AK-47. Luckily, she had learned to fire with either hand; something a lot of Marine Corps snipers taught themselves. For just this very reason; if one hand didn't work, the other sure as hell would.

As she peeked over the rock, she saw another Russian. He was racing from tree to tree, his rifle fixated on them. He was trying to get around to make them targets with the rock no longer a barrier between them. Lauren felt Morozov move. He was trying to sit up again, floundering weakly. She couldn't help him now. Her gaze followed the Russian closing slowly in on them. Lifting the AK-47, she waited until he broke cover and sprinted for another tree. Then she fired.

The man screamed, tripped and fell. His rifle flew in cartwheels out of his hands.

Lauren sagged back against the rock, barely able to breathe. She heard Morozov moan. How many more of them? Her mind was spongy. Losing count. Pushing herself, she felt faint, lack of oxygen. Two rounds to her Dragon Vest across her chest. She'd been hit once before, three years ago in Afghanistan on a sniper op that went bad. One bullet had struck her in the chest. She'd passed out from the pain and lack of oxygen, her entire chest wall heavily bruised.

Have to get up. Have to guard. The words swirled around in her head. Lauren couldn't feel her right hand, her fingers numb, barely responding to her command to hold the AK-47 up. She glanced to her right. Morozov had passed out, lying on his back, unmoving. Her gaze flew to his right arm that she'd put the tourniquet on. It was bleeding, slowly but surely. He would bleed to death. There was no help coming. None.

Rolling to her knees, she was gasping, trying to get enough breath into her pain-filled chest, looking up. Blinking, she saw two more men advancing upon her. Oh God! Where had they come from? Confused, she blinked, her mind tumbling. The one man. The one in the lead… His body; the way he moved. Lauren thought she was hallucinating from lack of oxygen, her mind loosing grasp of reality. It looked like Alex's shape. She'd recognize him anywhere.

Her knee scraped against the rock as she slowly tried to position herself, lowering her rifle at him. Pain drifted up from her knee.

Something was wrong. Terribly wrong. Her vision was fading. The men advancing on them wore balaclavas. But… she blinked unsurely as she tried to steady the barrel at the man advancing upon her, his AK-47 aimed at her. She recognized him. Or did she? Her mind spun and her vision grayed. Slowly, it felt like an eternity, Lauren felt the AK-47 slide out of her hand, and herself off the rockface. And she was falling… falling…

Alex saw the man hiding behind the rock fall backward, the AK-47 tumbling out of his hands. Alex was breathing hard, hearing Killmer order his team to fan out, check the Russians who were down. They were all accounted for. This was five and six. He kept in his crouch, advancing swiftly, silently, moving around the large rock. His eyes widened as he saw two men, both down, unconscious, behind it.

"Clear," Killmer growled, checking the first downed Russian near where Alex stood. With a knife through his neck, there was no medical aid that would bring the bastard back.

"Clear, but we got a wounded tango," Cunningham said. "Merrill, get your ass over here. I'm going to need help. Get your flex cuffs out."

Alex pulled the sweaty balaclava off his face, dropping it. Neither five nor six were moving. As a combat corpsman, through his NVGs he rapidly accessed them. Both Russians. Same uniforms as the rest of Petrov's team. What the hell had happened? He laid his AK-47 down nearby, hauling his medical ruck off his shoulders. The man nearest him had two holes blown into his chest, the fabric ripped and torn outward, indicating that he was shot at close range. Alex wiped his face, grabbing the man's balaclava, pulling it off his face.

Lauren!

CHAPTER 18

ALEX'S WORLD FELL apart as he hesitated for a split second, staring disbelievingly down at Lauren, who lay unconscious.

"Cunningham," he called, his voice unsteady, "I need your help over here. Got two down. One is Lauren." The Special Forces combat medic had gone through the vaunted 18 Delta program, the Army combat medicine training that produced the best field medics in the world.

He gently straightened Lauren out, tipping her head back to allow her air passageeway to open so she wouldn't suffocate. He quickly felt her slender neck. There was a pulse! A strong one. It gave him hope.

Nate Cunningham came on the run. He skidded to a stop.

"Take care of the other one," Alex ordered him, jerking his head toward the unmoving, masked Russian soldier.

Lauren suddenly gasped as Alex cut open her Russian cammo jacket that had been chewed into by the two bullets. Her eyes went wide.

"Lauren, it is me, Alex. Let me help you," he gasped, tearing the fabric aside, needing to see if the bullets had been stopped or if she was bleeding out. Her eyes were wild and shocky. Immediately, Alex saw she was wearing her Dragon Skin vest. Relief started to pour through him. He quickly lifted her into his arms, pulling her toward him, ridding her of the jacket. His heart was pounding with urgency. Had the bullets been stopped or not? As he pulled the Velcro on the sides of the Dragon Skin to one side and eased it upward, he could see her camisole beneath. *NO BLOOD. Thank God...*

Alex quickly hauled the vest up and over her head, throwing it aside. He had to see the damage to her chest. When a person took a bullet at close range, it could crack their sternum, break ribs, stop their heart from beating... She was gasping, choking, her hand flailing weakly, trying to reach up to her throat. He focused solely on the medical aid needed to save her life. He was vaguely aware of Nate working quickly over the other Russian.

"You're going to be all right, *malen 'kaya*," he rasped unsteadily. He laid her on the ground, gently pulling her flailing arm aside. Her gasps indicated severe damage to her chest cavity by the bullets. He might have to intubate her so she could breathe. And there was no way he could get her to a hospital in any short amount of time, which is what she needed to survive over the long run.

Killmer came up, growling, "I've called the Night Stalker Black Hawk from Cusco. ETA one hour."

The golden hour. If a person could get the necessary medical aid within an hour of their injury, it gave them a huge chance to survive their wounds. After that, Death took the greater percentage of possibility from the wounded person. Alex nodded. "Okay." Terror rushed through him.

Killmer responded, "We've got the one Russian who's still alive, flexed-cuffed and tied to a tree. He's not going anywhere. Nate patched him up first and he'll make it. I'm taking Merrill and we're going to scout a landing area for the Hawk. We'll be back," he said, gripping Alex's shoulder and then releasing it.

ONE HOUR. His hand shook as he took a pair of scissors, slitting Lauren's camisole up the middle, revealing her chest. Wincing internally, he saw two huge bruises, swollen so badly that her flesh was raised like two hardballs, each as large as the palm of his hand. The bruises met at the center of her chest, over her sternum. She'd taken two bullets over her upper-lung region. He talked to her soothingly, swiftly examining her rib cage, aware that she was naked. It couldn't be helped. He gently turned her toward him, brushing her back with his hand to see if there were exit wounds or bleeding. It was clear. Her gasping was hoarse and she was struggling, her eyes rolling in deep shock. He had to stabilize her but, as he slowly ran his hands to the side of her right breast, she cried out in pain, flinching, trying to pull away from his touch. *Broken or cracked ribs. Two or three?* His mouth thinned as he did the same to the left side of her torso. She cried out again. It hurt to hear and see her in such pain.

Grabbing her discarded jacket from the ground, Alex drew it across her and pulled a small reflective blanket out of his ruck. He tucked it beneath her head and shoulders, trying to get as much of her as he could risk moving off of the cold, wet ground. Swiftly, he reached into the ruck for a syringe and a bottle of morphine. He couldn't give Lauren much of the opiate because then she'd fall asleep and her ability to breathe would be compromised. He stuck the needle into the bottle, drawing out just enough. Dropping the bottle back into his pack, he rubbed an area of her upper arm with a medicinal swab to clean it off.

"It's going to be all right, Lauren. I'm giving you something to help ease the pain." Because, God, every breath she took had to feel like sharp-pointed knives digging into her lungs, the pain excruciating, stopping her from being able to take even half a breath, never mind taking in a full breath of air. He had no oxygen tank, nor oxygen mask, to support her continuing, deteriorating condition. And that was what he needed the most to stabilize her. *Pure oxygen.* Lauren was waxen, pupils black and huge, telling him she was low on oxygen. The thing he needed the most, the oxygen, he didn't have and it scared him. He gave her the shot, threw the syringe aside, drew Lauren gently toward his knees, spreading the reflective blanket beneath her from her hips to her head. Cold, wet ground would only suck the heat out of her body and, right now, she need to be as warm as possible to help her stabilize and stop the relentless shock that was overtaking all her organ functions.

He quickly ran his hands from her shoulders down each arm. He felt blood on her right hand and picked it up, looking at it more closely. Her long, beautiful fingers were swollen, deeply bruised. There was blood and bruising in the center of her palm. Manipulating each finger gently, Alex saw that Lauren moaned, telling him that there was a strong possibility all of them were broken. He quickly cleaned off that hand and wrapped it in a battle dressing. Continuing his examination of her, from her abdomen down to her feet, he found nothing else.

The real damage was to her chest, ribs and lungs. He worried that if a rib was badly enough broken, it could poke in through the side of her lung, deflating it or tearing it open, causing internal bleeding. Listening carefully with his stethoscope as he moved it beneath the jacket he'd pulled over her, Alex didn't hear any signs of collapsed lungs. Yet. For that, he was grateful. But, for the time being, it also meant Lauren couldn't be moved very much because a rib could still jab into one of her lungs. If a lung collapsed, it would mean a spiraling trauma going deeper. She'd have only one lung left to breathe with, half of her ability to get oxygen into her body gone. It would take major surgery at a hospital to repair the torn lung tissue so they could reinflate her lung. And there was nothing out here, in the middle of the jungle, they could do to help her. *Nothing.*

He knew Lauren couldn't see him; it was so damned dark. He could see her through his NVGs, her mouth contorted, head moving restlessly, trying to suck in enough air to survive. Gently, he pressed his fingers along each side of her throat, checking her trachea, making sure it wasn't compromised, that it wasn't causing her even more breathing problems. It was not. A small piece of good luck.

Alex heard a man groan behind him, and speak out in Ukrainian. That voice. He knew that voice! Lifting his head, he twisted around. Nate Cunningham was working on the man's bloody upper arm. He no longer wore the balaclava that had hidden his face. A gasp tore out of Alex. It was Nik Morozov!

"Oh my God, Nik?" Alex called to him in Ukrainian, and turned enough to grip his friend's shoulder.

Morozov reacted, pale, his face beaded with perspiration, eyes shocky. He slowly rolled his head toward Alex. A wobbly smile pulled at his mouth. "Alex... you're okay?"

"Yes," Alex said, suddenly emotional. "Why are you with Lauren? What happened?"

Nik swallowed, his voice a rasp. "Later... How is she?"

"Not good. Two bullets to her vest, upper chest. Rib fractures or breaks. Severe respiratory distress."

Frowning, Morozov said, "She saved my life... save hers..."

Alex squeezed his shoulder. "Just rest, Nik. You're in good hands. You're going to make it." He watched his friend of many years fall unconscious. He looked over to see Nate had put an IV into his arm and had attached the drip's saline pouch to the epaulet of Nik's jacket. The pouch had to be higher than the injection point in order to drip-feed its life saving fluid into the badly-wounded soldier.

"Is he stable?" Alex demanded of Nate.

"Yeah, getting there," he grunted. "He was starting to crash. Heavy loss of blood. Damn, wish I had some whole blood on me. Do you have any?"

Shaking his head, Alex turned, his hand on Lauren's head. Her eyes were closed and she wasn't gasping as much anymore. "Just Quick Clot. Nothing else."

"We're going to have to transport these two," Nate warned.

"We'll do it," Alex answered grimly. He took his stethoscope, sliding it beneath the jacket over Lauren, placing it gently on her chest, listening for breathing sounds. He placed two fingers against her inner wrist, feeling her jerky, bounding pulse. She was quieting now from the morphine taking hold, giving her relief from the pain. Her breathing was a little easier. She was able to take in slightly deeper breaths. When people suffered broken ribs, they couldn't fully expand their ribcage, which was composed of curved bones around their delicate lungs. And, if they didn't get enough oxygen, their entire system was at risk. Not enough oxygen meant the whole body plunged into deeper shock. And shock would kill.

Alex stroked his fingers across Lauren's brow, whispering her name, telling her everything would be all right. She was non-responsive, her thick red lashes laying against her waxen flesh. Alex was scared. But he kept whispering near Lauren's ear, soothing her, giving her hope. So often in the battlefield, a touch, a low calm voice from the medic made the difference. It could slow the downward spiral of blood pressure dropping, and then killing a person. He swore he could feel her respond even though she was unconscious.

Looking up, he wanted so badly for that Black Hawk to get here. In order to do so, those pilots would be flying in the worst possible weather conditions. He pulled the cover off his watch. It was 0400. The bird wouldn't arrive until 0500. Dawn. The start of a new day. The very hour the winds reversed and flying was easy, instead of dangerous. He shakily pulled the NVGs down off his eyes for a moment, wiping his sweaty face, wiping away the stinging salt running into his eyes, blurring his vision.

"How's Lauren?" Nate demanded.

"Critical." Alex said and heard the medic curse softly.

"GSW?" Gunshot wound.

"No... She took two rounds to the upper chest but the Dragon Skin vest stopped them." His voice grew hoarse with the emotions he could no longer constrain because he loved her. "She's got a minimum of two broken or cracked ribs on the right side of her torso, and at least three on the left. It's compromising her ability to get oxygen."

"Shit! I don't have O2 tanks in my ruck..."

Alex's heart plunged. "If Lauren doesn't start breathing a little better in a few minutes, I'm going to have to intubate her and then I will use the manual pump to get oxygen into her lungs."

"Okay, I'll try to help you," Nate said. "This guy is stable now. I've given him just enough morphine to stop the pain, and he's becoming conscious."

"Good," Alex whispered. "You need to know his name is Nik Morozov. He's my best friend. And he is a Ukrainian combat medic. He will not give you any trouble. I think he was trying to get Lauren to safety..." Alex leaned down and placed a kiss against Lauren's damp brow. He straightened, pulling his NVGs back over his eyes. Again, he slid the stethoscope beneath the jacket covering her and listened for breathing. Relief jagged through him. She was relaxed, the pain neutralized to a degree, and her ribcage was moving easier. She was taking in slightly fuller breaths. That meant she was getting more oxygen into her. He took her blood pressure, wrapping the cuff around her upper right arm. It was 300 over 60; not good. Her body was laboring to stabilize and wasn't finding purchase. Dammit! His heart ached. Alex wanted to cry but it wouldn't do anyone any good. He kept caressing her hair and speaking to her, urging that she must fight back. That he loved her.

Alex heard Morozov gasp, "Help me sit up," in English. He looked to his left, seeing Nate help his friend into a sitting position against the rock. Nate had put a sling around Nik's right arm, tight against his chest, to keep it stable.

"Alex," Nik gasped unsteadily, reaching out, gripping his arm. "The cave... where we keep everything. It's only a mile from here. There's four oxygen tanks and a cannula in my medical gear ruck…"

Alex raised his head, more than interested. Getting pure oxygen into Lauren could mean the difference between her living or dying. "Where is the cave? Can you tell us?" His voice was low with urgency.

"Y-yes," Morozov whispered, weak, tipping his head back against the rock and closing his eyes. Nate and Alex were intently watching the Ukrainian, hanging on his every word as he gave directions.

Did they have time to make the run? Alex thought so. "Thank you, Nik," he said, gripping his friend's hand, squeezing it hard.

Nik barely opened his eyes, his mouth stretched into what was supposed to be a smile, but looked like a grimace. "You can get there swiftly, Alex. Just follow the tracks. You can do this for her. She deserves it…"

Nate stood up. "I've got this," he told Alex. "You stay here and keep her as stable as you can." He picked up his weapon and leapt out onto the trail. "If Killmer comes back, let him know what's going down. I'll be back as soon as I can," and he turned, trotting down toward the ambush trail.

Alex dragged in a ragged breath, moving his fingers against Lauren's cheek. She was so damned pale. She looked like death. He'd seen it so many times on the battlefield.

"H-how is she doing?" Nik rasped, trying to move closer to them. He was weak, and every effort made him feel weaker.

"Critical," Alex rasped. Nik was a combat corpsman like himself. He knew what that meant. That she could die if her body couldn't stabilize at some point. So far, the blood-pressure readings showed her slowly continuing to decline.

"Do you have an oximeter on you?" Nik asked.

"Yes, wait…," and Alex dug desperately into his pack. He quickly found it and placed it on one of Lauren's uninjured fingers, his gaze fastened on the oximeter's small window. An oximeter measured how much oxygen was available to the body.

Fifty! He cursed softly and called it out to Nik, who grimaced. Her oxygen was at fifty percent. Normal was ninety to one-hundred. She had to have oxygen soon or she would die!

"She needs to be on a ventilator. The O2 will make the difference, Alex. You and I both know that…" Nik whispered.

Nodding, Alex's only focus was on Lauren. His heart ached with fear and terror. She lay still now, her lips parted, her hair badly tangled, thick strands having come loose from her ponytail. He gently tucked her in again, making sure the cammo jacket kept her warm, a nervous reaction, but there was little else he could do. He couldn't pull Lauren into his arms and keep her warm because it would potentially create more pain, or even lacerate one or more of her lungs by any of those potentially broken ribs. She couldn't be moved, except on a litter.

Looking around, that was something Alex realized he could do. He moved his ruck aside, getting up. "Nik? I'm going to look for some tree saplings for poles in order to make a litter for Lauren. We are going to have to carry her out of here. They have got a Night Stalker Black Hawk flying in to pick all of us up. We are going to have to transport her and you, and I don't know how far it will be to get to the helo," he told him. "Stay with her? Monitor her? If she takes a turn for the worse, yell out for me? I will return."

"Yes, my friend, I can do that for you. Go make her a litter."

Alex went, and swiftly searched around, locating some long, sturdy-looking saplings. He took out his combat knife, sawing off branches with its serrated edge, then gathering up the four of them, two for Lauren, two for Nik. He wasn't sure that Nik could make it out under his own power, weakened by his own heavy loss of blood. Within five minutes, he had four poles, and was carrying them back to the rock. He saw that Nik had inched over to where Lauren lay. His hand was on her shoulder and he was watching over her. Alex's throat tightened. Placing the poles nearby, he went to Nate's pack. Inside, he found two reflective blankets. They would do fine for the fabric stretched between the first two poles. Alex went to work with his knife, affixing them, along with some flex cuffs, to the poles to create Lauren's litter.

He wanted to look at his watch. Urgency thrummed through him as he finished the litter, setting it aside. The only other blanket he had was already beneath her. He hadn't had a pair of them in his pack. Not like he'd found in Nate's. Looking toward where the cave lay, somewhere out there in the dark, he resigned himself to the fact that he could do no more for now.

Alex knelt by Lauren's shoulder. He pulled the stethoscope from his pack, listening to her lungs again. Then, he inflated the blood pressure cuff on her left arm.

"What are the readings?" Nik asked quietly, his gaze on his friend.

"A little better. Two-hundred over sixty. Her oximeter is now sixty. It's a small improvement, but a good one." Normal blood pressure was 120/80.

Smiling a little, Nik felt woozy. But he kept his hand on Lauren's shoulder. He too, knew the value of touch on the battlefield. "It won't take that Special Forces operator long. He'll run like hell to get that O2 back to Lauren."

Alex nodded. "Yes…" He so desperately needed that tank of oxygen for Lauren. Feeling her face and slender neck, her skin was moist and clammy. Signs of deep shock.

"Her body is fighting back, Alex." And then Nik added, "She told me she loved you."

Alex snapped his head up, staring at Nik. "She did?"

"Yes." He shook his head. "She was the one who fought to get back to you." He swallowed hard, tears burning in his eyes. "Lauren told me everything, begged me to help stop the ambush. I promised her I would."

"And so, you dressed her in Russian gear to hide her from Petrov?"

"Yes. All our weapons, food and medical are in that cave. We've been working out of there for the last six months... after you... well... 'died'."

"This Special Forces team found me a few hours later, Nik. Nate is the one who stopped my slow bleed and saved my life."

"I'm glad, my friend." Nik closed his eyes. "I missed you. It wasn't the same in the team without you. It went from bad to worse under Petrov's leadership," and he slowly shook his head from side to side, the corners of his mouth deepening.

Alex couldn't even imagine, remembering the hell it had already been under Vlad Alexandrov.

"He's the only one left alive. Petrov is wounded, but stable. They're taking him in to interrogate him once we get back Stateside."

A sharp smile cut across Nik's mouth. "Exactly what the sick bastard deserves..."

Alex didn't allow his gaze to be anywhere but on Lauren. He felt on tenterhooks, knew that her body could crash at any second and there would be nothing he could do about it. He wouldn't be able to give her CPR, her chest cavity already as broken as it was. If he tried, he'd kill her by pushing down on her fractured ribs, sending them slicing like razors, ripping into her lungs. His only other option was to intubate her, slide a hollow tube down her throat, into her trachea and then use the manual pump to force air into her lungs by hand. He slipped his hand into hers, holding it gently, warming it. She was so cold. He wanted desperately to hold her, share his body heat with Lauren, but he didn't dare move her any more than necessary.

Alex was agitated inwardly. Restless. He wanted Nate back with those oxygen bottles and a canula for Lauren. And where was Killmer? He had heard neither of their returns. How far were they from the LZ, landing zone, where they could board the Hawk? Had the helicopter encountered terrible turbulence on the way up to them? Alex knew that could happen. That could slow them down. Worse, the helicopter could crash. The scenarios running through his mind were realistic but terrifying to him. Minutes counted where Lauren was concerned. Every second that she spent on the cold wet ground, her low oxygen absorption kept her at risk of crashing. And, once a person crashed, very few survived unless they were in the major emergency room of a Level

One Trauma hospital. And here they were out in the middle of a dark, wet jungle.

He noticed that the jungle seemed lighter and pulled his NVGs down around his neck. Dawn. Dawn was coming. Everything was a deep gray, but his eyes adjusted and he could see fairly well. Glancing up at Nik, who lay quietly, eyes closed, head resting against the boulder, Alex could see how pale he really was. He'd lost a lot of blood. Even he wasn't out of the woods yet, either.

Alex heard noise. He jerked his head up. Nate Cunningham was laboring toward them as fast as he could jog. He was loaded down with a huge ruck on his back, a Russian one. Under one arm, he carried two medium-sized oxygen tanks. Under the other one, as many blankets as he could manage. Alex got up and helped him unload everything once he'd halted at the boulder. The medic was breathing hard, sweat gleaming on his face. He'd also taken off his NVGs as well.

Nate unloaded the heavy medical ruck off from his back. Dropping to his knees, he tore open the Velcro on it. "The O2 cannula is in here," he gasped, pulling it out along with the tubing. "Good news, Alex. There's two more bottles in here. Damn, it was a motherfucker trying to run with this load."

Alex grabbed a bottle and the O2 mask. "You did good," he praised, kneeling by Lauren. He inserted a tube into the bottle, laying it down nearby. Gently, he eased the cannula around her head, fitting the two small oxygen tubes into each of her nostrils. Laying her down, he turned, twisting the knob, watching the hand of the meter climb. Setting it at the right level, he quickly listened to her lungs and took her blood pressure.

Nate moved around him, spotting the poles and the one litter Alex had prepared. "Hey, we're thinking on the same wavelength," he told Alex. "I brought extra blankets, thinking we could use them to carry these two."

"I got one litter done," Alex said, watching the needle on the blood pressure cuff. He was almost breathing along with Lauren, praying that the pure oxygen would begin to make a difference. He leaned over her, monitoring, listening, watching. There was no difference for nearly ten minutes. But then, he watched the color begin to slowly seep back into her waxen face. Relief, sharp and jagged, tore through him. He heard a difference in her breathing. Her blood pressure was rising. The oximeter read seventy! All good signs! For a moment, he squeezed his eyes closed, his mouth tight. Tears burned behind his tightly-shut eyes. Forcing them back, he watched the color slowly come back into her face.

"She looks better," Nik said wearily, his head turned toward them, watching Lauren in the gray light, peripherally aware of Nate working frantically off to one side, getting the second litter ready.

"Yes," Alex breathed thickly. "She is improving." He looked up at Nik. "You have given her a fighting chance. Thank you," and he reached out, gripping Nik's shoulder and giving it a hard squeeze. He saw his lifelong friend grin a little. It was a weak grin, but it was there.

"If anyone deserves to live, my brother, it's her."

Nate came over and said, "Look, there's Mace and Cale coming in," as he gestured in their direction.

Alex looked up, his heart pounding. The two men arrived swiftly, breathing hard, faces glistening with sweat.

"Just talked to the Hawk," Killmer said, looking around at the litters, and the medical rucks open around them. "ETA is forty minutes."

"How far to the LZ?" Alex demanded.

"One mile," he said grimly, shrugging. "Wish it was closer," and he was staring down at Lauren. "How's she doing?"

"Better, but still critical," Alex said. He gestured toward Nik, "This is Nik Morozov, combat medic. He is a FRIEND, Ukrainian, the only other one in their team who was a human being. He helped save Lauren."

Killmer nodded toward Morozov. "Thanks," he told him. "We need to get these two out of here pronto. What do you want us to do?"

Alex stood. He saw Nate had fastened a long green wool blanket around the spare poles to make a second litter. "Lauren has broken ribs on both sides." He saw the grizzled sergeant grimace. Killmer knew what that meant. "And Morozov has lost a lot of blood."

"I estimate two to three pints," Nate added, hauling the first litter near Lauren. "He's in no shape to walk. If he tried, he'd just slow us down, Mace. We can't afford that. Lauren has to be gotten to an ER, stat."

Nodding, Killmer said, "Alex, you and me will carry Lauren's litter. Nate, you and Cale take Morozov's litter."

Relieved that they were going to get Lauren to the helicopter, Alex had the help of all three Special Forces men as they carefully lifted Lauren and transferred her onto the litter. She was unconscious, limp, and as soon as she was laying in the center of the litter, Alex quickly covered her with the two warm woolen blankets they had left, tucking them in around her.

Nik protested about being carried, but Nate cut him off, telling him that Lauren was critical; that him trying to walk right now would put her in worse jeopardy. The Ukrainian nodded, lying down without further protest on the second litter. Alex came over and started to put a blanket over him.

"No," Nik growled, "put it on Lauren. She must be kept warm to stop the shock from worsening. I'm fine…"

Alex knew he wasn't. Nik's uniform, like everyone else's, was wet from the rain. He was chilled. However, ceasing any further argument with his friend, he quickly turned, knelt and placed the blanket across Lauren. Next came the oxygen tank, which he fitted between her lower legs. It would ride well there, no problem. The only thing he worried about was that Lauren might sink and sag into the litter. That could put undue pressure on some of those ribs, pressing inward, possibly disabling her ability to expand her lungs and get enough air into them. Everything was so tentative. So dangerous for her.

Nate came around as her litter was hefted up by Mace and Alex. "Hold up," he said. He quickly rolled up two of the reflective blankets. "I'm going to put one on each side of her lower ribcage," he explained to Alex. "To stabilize her so she's not rolling from side to side as you walk."

Alex was grateful for the 18 Delta corpsman's experience and knowledge. Nate quickly tucked in the blanket rolls and nodded. "Okay, let's boogie…"

They couldn't run. They couldn't trot. That kind of jagged up-and-down motion would harm Lauren's already compromised torso. It could send a rib jabbing into one of her vulnerable lungs. So, they walked carefully, using their upper-body weight to lift and hold the litter as steady and stable as possible. The sky was brightening, and Alex kept his gaze on Lauren as much as he could. He couldn't risk stopping to take her blood pressure or listen to her lungs again. All he could do was look at her skin tone. Her red hair had loosened more and was a crimson frame around her face and shoulders, her lips parted, unconscious. Without enough oxygen, a person lost consciousness and Alex knew this was the case here. As the light increased, he saw, to his relief, that her cheeks were becoming less pale. The more oxygen that got into her body the better her circulation would become; more oxygen dispensed to the red blood cells, which increased the pinkness of her flesh.

As they crested a small hill, Alex spotted the opening in the jungle. Grateful that their rescuers had found something so close, he heard the deep thumping of a helicopter's blades in the distance. His hopes rose. Lauren's chance of survival, which he couldn't do without, had just improved. But now, they were faced with another terrible challenge: the unstable air, the CAT, clear air turbulence, that ruled the night until dawn came. If the ride was rough, it could kill her.

CHAPTER 19

THE NIGHT STALKER pilot cut the blade power to bare minimum at the request of Mace, who radioed in that they had two critical casevacs coming on board. They loaded Nik first, the litter placed against the port bulkhead and locked in. Alex and Mace brought Lauren in, who remained unconscious and positioned her with her head toward the cockpit and feet toward the tail of the Hawk. They transferred her to an empty litter attached to the starboard bulkhead of the helo, locking her in, pulling a number of nylon straps across her to keep her stable so she wouldn't be tossed out into the cabin by turbulence. Everyone else quickly climbed into the crowded bird. As the air crew chief slid and locked the door shut, Alex pulled on his helmet and plugged it into the intercom mic by his lips. So did everyone else.

Alex recognized the pilot, Captain Jake Curtis, the Texan, as the man twisted to his left, looking down into the low lit cabin.

Curtis scowled darkly. "That's not that feisty little gal, is it?"

"Yes," Alex snapped, moving the oxygen tank off her litter. "She's critical."

"Damn, sorry to hear that," Curtis drawled. "Firefight?"

"Yes," Killmer grated. "Look, Captain, we need your experience here. She's critical. We need to get her to the best hospital in the area. Pronto! What do you suggest?"

Curtis nodded. "My advice is let me fly her directly into Lima. They have a Level-One Trauma hospital and it's the best in the country. She's lookin' pretty peaked to me. It would only be forty more minutes. I can redline this bird and we can lay contrails in the sky between here and there."

"Cusco is closer," Alex argued. Lima was forty more minutes away, and God only knew through how much rough air. "She cannot take turbulence, Captain. She's got broken ribs on both sides of her chest. Her breathing is not good. I cannot afford her to be beaten up by getting thrown around in this cabin. It WILL kill her," and Alex held the pilot's narrowing eyes. Curtis scratched his strong chin.

"Okay, here's a plan, pardner," he told Alex. "We're at that in-between point where the winds are shifting from the Andes to the ocean. If you'll agree to let me fly her into Lima, it's going to be a helluva lot smoother flight than the other route of trying to get her into Cusco, which is near twelve thousand feet. The LAST place that shift of winds takes place is in the Cusco area because of the high altitude. The shift's already well underway in Lima's direction. Lima sits at sea level. I promise you, it's a lot smoother ride for her. What do you say?"

"Forty minutes more?" Alex demanded, feeling raw and terrified.

"Yes, sir, forty minutes more but," Curtis drawled, "if you want your lady to have a quiet ride to the hospital, this is the only game in town for her. At least she'll arrive alive. What'll it be?"

Mace looked at Kazak. "Take it," he ordered.

Nik, who was also hearing all this through his helmet's audio, said, "Alex, it's the safest route for Lauren. Do it."

Alex nodded. "Yes," he told the captain, "let us get to Lima. As fast as you can…"

Curtis smiled a little, pulling down the dark visor over the upper half of his face. "We're gonna set a new air-speed record with my Hawk, here. Get ready to go Mach-three with your hair on fire, boys and girls… yeeeehhhhhhh-aaaaaaaaaaa…"

LAUREN FELT A dull ache all over her chest as she climbed slowly out of the darkness. She became aware of monitors beeping, of being comfortable instead of chilled to the bone. Where was she? As she tried to lift her hand, pain instantly plowed into her left side and she groaned.

Someone's warm, large hand captured hers. She relaxed, feeling its strength and gentleness.

"*Malen 'kaya*, try not to move too much."

Alex's low, deep voice vibrated through her like a fresh breath of life. Lauren forced her eyelids open, every slight effort feeling like she was running a marathon. His face was blurred at first but, after a few seconds, she saw him with clarity. Alex was standing by her bed, holding her hand, his hazel eyes dark with worry, exhaustion deepening all the lines across his grim-looking face. Dark circles hung beneath his eyes. His beard made him look lethal to her. His mouth was pursed, corners drawn deeply inward. He was worried about her. She tried to speak; her voice hoarse.

"Shhhh," he told her, leaning over, moving his fingers across her brow, brushing the clean strands of her red, recently-washed hair aside. "You are going to be all right, Lauren. You are safe. You will recover." And then he cupped her cheek, holding her drowsy gaze. "I love you, Lauren. I should have told you that sooner. I am sorry. You hold my heart forever. Hold onto that and I will hold onto you…"

Lauren closed her eyes, feeling the warmth of his mouth slide across hers. She absorbed his strength, his tenderness, as he moved his lips across hers, cherishing her. Loving her. Alex's mere presence reassured her. As he eased his mouth from hers, she tried to take a deep breath. Again, pain squeezed her chest and she frowned, riding it out, compressing her lips.

"If you take deep breaths right now, it will hurt," Alex told her quietly. He caressed her hair, watching her brow begin to smooth out from his touch.

"W-what… happened?" she croaked.

Alex squeezed her left hand. "You were hit by two bullets in the upper chest. Your Dragon Skin vest saved your life, Lauren. We got you out of the jungle. Right now, you are in a Lima, Peru, hospital. You are going to live." He watched as she barely nodded, licking her lips, trying to process what he'd said. Shock made the brain go offline. Alex didn't want to give Lauren too much information too fast. He checked the monitors, feeling a little more relief. Her oxygen absorption was up to eighty-five. It had been at seventy when they'd wheeled her into the ER on a gurney. She had been here for three hours. And she was continuing to improve. Her cheeks were flushed pink with life and her eyes, although dulled, still showed even greater life in their depths.

"…Nik…"

He smiled and caressed her cheek. How like Lauren to always think of others, not herself. She hadn't asked any more about her condition. Rather, more concerned about her team mate.

"He is going to be fine. He is up and walking around."

"Good," Lauren whispered. "And the Army guys?"

"Not a scratch on them, *malen 'kaya*. You were the most injured."

"And you look fine, Alex… really fine… We were trying to locate you… Petrov… he used me as bait. Nik… if it wasn't for Nik, we could never have found you…"

"Hush," he rasped. "You need to rest. We will talk more when you feel better."

Her red eyebrows dipped. "I-I'm so tired, Alex."

"I know you are. Are you in pain?"

A careless half-smile cut across her lips. "Only if I try to inhale."

"Broken ribs do that," Alex reassured her. Leaning down, he kissed her fragrant, clean skin. Two nurses had washed her hair and gently cleaned her up. Now, her skin smelled of life, not death. "Rest," he whispered against her lips. "I will not leave you alone, Lauren. If I have to go somewhere, Nik will sit in for me and be at your side."

His promise made her relax. It was so easy to close her eyes because she had no strength left to keep them open. Sleep claimed her immediately.

ALEX QUIETLY CLOSED the door. Nik was right there outside, now in civilian clothes, thanks to Mace Killmer, who was also back at the hospital after a run over to his Lima apartment to gather them. Morozov's arm was in a new, white sling. If Alex had never seen him before, he'd never have guessed that his friend had lost nearly three pints of blood out in that jungle.

"How is she?" Nik asked, turning and walking toward him, worry in his dark blue eyes.

"She just regained consciousness for the first time," Alex told him, more emotional about that than he'd realized. "She is going to make it…"

Nik gripped his shoulder, grinning. "That IS the BEST of news, my friend."

Tiredly, Alex rubbed his face. "She is going to make it." He took a deep, serrated breath and exhaled, emotion clearly written across his face. "I need to get cleaned up. Where is the men's shower and locker room in this hospital?"

Nik told him where they were located. "I'll stay with Lauren. Take a shower, get something to eat. I'll have you paged if anything happens, but I don't think it will. Sleep is the best healer for her right now."

Nodding, Alex gave him a warm look and gripped his hand. "Thank you… for everything, Nik. You saved her life and I will never be able to repay you for that."

Snorting, Morozov shook his hand and released it. "No, Brother, it's the other way around. We haven't had time to talk yet but, if your woman hadn't been there when I was jumped from behind by Burak, I'd be dead. We wouldn't be talking to one another right now."

"What are you talking about?"

"Petrov's team spotted us. I'm sure it was through an infrared scope. Burak was sent to come up behind us. You know how he loves knives? If he can use one to kill with, he'd rather do that than use a rifle." Nik gave him a grim look. "Lauren heard him first. She whirled around. Burak charged me. I evaded, but he cut my upper-arm open," and he gestured to his arm in its sling. "He sliced open an artery. I fought with him. I was losing because I was weak due to loss of blood. Lauren timed it right, and she struck Burak in the skull with the butt of her AK-47. She cracked his skull. I heard it." He took a deep breath, his voice low with feeling. "If she hadn't stepped in when she did, I would be dead. Burak would have gotten the upper hand, gutted me from neck to hips. That's what he likes to do: gut someone and then… watch them die. She had a blowout kit on her and she swiftly placed a tourniquet around my upper arm, above where the artery was spurting blood. She saved my life."

A coldness swept through Alex. "I… didn't know…," he whispered, looking to one side, his mouth working to halt the deluge of more emotions. Finally, he looked at Nik. "Burak was a monster."

"Well," Nik laughed a little, "your brave woman warrior killed him. She had the presence of mind to pull a tourniquet from her medical kit and stopped the bleeding from my upper arm. She's a lot stronger than I gave her credit for."

"Strong?" Alex said, a weary half-smile coming to his mouth. "She has a spine of titanium. Has anyone told you what she did after you made it to that boulder?"

Nik shook his head. "No, but you need to get cleaned up, Kazak. You smell like swamp," and he grinned tiredly, clapping him gently on his sagging shoulder. "tell me about it when you return. She is truly a heroine."

Alex took the suggestion. He rode the elevator down to the basement of the hospital. Getting off, he looked down the highly-polished hall and saw Captain Curtis, the Night Stalker pilot, ambling his way along with his long, rolling Texas gait. Alex walked down the hall toward him.

"How's your lady doin'," Jake asked, halting at the center of the hall with him.

Alex noticed the US Army pilot wore a single piece dark olive-green uniform but it had absolutely no indication of his name, rank, or any sign of what country he was from. It was typical black ops. Curtis was nearly six foot tall, lanky, and holding that lazy, boyish grin of his across his oval face. It was his hawk-like gray eyes, gleaming with intelligence, that made Alex smile a little back.

"She is doing okay. She just woke up a few minutes ago for the first time. All her numbers are going the right direction."

"Good to hear. Your team really rode a jaguar on that mission. The lockers and showers are that way," and Curtis pointed toward them. "You got any clean clothes?" and he looked at Alex's muddy camouflaged pants and mud-clumped boots.

Alex shook his head. "No."

"My copilot, Randy Henson, is about your height. A giant in the cockpit. Literally," and Curtis laughed at his own joke. "Come on, I know his locker number and I can open it up. He usually has three pairs of civvies in there. I'm sure you'll find something in there that will fit you… He won't mind loaning them to you."

Alex was struck by the camaraderie between all the operators. It didn't matter what branch of the service they came from. They were team players and thought nothing of helping out another one of their kind. "Thanks," he murmured, "I could use a shower and some clean clothes."

"If I had a clothespin," Curtis drawled, a quirky grin tugging at one corner of his mouth, walking beside Alex down the hall, "I'd be wearin' it on my nose right now…"

NIK JERKED UPRIGHT, awakened by movement. Blinking away the fog of exhaustion, his gaze instantly snapped to Lauren. He hadn't meant to doze off, but he had. Getting up, he quietly walked to her bedside. She was in pain. He could see it in her face. Looking over at the morphine pump at her bedside, he allowed the drip to increase just a little. If he hadn't been so well-versed in the use and application of morphine out on the battlefield, he'd have needed to call a nurse.

Almost instantly, the tightness in her face lessened as the drip flowed into her vein. She wore a white cotton gown, covered over warmly with several blue alpaca blankets. Unfortunately, there was nothing anyone could do about the fractured ribs on both sides of her chest. They were above her breasts. If she had been a man, Nik knew they could use supportive tape to help ease the pain that would be felt for a good three weeks afterward. A woman's breasts prohibited such a treatment. Lauren would be on a low dose of morphine for three to four weeks, to dull the pain. And she would require enforced bed rest. He didn't envy Alex because Lauren, from his experience with her, was tough, always on the move, and wouldn't be housebound. *At all.* That his friend had chosen a woman who was his equal, there was no question.

The door quietly opened.

Nik turned. Alex nodded to him as he entered, and was showered, shaven, wearing a dark-green polo shirt, dark brown chinos and his now scrubbed-clean combat boots. He nodded and made a gesture that they go out in the hall to speak to one another so as not to disturb Lauren.

Alex nodded and opened the door wider, stepping out.

Nik looked at his watch. He'd fallen asleep for a good hour. "You look better, Alex." He made sure the door closed without a sound.

"I am. Tired, but okay. How is Lauren?"

Nik told him about the small drip increase of morphine for her pain. Instantly, he saw his friend's eyes grow dark with concern. "She's okay. She went back into a deep sleep," he reassured Alex. "Her stats are stable and her oximeter reading is eighty-two. It is going the right direction."

Alex rubbed the back of his neck. "That is good. Sleep is always healing. It will take some of the shock out of her system, too."

Nik nodded. He sat down on a chair near the door. "You need sleep."

"Later," he growled. "I just talked with Sergeant Killmer. Providing Lauren is stable, the CIA is flying in a C-130 transport two days from now into Lima. They are taking all of us, including you, to San Diego, California. There's a Naval hospital there and that is where our boss, Gage Hunter, wants her to go."

"Me?" Nik wondered. "I've already been in contact with my CIA and DOD handler. At some point, I'll have to fly back to Washington, D.C. and talk with him, and fill out a lot of paperwork."

"I am sure the paperwork will be in volumes," Alex agreed. "Petrov is going to be on that same flight with us, but the Military Police will be coming on board the transport to take him off in chains. The CIA wants to talk to him for a long time."

Nik frowned. "I'm hoping my DOD sponsor will allow me to stay in the U.S."

Alex grinned a little. "I told the owner of Shield, my boss, Jack Driscoll, what you did for all of us. How you saved Lauren's life. He is working with the DOD, CIA and the State Department, to get you a temporary visa. The CIA wants to talk to you as well, but it will not be an interrogation. They want your intel, is all. Names, places, faces. You know the drill. And then, our boss, Jack Driscoll is interested in offering you a job with Shield Security when this is all over. That is who Lauren and I work for as a private civilian contractor."

Scowling, Nik said. "I'm glad my family lives deep in our country where Russia cannot harm them."

Alex held up his hand. "They are safe in Ukraine. But the US is granting this to you and your brother, Dan. There is a representative in San Diego who will meet you at North Island Naval Air Station, where we will be landing. She will be your escort, the person who will help you get your papers in order to remain in the US before the Russian mafia in New York City even knows what you have done."

Rubbing his jaw, Nik muttered, "Then, it must happen quickly."

"Listen, my friend, this same woman who helped me get Kira out of Ukraine, will get your and Dan's papers in order for both of you to remain in America. The CIA considers you a valuable asset in the war against the Russian mafia down in Peru. My boss, Jack Driscoll, is very interested in you if you want a job. Shield pays their employees very well."

Nik shrugged. "Much is happening quickly, isn't it?"

"Sometimes too fast," Alex agreed. "But I am here. Once we land on Coronado Island, near San Diego, I will make sure you get a burner cell phone, and then, once we separate, we can remain in touch. I will be there for you. You do not have to go through this process alone," and he clapped his hand on his friend's broad shoulder. "I hope you will take up Jack's offer to come and work for Shield. It would be a good thing, Nik. We have always been brothers, so why not work together again?"

Nik shared a nod with him. "It sounds good to me. I didn't like working for the CIA." He brightened and grinned. "You know, your woman in there isn't going to be happy being bed-bound for at least three or four weeks? Every time she moves or walks, she is going to be in deep pain." He saw Alex quirk his mouth.

"I know. I am going to have to be creative to keep her from becoming bored and then restless. She is not the type to sit around at all." He saw Nik give him a wry grin.

"Good luck on that one."

For the first time in ages, Alex laughed. It felt good, joy spooling up through him because Lauren was going to make a recovery. He loved her. And he looked forward to quiet time with her. Alone. Just with her. And equally important, his best friend, Nik, was going to be safe. "I think we will use the time well, brother."

ALEX DOZED OFF and on into the early evening. Lauren slept soundly. Shock was the reason. The pink of the sunset in Lima was casting a pale shade throughout the small, private room. He was just awakening when he heard Lauren's movement. Raising his head, he saw her lift her right hand with the moveable cast on it.

"How are you feeling?" he asked, slowly getting up, feeling stiff and sore. The efforts they had put out during the last twenty-four hours had been brutal on everyone's bodies. He saw Lauren looked more awake. Alert maybe. She was resting her elbow on the bed, staring at her hand.

"Better," she said, her voice rusty. "How did this happen?" She raised her hand, looking at it in its cast.

He shrugged. "None of us know. Your five fingers are fractured. You have a hematoma in your palm. Do you remember anything?" He slid fingers across her temple, easing strands of hair behind her ear. Alex could see she was having difficulty.

"N-no."

"Shock plays hell on our memory. I am sure it will come back to you in a few days. Are you in pain, Lauren?" because Alex was studying the monitors. Her blood pressure was up and so was her pulse; usually a sign of aggravating pain. He thanked God he knew these things because he knew Lauren wasn't one to show pain nor complain about it. He saw her lips quirk.

"A little."

"How long have you been awake?" He stood and adjusted the morphine drip.

"Maybe fifteen minutes… I don't know," and Lauren gazed up at him. "You were sleeping. You look so tired, Alex."

He watched the monitors, all the indicators starting to go down toward normal, simply because the pain was being reduced. He touched her hair, stroking his fingers through those crimson strands. Touch mattered. More than anyone realized. But he did. "Fifteen minutes. Hmmm, well you must have been moving around a little? Cannot stay still?" and he gave her an amused look.

Pouting, Lauren admitted, "I was trying to sit up and it didn't go so well."

"Ah, that is why you are in so much pain." Alex leaned across the bed, putting a drop more of morphine into her IV.

"I hate being in bed," Lauren muttered defiantly.

"You are getting better, *malen 'kaya*. You have your impatience back." And no one could be happier than he was to see it. Alex saw the cloudiness in her eyes, knowing it stemmed from pain. Wanting to distract her, he teased, "Are you hungry? Take a flesh pound from me?"

Lauren grinned weakly. "Pound of flesh, Alex."

He gave a good-natured shrug. "Thank you. I will need you around to help me with your bastardized American slang in order to speak it correctly." He saw her eyes dance with laughter, but she wasn't laughing. Lauren knew it would hurt.

"How long am I going to be down with these ribs?"

He moved around the bed and saw all the monitors had gone back to their normal levels. Love healed. Pure and simple. And he loved her fiercely. Sliding his hand down her left arm, feeling the warmth back in her flesh, he would never forget seeing her lying in the mud, unconscious, her jacket torn-up across her chest. "You will not like the answer." He saw her scowl. Clearly, Lauren was fighting the grip of the deep shock; more like her old self.

"Try me?"

"Your ribs are deeply fractured. You were fortunate none of them actually broke. It takes people six to eight weeks to have any bone in their body to heal."

"Six weeks?" Lauren rasped, desperation in her hoarse voice.

Alex grinned. "Three to four weeks is the initial stage. The first three weeks are going to be very uncomfortable for you, Lauren. Every time you try to take a deep breath, you will get the knife-cutting pain on both sides of your chest. If you try to walk, you will feel pain with every step. You will not be able to twist or turn. I have seen men faint from pain when they have tried to go back into their job, do it too soon after being injured," he warned her gravely. "You will have to be on some sort of pain medication, but no doctor is going to sedate you to the degree that you feel no pain and then go out and reinjure yourself."

She sulked.

Alex held back a chuckle because he could see how it was impacting her. Lauren was never still. Most operators were a restless breed at best. At worst, they hated sitting around. And, even though she was a world-class sniper, and could lay still for days, if necessary, this was different. If Lauren were on a mission, she had the patience of Job. In a bed and injured? The look glittering in her eyes didn't bode well for him. Or for her perhaps listening to his experience and wisdom in such matters.

Lauren took stock of herself. She had been catheterized; she had an IV in her arm. Her right hand had a cast on it to just below the elbow. And it hurt to breathe. It had made her pop out in a sweat due to pain when she'd tried to push herself into a sitting position earlier. And the pain had damn near made her pass out and she'd halted her struggles.

"I know you hate this," Alex soothed, holding her distressed gaze. He saw tears glimmer in Lauren's eyes and, immediately, he wanted to sweep her into his arms and hold her safe. But he couldn't embrace her. It would cause her so much pain. Lauren wouldn't look at him, pursing her lips, fighting back the tears, swallowing several times until she'd mastered her emotions.

Alex said, "We are only going to be here in Lima for two or three days. A C-130 is taking us to Coronado. From there, you will be seen to by the finest Navy doctors at the Naval Medical Center in San Diego."

"Damn," she whispered. She felt Alex's hand squeeze her own uninjured one gently, as if to reassure her. "Who knew cracked ribs could take me down like this?"

"I do," he said. "I have had them before. You must listen to me, Lauren. If you want to be able to get on your feet in three weeks, you have to respect my experience about such an injury."

"Are you going to be with me? Am I going to be left at that hospital? What's Jack got planned?"

Alex realized some of her being upset wasn't about being bedbound for three weeks. As a child, when Laura was hurting, no one came to hold her, care for her. She had been abandoned. As he searched her upturned eyes, he understood the root of her reaction. Leaning down, he kissed her cheek, inhaling her feminine fragrance. "You will not be left alone," he promised her in a deep voice, thick with emotion. "I will be with you, Lauren. I am not going anywhere without you…"

CHAPTER 20

"WELCOME HOME, LAUREN," Sky said, reaching out and gently squeezing her left hand.

Lauren smiled at her best friend. Alex had driven them from Reagan Airport to her apartment. It smelled stuffy, but it always did when she returned from a mission. Sky and Cal stood just inside the front door of her duplex bungalow. The early August heat was dry compared to the withering humidity of the jungle of Peru. Alex released her elbow so she could walk into her bungalow under her own power. Sky's expression was anxious, because her friend walked so slowly and carefully, focused on the floor in front of her feet. Lauren had nixed a cane or a wheelchair, although if she had used one or the other, either would have helped her a lot. Her pride hadn't let her go there and Alex, thankfully, had said nothing, but surreptitiously shadowed her movements.

"It's nice to be home, Sky," Lauren said, meaning it. On the coffee table sat a bright bouquet of summer flowers. She could see Sky's pregnancy showing through the loose tee that she wore. Her blond hair was continuing to grow and she looked contented. Lauren was happy for both of the lovely couple.

"Would you like to sit down over here?" Cal asked, coming over and giving Lauren a peck on the cheek.

"No, I'm going to aim myself at that other chair," and she pointed to the overstuffed dark green chair in the corner of her small living room.

Alex closed the door and smiled over at Sky and Cal. "Thank you for meeting us." And quietly moved once more into his covert support role behind Lauren once again.

Cal wore jeans his hiking boots, and a red polo shirt. "We got food in for you like you asked," he told Alex.

"Thank you," Alex said, holding the chair steady for Lauren.

She slowly turned and sat down very carefully. Two weeks' worth of healing on her ribs had taught her through lessons of pain: how to walk, how to sit and how to lay in bed. She hated it, but didn't let it show to her friends.

"Thanks, guys, for getting us food."

While Sky and Cal sat down in other chairs to chat with Lauren, Alex brought in her heavy canvas military duffle bag. Later, he planned to take it to Shield and stow it in her locker. Her small suitcase sat beside it. Lauren looked pale. She'd tried to do too much, pride making poor choices for her. But he couldn't blame her. She'd hated every minute of being in the hospital. One of Cal's teams, ST3, had gifted them an apartment because the SEAL it was assigned to was currently out on deployment. Alex had seen a huge and positive change in Lauren's attitude after that move. Those two weeks were no longer an incarceration for her. Staying at the condo was a newfound freedom. Even better, it was on a ground floor with a small yard filled with colorful flowers, blooming bushes and shade trees. She often sat outside, enjoying the view that overlooked the nearby bay. The sound of water lapping, in his opinion, was always healing to a person. Plus, the salt air was invigorating to the body's oxygen system in general.

"What else can we do for you?" Sky asked. "Are you thirsty? I brought some of my sun tea with me. There's a gallon of it in your fridge."

"Or," Cal asked, "are you hungry?"

Lauren smiled wearily. "No... not really. Thank you for meeting us. It's so good to see both of you." She hadn't thought she'd ever see her best friends again. Or see Alex. Her heart wrenched. Lauren wanted to cry so badly, but if she did, the pain would be overwhelming, so she kept stuffing her feelings down deep inside herself. "How's the baby girl coming along?" she asked. Sky was now five-months pregnant. Lauren saw her friend smile softly, her hand automatically smoothing gently across her swelling belly.

"No more morning sickness," Sky said, rolling her eyes. "Thank goodness for small favors."

Alex wandered into the kitchen, looking around as the three of them chatted in the living room. He'd never been in Lauren's home. It was stark. Without life. It was as if someone stopped by here every once in a while, but didn't really live here. He moved his hand across the gray granite counter, frowning. Lauren's whole life was tied up in being a private contractor for hire. As he wandered down the carpeted hall, he saw no photos of friends or family on the walls. He pushed a door open; it was her bedroom. Alex stopped, shocked. The bed was an antique metal-frame Army cot! Some olive-green military blankets and a lumpy pillow were piled on it, unmade. He quietly shut the door, peeking into the bathroom. There was a tub with a shower, the bathroom itself quite large and roomy. It too, was sterile-looking. There was another room and he saw it contained a lot of unopened boxes and a desk with a computer on it. It looked as if Lauren were either unpacking to stay, or packing to leave again. Alex knew a home always mirrored its occupant. Disturbed by what he saw, he began to realize that Lauren's life was very narrowly defined and focused. Her home told him that she had no apparent hobbies, and no close connections to others, except for Cal and Sky. And himself. This place that she lived in, was dead. There was no personality expressed here. No life to it. Lauren had not put her stamp on it. Made it her own. He felt pain in his heart for her. Being abandoned so young, she had never had a nest or place that felt safe to her. Or that she could honestly just relax in and let her hair down. She was living half a life, if that, Alex thought, anguished.

When he returned to the living room, he could see Lauren was becoming weary. Cal looked up and Alex nodded toward the door, a silent request.

"Hey," Cal murmured, standing, "you're looking like you need to rest, Lauren. Sky and I were just passing through. We'll keep in touch by cell or Zoom? Or maybe I'll see you over at Shield in a week or two?"

"Yes, sometime…" Lauren said.

Sky walked over and touched her shoulder, giving her a kiss on the cheek. "You can also, if you want, come up and stay with us. You always have a guest room. You know that, right?"

"Thanks," she answered, giving Sky a grateful smile.

Cal opened the door. "Let's stay in touch," he told her. He lifted his hand and nodded toward Alex.

"Bye," Lauren called.

The door closed. Lauren sank wearily against the chair, closing her eyes. She felt Alex come around and she looked up at him. He was crouched beside her chair. She liked the cream-colored shirt he wore, bringing out the green, sienna and gold in his eyes as he silently appraised her. And he always looked good in those Levi's, showing off his spectacularly long, hard legs.

Alex reached out and curled her left hand into his palm, resting it against her left thigh. "I have an idea I want to fly past you," he said quietly, searching her darkening eyes. Lauren needed to be held. And, God knew, he wanted to do it. And hadn't been able to. Yet.

He watched her rally herself into her response, "What?"

"Would you be upset if I asked you to stay at my cabin instead of staying here?" He saw Lauren frown, considering his request.

"Why? Don't you like my place?"

The corner of his mouth curved faintly. "I feel in my heart, Lauren, you would be happier at my place right now."

"Because?"

"I have all my medical equipment over there, and pain drugs if you need them." Alex shrugged, trying to not broadcast how much he wanted her to leave this dead-zone. "And," he teased, "I have my own pots and pans, too. I can cook for you. I wanted to make you some good, hearty Ukrainian meals my grandmother taught me to make as I was growing up." He squeezed her hand. "It means a great deal to me if you'd like to join me. I know you are tired. If you do not want to, I am fine with you staying here, too." Because he didn't want to push her. He could feel how emotional Lauren was becoming. She hadn't quite broken down yet from the trauma she'd experienced. "I want you happy, Lauren," and Alex searched her weary gaze. They had lived in that SEAL condo for nearly two weeks together. Separate bedrooms because he couldn't hold Lauren due to her rib injuries. But, at least they were together and she seemed happy having him underfoot.

"Okay," Lauren whispered, her voice unsteady. Giving him a glance, she nodded. "I guess I'm just really tired... my mind is fuzzy... I'm not thinking clearly, Alex."

He caressed her cheek. "You are still coming off that shock cliff," he murmured. "Let me pack our things into my SUV. I want you to stay here and rest while I do it," and he rose.

Lauren felt her eyes begin to burn. Tears! Dammit! She could NOT cry! Looking around her quiet bungalow, it didn't feel like it had to her before her brush with death. It no longer made her feel partially safe from that monster outside world that always threatened her. Only Alex made her feel safe. And, when Cal had mentioned to her about going back to Shield, her gut had knotted and fear had threaded through her like a poison. Lauren didn't know what was going on within her or her emotions. Or why. The one thing her heart needed... that *she* needed, was Alex. He was the *only* oasis of peace she had found a haven within after being shot twice. And the idea of going over to his home strongly appealed to her. She didn't know why, but was glad that he'd suggested it. So, they went.

Lauren almost gasped with wonder as Alex led her into his single-story home. It was a cedar cabin at the edge of a clearing, thirty miles from Alexandria. There were evergreens, white-bark Aspen with dancing leaves, surrounding it. She saw a small lake nearby. As she walked slowly across the creaking cedar floor it felt so homey, embracing her, and that fed her, making her feel emotionally stronger. Much like Cal and Sky's place; it was filled with life, with green plants here and there, and framed family photos on the walls. The couch was huge, overstuffed, with a small, colorful quilt hung across the back of it. There were two old-fashioned rockers with plump pillows on their seats and backs. A large gold and red cedar coffee table had lots of bright red, orange and yellow pillows set on the floor around it; as if people sat there and ate, or played a board game with one another.

The house smelled good. Fresh. Unlike hers. She halted, absorbing the quiet of his home, seeing that the living room and kitchen were connected to one another.

"Well?" Alex asked, sliding his arm gently around her waist, but not pulling her against him, "how does it feel to you?"

"Warm… welcoming," Lauren admitted. Aching for his nearness, she wished mightily she could lean into Alex and really be held. Damn her healing ribs.

"Would you like a tour? Or would you like to go lay down, Lauren?"

"I need to sleep, Alex…"

"I thought so. Come, down this hall," and he gestured toward it. "I am giving you the master bedroom," he added.

"I don't need it," she protested, giving him a stricken look. "I don't want to kick you out of your own bed, Alex."

He gave her a very male smile. "*Malen 'kaya*, I will be sharing that bedroom with you. Unless, of course you do not want me there?" he teased, kissing her brow.

"But… my ribs… you said I wouldn't be able to sleep next to you for three weeks."

"I lied."

She grinned and shook her head, seeing merriment dancing in his eyes. "Don't you feel bad?"

"No." And then, as they continued their slow walk toward his bedroom, Alex said seriously, "we can try it tonight. Some people's ribs heal faster than others. If you are not wrapped in pain when I dip the mattress to come and lay a foot away from you, then you know it will be okay. It is a king-sized bed, plenty of room for both of us. I can be nearby."

Lauren felt a little of her inner tension begin to dissolve. "Let's try it. I'm ready."

So was he.

It was nearly eight p.m. when Lauren awoke from her nap in Alex's bed. He had lain beside her, but at a distance, so as not to curve the mattress and put pressure on her healing ribs. Lauren felt more rested than she could ever remember. She heard soft classical music drifting down the hallway through the partially-open door. Inhaling, she swore she smelled baking bread. The hint of cinnamon was in the air, too. It all smelled so good. Peace. That is what she felt here, in his home, in his bed. She closed her eyes, her heart blossoming and a desperate ache filling her. What would it be like to be really held by Alex? She heard him padding down the hallway. When he poked his head around the door, she muttered, "I'm awake."

"I thought so," he said. "May I come in?"

"Sure," she murmured sleepily. Lauren had found ways to push herself up into a sitting position. Her ribs were cranky, but the jagged pain was no longer there. This aggravation she could bear without a problem. She watched as Alex entered. He had a plate in one hand and was smiling.

"What's that?" Lauren asked, watching him come around the huge bed.

"Cinnamon rolls." He carefully sat down, far enough away from her that the bed wouldn't suddenly dip precariously. Holding the plate out to her, he said, "I like to bake and cook. Have one. My Grandmother taught me how to make them. There are walnuts, raisins and bits of orange peel in them."

They smelled heavenly, those four huge cinnamon rolls slathered with white sour cream frosting, steam rising from them. "Mmmm, they do smell good," Lauren agreed.

"Fork?"

She took it. "Thanks."

Alex watched Lauren's thick hair move beneath the low light from the hall. It was dusk, the last of a pink and lavender-tinged sunset visible through the large window at one end of the room. He watched her pick delicately at the roll with the fork. Her right hand was now without the cast, but her healing fingers were still stiff and not always working as well as she wanted. She would be going to physical therapy shortly, to help regain full use of them once again. The physician at the Naval hospital in San Diego had confirmed that she had had a pistol shot out of her right hand, and that had caused all the damage and fractures. He had told her that she was lucky that some of her fingers hadn't been shot off in the melee... that she was very lucky. Lauren still couldn't recall the firefight in its entirety, but Nik had told the doctor that she'd had her pistol in her right hand when one of the Russians had shot at her, striking her gun.

"Here," Alex murmured, tearing off a small bit from another roll. He blew on it for a moment and then placed it near her lips. "Try this?"

Lauren opened her mouth and took the warm morsel. She closed her eyes, savoring the spices and the sweetness. "Mmmmm, you are hired," she whispered, chewing and swallowing it.

"More?"

She nodded, placing the fork on the plate. "I like you feeding me." She saw tenderness come into his gaze as he placed a second bit of roll between her lips. "There are many ways to love your woman," he told her thickly. "It is not always about sex. It is about cherishing her in many ways, small ways, every day..."

A keen desire to be held by him moved through her. Lauren knew then that she was still alive. That nearly dying hadn't deadened her everywhere else. It was a sudden revelation and an utter relief. "I'd like some more. Please?" She saw his eyes glint with happiness. Lauren's heart expanded wildly with love for Alex. He held her gaze, so calm, strong and quiet. She accepted the tidbit. Swallowing it, she whispered, "When I opened my eyes and saw you after… after… I almost died out there in the jungle…"

Alex hesitated. He knew survivors of trauma could suddenly drop into a past recall like this, the polite and previous topics of conversation erased. She was back in the firefight. This was one of those times.

The silence filled the space between them, but it wasn't awkward, just searching. He saw the struggle in her expression, the anxiety and terror come to her eyes. "What are you feeling, *malen 'kaya?*"

"I don't know how to say this, Alex," she began haltingly. "I've just realized how much of life I have missed… I've been living in a very small space within it. I laid out there on the ground after being shot… gasping for air, knowing that I was going to die… that I've never known love… but, whatever these feelings are in my heart for you, they're real and they're new to me." She barely had the courage to look up at him, afraid of what he might say, how he might react or judge her.

He gave her a tender look. "Sometimes," he sighed quietly, reaching out and touching her left hand, "it takes a trauma to break an older, usually worse trauma. Or, as my wise mother told me, a person had to have a breakdown so that they could have a breakthrough and get on with healing themself from the inside out. She called them inner wounds, and she was right."

Frowning, she managed to croak, "What do you mean?"

"You were traumatized as a young child. Yes?"

She gave a hesitant nod.

He held her hand gently, tracing each long, beautiful finger. "I have seen this same reaction you are experiencing. On the battlefield," he began quietly. "Men I knew and fought with, who I knew about their personal lives… their trauma they'd endured while growing up. How they tried to protect themselves from it, Lauren, by shielding themselves so they could not be hurt again. And then, they took a bullet. And it shattered them, again, but I saw something good come out of it, in some of them. They were close friends with me, like we are, and I watched them open up, cry, and talking with me, sometimes for hours, to share the story of their first trauma as a child. And later, I saw being shot became an opening for them to heal that older wound, even though they had been physically wounded the second time with a second trauma. Whatever this psychological mechanism? It inspired my friends to take on the challenge of healing themselves as best they could from the original childhood experiences."

He gently squeezed her hand. "Perhaps? This is a window of opportunity for you to reclaim the lost parts of your childhood, Lauren? Those parts that did not participate in world like most people do. Now? You are aware of what you have missed, and you want to know… perhaps immerse yourself into exploring those areas at your own pace." He gave her a sad smile. "It is like a second chance at life… an unexpected opportunity… filled with more hope, more happiness, for that person. That is what I have seen over the years as a combat medic. Being shot was a blessing in disguise because it pried open that vault of horrors, pain and terror that my friends had carried all their lives, and they were finally able to release it. And it cleansed them in a way that, to me, seemed like a miracle. As they healed from the first trauma, this second, physical trauma, their bullet wound, they grew hopeful, no more depression, no more hiding behind their shields, no longer afraid to test or taste the richness that life could offer them going forward. As they healed from that bullet wound, they healed the early wound and then turned around, and embraced all of life for the first time." He cocked his head. "Is this making any sense to you about your own trauma?"

She closed her eyes and nodded, her fingers tightening around his. "Yes," she choked out, opening her eyes and holding his tender gaze, "it does… and I feel like such a coward. I don't want to go back to who I was before this second wounding, back into my shell." Frustration tinged the words as they rushed out of her. "You have given me so much, Alex. It's the way you have treated me, been kind and helpful to me in large and small ways. I never thought a man like you could exist. I was always distrusting of most of them. Until you came along." She shook her head. "At first, I thought you were like them, but after learning so much more about you, and how much Sky and Cal trusted you. And because I trusted them, I began to trust and see you differently from the rest of them."

"And then," Alex offered, "the second trauma happened… you almost dying…"

She rubbed her eyes and her hands dropped into her lap. "I remembered thinking that I'd just found you and now, I was going to die…"

"But you did not. You are alive. You are processing a huge, life-changing ordeal, Lauren. It is a chance for you to change your life and, I hope, for the better. I am here. I will always be someone who you can trust, who has your back." He pressed his hand to his chest. His voice dropped to an emotional rasp. "Perhaps you do not want to hear this, and perhaps it is the wrong time to tell you this, but I must say it: As I was trying to save your life on that muddy hillside, in the dark, hearing you barely able to breathe, I breathed for you. I kept saying, I love you, do not die, please, let us have a chance to hold and love one another…"

Lauren stared at him, her heart thudding once to underscore what he'd just shared with her. She saw the turmoil in his eyes. He was suffering just as much as she was, she realized. "I didn't know what love was, Alex. I kept feeling this wonderful sensation in my chest every time I was around you. It felt like my heart was opening up, and it was so strange to me that it scared me. I've never been in love. I don't know what love is. But, since going to Peru with you, everything has changed. I just feel so tenuous right now, so unsure of myself and I'm afraid to trust how I feel toward you."

"Only one thing will cure you of that," he said, giving her a slight smile. "Hang around with me, Lauren. Get to know me, frog warts and all."

Her heart opened powerfully as Alex struggled to communicate with her on such an important, personal level. She didn't have the heart to let him know the slang wasn't correct. She whispered, "I *do* want to be around you. I'm afraid you'll get tired of me being underfoot."

He shook his head. "I promise you, that will NEVER happen. Ever. You move my heart, my soul, Lauren. I live to see your hair tumble around your shoulders when you allow it to be free from that horse tail. I live to see your eyes grow light because I know you are happy and at peace. I want nothing more than to hear you laugh, to see you smile, because no one, and I mean no one, deserves this gift of freedom to love me in return more than you do."

Tears burned in her eyes and she held his darkening gaze, seeing that, he too, had suffered just as much as she had. "Does love hurt, too?"

"If you love, then there is always a chance that if you lose the other person, or they are taken away from you, or they suddenly die… yes, the pain is the deepest I know of. If you do not love because of fear you may one day experience that kind of pain and suffering might happen? Not loving someone because of that? To me, that choice is not the answer. I would rather love and then lose the person I love, than never to have allowed myself to love them in the first place."

She straightened and looked around the room. "There is nothing but suffering, grief and pain in this world, Alex."

"That is true, but there is also love in this world to balance off that darkness, too, Lauren. No matter if you love your child that comes from your body, or you love your husband, or your dog, or the neighbor's children or some elderly person or the beggar on the street, it is worth it to me to feel that beautiful emotion. I can't answer that question for you. I wish I could because I believe we could share a wonderful life filled with love, with happiness, laughter and joy with one another. You have to make that decision. No one can make it for you."

Frowning, Lauren said quietly, "Sky told me that you'd lost your entire family, parents, grandparents and others and yet, you want to love me? I don't lead a safe life, Alex. Nor do you."

"All of that is true," he admitted heavily. He rubbed his chest. "But I guess I am an optimist, I always hope, I always see the good in people. Yes, I know there are bad people in this world. I want to always have hope alive in my heart. I want goodness for this world, for helping others, feeling good at supporting them no matter their age or who they are. I believe our heart, our ability to love, is the better choice."

Lauren's brow creased and she asked, "Do you really think there's hope for someone like me?"

"You, more than most, *Malen 'kaya*. We cannot erase your past, but we can put our energy and what is important to us, allowing your past to finally be healed, and us moving into the present with one another. When you love someone? There are two people involved. If they love one another? That is two times the love that they will share with one another. Love is the most powerful, the most beautiful and healing emotion we own as human beings. I hope that my love for you will support your heart to trust me enough to someday, reach out and love me in return," and he held her glistening gaze, tears moving down her cheeks.

Leaning forward, he cupped her face, and removed that moisture from her warm skin. Her pupils were large and black, that soft dove-gray surrounding them. Leaning over, he whispered against her parting lips, "This is what love between two people feels like…" and he met her lips that were moist with salty tears as he skimmed them with his own, waiting for her to respond. And she did, a low pleasurable sound vibrating in her throat. Alex felt her initial reaction as he continued to gently move his lips against her mouth's response to his overture. Joy surged through him as she responded strongly, taking him by surprise, a wave of pleasure thundering through his chest, his heart beginning to pound with such joy that he had to rein in his physical response to her reaction. Slowly parting from her lips, he could hear her breathing a little faster, as was he, their gazes clinging to one another, both drowning in the powerful feelings that they had unleashed through that simple kiss.

"This," he whispered against her lips, "is how love feels between two people…"

CHAPTER 21

THE LATE SEPTEMBER sun was low on the horizon, the day growing cooler as Lauren and Alex sat on the sundeck after the delicious barbecue meal. Being able to hear the birds sing their last songs before the cover of night was drawn across the sky, Lauren was content to sit in the two-person rocker with Alex. His arm was around her and she rested her cheek against his shoulder, her other hand covered his heart. Closing her eyes, she whispered, "This is perfect... all of this... I never dreamed I could ever be so happy, Alex." She opened her eyes, shifting her chin to catch his downward gaze at her. He gently squeezed her shoulder.

"I had so many dreams of you after I met you and you wanted nothing to do with me."

She sighed. "I was awful toward you."

"Well," he murmured, kissing the top of her head, "I survived."

"Because you dreamed?" She studied him as he looked back off into the distance across the darkening lake.

"In my heart," he said, "I knew you were the woman I had been waiting for all my life. It did not matter to me that you did not like me at first. I knew with time and patience; I could show you I was not someone to dislike or see me, a man, as a threat."

"Even back then," Lauren mused softly, moving her hand gently across his massive chest, "you knew..."

Nodding, he smiled a little. "My instincts have never led me wrong and I trusted them. And, look what happened. Are you happy about it?"

"A hundred percent." She sat up and whispered, "I want to love you, Alex. Right now."

"I like a woman who knows her mind," he murmured, catching her hand, pulling her gently to her feet. He led her into the cabin and shut the door for the night. Leading her down the hall, he drew her into their bedroom. While Alex divested himself of his shoes, socks, Levi's and black t-shirt, she disrobed as well, placing her clothes over the top of a nearby chair. Lauren felt him come up behind her, turning her around in his arms and drawing her lightly in against his naked body. The look in his eyes melted her heart, her soul. There was such raw love shining in his green, sienna and gold eyes, that her throat tightened. As he reached up, loosening her top knot so that her hair fell and flowed like a crimson river around her shoulders, she saw predatory lust come to his eyes, too.

"You are a warrior's woman. Do you know that? So proud. Brave. Strong and fearless."

His words were as if they were touching Lauren physically, his voice roughened with need. "All I need is you. My other half," she whispered, sliding her hands around his thick, broad shoulders, "to make me whole…"

Alex nodded and picked her up, carefully placing her on her back in the center of the bed. He joined her, propping himself up on his left elbow, his hand trailing down her left arm, her hip, to her long, curved thigh. Closing her eyes, Lauren wanted to remember every touch he shared with her, her skin riffling with sparks of heat wherever he trailed those roughened fingers across it. As his lips moved slowly across her hairline, she felt his hand settle against her hip.

"*Malen 'kaya*," he breathed, "you must tell me if I make you scared?" Lifting his head, Alex held her soft mourning-dove-colored gray eyes that were barely open yet simmering with so much arousal. "Tell me no, and I will stop immediately." This was something he'd kept saying ever since they had begun slowly introducing her into the realm of loving one another. To him, it bared repeating, wanting her to always know that she was in control. Caressing her flushed cheek he scowled, feeling his own fear of doing something that would trigger a flashback, or loosen a terror from her childhood that could overwhelm her. So many things could happen, and *had* happened between them already. They went at her pace so that she was in control of the situation at all times and it was working well for them.

Understanding that the past was still alive and being slowly healed, there were moments he hesitated; those where he sensed she would experience a flashback. Lauren had no power over them, so they would stop, communicate with one another, talk some more, and sometimes cry and hold one another. More than anything, his way of seeing her was not as a woman to have sex and self-gratification with. Rather, that he loved her and wanted to share that love with her—on her own terms and needs. That decision between them had made these rocky times far easier to deal with for both their sakes.

Once Lauren had understood his perspective on her, and them as a couple, it had made it easier for her, too. When his touch set off a flashback, she would freeze and he would wait, listen to her needs, and give them to her. Most often, when these times occurred, she reverted back to that frightened, hurting little seven-year-old girl she had once been and he would gently wrap her up in his arms, hold her safe and protected, giving Lauren the opportunity to then work through all this, instead of being paralyzed and overwhelmed by it. He was her partner. He would never allow her to go through one of these episodes alone.

"I will tell you if I get scared," she promised, her voice husky. Sliding her fingers across his jaw, his stubble of beard making prickles of heat leap through their tips, she smiled up at him. "You look so worried. Don't be? It will be all right. We'll take this next step together, Alex?"

Swallowing, Alex nodded, pressing his brow to hers. "I am afraid, Lauren. For you. For what I might do without knowing that I have harmed you."

"You love me, you big teddy bear," Lauren whispered, gripping his shoulder and giving him a small shake. "Sometimes, I feel scared too, but not for those reasons. I'm such a neophyte at this; learning the ways of how to love someone… I know so little…" She saw him give her a very confident, male smile.

"Teaching you about your body is one of my greatest joys, *malen 'kaya.* I want you to always be natural, flow with your body's desires. Do not be afraid to moan or cry out. It is healthy. Wonderful. But," and his brows dipped, "There is a way to do this, that gives you all the control. All right?"

Nodding, Lauren had never felt as safe, as cared for, as right now in his arms. "It will be all right. I feel it, Alex, here, in my heart. Because we love one another, nothing bad is going to happen tonight."

"Still," he whispered, his mouth barely grazing her lips, "talk to me. Tell me what feels good. What you want. I will go only as far as you want me to go. I will never force myself on you."

"I know that," she quavered, feeling tears enter her eyes. Of all times, Lauren didn't want to cry right now. Just the tenderness in his gaze, in the grave quality of his rumbling voice, made her heart fly open on wings of such joy that it took her breath away. "You have always been my teacher. Teach me more tonight?" and she leaned up, capturing his mouth, deepening their kiss. Lauren might not know everything yet, but she knew how to incite Alex into groans of need that shook his entire body. It was an amazing discovery of her own power as a woman influencing her man. And it was done with love for one another.

His tongue moved boldly against hers and Lauren squirmed, thrusting her hips against his turgid erection. He felt like warm steel pressing insistently into her belly, making her channel contract, more fluid collecting between her thighs. She lost track of time, centering her heart, her mind, her soul, on his hand moving down the length of her spine.

Lifting his mouth, he gently caught the nape of her delicate neck between his teeth, sending a wave of teasing electrical jolts downward, tightening her breasts, making her nipples throb and become erect. And then he released his teeth, slowly licking the fading pink welt he had left behind, his warm breath moist, then kissing it. Lauren felt the deliciousness of his tactics, her body melting, reacting, wanting…

As his hand curved around her breast, she felt its calluses inciting her flesh to grow taut. Moaning as he dragged his thumb across her nipple, she pressed wantonly against his erection. His lips left the tingling flesh of her neck, moving languidly across her super-sensitive collar bones. It was a movable feast of heat combined with raw pleasure and Lauren couldn't just lay passively next to him. She arched her breast deeper into his large, roughened palm. It was then that he lifted his head, and his lips captured that taut nipple, suckling her. Lauren's world flew apart as she felt wild slivers of heat boiling down through her, making her cry out. It was a cry of utter surprise, woven through with savage unexpected pleasure for her. Fire rippled out conically from around her breast, widening, making her arch hard against him, her hand gripping his back, her leg tangling with his.

Smiling to himself, Alex lavished the other nipple with the same kind of attention, and he felt Lauren dissolving, becoming wild and restless against him. She was not trained or studied in how a man could love her. Instead, her reactions were natural, and his heart soared as he felt her move sinuously against him, her warm, velvet flesh against his toughened skin. She was all softness, curves, hunger, her mewls like sweet songs making him so damned hard that he could barely control himself. Her hair moved in ripples of crimson and gold, strong, silky, and free, like she was. Reveling in her entrusting her body to him, Alex moved his hand downward, sliding his long fingers over the curve of her thigh, gently opening her, making her available for the further delights that he could gift her with. He suckled her while he eased his fingers around to her inner thigh, feeling how wet it already had become. She was more than ready but he wasn't going to take any chances.

The moment he traced her outer entrance, she stiffened against him, a low sound of pleasure rising out of her, fingers frantic against his back. Easing inside her, stroking that swollen knot, she sobbed his name, clinging to him. Pleasing this woman—his woman—allowing her to be the wild, instinctive Steppe pony from Mongolia that she had always been in his heart, was all he wanted. He lived to give Lauren full knowledge of her body, to give her the confidence in herself to enjoy these treasures. Alex had always hoped her past could remain behind her and that they could build a new foundation based upon mutual pleasure and their love, instead. Maybe? Maybe this was one of those times? He hoped so.

She was going to orgasm. He held her close, suckling more strongly upon her nipple, boldly stroking her, and Alex felt her entire body clench from the inside out. Her fierce cry surrounded them as he felt a hot rush of fluids, feeling her body spasm. Lauren was frozen in ecstasy, and he continued to milk her. Sobs tore out of her, and he placed his teeth on the other nipple, squeezing it just enough to walk the line of that pleasure-pain threshold. And when he did, a second orgasm flooded through her, making her gasp in surprise. Alex could feel the fine quiver running through her damp, tense body, her back arched, head thrown back, her eyes closed, a flush spreading swiftly up across her chest and into her neck and face. He felt damned good being able to bring her willingly, without fear, without reprisal, to this climatic moment, for the first time in her life.

Easing out of her, he soothed her hip and thigh, as if calming a fractious horse. Her breath came in pants, her fingers dug deeply into him, a sign of how much raw pleasure she was still experiencing. Alex knew he had to give her time to ramp down, her body now over-sensitive and in need of a rest for a bit. Laying her gently onto her back, her red hair flowed like molten lava around her flushed face still filled with ecstasy: her eyes closed, her lips parted, nostrils flared, drinking in great draughts of air like a wild Steppe pony on a hard run. She was indeed his untamed woman, and he kissed her damp brow, inhaling her scent, the ache in his own body intense. He wanted nothing to take away from this precious moment of discovery for her. Each time they loved one another was new step for her, and Alex was determined to give her the time she deserved to absorb all of it.

Lauren's heart was beating like a fluttering bird in her chest. She felt Alex's lips on her brow, her temple, soothing her, giving her time to recover, to satiate herself with the scalding splendor of her own body. She was floating, no longer tethered to the earth, only to his arm beneath her neck, his large, roughened hand moving slowly up and down her hip and leg. His moist breath feathered across her cheek and temple as he gently took her mouth, relishing her lips, her instant response, her woman's heat meeting his male hunger.

Alex knew he would not lay over her in order to enter her. It was just too much weight on her newly healed ribcage. He slowly released her.

"Come," he urged her quietly, helping her to sit up. Her gray eyes were blown; pupils huge, silver in their depths, telling him of the utter pleasure she was still experiencing. Settling himself up against the headboard, he eased one of her thighs across his hips and then brought his knees up, supporting her back, his hands resting lightly on her upper arms. She was flushed, nostrils still flared, lips moist from the hungry kisses they had shared. She settled her wet, hot core against his thickened erection. Alex gritted his teeth, his fingers tightening momentarily on her firm upper arms. Lauren hadn't realized how much this would affect him. This was their first time introducing her to this particular position. And it was the only way to control her descent into another way to love one another. To give her even more orgasms.

She placed her hands on his wide shoulders, her red hair like a waterfall cresting her shoulders, flowing down over her breasts. Alex smiled into her half-opened eyes, liking what he saw. He settled his hands around her flared hips. "Do you feel me against you, *malen 'kaya?*"

Nodding, she licked her lower lip, barely coherent, still floating in that nether-world of heat and sensation. "Y-yes..." She felt his fingers grip more firmly against her hips, drawing her a little forward. Instantly, she moaned, sudden jolts of pleasure emanating from where they slid against one another. Oh, that felt electrifying! Wonderful! And she saw Alex smile up into her eyes.

"Good?"

"Umm," she managed, stretching her torso upward, allowing him to slowly ease her back and forth across his hard length and thickness. "Ohhh..." and her eyes closed as she lifted her chin, lost in the wickedly scalding heat boiling within her from their newest connection.

"Now," he rasped thickly, "lean toward me, Lauren." She did so, their mouths meeting, clinging to one another. And, as she moved forward, Alex felt his tip pressing hotly against her wet gate, asking for entrance. A quiver flew through her as they met. Her mouth lifted from his. Her hands knotted into his shoulders. "That's it," he growled, "take as little or as much as you want of me into you, *malen 'kaya.* Do not hurry it. Just... appreciate the sensations... let your body be your guide as to how little or much you desire of me..." and he gritted his teeth as she boldly moved her body, allowing him entrance into her welcoming depths.

His fingers dug convulsively into her hips as she moved the first few inch-es, easing back and forth on him, her body acquainting itself with his, with all these newly discovered sensations. He didn't have to worry about protection because Lauren was on the pill. And every sweet movement of her core against him made him groan with an intense feeling close to pain, and yet far from it. His entire body was galvanized, the throbbing ache building until he pressed his head against the headboard, trying to control himself. He could feel her breath hitching, enjoying the new pleasure she was delighting in, and he could feel her walls begin to grip him even though he wasn't even halfway into her loving body. He knew he was large, and she was so tight and small. Keeping up the gentle rhythm, the back-and-forth movement along his length, he saw her lashes sweep down across her cheeks, her lips parting, her back beginning to arch. She was going to come again and, this time, he wouldn't be able to stop himself from coming, either.

Just as he thought she would orgasm; Lauren drew nearly all of him deep within her. The movement surprised him, took him off-guard for a split second. He heard her moan, felt her fingernails dig into his flesh, realizing it wasn't from pain. Instead, it was him filling her in every way, triggering even more pleasurable sensations that she'd just discovered. When he felt her body relax around him, accommodate him, he began to move her gently once more, to show her how much more enjoyment they could both gain by being deeply seated into one another. Sweat popped out on his brow. His nostrils flared. He felt Lauren realize it, too. Those sweet sounds spilling out of her exposed throat sent him into a special heaven and hell. He fought to control himself so that she could fully experience her body singing with the lush delights of being loved.

Just as he felt Lauren tense with a swift intake of breath, her walls contracted around him so tightly that Alex couldn't control himself any longer. Just as the white-hot orgasm shattered through her, scalding him, he felt his own avalanche of heat erupting through him, flooding her with himself. Drowning in her heat, in her cries of exquisite surprise, Alex allowed her to ride him as never before. He moved her firmly, giving her even more stimulation... raw, unbridled sensations... until he heard her crying out in utter satiation with each stroke.

Lauren felt her entire universe shatter and explode into billions of shards of light reflecting behind her tightly-shut eyes. She felt the thrust of his erection deep inside her, feeling her body give way, thirsty, hot and wet. All she could do was hold onto his broad shoulders, hearing his groan and the hiss of air between his clenched teeth as she rode him. The movement was like hot silk building into another explosion, and the lavishness of sensations tore through her once more. With a groan, all she could do afterward was sag limply against his damp body, her silky hair spilling across his chest and shoulders, tangling teasingly around her sensitized nipples, sending even more charged currents through her and down to her orgasming lower body. It was just too much and she felt hurled into timelessness, where she was held in light, boiling heat by rippling sensations that deepened with each of his wave-like thrusts. Feeling lightheaded, Lauren collapsed fully against Alex, the ongoing undulations of pleasure flowing vibrantly through her.

Alex couldn't move. He felt drained in a completely good way as Lauren sank against him, her head on his shoulder, her breath coming in sobs. It had been good for both of them. *The best.* Skating his large hand down her damp back, she felt boneless to him. Fully satisfied. Slowly, he carefully eased out of her and then placed her onto the bed beside him. Lauren moaned, as if not wanting to lose that living connection with him. She would be sore enough, soon enough, and Alex knew her body needed the rest.

He brought her into his arms, and held her safe. Held her forever. She made a humming sound of satisfaction deep in her throat as he brought her against him, his leg wrapping around hers, fully pressing her against him in every possible way. The fan of her silky red hair felt cool in contrast to the damp heat of her skin against himself. Lauren's breath was stabilizing. She nuzzled her face against his neck and shoulder, as Alex felt her fingers glide through the dark hair across his chest. She was still boneless. Utterly relaxed, all the tension she'd carried dissolving beneath the orgasms and loving him. He absorbed her soft, moist breath, felt her lips form a kiss upon his flesh. Smiling, he rasped, "It was good, *malen 'kaya*. The best... I love you..."

LAUREN DROWSILY OPENED her eyes. She was laying against Alex. No longer damp and hot, she felt the dry warmth of his arm around her shoulders, holding her close to him. Dusk was upon them. What time was it? Did she care? Closing her eyes, she could feel the heat and subtle ripples still ongoing in her lower body. It was such a good, clean feeling. Wonderful. Lauren wasn't sure she was even back in her body yet. She felt Alex's fingers move lightly across her shoulder, letting her know he too, had awakened.

Lifting her head, she met his hooded eyes, seeing the gold dancing in their depths. A soft smile came to her lips and she leaned upward, kissing the corner of his mouth. "I love you, Alex Kazak. You've given me something so incredible... I just can't give it words."

He smiled lazily and nodded. "Love needs no words, *malen 'kaya*. We talk to one another in a different way. Real love like this is to be savored and enjoyed." Opening his eyes more, he drowned in her soft gray gaze. "I love you..." Her tremulous smile undid him in every possible way. Alex had seen the question in her eyes, asking if she was good enough, if she had pleased him, too. Understanding Lauren's lingering lack of confidence, he slid his fingers through her hair, moving strands away from her face. "You love like a wild woman. You are hot, hungry and unafraid. You are the kind of woman I will spend my life with, exploring you, your beautiful, sensitive body and loving heart." He saw tears come up into her eyes, and her doubts dissolving.

"It was so good, Alex. I never realized all of this until just now, with you," and she sighed, resting her brow against his chest.

He drew her up and settled her along his length. It would be at least another month before he would even think of lying on top of her with his considerable weight. For now, he was perfectly fine with her long, lean, firm body like a blanket covering his. She liked it too, snuggling her face into the crook of his shoulder. Lauren moved her hips suggestively against his growing erection, realizing that doing so, and feeling his response to her sinuous, teasing movements only increased her confidence. Smiling, Alex closed his eyes, gliding his fingertips down her long, strong spine. He wanted Lauren to show, in her own way, what she wanted from him. The clock on the dresser read nine p.m. Two hours had passed. He was more than ready to please her again if that's what she wanted. Right now, Alex wanted her to choose her own pace. In the months to come, he was going to enjoy showing her all the ways a man could love his woman. The mere thought of the deep joy of sending her into that bright, hot light where one was mindless, her body burning with pleasure, and then, languishing in the fire of love their hearts had created, made him smile.

He thought about how they had met, and how much she had disliked him, but now, so many months later, he knew the whole story of why she'd reacted to him the way she had. Stroking his hand gently across her hair, he felt her relaxing against him, indicating that she was falling asleep. Alex knew that the shock and trauma of almost dying were still working their way through her. The bright spot was their love for one another. Smiling to himself, holding her gently, he closed his eyes. When the time was right, he would ask her when they should get married. That would come, and for him, having the woman he'd so artlessly fell in love with, to have their home, living together, mattered the most to him because of the loss of his own family. Yes, everything he'd lost, and everything Lauren had had equally taken from her, was being given back to them. Only this time, it was good news wrapped in a bow of happiness. Their lives were already as one and, soon perhaps, after Sky gave birth to her baby girl, Lauren would want to set a date for their marriage. It was something to look forward to and Alex closed his eyes, resting his jaw lightly against her red hair, at peace as never before. Together, they had so much to look forward to—together. Forever.

EPILOGUE

ON FEBRUARY 14th, Valentine's Day, Alex married Lauren in St. Sophia's Orthodox church near Alexandria, Virginia. Sky was Lauren's Maid of Honor, and Cal was Alex's Best Man. The entirety of Shield's employees were all there in happy attendance. Cal's ST3 SEAL team members also came. Jack Driscoll, having volunteered to hold Cal's and Sky's two-month-old baby daughter, Makayla, smiled broadly, cradling the sleeping tyke. And sitting with him was Kira, Alex's sister. She was coming along well in her recovery from her own trauma and wanted to be there to see her big brother happily married. It meant the world to Alex, a huge load of worry lifted off his shoulders as his sister finally turned the corner, her mental and emotional health beginning to improve.

Lauren looked positively glowing in a white wedding dress that was was a simple sheath, the top of it beaded with small white and black rainbow-colored pearls adorning the bodice. Her red hair was a burnished and shining red cape around her shoulders. A delicate headband of small pink roses, and white rose buds with purple stock, encircled her head, with their green vines woven into the long lengths of her hair. Her bouquet mirrored her headdress, consisting of fragrant white lilacs, pink roses, one large white peony, and touches of fragrant purple stock. She wore a pair of black Tahitian pearl earrings set in gold, gifted to her from Alex the day before the wedding.

When Alex slipped the gold wedding band onto Lauren's finger, with the single black Tahitian pearl set into it that she'd worn since he'd given it to her months earlier, she felt hot tears leaking into her eyes. The expression on his face was tender with love for her alone. It only made her love him even more than ever before.

Jack Driscoll sat there, shadowing Sky and Cal's baby daughter during the wedding. Kira Kazak, having flown in from San Diego, took over the major duties of holding and feeding the baby, and was more than happy to do so. Jack had caught a lot of jibes later, at the wedding reception, but took them all in good stride. After all, he'd remained single, so it was an interesting curiosity to the other nosy males as to why he'd wanted to be a babysitter for the wedding occasion. Driscoll merely grinned and said he was Kira's and the baby's bodyguard for the day. Kira carried Makayla around, changing diapers and rocking the tyke asleep in her arms after feeding her. Jack made sure she got a piece of the wedding cake and took over the holding duties of Makayla while they sat in a quieter corner of the massive building that held the party, discovering one another.

After the rousing reception, there was dancing and merriment, and then Alex took his new bride home to their cabin. It was there that he gave her one last wedding gift: a necklace of black Tahitian pearls that she had, at one time, confided to him of dreaming all her life of owning a complete strand of. Knowing that the cost of such an extravagant necklace was beyond nearly any operator's ability to buy, she had drawn in a sharp breath upon opening the long white jewelry box. A triumphant look came into Alex's eyes, the grin on his face widening as she gasped with delight at the unexpected gift. The pearls were graduated, a dark gray-black with the rainbow colors of pink, purple, blue and hints of yellow and green, glinting and reflecting from each one as she held the warm, living necklace in her hands.

"They are like you, *malen'kaya*," he told her, his voice roughened with emotion as he sat on the couch next to her, holding her tearful gaze. "Out of the darkness of your young life, you chose to become like the pearl through the grit and sand of those painful early years. You began to build the nacre, the fluid created by the oyster to protect and internally heal itself, and surround that wound. You became a beautiful pearl yourself, a woman with a good heart and soul, despite it all." He touched the pearls, holding her gaze, and then lifted his hand, cupping her damp cheek. "We have nothing but goodness on our path together in front of us, and I am so grateful that you are sharing your life with me."

END

Don't miss Lindsay McKenna's next Shadow Team series novel, *Unforgettable*.

Available from Lindsay McKenna and Blue Turtle Publishing and wherever you buy eBooks.

Excerpt from Unforgettable

D ARIA FELT HER entire life shifting on its foundation as she sat next to Ukrainian combat medic, Nik Morozov, in an ancient Spanish church in Aguas Caliente, Peru. This was where she was to meet her black ops partner in order to complete the coming, deadly mission. She felt the heat of his tall male body, more than a little aware of his powerful shoulders that she knew carried so many loads. His profile consisted of light and dark, emphasizing the high cheekbones to his oval face, full mouth that was pursed and ending in a strong jawline and chin. There was such steadiness and grounding energy around him that Daria sat in silent awe of it. Maybe this is what had gotten Nik through five long years in this green hell, as Alex Kazak, his Ukrainian friend and brother combat medic, referred to Peru's jungle areas. There was such quiet strength in his face. He was not handsome. His face showed the ravages and stress of his life, slashes on either side of his mouth, fine lines at the corners of his eyes, horizontal wrinkles across his brow, as if he frowned a lot. There was no joy in his face. But why should there be with his past and present? All Nik knew was work and bone crushing responsibility not only for Dan, his wounded brother, but to survive and remain a CIA mole under Russian Korsak's drug team in the Peruvian jungle. He worked to make enough money to help his brother Dan.

The first time she met his eyes, she felt her entire lower body quiver, like a deer that had been spotted by a stag during mating season, that palpable sensation vibrating through her like a tuning fork. Those azure colored eyes with huge black pupils of his, saw so much more than most people realized. Daria acknowledged it and for whatever reason, she did not try to hide herself from his nearly x-ray looking intent gaze as his gaze caressed hers. And it was a caress, not a threat. That was the defining difference as their gazes briefly met to acknowledged one another's connection in this dance with death. The CIA had given Nik had a photo of her, and she felt every cell in her body vibrate with the awareness that he knew who she was.

Daria put great stock into looking deeply into another person's eyes. They were the mirror to a person's soul, no question. And as she intuitively plumbed the depths of his, she felt a terrible, wrenching sadness embrace her. She could feel the grief he carried so darkly and deeply within himself. He had seen too much, lived through so much, and was a survivor, like herself, she realized. They were two badly wounded animals, heavily scarred and yet, still ambulatory, still able to survive in a world that was never friendly or safe. Daria didn't know what safety felt like. She never had.

Until this moment when Nik's gaze met hers, Daria recognized him as from the same herd of humans who had shared similar life experiences. It wasn't a bad thing at all. In fact, it sent a frisson, a sensation so sweet and unexpected through her, that her breath jammed momentarily in her tightening throat. The sadness she saw in his eyes made her tear up and she turned away, swallowing several times, pushing her reaction deep down within herself. She did not want to cry. She would not cry! Her tears had been spent on that unnamed hill in the Hindu Kush Mountains as the sniper, as she sat there with Melissa, her spotter, dead in her arms. Her own life was flowing out of her as she waited, prayed that the Black Hawk medevac would get there in time before they found her dead, also. In the darkness, she cried so hard, the sobs ripping out of her as she held on to her friend who had fought so bravely and fiercely to save her life. And Melissa had. She'd stood up and took the brunt of the initial attack, two curved daggers penetrating between the plates of her body armor, finding her lungs, tearing into them. It had given Daria time to pull her own knife and fight off the other Taliban soldier coming to kill them.

All those horrifying moments unrolled slowly in front of her and she no longer saw the church they sat in, or its inhabitants, or hearing the priest speaking in Latin, dressed in his white and gold robes. She saw nothing but those long, tortured minutes as they fought off the Taliban group who had accidentally come upon them in the darkness. Their intent was to murder them without remorse.

As she had looked into Nik's large, intelligent blue eyes, she saw and sensed similar horror that he'd witnessed in his life. Maybe more than once? He was a mirror reflection of her and that gut punching knowledge staggered her. It was just too much for one human soul to absorb, much less carry by itself. And in that second, she realized Nik would become her ally. He was someone who had experienced similar horrors in combat. She saw it in his gaze even though he fought to recess it, keep it in the background, just like she did. Daria wondered if he saw the same thing in her eyes as they made that second connection with one another in order to complete a deadly mission together.

Available from
Lindsay McKenna

Blue Turtle Publishing

SHADOW TEAM SERIES
Last Stand
Collateral Damage
No Quarter

NON-SERIES BOOKS
Down Range (Reprint)
Dangerous Prey (Reprint)
Love Me Before Dawn (Reprint)
Point of Departure (Reprint)
Touch the Heavens (Reprint)

WOMEN OF GLORY SERIES
No Quarter Given (Reprint)
The Gauntlet (Reprint)
Under Fire (Reprint)

LOVE & GLORY SERIES
A Question of Honor, Book 1 (Reprint)
No Surrender, Book 2 (Reprint)
Return of a Hero, Book 3 (Reprint)
Dawn of Valor, Book 4 (Reprint)

LOVE & DANGER SERIES
Morgan's Son, Book 5 (Reprint)
Morgan's Wife, Book 6 (Reprint)
Morgan's Rescue, Book 7 (Reprint)
Morgan's Marriage, Book 8 (Reprint)

WARRIORS FOR THE LIGHT
Unforgiven, Book 1 (Reprint)
Dark Truth, Book 2 (Reprint)
The Quest, Book 3 (Reprint)
Reunion, Book 4 (Reprint)
The Adversary, Book 5 (Reprint)
Guardian, Book 6 (Reprint)

DELOS

Last Chance, prologue novella to Nowhere to Hide
Nowhere to Hide, Book 1
Tangled Pursuit, Book 2
Forged in Fire, Book 3
Broken Dreams, Book 4
Blind Sided, BN2
Secret Dream, B1B novella, epilogue to Nowhere to Hide
Hold On, Book 5
Hold Me, 5B1, sequel to Hold On
Unbound Pursuit, 2B1 novella, epilogue to Tangled Pursuit
Secrets, 2B2 novella, sequel to Unbound Pursuit, 2B1
Snowflake's Gift, Book 6
Never Enough, 3B1, novella, sequel to Forged in Fire
Dream of Me, 4B1, novella, sequel to Broken Dreams
Trapped, Book 7
Taking a Chance 7B1, novella, sequel to Trapped
The Hidden Heart, 7B2, novella, sequel to Taking A Chance
Boxcar Christmas, Book 8
Sanctuary, Book 9
Dangerous, Book 10
Redemption, 10B1, novella, sequel to Dangerous

Kensington

SILVER CREEK SERIES

Silver Creek Fire
Courage Under Fire

WIND RIVER VALLEY SERIES

Wind River Wrangler
Wind River Rancher
Wind River Cowboy
Christmas with my Cowboy
Wrangler's Challenge
Lone Rider
Wind River Lawman
Kassie's Cowboy
Home to Wind River
Western Weddings: Wind River Wedding
Wind River Protector
Wind River Undercover

Everything Lindsay McKenna

My website is dedicated to all my series. There are articles on characters, my publishing schedule, and information about each book written by me. You can also learn more about my newsletter, which covers my upcoming books, publishing schedule, giveaways, exclusive cover peeks and more.